THE DEARORN TERRORIST PLOT

2 Novellas & 6 Stories
Thomas Haftmann, P. I.

Book 6

Habent Sua Fata Libelli

Manhanset House
Shelter Island Hts., New York 11965-0342
bricktower@aol.com • NewPulpPress.com

The New Pulp Press colophon is a trademark of
J. T. Colby & Company, Inc.

Library of Congress Cataloging-in-Publication Data
White, Robb
The Dearborn Terrorist Plot—A Thomas Haftmann Novel
p. cm.
1. FICTION / Mystery & Detective / Hard-Boiled.
2. FICTION / Thrillers / Suspense.
3. FICTION / Noir.
Fiction, I. Title.
ISBN: 978-1-955036-91-7 Trade Paper
Copyright © 2025 by Robb T. White
Electronic compilation/ paperback edition
copyright © 2025 by New Pulp Press

October 2025

THE DEARORN TERRORIST PLOT

2 Novellas & 6 Stories
Thomas Haftmann, P. I.

Book 6

Robb White

For Dave Perkins

CONTENTS

The Dearborn Terrorist

PROLOGUE

Children see butterflies, men with beards, giraffes, and dragons in clouds on a summer's day. A silly game we outgrow, but we forget the mind craves patterns because the brain is an image-making machine. The International Space Station, for example, does not zigzag across the velvety black sky as our eyes would have us believe. Its coordinates, degree of altitude from the azimuth, and speed are as precise as modern computers can achieve and as accurate as an astronomical chart of the motion of the stars in the celestial coordinate system. It is simply the mind seeking an explanation—a narrative, in a word—for the shiny object two-hundred-fifty miles above our heads shooting across the night sky so fast that it transverses the entire American continent in seconds.

Looking down from the ISS, an astronaut might say the Great Lakes doesn't look much like the maps of cartographers—for example, Lake Superior, the largest and coldest of them with its emerald-green waters, resembles a swordfish breeching. Its upper snout appears to have embedded its bill into the sister cities Duluth, Minnesota, and Superior, Wisconsin, the terminus for shipping the iron-rich deposits of the 80-mile-long Gogebic Iron Range. The resemblance fails here because what would be the eye is too small, a speck of island in a chain called the Apostles, and the place where the swordfish's eye should be located is Devil's Island rather than either of the largest two, Stockton or Outer Islands. Somewhere around Sault Ste. Marie, with its famous Soo locks, is the fish's anus. To the left is Canada, to the right is the United States. The International Bridge spans the two nations above the St. Mary's River. Ice shuts down shipping on the lakes in the winter, of course, but 10,000 vessels make the annual journey and hundreds of men and some women make their livelihoods from these inland seas carved from glaciers eons ago, and like the earth itself, are destined one day to disappear.

In the years before smart phones, googling, *Tik Tok*, and constant emailing, sailors looked forward to arriving at the Soo to pick up mail, especially if there had been too little time in port to get really drunk or find a willing woman, usually a barfly with problems, or talk to the wife or children. Besides the letters, captains used to complain to deckhands about all the Swedish pornography sailors ordered that would arrive at the Soo Canals for pickup. Today, the typical Great Lakes sailor is a family man proficient in online chatting, Skyping— and yes, downloading the cornucopia of pornography from sites like *YouPorn* and *Dr. Tuber*. The hard-drinking renegades and tattooed mavericks are fewer nowadays. Most have sought berths on fishing vessels in the Bering Sea.

At the Soo locks, operators use computers to control the valves and pipes to raise or lower water levels for the big lakeboats to traverse uplakes or downlakes. Those coming down from Lake Superior have massive cargo holds loaded with tons of limestone, coal, gravel, and iron ore. In an earlier era, they hauled wheat and other grains. Boys once prowled the trainyards for spilled cargo of pellets ideal for slingshots for killing birds and small varmints. This taconite from the iron-rich fields in Wisconsin and Minnesota are the same ones Andrew Carnegie once held a monopoly on.

One sailor, in the years shortly after Nine Eleven, emerged from belowdecks for his shift aboard the Great Lakes freighter, the *Barclay N. Mathers*. Slender, unshaven for weeks, nondescript in his heavy work attire, Ammar Habib looked like any other sailor on deck. Not even the conveyormen could be picked out by the sightseers in the grandstands watching the lakeboats pass by. They would be covered in gritty dust and sweat hours after docking in port and the unloading system of moving everything out of their vast cargo holds with the conveyor system. The thick plates at the bottom of the deck would be scraped clean by the bulldozer shovels lowered down to finish the job.

Huge stripes cut in the metal glistened from the light pouring down into the holds. By day's end, every conveyorman would be tinted white, or black, or red from their heads to their steel-toed boots—depending on whether limestone, coal, or iron ore had packed the vessel that trip.

This ordinary seaman received a single letter at the locks, his first letter in a month from someone who had assisted Ammar and arranged for him to go to America. Most of the rest of the mail the captain of the *Barclay N. Mathers* were handmade items from wives and children, treats that could survive the roughshod mailing system of the locks. It was no letter from a cousin back in Lebanon, as he told his shipmates. Its Arabic was tender, flowery. Not a word written meant what it said. That letter meant Habib was to supply the author of the letter with specific information about the Soo locks and its operating procedures.

The author of the letter was a wealthy citizen of Lebanon, who belied his sophisticated lifestyle by praying five times a day to Allah for guidance in accomplishing a *muhimat muqidasa*, a "holy mission," one he knew would come to him in a dream. He believed fate was thrust upon him by Allah since his birth. If he were to be successful, *Inshallah*, no one in America would ever think of a recreational boat or a working vessel on any one of the five Great Lakes the same way again.

This sailor's lakeboat was preceded through the locks by the *J. Beaufort Göttlieb*, one of the few and largest freighters sailing the Lakes known as "footers." The steamship carried stone, ore pellets, and coal to either Sandusky or Northtown, Ohio coal storage facilities on Lake Erie.

Ammar was happy to supply his cousin in Lebanon with whatever he could. He wasn't even curious why his cousin wanted to know all about the Soo. He owed him for providing the means to make the passage to Dearborn, Michigan years ago. He could not have known that one deckhand on the *Gött* behind his boat would play a crucial role in his cousin's plan to make the infidels of America weep and gnash their teeth for generations.

* * *

CHAPTER 1
Bob Lo Island in the Detroit River, MI/August 10, 12:05 p.m.

Mitch Grebski waited until his boat, the steamship *J. Beaufort Göttlieb*, with its load of iron ore pellets destined for Northtown Harbor on Lake Erie, was fogbound in the Detroit River before he opened Libby's letter. He had no expectations of finding anything interesting in it. He tried to insinuate she wrote too much while he was on the water and he didn't like being obligated to write back. He refused to waste money on a cell phone. He told her the crew complained all the time about no reception on the water and how lousy it was in port.

"You want to write letters, find a convict in Lucasville. Lots of lonely guys there."

That was a dig at her husband, a jailbird and lowlife Grebski despised. Lucasville was where Ohio Parole Board sent its worst criminals.

"See if I write you when you wind up there, asshole."

Libby's rebuke had some merit. Grebski had a violent temper and a propensity to unleash it. He knew how to scrap and he was possessed of a rat's cunning when it came to evading punishment.

She lived in Riverton, a small, depressed town near the Ohio River once named Mystic in error when English residents coming after the first French trappers mistook their gruff, dismissive term "infesté moustiques"—"mosquito infested"—as a term of approval. The town's name was changed to Riverton in the early nineteenth-century, and there it remained for decades: a semi-industrialized city with a plastics manufacturing base for the Michigan car companies with a few farms holding with rotting barns and empty corn silos tucked between.

When the car companies outsourced parts from Mexico and China in the nineties, the town collapsed. Riverton led all Ohio cities in meth labs, most built on abandoned farm property, some in the backs of cars, behind housing projects in the woods, and once, memorably, to the town's infamy, inside the room of a patient's nursing home. When it exploded and killed the cook, the newsfeeds and TV late-night comics in New York and L.A. had themselves a witty sound bite.

She occupied the house that was left them when their mother died. It was never discussed between them, but it was understood she would move her family into the place right after the funeral. The letter was handwritten, although he knew she could afford a laptop because he was sending her half his paycheck and had been for years. Because her husband was a criminal who went in and out of jail and part-time meth cook, he knew the money helped and besides—he told himself—he had no use for it aboard a lakeboat. Grebski didn't gamble unlike many of the crew in the forward end, and he rarely went ashore. When he did, it wasn't to get as drunk or find sex before his shift came on. This fact alone made him something of a freak among his shipmates, not to mention his unfriendly demeanor and size. He was bulked up with weights and when he was ashore near Northtown, he had a contact for cycling steroids. On his days off, he could be heard slinging iron in the dunnage room as early as five in the morning. The "lunk" alarm wake-up call, his roommates called it behind his back.

The letter was full of Libby's misspellings, which he overlooked despite a quirky fastidiousness in his sensibilities that avoided slovenliness of any kind. She mentioned Frank, her husband, getting released in a couple weeks from Youngstown State Penitentiary and the deeper concern that her twelve-year-old son, a boy with special needs, was being taunted at school. He vaguely recalled the boy's vacant, lopsided grin, none-too-clean clothing, and a ferocious nose-picking habit he had tried to call to his sister's attention one afternoon at McDonald's on a rare visit:

"Mitch, holy Jesus, now what?"

"Your son, Libby," he said. "He's a regular nose miner."

"What?"

"Tell him to stop pointing at his brain when people are eating."

Libby was an indifferent mother like her own mother whose drug abuse characterized her own and her brother's upbringing. She watched him for signs of aberrant behavior, was given pamphlets on children on the autism scale by the boy's teachers. She told Mitch she expected unusual features to appear on his body, as if their mother's drug binges would result in generational tumors, or fibers sprouting from his hands or a tail developing at puberty. She laughed about it.

The father of the boy was not her current husband who, by Grebski's reckoning, was the third or fourth man she was involved with since he had left home after his last concussion from the old man's boot. Libby would drop their names into her letters casually without introduction and he assumed any male's name appearing twice in sequence meant a serious relationship with his sister. Her promiscuity matched his own. He didn't know why he kept coming back home. He was a stranger to the town that once celebrated him. He hated everything about her that reminded him of his failure, yet he was a fly on one of those yellow sticky strips when it came to revolting. Being his twin, Libby was able to swim under the sharks belly without fear. Anyone else would have wound up in its maw.

Mitch's body responded to her annoying prattle; the muscles in his shoulders bunched up. Another familiar sign was the fist-clenching that had a will of its own like cadaveric spasm in a dead person's hand.

Sometimes an image of Libby would crawl into his brain and sit mocking behind his eyes. Libby was sexually active in their neighborhood by the time she was fourteen. At fifteen, she had the fully developed body of a woman. Libby's hair was dark, unlike their Nordic mother, a translucent Swede, but like their mother, she had full-sized breasts that drew the eyes of every boy and lowlife stud in a twenty-block radius of their home.

Riverton High was an anomaly with a large Appalachian population and a smattering of blacks, descendants of families drawn south from Cleveland to the Ohio River back in the Roaring Twenties when a proposed steel mill promised to employ thousands with high-paying jobs. Then came the Depression. School was a catwalk for Libby. Grebski let it be known to the cliques of black girls who ridiculed her that he would be in their faces if they tried anything.

Some of these girls were themselves physically prone to violence. Starring on the football team, and given his impressive size, he held authority around school despite his below-average IQ.

Grebski's jaw clamped at the memory of her skirt riding up her thighs, and the swaying breasts she didn't have to exaggerate. Heads swiveled on necks when she passed. The sexual innuendo and catcalls were a daily gauntlet she created and thrived on. More than once, a cat fight behind the track field was attended by as many as a hundred students when word got out that she pissed off another girl because her flirty behavior to the girl's boyfriend. The winks, smirks and *double entendre* were often made by the male teachers, and Grebski burned with a hot anger he could do nothing about their sly exchanges when his sister entered or left a room. One prude who didn't even have her as a student turned her in to the principal for shaking her boobs at a student from the stairwell beneath her bulky Riverton High sweatshirt. That earned a week's suspension and even more notoriety as word spread. She was pleased that, when she came off suspension, she learned she'd won the challenge by a huge margin.

That made the whole letter-writing puzzling. Being twins, they should have been close but they were strangers growing up. He forced himself to breathe evenly, relax. He headed down the starboard deck and found a hatch cover to sit on to read the letter. This far away, nothing of the boat's stern could be viewed from the pilot house. On days like this or in rough weather, men traveling the length of the ship preferred the portside tunnel that led to the engine room. His eyes strained through the fog. He knew from the silence he was completely alone, nothing to see but ragged wisps coiling about the railing running lengthwise down the vessel. The top of the pilot house looked as if it were floating in air, detached from the Texas deck.

Every other moment, the fog lifted to expose a patch of blue sky. The water below the deck was invisible, shrouded in white. He smelled its oily murk . Sudden noises reached through the fog everywhere at once, appearing overhead like words in a cartoon bubble. They might be coming from downtown Detroit or Grosse Isle off to port for all he could tell. He could barely make out the wire railing from where he sat. The fog curled over the boat and made a figure eight amidships caused by the warmth of the steel and the draft of air that circulated in ribbons of white sheets overhead.

The triple blasts of the *Göttlieb*'s horn in one-minute intervals did not disturb his solitude on deck. He was alone all the time anyway, alone in his mind. His shipmates called him a cold fish. Suddenly, both the pilot house and the boat deck of the afterend were lost in the tattered gauzy of fog.

He returned to her letter, squinting in the hazy light. Libby somehow knew his boat's arrival was expected at the dock in Northtown on Sunday at 1:00 p.m. before heading back uplakes for a backhaul of coal in South Chicago. She kept tabs on him but not out of concern or love. Libby was a colder fish than he was, and she always had a reason to do what she did. She said she would be at the dock in Northtown if he wanted to spend some time "at the funny farm," their childhood name for the family homestead. Mitch knew her husband's absence or presence meant nothing as far as the invitation to visit. For all her manipulating of men, she could not influence him that way. Something else could: his fever dream that woke him up at dawn weeks ago and gripped him constantly at work or in the idle moments between shifts. It began as a dream but it evolved slowly to become a plan. It was simple: Mitch planned to kill everyone aboard the *Göttlieb*. The bonus was to kill as many civilians on shore as possible while doing it.

Sailors of all waters, fresh and salt, speak of "channel fever," that gut-wrenching desire to get off the water and onto land as soon as possible. In Mitchell Grebski's case, it was the opposite: leaving the boat filled him with a squirmy distress that turned to rage as soon as he found himself in close contact with people. It could be a woman pushing her kid in a grocery cart across a parking lot or a teenager on a skateboard with his pants around his knees or a harmless-looking guy on the barstool next to his saying something wrong, saying *anything*, that would make him want to grind broken glass into his face. Back in Duluth, to avoid a murderous encounter with the third mate, he had gone for a long, exhausting jog up the steep hillsides enclosing the harbor, following the twisting roads ever higher, until he could see the "*Gött*" far below in its berth, tied by cables to the bollards beneath the huge insect arms of the black Hewlett cranes plunging into the open cargo hold. The dock boss somewhere above on his platform giving signals to their operators to move the massive steel booms.

When he left his last foster home in Cleveland fifteen years earlier to go sailing (his foster "father" was a retired ore boat captain for Interlake Steamship Company and wrote him the reference letter to the Coast Guard), he thought he had found something that resembled a safe life away from people, Libby especially. Growing up in a dysfunctional family, in which the other was a heroin junkie and that father a biker who sold drugs and supplied the mother, made him want to escape it all the time—until the dream came to him like a succubus in the night. His red dream of mayhem aboard a lakeboat.

When the telephone call came from the Great Lakes Seamen's Union, he learned he had been assigned a deckhand's berth on the Str. *Col. James Pickands* as an ordinary seaman. He paced in his room wondering how to tell his foster parents, kind people but religious zealots, he had crashed the family car when another car full of teenaged boys had come flying at him out of the dusk just as he was turning into the drive-in theater. He just missed being killed. The only damage was a crumpled front fender turned into instant sculpture when the other car swerved at the last second to avoid him. He and his girlfriend weren't hurt, but he was cited for failure to control and would have to go to court. He decided to hitchhike on the Memorial Shoreway east to meet his boat in Northtown, a small port town of red-brick roads. He spent the night sleeping in Point Park overlooking the harbor as a teenager. It was the same place where Libby said she'd meet him. It wasn't an invitation after all but a summons. Whatever her reason for inviting him, he now had his own. He crumpled the letter in his fist and tossed it over the side.

Grebski did not like the feeling that he was caught in a loop and was returning to the starting point of his escape. He had a memory of himself tying down clamps on hatch covers on the old rust bucket, long since converted to scrap. The boat was loading coal and the piles of it on deck had to be scraped up and hosed off. The wind coming off the harbor blew coal grit into his skin and left raccoon circles under his eyes for a week. He felt free for the first time in his life. The canker worm of rage lay dormant in his brain for years until it started to gnaw its way out. It started with accusations, then open quarrels with shipmates who said something or looked at him a certain way. He had to wait until he got into port before getting into fights. After a while, the mates ignored the bruises on his hands and left him alone.

Grebski's reading stopped in high school. He found biographies dull and most literature not pornographic time-wasting trash, a notch above the skin mags and fuck books his shipmates left lying around the galley. No one had ever seen the journal because he kept it well hidden in a lock box behind the mattress in his bunk in the fo'c'sle. His two deckhand mates knew better than to disturb the green "jackoff curtains" that afforded sailors' privacy in their bunks. Grebski kept them closed and told both men if he ever saw one of their hands moving to disturb them, that individual would be pulling back a bloody stump. Nobody took it as a jest or accepted the challenge.

He also placed certain objects, such as a homemade garrote with steel wire and wooden block handles, an old-fashioned belaying pin he had bought in an antique store on the waterfront in Milwaukee, and a deformed piece of short-length rebar, about two feet in length with ridges for gripping. He kept two knives in his boots: one a twelve-inch buck in a scabbard, the other a filleting knife for slicing the carotid or iliac veins. Hit the right or left branch of the common iliac vein and the entire pelvis region drained. With a good aim, he would hit the ascending anterior at an oblique angle, smash "the inferior vena cava," whatever that meant in the anatomy book he stole from the steward, a college boy hoping to go to medical school. The man sleeping in his bunk would feel the blow back there and would be awash in spurting black blood—an abstract painting in red gore on the bed covers.

His main weapon of choice was the rebar he had found near a construction site in Lackawanna, New York. He was running full tilt from a gang of black men who had bad intentions for his insult to some pimp's whore, who kept demanding he buy her expensive cocktail drinks. The blow job was only fifteen bucks, but the three-drink minimum goosed the bill to $46. She expected a good tip if she let him give her a facial or swallowed.

As the dream intensified over time, he added items beneath layers of coiled tow rope attached to block-and-tackle pulleys and various-sized gambrels for hauling. His crude journal outlined a plan for killing every member of the *J. Beaufort Göttlieb*, starting with the captain and first mate. He knew every bunk aboard ship, every sailor did. All thirty-seven crew members, their shifts, and their positions on his floating factory, and he knew, to a man, the order, and the places he expected to find them in to kill them in the right sequence.

Being fogbound for the last three hours wouldn't put more than a slight hitch in his plans. Sleeping men were easier to kill, after all. He was saving that old fool, the old wheelsman, "Buck" Liberty, on duty in the pilot house for last. Somebody needed to steer the boat through the channel straight into the Bascule Bridge in Northtown at a fifteen knots full speed.

With good timing, the bridge will be at an angle that the bridge operator wouldn't get the traffic gates down in time. Grebski wanted as many as possible. It was all laid out in his "project" as he conceived it growing grander every time. He had a fatheaded football coach who was obligated to teach history for his salary. He told Grebski's class about the Japanese attack on pearl Harbor half-a-dozen times, all he remembered from his own college courses. He gave them a word for a noble suicide: *seppuku*. Grebski's A in class wasn't because he passed any tests. It was all owing to his touchdowns on Friday nights. He kept the word and rolled it around in his mouth with his dream of vengeance. His would be a grand *seppuku*, one with the difference that instead of a ceremonial dagger, there were 75,000 tons of bulk cargo powered by Enterprise DMRV-16-4 diesel engines driving twin propellers and rated at 19,500 brake horsepower, making the *Gött* one of the most powerful lakeboats plying the five lakes.

Mitchell Grebski was more than a social misfit who adapted to the isolation of a Great Lakes sailor. He was beyond what TV psychologists referred to when they spoke of certain people with "anger-management issues." In Grebski's case, that was like comparing a summer cold to the Black Death. Grebski devoted all his off time from assigned duties to his project. He stopped going to bars to obliterate the pain. He knew he was out of his depth. It was moving from checkers to grand master chess. He couldn't do it. He needed someone who could help him bring it off. Someone smarter, someone like those crazy towelheads overseas who massacred people right and left. *How to find one?* Libby had a computer. She could show him how to find people. His moron shipmates talked about it all the time. Some of them met strange women on it.

Grebski was one of those "angry loners," as the FBI described them. The galley TV worked in port and the news was always talking about the threats to the homeland. Normal people ashore stepped aside when he approached on the street. Store clerks twitched when he bought something, even if it happened to be from the bum boat. Women on the street or in bars were immediately wary, as though they sensed something off in his personality. Lately, his attempts to play down the bristling violence that simmered in him failed. His sexual encounters were becoming sexual assaults. His latest told him he'd be lucky if she didn't report it as a rape. Grebski took her bra and panties as trophies before tossing them in a dumpster on his way back to the boat.

He remembered what it was like to be cheered. He knew what it felt like when the cheering stopped. He felt betrayed by everyone in his life. He wrote *My Project* on the front of a school notebook and kept it in his footlocker beneath his bunk. Mitch Grebski let it be known you didn't fuck with him or his things. If he were working on shore in an office, Grebski would have been terminated by HR within weeks for his displays of anger and intimidation of his co-workers. But the Steelworkers' 5000 was still a strong union. Grebski, loathed though he was by his crew, was bull deckhand and had seniority on his boat. No one in the company would have dreamed of promoting him. He had failed his Able Seaman's test twice. Grebski blamed his football concussions—and even more than his lack of intelligence or outbursts, he was a baleful presence on board a lakeboat that no Great Lakes captain would have wanted within a hundred yards of the pilot house.

* * *

CHAPTER 2
Residence of Thomas Haftmann,
Northtown, OH/Aug. 10, 12:22 p.m.

At the same moment that Mitch Grebski was wadding up his sister's letter and tossing it over the side into the Detroit River, Thomas Haftmann was rolling out of bed with his third hangover in four days. Today was the day his uncle in Prescott, Arizona was calling to check up on the business—*really to check up on him*, he realized, so he had to clear his head.

His uncle was down there drying out in the Arizona desert heat, probably cranky. He also had a sharp nose for a fellow lush, so Haftmann headed for the shower and accepted the hot water until his back felt scalded; then he took the full blast of icy water for a full minute, counting *one-Mississippi, two-Mississippi,* until his teeth chattered. When he had shocked himself into full wakefulness and reasonable sobriety, he stepped out to face the new day. It was just another day without hope or prospects for someone who had achieved an early and excellent start in life.

It was nearly one o'clock and the call was coming at two. He guzzled mouthwash but it did little to dissolve the coating of his mouth. He winced when he recalled the three cigarettes he had smoked as a capper to his debauch. Disgusted with himself, he brewed a strong pot of Verona coffee and eyed the opened pack of Marlboros on top of the fridge.

Fuck it, he thought, *I'm done.*

He intended to tell his uncle he was quitting the private-eye business. All he had been doing for ten long days was sitting behind the desk, opening mail, answering the phone, and talking to a few people. It added up to zero. Not one paying client showed up, called, or emailed. His uncle was old school, didn't believe in advertising with a website. The only semblance of a case occurred when a girl, young-sounding, in tears, called to see if he would finding her missing dog. She broke off crying and hung up before he could formulate a polite refusal. *A missing dog, for God's sake. This dog returneth to his vomit,* thought Thomas and his self-contempt grew a notch when he realized he was yearning for a drink already. Now: *The hair of the dog.*

Despite last night's frivolity in the Penguin Bar, this was the lowest Thomas had felt since his firm let him go. Not *let me go,* Thomas corrected himself. *Fired two months into my probationary period.*

All that promise, all that hard work in law school, then the amazingly good fortune to clerk for Judge Ladd with his contacts in the Northern District of the US Attorney's Office. A man who took the President of the United States' phone call. Hired by Mister Robert Jackson Plummer the III of Plummer, Fuqua—and the firm's legendary trial litigator Alexander ("The Great") Leasson himself—a man reputed to have taken in more than forty million in tort cases for his clients, forty percent of which went to his firm.

Then it all went up in smoke because he had missed two depositions in three weeks. Thomas kept telling himself that no one was hurt by it, not a fraction of an iotum lost over it, and he had rescheduled both for the next day, apologized profusely to the clients, and was even convinced that the firm's other partners were altogether unaware of it. The fact that he won the first case and the second was settled with very generous terms for his client, the billable hours for the firm, and his own prestige did nothing to assuage his feeling of shame and regret.

Now instead of drinking and rubbing shoulders with some high-profile people in the best bars in the Cleveland Warehouse District, he was languishing fifty miles away in this godforsaken, second-rate resort town drinking in third-rate dives and sitting behind his uncle's scarred desk watching tourists amble past and ogle him through the plate glass window as if he were some kind of freak. Rubbing his eyes to dampen some of the pain warbling like a band saw across his forehead, he looked up to see a skinny goth girl with red hair and a nose ring drag a little boy away from the window. She wore a halter top with twin tttoos over the tops of her breasts—Batwoman and Catwoman appeared to be staring at each other. Her arms were tattoo sleeves in blue and red with designs that intertwined female Marvel superheroes with Valkyries and witches. Her mouth moved with the boy's behind the glass. Both laughing at him.

He watched them skip off. He checked the time—twenty-two more minutes to be on display for the passing yokels.

He grabbed a notebook and began preparing a list of reasons. His head throbbed as he wrote down several excuses for quitting. He thought he'd lead with the best, the one his uncle would be most interested in: *My working here is costing you money and I'm not bringing in a dime.*

Then a wave of nausea roiled through his intestines, and he felt acid bile creeping up his esophagus. His throat burned and he realized the gaseous vapor he exuded would offend any soul who happened to walk in the door at that moment, albeit not a likely possibility. He looked down at his paper as if the letters of the words he had just written transmogrified magically into Aramaic or Old Irish some other lost language; then he scratched out all his excuses and wrote:

Because I'm a hopeless alcoholic and I can't control my drinking.

Thomas put down the pen and looked up at the wall where his uncle's licenses were framed: Ohio Peace Officer Training Commission (OPOTC), to note his qualification to bear a firearm, and the Private Investigator Security Guard Services (PISGS), for his class A license. There were no photos on the wall, not even one of his ex-wife Roberta, Thomas's aunt. A lawyer, she worked for the Jefferson County DA's Office and once handled all the big criminal cases until the divorce. Marital infidelity ran in the family. It became his uncle's profession.

Thomas assumed his uncle's wrath for the law in general and the minions of the legal profession were in no small part owing to his wife's betrayal. They had no children, but he was the favorite nephew of his aunt. The big wall clock next to the framed certificates ticked with a menace as two o'clock drew closer. When Haftmann attended a Catholic elementary school in Riverton, one old nun, probably senile, told him he was destined for hell where a big clock, somehow

17

miraculously unconsumed by fire, boomed: *You'll never get out, you'll never get out.* He told himself to man up and wait for the goddamned phone to ring.

* * *

CHAPTER 3
Residence of Dean & Libby Boatwright,
Riverton, OH/Aug. 10, 12:44 p.m.

While her brother was savoring images of mass slaughter in his head, Libby (née Grebski) Boatwright was engaged in coitus in her marital bed. Theirs was an open marriage and she was actively bisexual with her husband's consent whenever Boatwright himself was out of the picture, which usually meant out of town on one of his criminal pursuits or doing time in the crowbar hotel. He liked the idea of his wife taking women into their bed and bragged to his jailbird cellmates what she was like. He didn't relish her sharing their bed with another man, but he was a realist. He knew his wife's sexual appetite.

This woman, however, was unusual in that she happened to be Boatwright's first wife, a fact that made Boatwright smile every time he thought of it. The fact that Libby had taken her man from her didn't seem to faze any of the parties involved. Libby enjoyed seducing her lovers' partners, with or without their consent.

Marissa Toensing was a petite one-hundred pounds with much of it concentrated in her lower half. Her heart-shaped ass made her nursing pants snug, and she exploited it by shopping in the teen section owing to her small size. On the job, she wore a print outfit that emphasized her backside, which was the subject of much male commentary. Marissa was a med-surg nurse at Riverton Memorial. She had a fierce addiction to Percocet and Vicodin during her marriage to Dean Boatwright, a transplanted Appalachian, whose own addiction to meth was at that time at its worst and often manifested itself in bouts of full-blown paranoia and spousal abuse.

Libby was one of her seven patients during a week-long stay at memorial for an abscess in her colon. Marissa raced through her duties to her other patients to spend as much time as possible at Libby's bedside. On her last day, just before the male nurse was preparing to wheelchair her out, Libby's hand slipped through the bed rail and felt the front of Marissa's pants. Before Marissa could react, two of Libby's fingers slipped inside the waistband and fondled her labia, caressing the extra-large clitoris. Libby looked up at her and smiled.

"Hey, you wouldn't be a guy, would you?"

Marissa, exhilarated and shocked at the same time, flushed with pleasure. The size of her clitoris was something that had embarrassed her since middle school when two of her gym classmates snickered behind their fingers watching her undress.

As the male nurse entered the room to take Libby to the elevator, Libby thanked Marissa for her care and shook her hand. Marissa felt the folded paper she put there and waited until her heart stopped thumping to read it. "Dean's away. Call me," she wrote.

Within a week, Libby had taken her to bed and given her five shivering orgasms with her tongue and fingers.

Libby was a more sexual being than even her brother knew. That wasn't insignificant. One of Libby's older friends, a girl named Donna, also from Riverton High, had bragged in homeroom about the number of "virgin cards" she'd collected over the summer vacation. Being sophomores, she and Libby had enjoyed a steady sex life with boys their age and one or two older ones. They knew the senior boys would be coming around and they wanted to upgrade their skill set.

Libby talked her twin brother into letting Donna use him for a little practice.

"What kind of practice, Lib?"

"Donna's tired of sucking on bananas. I told her none of the guys had one your size."

"You're a slut, Libby. You know that?"

"You didn't say that when you finger-fucked me last summer. Or when you begged me to jack you off."

"You bitch."

"I wanna watch her go down on you."

20

"That shit ain't right, Libby." His accent, like most of the white boys at school, was infused with a blaccent.

"Don't go beating off beforehand, either. I got to listen to that moaning shit every damn night while you shoot off."

"Christ, you're a pig."

"Make sure you shower tonight, stinky boy. Wash that cock good."

Grebski had never thought much about his cock size. His biker old man was always walking around the house naked and stoned, no matter who was in the house. His penis was always flapping from one side of his shorts to the other. His idea of humor was to take it out and let it hang over the elastic band when people collecting money dropped by on a Sunday. One time he set up some Jehova's Witnesses who came to the door, two young women in old-fashioned dresses without make-up. He listened to their godly spiel and bible quoting. Then he pulled the belt of his bathrobe open. Both women screamed and nearly fell down the porch steps to escape. The words "Satan," "devil," and "God forgive you" hung in the air as they raced down the block.

Grebski enjoyed his athletic homage at Riverton High. Since his sophomore year, he was already talked about by football and track coaching staffs at the big colleges. Some grade-fixing was required to make sure he could suit up for all four years but his low intelligence precluded a collegiate scholarship, although one Florida college was hopeful enough to send up a team of tutors and education specialists.

Libby watched her friend Donna, gave her advice, and told her how to hold him at the base as she guided Donna's head onto the swollen glans. "Go forward, like this, you sexy bitch," she'd say, and motion with her own head. "That way you won't gag on it." Libby looked old enough at sixteen to get past the cashier at Adult Videos on Salem Street to watch videos.

Donna released it, gasping for air, and complained her mouth was sore from stretching. She repeated what she said at first: "Don't come in my mouth, fucker."

Libby or Donna took turns pumping him. Donna's hands were always too dry and she would chafe the skin. The big vein running down the center of his member would wiggle from the pressure. "Put some spit on it," Libby ordered her. Her sex tapes showed her all the tricks. Grebski himself would show off by placing his hand over hers to make the ejaculation go farther.

After some weeks of this, whenever the girls weren't on dates, or whenever Donna was with her, the object of their sex game became hit-the-Bon Jovi poster on Libby's bedroom wall. Whoever made a head shot would have the other one lick it off.

That was Grebski's introduction to sex. Donna was a natural blonde with a caramel-colored twist of pubic ruff.

"You want to lick my snatch?"

Grebski wasn't sure about making love with his face although he had seen his old man's jackoff magazines all over the house. "C'mon, man," she urged him once they were both nude in Libby's bed, "I've sucked your dick until my jaws ached. How about a little payback?"

Grebski obliged her. He was grateful she had no taste down there, even when the labia opened to his probing tongue. Guys at school talked smut about the taste of a woman's cunt smelling like rotten cheese. He learned to move his tongue around, not just jab at her pussy. Her moans told him when it felt good. When she lay back on the bed shuddering from another climax, he lay beside her, thinking she would finish him with another blowjob.

"Not this time, baby," she said, and kissed him tenderly on the lips. "I want that cock inside me. See if you can fuck me harder than DeAndre."

"And what if I do?"

"I'll let you put it in my ass when you come."

"Deal."

Grebski's supercharged sex life took an unorthodox turn in those early days of puberty, but it wasn't altogether owing to his libertine sister or his mother sitting in front of the TV in a stupor, moving only in her junkie nod. Libby and Grebski were used to these odd twitching movements and ignored them. Somewhere in Grebski's psyche, grafted onto the dynamics of sex like bagworm larvae on a tree, was this other dark thing—to hurt, to humiliate, to conquer. Grebski with a football tucked under his arm was a formidable opponent. He didn't run to gain yards, his smiling coach liked to say, he ran to hurt people.

Grebski imagined it living and breathing inside him like a tiny fetus in a mother's womb. As he got older, he saw it grow, too, and thought of it more as a medieval homunculus with a gargoyle-shaped head, something he'd glimpsed on TV about cathedrals in Europe. It never spoke to him, but at times, in the early hours before dawn, while he stroked his erection to climax, he heard its whispered hiss inside his throbbing head.

* * *

CHAPTER 4

Haftmann Investigative Services,
Jefferson-on-the-Lake, OH/Aug. 11, 1:34 p.m.

"**Hey,** Uncle, how's it going out there?"

Thomas suspected his uncle could hear the false jollity in his voice and feared the worst: *He'll know I'm drinking again despite my promise before I left.*

"I'm OK," he said. He wouldn't use ten words when one or none would do. "Saw a whitetail deer near my cabin this morning."

"That sounds—therapeutic," Thomas said. The implied accusation made him wish at once he could take that word back. "I meant fine—"

"I know what you mean, forget it. The heat out here is intense. If this doesn't kill the booze sweats at night, nothing will. Hell couldn't be hotter."

"That's fine, I'm really glad to hear it."

"How's everything in the office?"

"Fine, you know . . ." *How many times did I just say "fine"?*

"How's everything else?"

He means: am I getting shit-faced every night on the Strip?

"Quiet, you know. A few calls about a missing teen, one sounds promising. Another one about a missing dog—"

His uncle's cigarette-bray laughter surprised him. "A dog, you say?"

"Yeah, I told the party to call the county animal protective services."

"Unworthy of your time, Thomas?"

"No, that's not what I meant." *What the fuck, he expects me to take on a case of a missing dog? The heat must be baking his brains out there.*

"Little things, Tom, are important. Maybe there's a real case behind it," his uncle said. His voice sounded laconic, part-mockery, and this shortened Haftmann's temper more but he kept his voice even in reply.

"Sure, I'll call her back today." *The fuck I will.*

"Anything else I should know?"

Thomas was on the verge of telling him just how much he hated this private-eye business, its short money, the sleazy or dopey clients, and endless phone calling for information from bored, hostile, or uninterested people. He had fallen to the bottom of the barrel: a telemarketer who couldn't persuade anybody to buy anything he was selling. His sore neck from staring at a phone pr a computer screen would probably bend him over in his old age and make him look like a doddering old fool shuffling along, staring at his shoes.

Haftmann already knew all this from doing the apprenticeship with his uncle during law school breaks years ago. Because his uncle's business was a licensed private investigation provider, he being an employee required no license. During his last summer working for Sam Haftmann's Private Investigation Services before heading off to law school in Cleveland, he hit his first-year books every moment in the office when he wasn't answering phones or writing out bills or doing night or daytime surveillance of some husband on the make. Just before leaving for Chicago that August years ago, his uncle asked him to take the simple test for a class B license—"You never know how things turn out"—but Thomas had no more stomach for this wretched job and the sordid catastrophes his uncle's lowlife clientele involved. He wouldn't dignify it by calling it a profession.

"Let me check. I have a list . . ."

Thomas glanced down at the list of callers, the bills paid, and tried to summon enthusiasm for the one client who called three times to leave messages (twice while he was across the street boozing) and who wanted to know if he would follow her husband. Her second message was blunter: "I know the lying fucker's seeing that whore of an ex-wife of his."

They talked briefly about this, and then a silence. Thomas was afraid his uncle was on the verge of giving him fatherly advice, even though it wasn't in his character to micromanage. Thomas thought he had pulled it off when his uncle said: "You have to do the little things well. I mean every day. It's hard."

"Yeah, I know," he replied. He had no idea what his uncle was talking about.

"It's getting back up after you've been knocked down. That's what matters," his uncle said.

Fuck me, there it is. "Sure, Uncle, I know that. I'm looking into some opportunities in Cleveland right now."

"You'll have to pass the Ohio bar."

"I'm not worried." *Too cocky . . .*

"I've got, maybe, a couple more days to do out here," his uncle said. "I'm in a Motel Six just off Highway Eighty-Nine. "It's in the Frontier Plaza."

"That sounds fi—nice," Thomas said.

He made it sound like a prison sentence. Haftmann knew his uncle wasn't your typical snowbird tourist in Arizona. One strange way to rehab a drinking problem. He probably stayed inside all day and never did anything but sleep and stare at the walls. *I could just as easily have saved the expense and rented a cabin on the lake a block from here . . .*

"I'll bring you back some turquoise," his uncle said. "The Indians sell them to tourists by the roadside. There's one near the motel. It's next to a plaque the town put up for the firemen killed in a burnover."

Thomas remembered it: nineteen Granite Mountain Hotshots burned to death in their aluminum foil blankets like human pot pies in a microwave. A horrible way to go.

They said their goodbyes and Haftmann realized he was dripping with perspiration from last night's booze and this miserable conversation—half-moons of sweat under his arms, the back of his shirt damp, even his hands felt slippery. *Jesus, fuck—I'm falling apart.* He sounded like half the country-western tunes playing on the jukebox across the street.

He knew his body worked overtime to expunge last night's alcohol from his system. There were two of him now: the promising young lawyer whose grades let him wipe the muck of Jefferson's shitty little resort town off his shoes and beeline right back to Chicago, where he had promptly botched his first professional job. This Thomas, the one under control, took and gave orders from the citadel of his brain where he went through the motions and didn't think about life, failure, or success anymore.

He recalled the poem from some lit class he took as an elective years ago. He'd memorized a passage to impress a pretty English major he wanted to date:

Take me to you, imprison me, for I
Except you enthrall mee, never shall be free,
Nor ever chaste, except you ravish me.

Haftmann noticed a fruit fly crawling across the notepaper. He canted his head slightly so that the angle of the droplets still forming on his forehead bombed the tiny insect in steady drips until it puttered in circles like a tiny motorboat.

Cohesion, the attracting forces of molecules, stuck the sweat-entombed fly to his fingertip and he turned it back and forth under his eye.

Battered your heart, didn't I, motherfucker?

* * *

CHAPTER 5

Lake Erie, lat. N 41° 46'; long. W 82° 39'/ Aug. 1:47 p.m.

The *J. Beaufort Göttlieb*, currently moving along at ten nautical miles north of Pelee Island, Canada's southernmost piece of property, was a handsome vessel by standards of nautical esthetics adapted for the bovine ore carriers of the Great Lakes. Not just big but a massive thousand-footer, one of the fastest on the water, capable of maintaining a fifteen-knot speed twenty-four/seven. Lakeboats don't stop. They wait outside harbors for tugs and use a system of horn blasts to communicate. The more cautious of captains would never dream of depending on their bow thrusters alone to tow them in. But like every profession, there are a few cowboy-types in the pilot houses here. The dock boss communicates by walkie-talkie to signal to the radio dispatcher when the berth is ready and the shift dock workers are ready for unloading. They are basically floating factories with very little bright work on display outside the electronic equipment you'd find inside and on top of the pilot house.

The *"Gött,"* known around the lakes by that nickname, was christened after some long-dead company big shot, a tradition of lakeboats to use the masculine, perhaps because they are so mulish and unfeminine by nautical boat design. They don't slice through waves. They punch and beat them back like a bar brawlers.

The *Gött* made the last of the normal series of turns south-by-southeast on a heading for its port-of-call in Northtown Harbor. Grebski had sailed this shipping channel so long he could tell when the turn was coming whether he was on deck or half-asleep in his bunk from the slower-pitched *thrum* of the screws. On deck, you could always feel it in the vibration of the deck plates. Even as he dropped off to sleep in his bunk, the waves lapping against the bow gave away the wind direction. With no headwind or chop, they would make good time. Seven, eight hours at most, close to peak bar time on Bridge Street where most of the town's bars were located.

He was back on deck, his spot slightly aft of midships, his belly full of the galley's starchy fare. Prisoners and sailors put on weight for the same reason. He was going to take great pleasure in killing one steward in particular. The man was a moron, who couldn't get Grebski's orders right no matter what he said. Grebski wondered if the other men put him up to it. He was barrel-chested, bald, and had an ex-con's mean-mugging look about him. Grebski considered the garrote for him, time permitting, but it might come down to his rebar club with one end wrapped in electric tape to reduce the shock up his forearm. He could always stun him and then return to finish the job once the rest of the crew in the afterend was cleaned out. The oilers and chief mate in the engine room had to be last. He couldn't be sure where every man would be when the exact time came and his "schedule" depended entirely on no one discovering the ongoing massacre. That thought thrilled him deep in his belly every time it bubbled to the surface.

When the *Göttlieb* made its shoreward turn, he could see land in the distance. One of the deckhands, a twenty-five-year-old from Traverse City in the U.P. joined the steamship when his union card allowed him to bump another deckhand. He approached Grebski on his way forward from the galley. It was Grebski's job in port to swing him over the side in the bosun's chair. He averted his eyes from Grebski after grunting something about "green bloom" in the distance. Sure enough, a vast neon green blanket of scum extending out from shore about twenty miles in all directions.

"They can't even drink their own water now," the deckhand said. "All those people, everybody living in Toledo, man. Farmers did it with chemical spilloffs into Erie."

"Tough fucking shit," Grebski grunted back, uninterested. "I hope every motherfucking one of them chokes on it."

The deckhand moved off. They'd warned him about Grebski.

Grebski knew he had to be more careful. This was no time to alert anyone to the looming apocalypse. He breathed deeply, relaxed his shoulder muscles. His growing irritation and restlessness threatened to expose him. He had until the end of the shipping season for his project timeline. When the weather turned, it would make things more difficult. He considered stopping lifting for max, not take unnecessary chances on pulling a muscle in his biceps or back. Down in the dunnage room, he had practiced short, vicious strokes with the rebar. He used a coil of thick rope for tying up as a practice head and brought the bar down in an arc just above the occipital bone's position. One end wrapped in a tape for gripping. He kept baby talc for his hands in case of sweating. He didn't think where he hit them would make much difference anyway because the force of the blow would be sufficient to kill outright or, at the least, incapacitate until he could finish them off at leisure.

Grebski studied anatomical books in the public library on his last shore leave in Two Harbors, Minnesota. He avoided anything that had to do with concussive trauma, fearful of what he'd find. He tried to understand the effects of blunt force trauma on the neocortex, but the lingo was Martian, incomprehensible medical jargon. One of the textbooks was written by a neurologist who bashed in the heads of small mammals with a tiny wrecking ball while they were fixed to an apparatus that looked like medieval stocks. The momentum of the swing would produce different effects on the gray matter, such as the hippocampus and the amygdala. Some of these brain-damaged animals would repeat their movements through a maze the researcher built and clocked them while they bumped into walls and staggered along. His conclusion was that the brain's older structure, the paleocortex, would kick in when the neocortex was damaged and the animals would repeat their memorized rituals of behavior.

Grebski loved to fantasize during his shift with the idea of a boat full of zombies with bashed-in skulls shambling about in their respective duties. He wondered if asking the forward crew of officers to line upon the Texas deck to kiss his ass would work.

He fussed over the problems the necessity of a second blow would bring. First, because he needed to conserve muscle strength. He'd be running to and fro between the bow and stern to account for every man, and he couldn't count on that because being in port and being on the water involved a variety of work tasks that had men moving all over the deck besides being at or near their workstations. Besides, he wasn't going for a *coup de grâce*. He wanted more of a slaughterhouse effect, something to jolt the viewer's senses, and his penis thickened at the thought of the news people and videographers combing the ship in the wake of his masterpiece.

Every crushed skull, every bloody handprint would be immortalized in some documentary. He even thought of slicing off a few testicles and hanging them from various places like the VHF aerial above the pilot house. Grebski had the sheer physical power required to sever whole heads in less time than it took those Al-Qaida crazies. He knew places on the forward bow where he could lash them to port and starboard. He played with the notion of tossing a few bodies onto the conveyor belt for good measure as they entered the harbor. Let the rubberneckers on shore get a gander of headless bodies pitching onto the pier or dropping into the water while the gulls dive at them for food. He would be standing in the pilot house pulling down the air horn lever with earsplitting blasts.

. . . *Come see what I have for you, rubberneckers.*

Time permitting, the steward was going to be dragged forward and hanged by the ankles from the bowsprit just before the collision. He hoped those people trapped in their cars on the bridge would be able to see him swaying there, bearing down on them. The heads decorating the gangways with rictus expressions—*Jesus*, he could feel blood surging south. Those unbelievable, precious moments before impact. The *Gött* bearing down on the bridge and its trapped occupants like the fist of God. He'd send them all screaming to the filthy river bottom in their metal coffins. All of it, he knew, with hundreds of pedestrians on Bridge Street, witnessing his deed from a dozen angles. The news channels would gourmandize on it for weeks.

The news channels all used that word, *souls*. Grebski knew he had to be content with a much more modest body count. It was really about style. Making a statement. Searing it into the memory of every human being in the country—maybe even the world.

Libby's half-retarded brat notwithstanding, that should suffice for carrying the family name into posterity. The bleachers hadn't rung with cheers for him in a decade. He'd give them all something to remember.

Motherfucking people, you'll pay—you'll all pay.

* * *

CHAPTER 6

Haftmann Investigative Services,
Jefferson-on-the-Lake, OH/ Aug. 11, 2:09 p.m.

"**Hey** you, remember me?"

"M-Marissa? Marissa Toensing? Oh my, it's been a few years. How have you been?"

"Great. I'm a nurse in Riverton. Word is, you became a big shot Chicago lawyer."

Haftmann winced. "Not exactly. I'm holding down the fort for my uncle while he's on vacation.

Her smile turned flirty-pouty. "Had a rough night?"

"A whole bunch of them," Haftmann said. "What brings you all the way up to Haftmann P.I. Investigations? Got a cheating husband you want spied on? Sorry, that sounded funnier in my head."

Haftmann has the vaguest recollection of being drunk with her years ago after high school graduation when the drinking and partying all night were at a peak. He remembered being with her in a bar and being the happy recipient of a blow job on that drunken weekend, but he wasn't sure she was on the end of his tumescence.

"No, not *my* husband."

He gestured her to the lone chair in the tiny office.

"I want you—I want you to follow Libby Boatwright's husband. I want a report I can present to his parole officer."

Libby Boatwright. The last name didn't tick any recollections. There was only one Libby from their mutual past.

"Libby . . . Grebski?"

"Her husband's a criminal. He's going to do something stupid. It's all he ever does. It's just a matter of time."

"You want me to find him doing something to get him violated?"

"Sorry?"

"I meant whatever his parole conditions won't permit, like carrying a weapon. Then he'll have to return to prison to serve out his sentence—is that it?"

Haftmann wasn't sure about the ethical implications. "What, if I may ask, is your interest in Libby's husband going back to prison?"

"I'm in love with her," Marissa stated flatly.

"OK."

Haftmann hoped she would amplify her statement. His uncle liked to say that love got more people killed than greed.

Sensing Haftmann's confusion at her abrupt declaration, she added: "If he's out of the picture, she'll come to her senses about her marriage. She has a son. He's in danger in that house. Boatwright's a horrible influence."

Haftmann didn't put much stock in her reply. The kid might be a good reason to interfere in another woman's marriage, yet it didn't sound genuine. He was still having a hard time wrapping his mind around the fact of highly sexualized Libby Grebski, convert to lesbianism. She was as much of a sexual athlete in high school as her infamous brother had been a couple of years earlier. All-state this and that. A thug on or off the field. An ugly story about an opponent's eye gouged in the district championship surfaced in his memory.

He thought the brother left town to play college ball but didn't remember any newspaper stories after high school. He did recall that the Grebski household was notorious throughout the town for all kinds of bad reasons—the mother a gorgeous, tall beauty with a drug habit, dead with a needle sticking in her arm. The father was so violent that Grebski *fils*, built like the proverbial brick shithouse, used to come to school sporting a black eye or chipped tooth from a brawl with his old man. Another ancient rumor popped to the surface: the head coach went to speak to the old man about clobbering his son because concussions kept him out of practices before the Friday game. The coach, a blustering, half-literate buffoon, came back and hid in his office all day; when he did appear for his obligatory afternoon classes, he turned them into study halls and remained ashen faced behind his desk.

"What do you think Boatwright is currently involved with that might help me out?"

Marissa didn't need to think about it. She pulled out a folded piece of paper and handed it to him.

Haftmann unfolded it and read: *steels heavy equipment from construction sights—makes and sells meth—has a skimmer that captures credit card numbers—sells these to an ex-con in Flint, Michigan . . .*

Haftmann read through the list and found a couple items at the end of Marissa's list that looked promising, especially the dogfighting ring.

"He goes to bars and drinks like a fish. Keeps guns around. He knows he can get away with it. Nothing but toy cops down there. You remember the place. Nobody ever checks up on him."

"How does he pass a urine test? They watch."

"Libby told me he uses some guy's piss, but she doesn't know how he manages to do it. Boatwright loves to brag on himself. He's never said how he works the system."

"Libby gave you this list?"

"I wrote it down from memory," she said. "Libby doesn't know I'm here."

"Would she . . . approve of what you're doing?"

"It's a chance I'm willing to take. He has her under his spell, the pig. I'm afraid he's going to hurt her bad one of these days. Worse than a black eye."

Haftmann asked her what Boatwright thought of his wife's sexual involvement with another woman. Neither his smattering of Latin nor his legal training went far into that area of human activity. In any event, he was going to have to speak to Uncle Sam about the ethical implications of a case that involved two parties.

Marissa Toensing wasn't the sharpest cookie in the jar back in school. Her gentle ways and pretty smile smoothed the way for her to move easily from one clique to another—not an easy thing in any high school at any time. No question, she evolved sexually since then. He gave her the standard contract, went through it with her while she listened politely, never asked a question. They concluded by talking of old friends and times past.

"You missed the last reunion," she said.

"I was working on a case and was out of town at the time."

But he thought: *that was a lie.* He had tossed the invitation in the trash as soon as he read it. He believed then and now he was past such sentimental foolishness, and he pitied his stuck-in-place classmates and their humdrum jobs and lives, and predictable marriages to be followed by predictable adulteries and divorces. He, on the other hand, was going places. His career path was just taking flight.

Haftmann watched her leave the office with a smile and wave through the plate glass. He thought of her going down on Libby, but that picture was wrong. He hadn't seen Libby Grebski since graduation, not counting two times he'd bumped into her at bars on the Strip up here. Marissa Toensing's decade since high school had been kind to her, rounded her in womanly places, and softened an already pretty face with maturity.

Lord help me, Haftmann thought, *that's another thing adding to my distress.* His protracted celibacy that seemed to stick to him like a scent that turned women away. He'd made a couple half-hearted plays in different bars and been rebuffed. Last night, for instance, the girl he was hitting on acted as if he were some forty-year-old perv. She liked rap music. He told her about the music coming out of Chicago's warehouse district. She never heard of deep house music.

Back to work, he told himself. *Uncle depends on you.* He smoothed out the notepaper Marissa had given him and looked at the list again.

OK, he said to himself, *dogfighting it shall be.*

* * *

CHAPTER 7

Lake Erie, lat. N 41° W 53'; long. NW 80° 48 '/Aug. 12, 1:16 a.m.

Thirty-four minutes left of dogwatch and he was within sight of the blinking shore lights of Northtown Harbor. Grebski was practically levitating on deck; he couldn't stand still for thinking about what was coming to these stupid bastards.

He leaned against the portside mooring winch and looked out across the water. It was a rare confluence of events in the night sky. The Perseid meteor shower was in full glory, those pea-sized meteors bursting in streaks every few seconds from high above in the southwest. In the east, a massive supermoon at its perigee, so brilliant it illuminated the ice crystals in the clouds in a display that would have thrilled him if he were not so tense in these final hours before the Big Get Even.

Back in June, waiting for the cable to wind up on the drum as they were leaving Indiana Harbor, the young deckhand, an obsessive gamer, asked Grebski if he was familiar with the arcade game *Mortal Kombat*. Grebski blurted out that he wasn't but was going to master it before they tied up for the winter. He had been deep in his reverie about slaughter. The deckhand looked puzzled and moved off. Grebski had no feelings about his shipmates. He had a deep loathing for the third mate and the boneheaded steward, but they were all going to die in the end just like the new deckhand.

Nobody comes out of this alive. Not even me . . .

The thrill that knowledge gave him made him leery of going belowdecks for fear of saying something that might alert someone. Third Mate Johnson, the wheelsman, the bosun, and the two members of the "conveyor gang"—the *Gött* being a self-unloading bulk

37

freighter—were having another loud game of Texas Hold 'em with monthly paychecks risked in the jackpots. Even in a poker game, the former jarhead of a third mate had to flex his muscle around Grebski. In the galley for supper that night, he wore a t-shirt stretched tight across his deltoids that had *I Do Alpha Male Shit* written across the chest. Grebski was going to make him the sole exception. He wanted this prick to know he, Mitch Grebski, was going to kill him before he killed him.

The wind, as usual, was from the northwest at his back, with swells of three to four feet—just a gentle rolling as the boat cut through the black waters and curled a white comma of foam against the hull.

Grebski looked at his watch again. Just two minutes had passed since he last checked. His stomach growled from hunger because he ate little, fearing a full stomach might make him slow when the time came to strike, and *strike* was the operant word. The card game presented a problem if it did not break up soon. The third mate's high-and-tight buzzcut shone under the generator lighting. He was sure he could take out the two guys from the engine department, both little men with stick arms and beer bellies. The older of the two was a grizzled veteran of the lakes who liked smutty talk and bragging about being a confirmed bachelor.

"I never get nagged, I hunt and fish whenever I like," he liked to say. "I can snort coke off strippers' asses unlike you married jerks." Grebski would think: *The only thing you'll be snorting will be your brains coming through your nasal cavity and sooner than you think . . .*

Torn between going all the way down the deck to the galley for some food or having a lie-down to settle the riffs of nervous energy, he chose the latter. He'd have to run a gauntlet past the card players and hear some veiled insults in passing, especially from the wheelsman and the mate, the two members of the deck department he had the most dealings with.

Drinking and drugs were forbidden on board all Great Lakes freighters, but that policy needed to be enforced. The third mate wasn't one to enforce any vice he enjoyed. He was a notorious whoredog who cheated on his wife not only with an Ojibway Indian girlfriend from International Falls but also a forty-year-old married woman from Cheboygan Harbor he brought on board in port stops. Just the day before, he had taken a ride on the bum boat to Mackinaw Island to spend an afternoon with his wife and three daughters before rejoining the *Gött* on Lake Huron.

He'd chance it, he figured. He stepped down the ladder into the common area that split off into separate deck crew's quarters on either side. His foot no sooner touched the bottom plate than the steward, drunk, hollered: "Hey, Grebski, something wrong with the Beef Wellington tonight? I noticed you didn't eat nothin."

"That what you're calling it? Looked like dog food." Grebski kept his head down and feet moving toward the deckhand sleeping quarters.

He heard his name called again—Johnson, the third mate, who else?

Grebski clenched, expecting another jibe, his name being a favorite target—that and the fact that he'd remained a deckhand all these years, refusing to try the Able Seaman test again. Reading word had steadily become more difficult since high school. It gave the mate fodder to ridicule him. He hesitated at the door, hand squeezing the handle so hard his knuckles were white like the "diamond points" of boxers' hands.

"Grab-ASS-ki."

"*Grebski*, mate."

"Kind of fuckin' name is that anyway? Polack? Hunky?"

Slurred speech, drunk obviously. The captain didn't have the balls to discipline his ship despite the No Alcohol signs all over the place.

"Sounds like a bug's name," the mate said. "Hey, Grab-ass, I'm talking to you. Don't walk away from me!"

Grebski turned, faced the table but didn't make eye contact with the mate for fear something might happen he could not control. His hands shook. *Not now . . . not now*—

"The first, he wants to see you," the mate said.

"Right now?"

"Who the hell do you think the first mate is, moron? Right fuckin' now!"

A tinkle of laughter, a cough here and there. The jump in electricity in the room was palpable. The testosterone in Grebski fought his recent vow to lie low, be calm.

The third mate made a mistake: he decided to play to the boys at the table.

"McElroy says, he says," —

The mate attempting the basso-profundo New England accent of the first mate: "You see that lazy sonofabitch Grebski, send that big dummy to me, chop-chop."

Nervous laughter, louder, some coughs into fists. Grebski knew this was the moment he would hold it or lose it for good.

"Speaking of big asses, mate," he said with slow, careful enunciation; "why don't you go topside and look at the moon? It'll remind you of something."

"Remind me of what, fucker?"

"How many craters it has as like your wife's ass."

The words slipped past his teeth, greased on a half-season's worth of contempt. The second big dog answered the first's challenge, and it was on, no stopping it now. Everybody in the room knew it. A man at the table snickered at Grebski's cheap wit. Without another word, the mate's big fist slammed the table sending cards, chips, and drinks jumping and flying about as if the table had exploded from below. No more laughter from the men present. All eyes were downcast looking at their cards in their hands—except for the bosun, who stared at Grebski in outright shock. A bland, company man, he talked too much. Grebski always avoided him on deck.

The mate roared: "What—what the fuck did you just say to me, you asshole?"

Grebski tried to walk back the comment: "Forget it, mate."

It didn't work. "Like fuck I will!"

The mate's forehead became a single-browed, prognathous ridge of fury. His eyes lasered Grebski, tracking him as he quick-walked back to the ladder steps. Grebski had both hands on the iron railing when the roar erupted from behind followed by the crash of the table and the clattering of its contents across the metal deck. By the time the sound registered in Grebski's brain, it was too late. The mate's hand

40

was a claw digging into the fabric of shirt at his shoulder, spinning him around. The cocked fist that the mate hurled at his nose missed but caught enough of Grebski's cheekbone to puff it up the skin almost to his eye in an instant. Grebski kept his balance only because he slammed into the handrail just above his kidneys.

Before Johnson could launch another haymaker, Grebski stepped up the ladder to make his escape. A brawl right now would ruin everything. Before he could take another step, his ankle was grabbed by the mate and he was pulled down to the deck in a heap. Reaching out to seize the rail, Grebski felt knuckles pop and a bone shatter when the mate's boot smashed his hand.

Grebski rolled sideways but couldn't avoid a second kick to his back. The mate was already measuring him for a third kick that would have meant lights out. He shifted his feet like a boxer and drew his right leg back. Grebski glimpsed in that moment the blood-mottled, shiny face of the man who was about to destroy his project. Grebski rolled into him, hard, and caught his leg at the knee just as the kick's inertia was at its maximum velocity. The leg went sideways even as the momentum of the kick propelled the rest of the mate's large body forward right over the prone Grebski.

Everyone heard the sound. It had the deep resonance of a clapper in an iron bell except that the handrail was a steel pipe, and it caught the mate viciously across the neck before he could get his hands up to break the fall. Grebski scuttled away, ready on his feet for the mate's next attack. But there was nothing coming. The mate's hand reached up in slow-motion to clutch the rail, but he didn't get up. When he shifted his body to turn around, his face was drained of blood and there was foam issuing from a corner of his mouth. Then he began flopping, a hideous parody of a fish reeled into a boat, and a gurgling noise came from him. The other men stood around like kids watching a playground fight.

The bosun bellowed: "He can't breathe! He's choking!"

Grebski stood rock still, waiting for what came next. His mind went numb. Vicious pain throttled up his arms.

The bosun was safety officer for the *Gött*. He knew first-aid.

"Hold his arms and legs!" he demanded of the others who'd backed away into a tight circle away from the combatants. "Give me some help here!"

Jolted into action, everyone except Grebski moved in on the mate simultaneously and held one of his thrashing limbs. Unseen, Grebski reached down to his boot and took out his filleting knife. His right hand was too damaged to grip the knife firmly, he realized, and this hesitation for what to do next sent his thoughts into hyperdrive: *wait, stop, no, go, go, head for the stairs, right now, get the bar—climb the stairs, do them one at a time, as fast as you can. Swing, swing, keep swinging away until the floor is awash in brains.*

His confused thoughts sent him stumbling forward toward the mass of men crouched around the thrashing mate. He was going to have to kill them all *right now* or else it would be too late. He knew when the third mate said he was wanted in the pilot house by the first mate that they were going to fire him for that business back in the *Gött's* last port stop.

The bosun jerked his head sideways and Grebski approaching with the knife in his hand. He reached out for the bone-handled knife from Grebski's swollen hand. It clattered to the deck and the bosun scooped it up. Grebski watched him slit a two-inch incision in the mate's Adam's apple.

Pawing around the floor like a blind man, he grabbed one of the playing cards off the floor and folded it into a funnel which he jammed into the hole. Immediately a gout of blood shot out. The wheelsman holding down the mate's right arm was sprayed. He let go of the arm. The mate began bucking off the floor, clutching at the thing in his throat, no doubt blaming it for the panic flooding his limbic brain. His face turned from cherry-pink to a grayish-blue tint. His powerful body thrust the men in several directions; they barely managed to control him.

The mate surrendered to shock. The bosun worked at his throat and then he shouted to the others: "Hold him down, or he'll choke to death!"

Grebski reinserted the card into the mate's throat and another tiny crimson geyser shot forth. Finally, a bubble of air and an eerie noise of struggling lungs trying to compress, straining for precious air. Grebski leaned toward the card the bosun pinched into a funnel shape and blew the breath of life back into his enemy's body.

With his damaged hand limp at his side, he continued to blow air until the mate, insensate but alive, lay still for the nourishing oxygen. Grebski could not cease his life-giving ministration to see what was going on, but the men came to their senses and began to talk among themselves as they eased their hold on the prone body now twitching at intervals. Grebski kept him alive, timing his head bobs to make sure the lungs were inflating.

Grebski's own brain seemed fully alive, getting that squirt of protein from the amygdala to keep him in perfect synchronicity. Theta and alpha waves conjoining, meshing, like athletes in their zone, he would not let himself think ahead of the moment-by-moment resuscitation. When the bosun returned to pull Grebski away from the mate and insert a plastic tube from the first mate's medical kit, Grebski's neck was kinked with stiffness. He noticed a dozen men, some freshly awakened, all staring at him. His shirt front was blood-spattered; his face was swollen on one side and his eye sunk behind bruised flesh.

Hands gripped him under his shoulders and pulled him upright. Grebski, who had avoided these men as the fox avoids the groundhog he intends to kill, found himself the cynosure of all eyes and full, hostile attention. Someone in the crowd kicked him in the stomach. He could not focus on the first mate, standing in front of him and whose mouth was moving without sound penetrating Grebski. His legs tried to walk him away from all this attention, but he could not free himself from their collective grip. His brain screamed at him to flee, get into his bunk.

He thought somebody behind him did something to him, inserted a wire into his ear, or rammed something under his ribs, because he lost all body control at once. In a terrified flash, he suspected they had discovered the journal and knew all about the project. They were ganging up to kill him. Liquids gushed from him—his nose leaked, saliva frothed from his mouth when he tried to speak, tried to tell them he was fine, he just wanted to sleep for a while. *Before I kill every motherfucking one of you . . .* Then, he realized he could do nothing with a broken hand, and with nothing left of his project to salvage, his knees buckled. Tears fell. The ducts flowed freely, like broken pipes, his snot and phlegm gagged him, and his eyes stung from the salty flow, but he could not speak words that made sense.

Images of all that had ever tormented him as a boy tumbled through the lens of his neocortex: his dope fiend mother's teats spilling from her bra, the rutting from her bedroom with any man who could supply her, his father's beatings, and one he culled from the abyss as his most painful: sitting in history class in the last seat of the second row while tears fell down his face from the concussion of his last clubbing by his father, the girl whose name he cannot recall, a dark-eyed Italian girl, gets up and takes him by the hand while everyone stares—his trashy family known to all—and gets him to sit down in the hall. Nausea fills his stomach with hot bile; sobs of pain and suppressed fury shake his body. The girl, a classmate he never spoke to before, pats his hand gently, and he feels he has hit the bottom rung of hell.

He heard the wheelsman say, "Look, he pissed himself."

Someone else mumbled about "an epileptic seizure."

The first mate said: "Get him into his bunk. Strap him down."

Before they tied him with sheets to the corners of his bunk, he raved. Hours later, when the first mate came down to check on him, the *Gött* blew the signal for entering Northtown Harbor. Its bow thrusters obviated the need for the tugs to lead the boat to harbor. Just another routine run. There'd be a few bouts of heavy drinking at the Wyandotte Bar on Bridge Street and a few hangovers back on board, some wives and girlfriends would meet their husbands and boyfriends for a rendezvous at the new hotel on Goodwill Avenue. A normal port of call for a lakeboat freighter. If it weren't for the brawl belowdecks between two shipmates, there would be nothing to text home about.

* * *

CHAPTER 8

Residence of Thomas Haftmann, Northtown, OH/Aug. 14, 9:04 a.m.

Thomas Haftmann woke with his temples throbbing like a bongo being sporadically hit with spoons. *Oh my fucking God. Not again, why—why do I do this to myself?*

His disgust was leavened by the shocking ease with which he had wound up closing down Hanratty's Irish Bar on a weekday night. Hanratty's was his uncle's favorite watering hole just across the street. Haftmann had never seen his uncle get even slightly drunk in the bar. He had never left it sober enough to drive a vehicle legally. Last night, he barely managed a walk across the street to collapse on the cot in the office. All his newly minted vows to stay sober like do much confetti in a wind tunnel.

I am destined to be nothing more than a drunk in my life.

He stood up too abruptly. Dizziness forced him to sit back down. The rickety, fold-up cot collapsed around him, and he hit the floor. One retractable brace pinched two of his fingers and let out a yelp of pain. A young family strolling past pushing a stroller swiveled their heads to see him through the plate glass. The man and the mother laughed in sync as they moved out of sight.

It took Haftmann a full thirty seconds to extricate himself from the tangled wood and torn fabric pinning him. His personal antic farce was prolonged when he kicked the broken legs of the cot wrapped around his ankles free. It flew into the small bookcase where he kept some law books he couldn't part with but which pierced him like arrows when he glanced at them. A loose paperback fell to the floor.

Haftmann didn't recall putting it there, much less reading it. A collection of essays by twentieth-century existentialists with names he barely recalled: Sartre, Camus, Heidegger, de Beauvoir, Marcel, Tillich. It must have been one of his many books from college that he never got around to reading.

What have I got to lose? He figured.

He opened the book at random and began reading: "There is but one serious philosophical problem, and that is suicide. Judging whether life is or is not worth living amounts to answering the fundamental question of philosophy."

Despite his hangover, he finished reading it. At the end, where the demigod is pushing his rock up the hill again, his eternal punishment, yet happy, Haftmann was overwhelmed by a feeling he had not experienced before. Suppressing a sob, he returned to the beginning and re-read the essay, lingering over passages, and oblivious to the stares of people passing by.

* * *

CHAPTER 9
Coast Guard Station, Northtown Harbor/ Aug. 15, 2:00 p.m.

The hallucination was so real he thought he was drenched in blood, his blood. His olfactory senses had sharpened to a keen pitch where he could smell the stink of his own intestines. He believed he heard the billions of bacteria festering in there, breeding and popping into seething life like so many bubbles swirling a drain. Like maggots feasting on roadkill.

Grebski ripped at his leather straps before more clawed hands could get to him. He couldn't see their faces behind the terrorist-style masks. He didn't remember every detail of how he got here, but the out-of-body experience he recalled somewhere in his battered psyche have been the men carrying him on a stretcher to the Coast Guard patrol boat. He thought he was flying above them at one point, but it must have been the stretcher basket he was lashed to and then lowered over the side. When he closed his eyes, he saw himself floating above the deck, an avenging angel with his rebar club in one hand and the garrote in the other. The image dissolved and he felt an enormous hand, clawed like a giant owl's talon, pushing his face down through the mattress and bedsprings into the cement floor.

Time passed. He didn't know how much. A four-block window panel of sea-green glass let little light into the small room, which housed the detainees (the preferred term of the emergency manual) for anyone the Coast Guard believed was in its authority to hold. Everything in this small detention cell—walls, floor, ceiling—was a depressing pewter gray.

A man with a bag and a stethoscope draped across his neck entered without knocking. He was accompanied by the Coast Guard station commander if the chevrons on his sleeves and the egg yolk on his cap meant anything. Grebski looked into the face staring into his face: foreign-born, Iranian, or Middle Eastern visage, fortyish, black-frame glasses with thick lenses, and hair growing out of his ears and nostrils. His cologne was citrusy and Grebski felt his stomach churn. The man's pen light hit him square in the iris and he was ordered to "follow the light with his eyes." The man spoke softly to the commander and gave him a script for a prescription. Grebski did not fathom the words except every fourth or fifth one. He heard "metacarpal fractures," "seizure," "MRI," and watched the doctor hand a business card to the commander.

That afternoon (the light from the cubed glass told him the time) a detective entered the room. This time the commander did not accompany him. The man introduced himself as a Det. Sgt. Peter Moisio.

Grebski was back in control and had stopped chafing against his bonds. The big cop told him no charges were being filed against him for the assault. Witnesses to the fight testified he was attacked and had defended himself.

"Will charges be filed against Johnson?"

"The third mate? The FBI has jurisdiction over maritime vessels. But not as far as I know. I'm a liaison officer in this capacity, so you needn't fear any trouble from me, Mister Grebski."

"Where is Johnson?"

"I was told he was life-flighted to the Cleveland Clinic. His hyoid bone was crushed when he hit the railing."

"When can I rejoin my vessel?"

The lieutenant looked at him hard, a cop's auger. He was well dressed in a suit and tie, but the thickness in the shoulders and arms made him look uncomfortable in his clothes. His brown eyes revealed no pity, and Grebski wondered for a moment if his journal has been discovered.

"That's not for me to say. The captain told me you've been fired for cause. Besides, the commander here tells me the bone in your hand is broken. You're going to be one-handed for a while."

"Then I'm not under arrest?"

"No, you were sedated for your own good. You were thrashing around and screaming. As soon as the doctor clears you, you can leave."

"Then fuck off and tell the doctor to get in here."

"He's outside the door. I'll tell him to come in."

A long minute passed in which Grebski figured the doctor was picking the cop's brain for something to delay his release. Finally, he came inside. This time he knocked.

"Mister Grebski, good to see you up."

"I'm not up, doctor. I'm strapped down."

"That was quite a fit you threw, they tell me." *Big fake smile, bedside manner horseshit.*

"I'd like to leave now."

"Of course. The commander has called your sister, I believe. She's on her way up from Riverton. She'll take you home to recuperate."

"Can you take these fucking straps off?"

"I'll have the officer do that as soon as I leave. I'd like to recommend someone for you to see. I'd also like you to come to my office for a check-up. We'd like to schedule a scan for you to see if there's any damage from the fight."

That was horseshit, too. They want to know if they can use it to get me fired.

Grebski said nothing. He wanted the man to go away.

"When you're sufficiently rested, that is." Another loopy smile, the fidgety mannerisms with the fingers. Grebski figured this guy was a candidate for seducing women patients. Something desperate about him. He imagined his rebar club punching through his skull, cleaving the brain hemispheres neatly into two. A second blow to pound all the way to his limbic brain at the top of the spinal column. Maybe a third to take it down to the jawbone. The mandible flapping like a ventriloquist's dummy's mouth.

"Ah, it's good to see you smiling. This good friend of mine," the doctor said. "He's a psychiatrist, you know. I'm going to leave his card for you with his office number. I'll put it on the table—yes? For when you get ready to leave."

Grebski remained silent but he his own eyes drilled the man.

"OK, right. I'll just be on my way. Please make that appointment as soon as you are able, Mister Grebski."

Grebski watched him leave. He let out his breath. *No charges on me, free to go.*

Two Coast Guardsmen whose badges meant they were both unrated apprentices entered the cell and undid his wrist straps. They told him to get dressed and said that they would escort him off the premises where he could wait for his ride. One of them saw the card on the table and handed it to Grebski while he laced up his boots. Grebski snapped it from his hand and tore it in half.

All those beatings, all those years. One concussion after another from the time he was fifteen and big enough to get punched in the head or play contact sports. Even going back into a game with a concussion that left him with a blinding headache all day afterward and non-stop vomiting for the rest of the weekend. Then football practice on Monday: the fuckhead coach lining up his players for what he called "Round-the-Mulberry-Bush" drill. At the edge of the practice field, two players run around a stunted bush at top speed to collide helmet-to-helmet. Grebski, being the bull of the team, was chosen to go several times with players the coach wanted to test or punish.

Where the fuck was all this shit about MRIs then?

* * *

CHAPTER 10

Residence of the Boatwrights, Dean and Libby,
Riverton, OH/Aug. 18, 4:40 p.m.

"**Place** is a goddamn dump, Lib," Grebski said with disgust.

Shutters were hanging from one hasp latch, the whole place needed paint. On the west side where the sun hit, the entire side of the house had serious wood rot and alligatoring. The gutters and drainpipes were either missing or had gaping rust holes you could put a fist through.

"Dean's not much of a handyman."

"That cocksucker. If this was an ore boat, it'd sink."

"Watch your mouth around my husband, Mitch. I mean it."

Grebski grunted. He was already missing the orderliness of life aboard a freighter.

"Who'th'fuck are you to complain? I'm the one stuck here in this shithole," Libby said.

"What about all the money I been sending you?"

"God damn, I wrote you about that, man! Lawyers cost a freaking shitload of money. Dean's been doing time the last three years. You know that. He don't have a job yet. Nobody wants to hire an ex-con. We're on welfare, SNAP card—the whole nine yards of government bullshit. I've been sending him commissary money. He said the Aryan Brotherhood will kill him—"

"That's what he said? Lying sack of shit. Fuck him," Grebski said. "What has that hillbilly contributed to this shitty marriage of yours?"

"Oh, fuck it, Mitch. I'm so tired! We ain't even in the goddamn house yet, and you're badgering me. You don't like the fuckin' house, you fucking fix it up."

He watched her walk up the broken porch steps and experienced that old thrill in his belly. Her womanly ass stretched the fabric of her jeans. Wore them with the big gaping fashion holes like a teenager. That old poison in his blood coursed through his veins once again as if time had not lapsed a day since high school.

Half my paycheck for the last three years while that shithead Dean was doing his bid at the Youngstown penitentiary, Grebski figured. *That added up to more than lawyers' fees.*

Mitch knew that loser husband always had a new Ford F150 or Silverado with all the electronic gadgetry and decorative trimmings. Libby's Honda was pocked with rust and had a crack that zig-zagged across the windshield. His foot nearly went through the floorboard on the drove to her house. He could see the dusty blue tarp covering Boatwright's latest acquisition sticking out of the garage and was tempted to go over and key the finish from stem to stern.

Patience, he told himself. *Killing shouldn't be done like whack-a-mole.* Besides, Dean was going to take it out on Libby if he was still in the house whenever he got back from his latest half-assed caper that got him jugged again. He didn't buy the no-job spiel Libby handed him, either. That hillbilly shitsucker would sell Brazilian butt lifts in a nursing home.

One spectacular event is all that's required, Grebski believed. He would not forsake his vow to get revenge with a big body count.

Be like nature, he told himself; *one major earthquake followed by aftershocks. If time permits, add him to the tremors.*

* * *

CHAPTER 11

Three miles from Cato Springs Road,
Northtown Township/ Aug. 22, 11:14 p.m.

Haftmann was being eaten alive. The mosquitoes and deer flies were biting chunks of his flesh despite the bug repellant he had applied lavishly before setting off.

He'd been following Dean ever since he left Chick Brown's bar with a six-pack tucked under his arm. So much for that parole violation, but Haftmann didn't bother to snap a shot with his crap camera, much less waste a shot with the bulky telephoto lens he brought along. Marissa wasn't interested in anything trivial. She wanted him back in the slammer doing hard time for a major violation.

Haftmann wasn't sure where, exactly, he was. This part of the county was all abandoned farmland with wind-stunted apple trees bending in the winds roaring down from Canada. The farm was six miles outside the township in the real boonies. The Jefferson paper called it a "haven for meth cookers." Deserted farms overgrown with dockweed and stunted trees of heaven, trailers on cement blocks you wouldn't want your dog to live in, and coyotes who prowled the marshes for ducks.

Dean's pick-up was evidence he made money somewhere. Out here in the sticks there weren't many legal opportunities. Back in the nineties, a Cleveland serial killer used Cato Springs Road as a body dump. The *Plain Dealer* reported four crack prostitutes from East Cleveland had been found by deer poachers, all rotting within a thousand yards of one another.

Haftmann secretly hoped it was meth cooking, not dogs. One snap, bleary or not, of the cooking operation in some ramshackle shed or hideaway should do the trick. When he called his uncle about it, he got a lecture on f-stops and bokeh. He was more worried about Lyme disease from the ticks that were no doubt feasting on various parts of his body. He had taped his trousers to his legs but left the back of his shirt collar open. It was either itchy sweat from his boozing pouring down his back or he had some insect life going on back there.

He maintained a good distance so that he could keep the binocs on Dean Boatwright without fear of twigs snapping and drawing attention to him. He parked his Jeep into a thicket of overgrown vegetation off the road as soon as Dean made the turn down an unpaved gravel road—little more than a four-wheeler path with ankle-deep ruts. He'd never have been able to keep him in sight without riding up his backside. His uncle neglected to train him or give him advice about surveillance. Any imbecile can do a stakeout, Haftmann would have told him, and in fact it never even occurred to him to ask about this part of the job.

"I'm just a secretary with a drinking problem," he muttered with the binocular lenses steaming up from the perspiration on his forehead. The salt sting in his eyes made him curse. He imagined the carbon dioxide he was exuding with every breath encouraged every mosquito within a mile to zero in on his prostrate form. The Beretta he'd brought along irritated his hip bone. He bought it on the Strip from a biker with a serious drug addiction. Taking a gun on the job would have sent Uncle Sam into a frenzy had he known.

"C'mon, Dean, you wife-beating jailbird, do something," he muttered.

Dean appeared to be walking off distances from old fence posts attached to the gray-black boards of what had once been the side of a farmhouse. Haftmann could see the roof was caved in and shingles had dropped into the upper floor—if there was an upper floor left. It didn't look like a place where you'd want to hold dog fights, but it was well hidden from the roads and safe from noise traveling on the wind.

It wouldn't get dark for another hour at this light. He assumed the party wouldn't get started until then. He was wrong. Within twenty minutes, the place was rocking. He heard more than saw a pair of Harley Fat Boys and three rusted-out Ford and Chevy pickups amble and buck down the rutted path Dean had followed to the clearing. Fifteen minutes later, he heard dogs growling but couldn't see the kennels.

He lay still and breathed evenly. The pungent stink of swamp muck was nauseating. His original plan had been to creep up close and snap a shot of some illicit activity. He hadn't counted on so many people milling about. Two men carried folding tables; others loaded them with beer. Some were set up with booze and snacks and kegs of beer.

Dean, meanwhile, directed the rigging up a square of light bulbs and looping the wires from two corners of a decayed farmhouse to one limb of a birch tree and back again to a rusted pole that might once have held a home for purple martins. Inside the window of yellow light were dozens of people, mostly bikers and their women.

Probationer bikers ran around fetching beers for their gang brothers-to-be. Haftmann's face itched from going unshaven and sweating. Most of the men had beards or elaborate moustaches. The patches on the cutoff vests bore the diamond one-percenter's symbol and other signs of achievement for the ones who had put in the serious work of biker mayhem. Greasy jeans, beards, ponytails, and tattoos—it looked like Altamont, 1969, to Haftmann.

He zeroed the binoculars on Dean again. He walked over to one of the tables and casually liberated one of the beers from its bucket cocoon of ice. The he sauntered over casually while work went on around him to chat up a blonde and brunette. Both teenagers from the looks.

They weren't the usual hatchet-faced slags on the backs of Harleys roaring down the Strip on summer nights. Haftmann put them in their early twenties—local girls. Some of them, not just the runaways at the resort, liked to play with fire and hung out with the various biker gangs riding through the resort town. They sported cleavage and showed off butterfly tattoos. Dean was tracing one on a girl's back shoulder while she giggled.

The girls giggled and hip-bumped him, flirting with their bodies. It made Haftmann think of remora fish coasting safely beneath a shark's belly.

Dean grabbed an ass cheek of the blonde. "What's yer name, sweetie?"

Giggles, name-calling, laughter. Old Dean, comedian on probation.

Then they arrived in steady intervals every few minutes. Haftmann counted twenty big engines droning along. It was like waiting for the last kernel of popcorn in the microwave. It was five minutes since the last one. All trucks, Silverados and F-150s, he guessed—Dean's crowd, not your sporty SUV suburbanites.

He grabbed the bag and worked his way in the darkness toward the sounds. Truck doors slammed in the distance, loud men hooted. Finally, the dogs. He saw the lights speckling the blackness. Dean had rigged more lights just beyond and strung them in a square. Haftmann made out the edges of the plywood shanties he had constructed for the dog pens.

When he was about fifty yards to the lit square, he took out the night-vision binoculars. He could make out an area of churned-up earth bordered by the jerry-built cages of the fighting dogs. Nearby was a bigger plywood cage hut with chicken wire stretched across the front. That was where he guessed Dean kept the bait dogs. He detected a glowing, squirming, huddled mass of hind quarters, muzzles, and tails in the magma glow of my lens, but it was impossible to tell one kind of dog from another.

He counted at least twenty men and five women. Nobody looked to be packing, but they were a rough-looking crowd. Some of the trucks had wire cages in the beds for their dogs they had brought to match up. The women were all around thirty, mostly chainsmokers, and wore sweatshirts with goofy or obscene sayings on them.

Around ten o'clock Dean started the festivities with a prelim meant to lather up the crowd and whet their betting appetites. He grabbed a short-haired dog by its tail from the coop and dragged it to the center of the pit. He held it between his legs and wrapped duct tape around its muzzle; the dog sat abruptly on its haunches in the center of the ring, jerking its head all around. A urine stream jetted from its nether region in a bright arc made fluorescent by Haftmann's binoculars.

The shouting grew a notch in volume and then a black blur streaked to the center of the ring. The action was intense, hard to follow unless you had the shutter speed of a fly's vision. With the glasses, it was even harder but it was evident what was happening to the bait dog—it was methodically butchered by the pit bull, ripped from stem to stern. He tore open its throat with some lunges and shook it like a hunting dog trying to break a muskrat's neck. He remained clamped down on the dead dog's forepaw even when Dean beat the dog on the head to force its jaws open. Haftmann saw the slavering fangs appear ghostly white.

Another dog was brought out, a large poodle from the looks of it. This dog was equally terrified, but it ran from one end of the ring to the other before its attacker, another brindled pit bull, cornered it. The poodle thrust its own taped muzzle at its deranged enemy but that didn't deflect the charges which drew blood or knocked the animal backwards. The crowd's cheering was heightened every time the pit bull took a chunk of flesh or fur from its helpless victim. The end came when the attack dog rammed the poodle into the corner like a linebacker sacking a quarterback and worried its dying body with shrugs of its bunched-up shoulder muscles.

Haftmann felt his stomach turn to water as he watched the dying dog's legs spasm and twitch until Dean entered to pull the dog off the carcass.

The first match was between some bearded redneck's dog and the first dog Dean loosed into the ring. The betting commenced and the men's wallets opened for the contest. From where he was, Haftmann couldn't tell one dog from the other. The fight lasted twenty minutes. Neither dog wanted to quit but they were both bloodied and foaming blood and saliva by the time it was called off.

The redneck's dog was declared the winner. He received a wad of bills from somebody acting as bookie and several claps on the back from a few spectators. The man took his bruised warrior off to the side where a piece of tarpaulin lay on the ground near some buckets. He emptied one of the buckets over his dog to clean him of blood and drool. The dog whipped its tight body and sent a drizzle of spray in all directions.

Haftmann tensed. He heard a commotion near the opposite side of the ring and put the glasses on a cluster of men surrounding Dean. He moved off a distance. Then he returned carrying a long-barreled Ruger he slipped into a holster tied to a post. The dog that lost the fight lay dead between the legs of the men who had witnessed the execution or the *coup de grâce*, although that, Haftmann felt, was too good an expression for this spectacle.

The second fight was a replay of the first one except that one dog was clearly more the aggressor. It looked like the dog which had killed the poodle, but he wasn't sure. It was obviously one of Dean's because he took the congratulations and pocketed a wad of bills just like the other man. He didn't bother to wash off his dog. He simply hoisted it by its stub tail and chest into a top cage behind the ring.

Haftmann didn't know how many of these he'd be forced to watch until he found the courage to act. His new plan was to bellycrawl his way to the cages after the fights, snap whatever he could without a flash, and haul ass back to the Jeep. Not much of a plan, and the photos would be clear in this light, but it was proof enough to get the Sheriff's department involved and Dean remanded.

Haftmann's plan changed drastically when Dean loomed into his binoculars' view holding another whimpering, small dog he was drawing out of a cage on a pickup bed. He zeroed in on the dog's white chest markings.

"Fuck me," Haftmann said pressing his face into the dirt. "Nothing's ever simple."

He already knew there was at least one gun around. He had no time to call the sheriff's because Dean was already gripping the Corgi's muzzle. His binoculars picked out the tape in Dean's other hand.

Haftmann was up and running, stumbling through the brush. He ran headlong toward the lights, giddy with fear—a real ass-puckering fear—and screaming "Police! Everyone! Don't move!"

Haftmann thought of Sisyphus when he ran blindly into that crazed, dogfighting mob. His uncle used to warn him about physical danger on the job. "They don't give medals to private eyes killed in the line of duty because they're mercenaries, and that fact makes them less valuable and a whole lot less brave than cops," he told his nephew.

Haftmann's youth notwithstanding, he was out of shape and fueled entirely by adrenalin. When he came into view, Dean's hand was still gripping the dog's fur to steady him. Haftmann had his full attention. He also had the attention of everybody else in the squared circle and their silent, menacing stares, once the surprise vanished, would stay with him forever. But he had the gun free of the holster and he was holding it out and swinging it in an arc.

"I'm taking that dog, Dean," he said as soon as he found his voice. He was about to add "Don't anybody try to stop me" when he recalled that's what the stooges in bad cop dramas always say before they get the shit beat out of them.

The problem was the Corgi. He didn't know Haftmann from Adam, and he was in such primeval fear that when Haftmann reached down to hoist him into his arms from the stupefied Dean, the dog jerked its body free of the duct tape, whirled around and bit Haftmann on the chin. Then he put his low-slung body into high gear and bucked out of his grasp. Dean and Haftmann, like two sitcom actors, looked at each other and then both turned to watch the fleeing dog bolt past everybody. The Corgi was gone like smoke, his little alligator legs churning like wheels.

Dean took advantage of the distraction. He threw out a fist that caught Haftmann on the side of the neck. It wasn't enough to take him down but it sent him tottering sideways. That was the signal for everybody to cut and run. Some fled this way, some tore off in the direction the dog had gone, and a couple bigger men balled their big fists and took a step toward Haftmann, who raised the gun in their direction.

The first shot snapped past Haftmann and thwacked into the plywood. He never heard the shot, but he felt the air sizzle beside his left ear lobe. This was getting into nightmare time way too fast, he realized. He saw himself in a gunfight with twenty hillbillies shielded by their mud-spattered trucks and armed with deer rifles and .357s. He wasted no more time with stupid heroics and took off between the dog cages and ran as fast as his legs could carry him, which is to say, not as fast as his limbic brain was urging him on.

He took a roundabout way back to the Jeep, remembering the woodsman trick of compensating if you're right legged so you wouldn't wind up circling back where you started.

He called the sheriff's office from the highway and gave them directions and descriptions of the place. The dispatcher sounded bored. Illegal dog fights didn't impress her as any kind of big-deal emergency.

"You weren't there," he said and thumbed off. He left out the part about pointing a weapon at people and identifying himself as law enforcement. If it came up later, he figured he'd deal with it then. Meanwhile the adrenalin had subsided to a bad-tasting lump in his stomach.

He made it back to his uncle's office by two in the morning, bedraggled, muddy, with a dozen facial lacerations from stinging branches whipping at him from all directions, his clothes full of brambles, seed pods, and rips as well as a limp acquired from a gopher hole. He left the Jeep parked in front of the office and crossed the empty, rain-glazed sidewalk. He crashed on the fold-up cot kept in the closet for emergencies, too tired to drive home and shower. In the morning, Haftmann told himself he'd clean up. He fell asleep thinking of the fleeing Corgi and hoped he made it home, wherever that was before Dean stole him out of his yard.

He woke at seven, an hour past the alarm setting. He called Marissa and left her a summary of what he had found out there in the abandoned orchards when he halted his much-abridged progress report in mid-sentence. Haftmann had a brain flash, a satori, as the Japanese called them. He wasn't sure why he'd stopped in mid-sentence but something was wrong. He knew she was going to be with Libby at her house because today was the day Dean was getting out.

Hanratty's wouldn't be serving for several more hours, anyway, which fact gave him time to kill. He also had a personal score to settle with Dean, so he drove down to Riverton and found the address

Marissa had given him for Libby Boatwright's and saw a half-dozen police cruisers and sheriff's cars already there.

When I saw the flashing turquoise and cherry lights of the cruisers parked in front of the house, his rage evaporated. A deputy fast-walked toward him when he saw Haftmann getting out of my car behind the EMT ambulance.

"This is a crime scene," the deputy said. "You can't go in there."

"That's all right, Officer," Haftmann said with a surge of pride. "I'm the one who called it in."

"Wait here," the deputy replied. "A detective will be right out."

When the detective came out, Haftmann shook hands and repeated what he'd said to the deputy.

"You called in the suicide?"

"What—suicide?" Haftmann asked the detective, stunned.

The detective looked down at his notebook. "Marissa Toensing— if that's how it's pronounced," he said.

Haftmann recalled that *frisson* running up his spine when he left the partial message on her phone just minutes ago; the phone was probably ringing in her purse while the detectives were examining her body in the house.

One of his law school professors surprised a class on torts with a Latin expression, and being a third-year law student, Haftmann translated it: *Homo homini lupus est.*

Haftmann said it to himself, not Latin this time but in English, watching two deputies escort Dean Boatwright, hands cuffed behind him, to a cruiser.

"Man is a wolf to man."

* * *

CHAPTER 12

Haftmann Investigative Services,
Jefferson-on-the-Lake, OH/Aug. 23, 9:46 a.m.

Haftmann was composing the third draft of his resignation letter to his uncle. He outlined some talking points so that his uncle, upon return, would see his nephew's basic unfitness for this kind of work. *Any kind of work that involves people*, Haftmann thought morosely, still reeling from the shock of Marissa's death. His brain wasn't letting him say the word *suicide* yet.

She walked in. Haftmann looked up as if the room had been supercharged with a jolt of outside energy. She could have been anybody, but he knew who she was before she sat down on the chair facing him: Libby, Marie Toensing's lover—former lover.

"I'm Libby Boatwright."

She crossed her legs, placing her hands, one over the other, on her lap. Haftmann noticed women's hands. The skin of her right hand was reddened as though burned.

Libby noticed Haftmann's glance and held up her right hand. "You're staring at my psoriasis," she said. "I'm not disfigured. I grabbed a hot pan—silly of me."

"Sorry. You don't remember me, I think. I'm Tom Haftmann. I'm just filling in for my uncle while he's away—"

"You followed my husband," she interjected, "and now he's going back to prison."

Haftmann appraised her in the pause that abrupt accusation gave him. Women over twenty-five, especially with kids and abusive husbands, weren't supposed to be this gorgeous, this perfect in the face, and the body carriage. She was obviously tall, obviously blonde with long hair shaping her symmetrically perfect oval face, sexually attractive, but it was more than that: she stopped you in your tracks. The first thought Haftmann had in his head was *No wonder Marissa fell in love with her . . .*

"Who gave you permission to do that?"

"I'm sorry, Libby—Ms. Boatwright, but that's confidential."

"Fuck you, confidential! I've lost my husband again. You had no right to do that! Sneaking around, prowling in the grass like a dirty animal."

"Won't you let me explain why I can't speak of this? And as far as animals go, your husband was engaged in slaughtering dogs for entertainment."

"Fuck you, you scum-sucking dirtbag . . ."

Her litany of abuse was such a counterpoint to her sheer physical beauty that Haftmann shifted back in his seat as if he'd been hit by a man.

"Now, wait a second, Mrs. Boatwright, Libby—"

"I remember you from high school. You twerp! If I ever see you sneaking around my property again, I'll blow your fucking head off. You think Marissa was thinking of me? Here's something you should know about Marissa Toensing."

She tossed a color print, folded over, onto his desk.

"I already know that you and Marissa were lovers."

"I let her go down on me while my husband was in prison. That's all she was to me. A fisting, rug-munching dyke. I can't help it if the cunt wouldn't get that idea into her head."

Then she did something Haftmann had never seen a woman do in his life. She leaned over his desk and intentionally gave him a view of her ample cleavage before spitting a gob of phlegm on the paper in front of him."

She straightened up, stared at him, daring him to say a word, say anything. Then she turned around and left his office. Her scent lingered in the confined space—sweet with a tang of something waspish.

Haftmann got up and went to the big plate glass to track her walk down the Strip until she was out of sight.

He went back to his desk and wiped the spit off with a paper towel. He wasn't aware of her perfume while she sat opposite him. Now he couldn't breathe anything else but the musky scent lingering in her wake.

He unfolded the paper and saw Marissa Toensing wearing a black *domme* outfit. A black hooded mask complemented the Lycra spandex bodysuit replete with thigh-high shiny black boots ending in stiletto heels. Marissa was poised as if cracking a flagellant's whip at the website's spectator. There were descriptions of services for slave contracts and other specialty services Mistress Angelique would perform or accept.

Haftmann spun his chair to the computer station and googled *Mistress Angelique* but the page had been taken down. He called the Jefferson precinct and asked the desk sergeant, a guy his uncle knew well and bought drinks for at Hanratty's, what news he could release about the Toensing death. The sergeant was leery of giving information to Haftmann despite his name-dropping. The sergeant said the case was under investigation and couldn't be discussed.

"I'm not a reporter," Haftmann began, but the sergeant ended the connection.

Haftmann spent the next hour musing about the events of the preceding day. He had liked Marissa. He didn't judge what she did. It made his stomach churn to think how fast she had entered and left his life after a hiatus of ten years. *Gone, like that. Nothing.* He hoped that slimebag Boatwright was implicated and would never see another free day or that slutty wife of his again.

Libby Boatwright. He recalled Libby Grebski from years back when they were seniors at Riverton. A similar image like the avatar of the real thing popped up in his memory banks: big-breasted, sultry walk down the corridors that stopped the boys in mid-sentence to watch those swiveling hips. The little judder of movement from her bra holding in a pair of breasts every one of them would have sacrificed a testicle to be able to fondle. A woman among girls, rumored to be sexually active with adult town boys. They ran in different circles and rarely intersected except for the hallway passing but you couldn't attend the same school as Libby Grebski and not know of her. She was an indifferent student, he heard, but not stupid. She never did the dumb blonde thing even when she dyed her hair one year. He couldn't recall any rumors about instructors grilling her over the fact she never came prepared or made any attempt to answer when called on. Her brother's sports prowess explained some of it but not all of it.

There was something about her today that struck a chord from far away and long ago. A girl fight between Libby and a big-boned, masculine black chick with an amateurish *Black Power* tattooed on her biceps. The girl was different after that fight with Libby Grebski. She followed her around like a lapdog. It became a joke around school not to mess with Libby. It wasn't the brother who'd show up to kick your ass now, they said. Davonta Byrd was Libby's personal enforcer after that fight.

Haftmann remembered stories about the mother—the tall, statuesque blonde with the sad eyes and the drug problem, the husband a violent biker enforcer and drug dealer. He recalled Grebski, the sports star breaking down in tears in class one afternoon in early fall. *Nature throwing the dice here*, Haftmann thought: the boy got the old man's powerful physique but inherited the mother's soft nature. It was the daughter who inherited the beauty from the one and the violence from the other.

He called a reporter at the paper his uncle used for information or gave information to for future credit. He knew him slightly and his call this time had better luck.

"You don't have to worry," the reporter said. "Your name isn't coming up. You're the 'anonymous source' who reported the dogfighting."

"I don't care about that," Haftmann said. "How did Marissa Toensing die?"

"Autopsy's not been released but I know the lead detective," the reporter bragged. "He told me she guzzled from a container of Red Devil Lye."

"Fuck," said Haftmann.

"Fuck is right," the reporter added. "That must have burned going down."

"Listen to me," Haftmann said. "I don't think she—I don't think Marissa killed herself. Did the cops check for fingertip bruises? She could have been held. Look, I had a woman in here, in my office—that is, my uncle's office. Her name's Libby Boatwright—"

Jesus, I'm prattling like a nitwit, Haftmann thought.

"I know who she is," the reporter said.

"She had a burn—what looked like a burn mark on her right hand—I mean, it could have been a burn, you know, from getting splashed with lye while she's pinning someone down. Doesn't her husband have a reputation as a meth cook? It's not a stretch to assume—"

"Yes, it is. Hey, pal, you want to watch it with reckless accusations like that."

"I'm just saying why not get your detective to consider the possibility."

"Marissa Toensing killed herself," he replied. "According to the owner of the house."

Haftmann cut in: "I thought you said she was alone?"

"That's what the owner said. She was taking her child to the doctor's."

"You keep saying 'owner.' Would that owner by any chance be a certain Libby Boatwright?"

"You're jumping to conclusions, my young gumshoe."

"Am I? You say the cops have a suicide note?"

The reporter, clearly anxious to get Haftmann gone, said, "What? The guy's wife, for no reason at all, decides to off the girl she's hooking up with while her husband's in the slammer. Boatwright probably arranged it so he could count on her not running off with some guy who knows how to stay out of jail."

"That, my old journalist friend, does not pass the smell test even for these rent-a-cops we have here."

"You're way off base here. If you're done playing homicide cop, I've got real work to do."

Haftmann decided to get drunk. It was the one thing he was good at.

* * *

66

CHAPTER 13

Hanratty's Irish Bar on the Strip, Jefferson-on-the-Lake, OH/ Aug. 25, 1:01 p.m.

Haftmann didn't turn from his stool at the bar to glance at whoever had just taken the stool to him. Plenty of empty stools so the guy must want something, he figured. He knew it couldn't be a woman from the heft and creak the stool made when it took the weight.

"Kind of early to be getting shit-faced," a deep, pleasant voice said next to him.

"Never too early," Haftmann responded. He thought: *Shit, a barfly who wants to have a conversation. All of you just leave me alone . . .*

"I understand my sister came to see you," the pleasant voice said without a change in timbre.

Haftmann tried too late to disguise the little jump *that* gave him. *Oh fuck. Now I'm going to get the shit kicked out of my by her bruiser of a brother.*

Haftmann turned in the voice's direction, half-expecting a sucker punch.

It was the same Mitchell Grebski, high-school jock and ex-football hero, with a lot more meat on him. Bigger arms, for sure. *Christ Almighty, his forearms are thicker and more muscled than my thighs,* Haftmann realized.

"Yes, she did stop by the office a few days ago," Haftmann said, the quaver in his voice making him blush. Haftmann was relieved Grebski couldn't see it in the semi-dark bar light. "I didn't get to say all that much, though. She kept interrupting me with curses and then she spit—spat—at me on her way out the door."

To Haftmann's relief and no small surprise, Grebski laughed. A short, sharp bark.

"Yeah, that sounds like Libby. You put that worthless piece of shit back in the hoosegow, and I hope he fucking dies there," Grebski said. He held two fingers aloft and waggled them.

A short dark man in a white apron sidled over from the end of the bar and poured two drafts. He set them in front of Haftmann and Grebski, his gaze lingered over the bigger man, and then disappeared back to where he had come from.

Grebski stared after him. "Who's that? The sign said Hanratty's?"

Haftmann said, "His name's Tico Gutiérrez. He's from Guatemala. He and his wife bought the place a few weeks ago from Hanratty."

Relieved at feeling he was off the hook as far as a beatdown went, Haftmann said, "Hanratty wasn't Irish, did you know that? His real name was Majka. I think he's Hungarian."

Grebski didn't respond or bother to acknowledge the trivia. Haftmann had another flash of insight: he's got his mother's features, not his old man's. The obit photo must have lurked in his neocortex.

Grebski surprised him by what he said next. "Things are never what they seem."

"I'll drink to that."

Grebski spun his glass of beer around between his heavy hands, spilling some, and wiped it with the edge of his hand.

He's thinking how to say it, Haftmann realized.

"Libby's—different," he began. "I've tried to look after her but she's headstrong."

He seemed satisfied with the word choice. "Her husband's no good for her. But there's nothing I can do. When he first put his hands on her, I beat him up so badly he couldn't leave his house for a week. I wasn't trying to kill him. It was a lesson. Libby, she wouldn't talk to me for a month. She doesn't even love the asshole. I know that."

Haftmann instinctively sensed he needed to be careful in speaking of her. "She seemed upset with me he got violated for the dogfighting."

Grebski turned to look at him. It wasn't friendly, it wasn't hostile. Haftmann's high school took a day trip to the Perry Nuclear Power Plant fifteen miles west when he was a senior. It was intended for the

68

shop class students, but he went along to get out of algebra. Grebski brought the memory back to him. All that power humming along. A bucktoothed guide told them: "Just make sure the fuel rods stay submerged."

"God damn if I understand it. She picks up men, women—then drops them when she's had whatever she wants from them. Boatwright's not the father of her kid, either, so why she hasn't thrown his ass out is a mystery to me. I'm sure Libby will dump him one of these days."

"He fired a shot at me," Haftmann said. *Christ, I'm looking for cachet with this thug.*

Grebski snorted. "Boatwright's a pussy, come right down to it, but he likes his guns. You're lucky he didn't put one in your head when you come charging out of the weeds."

My maniac moment, Haftmann thought. Dread hit him in the belly, a tiny aftershock of remembrance. Haftmann said with forced jollity, still tiptoeing around the reactor. "It was definitely the dumbest thing I did this week." *So far . . .*

Grebski seemed uninterested in talking about it further. The air between them chilled.

"She's a Black Widow spider," he said. "I'm the only thing permanent in her life. I stopped by this shithole of a resort town to let you know that."

Haftmann had the ominous feeling that the man on the stool next to him had just made one of the longest speeches of his life in those three sentences. Grebski's longest speech was a series of obscene-laden threats to his father after the cops showed up at the house to inform them Lola Grebski had been found dead in a fuckshack motel on the interstate with a needle in her arm.

Haftmann was staring at the bar mirror when Grebski left his stool as silently as he'd taken it. He wasn't sure he'd just been threatened; deep in his brain he knew he'd just been told something Grebski had confided that he'd never told anyone else, not even Libby. Haftmann was still pondering the spider image when he saw the rectangle of light flicker out with a bang as the door closed shut.

He's as fast off a bar stool as he was out of the starting blocks in high school.

Haftmann did not know what to make of it. He had sobered up considerably, however, and this was something positive for once in this weird, up-and-down week. He experienced that involuntary shiver up his back. It wasn't the mugginess of a late summer day in August or the morgue-chilled air conditioning in the bar. Then he had it: a *satori*. An epiphany—something that broke open like a tiny door in his head: Libby and Mitchell Grebski were twins, sired in the same womb at the same time. They breathed the same amniotic fluid and looked at each other across the unlit cave of their mother's womb, separated by inches for nine months.

How the hell had I not known that? They were rarely together, never had the same classes. Like two different people with the same last name.

Something else had communicated itself in the short time he and Grebski sat side by side in a dark bar—a small, ugly thing, menacing like those stone gargoyles on cathedrals. On reflection lubricated by another boilermaker, like a homunculus covered in pigeon shit sitting on Grebski's shoulder, gaping at Haftmann the whole time.

* * *

CHAPTER 14

Crestview Cottages on Duquesne, Jefferson-on-the-Lake, OH/Aug. 29, 5:43 a.m.

Grebski's recurring nightmare returned. He has left his sister's place, saying he wanted to spend a few days unwinding at the shoreline. He couldn't look at her when he said it because they both knew where he was going.

He moans in his sleep in the false dawn: "Oh, no, noooo." Libby is being strangled by two bikers, begging for her life. These are men who had raped her when she was sixteen. Libby's fake ID was never questioned by any of the bouncers in any of the bars on Jefferson-on-the-Lake. She could have passed for twenty easily. This time was different because she had gotten drunk fast and her girlfriends, older, both high-school dropouts, left her behind when the boys drawn to their table all had eyes for Libby alone. They might as well have been chopped liver. Mitch and Libby's mother is off somewhere in a dope haze. Their old man is finishing his last year of a three-year bid in Lucasville for aggravated assault. He was at that time sitting in SHU, out of general population, because the Gang Intelligence officer learned from a snitch the AB had ordered up some "hard candy" for him—their term for a severe punishment. The shotcaller on Grebski's tier was angry about getting busted and blamed Grebski's father for messing up a big dope deal.

Grebski found Libby Sunday morning wandering in a daze on Duquesne and the "Little Minnesota" intersection, beat up, and half-strangled from the towel the men had braided and used to wring the life out of her. Libby, lie her twin, was genetically a freak. A doctor at the Jefferson clinic examined her for an ankle sprain from gym class.

He was startled by her weight despite the lush feminine body sitting on the examination table looking at him. He told her she was "sthenic" and said under a microscope he'd see the fast-reflex, twitch muscle cells of long-distance runners and weightlifters.

When she could talk about it, she told her brother what happened. Grebski went berserk. He took a Louisville slugger from under his bed, the same bat he'd clocked three home runs with during the state championship game the weekend before. His track and baseball coaches shared him like a prize racehorse. He went looking for bikers of the description Libby had given. He never saw the two he sought every hour of his free time in his lone patrols after the bars on the Strip closed. Following one pair of suspects down a gravel road to some decrepit, low-rent cottages on Erieview, he accosted the bikers. When they turned on him, he beat both into the dirt. Only the darkness prevented him from landing blows that would have killed both men. Grebski thought he had killed them. When he read of their survival, he begged Libby to forgive him.

The bikers who assaulted Libby were long gone. Libby was so intoxicated that she didn't know if her rapists were Pagans, Mongols, or Hells Angels. All three gangs rode tandem through the Strip during that summer and agreed to parcel out certain bars as being theirs and off-limits to the others. For the most part, the peace was maintained but there were exceptions.

The dream left him sitting up, shivering, and sweat-soaked.

Grebski showered and made coffee. His new day was promising. The mail yesterday brought a letter from the chief grievance officer of United Steelworkers - Great Lakes Seamen Local 5000. Grebski's boat was owned by Inland Steel Company and therefore he was a dues-paying member in good standing regardless of what his shipmates thought of him. The union insisted he be reinstated as ordinary seaman to the *J. Beaufort Göttlieb* at its next port of call.

Grebski was going back to his boat. More importantly, he was going back to the *Gött* with a new plan, one that he had been mulling over in his brain since his enforced time ashore.

Grebski never watched anything on television while aboard his vessel. He didn't want to associate with his shipmates; for another, he didn't give a flying fuck about television programming and the steady diet of talk shows and mindless sitcoms.

As far as news of the world or country went, fuck the world and everyone in it. Whenever he did catch a local news item, it had to do with a robbery or a carjacking. He'd played sports with plenty of blacks and had a grudging respect for their athleticism. He never understood his sister's friendship with blacks. The fact that she hid from their old man she had black lovers saved her from a beating. That would have made his father grind his teeth in fury.

Being idled ashore and champing at the bit to get back on the water and away from Libby and her dysfunctional family made it possible for him to absorb more news about current events. He saw how those raggedy-ass terrorists from the poor countries of the Middle East fought back against the powerful countries. He understood the allure of what they accomplished in drawing young men to their cause, even though Grebski could have put his entire knowledge of Middle East politics into a shot glass.

He didn't give two fucks for their politics or any of jibber-jabber they proclaimed in manifestos before they blew their dumb asses up. He did like the idea of killing on a mass scale. One afternoon, he concentrated his attention on a pert young woman on CNN interviewing an older broad with an eighties sheepdog hairdo who babbled on about terrorists. A panel of talking heads replaced her and they all said the same things to one another, nodding sagely at each other's wisdom.

"These apostles of terror are among us every day," intoned one retiree from the FBI's Counterintelligence Task Force, "encouraging other gullible young men to commit acts of violence *right here in the United States . . .*"

Grebski repeated the phrases to himself: *. . . apostles of terror . . . gullible young men . . .*

The words resonated in his head. He had already taken care of his union business and notified the ship's company with a few phone calls that morning. He would return to his berth. His last call to the head office revealed his boat would be picking up coal in Sandusky in two days and delivering it to South Chicago.

Once Libby showed him how to locate chat rooms, Grebski prowled the web hours every day looking for someone for his project. Time was running out now that he was going back to sailing the lakes. A lakeboat smashing into a small-town bridge on Lake Erie wasn't big enough, not nearly big enough or grand enough, to make everyone in the country—*in the fucking world*—pay attention. Now, a massive lakeboat, a thousand-footer like *the Gött*, pride of Inland Steel Company, crammed with barrels of ammonium nitrate and fuel oil in the windless room set to detonate at the Soo Locks with grandstands full of people young and old looking on at the big boats being raised or lowered—*now that was something worthwhile.*

His brain supplied more details: scatter a couple dozen buckets of taconite pellets or steel ball bearings for projectiles for good measure. Set it off on Labor Day when the picnickers and crowds are at their peak. That was something so big that even Libby, who couldn't name a single president of the United States after Washington, would take notice. It would be glorious. It would be his manifesto to this rotten world.

All he needed, he figured, was three or four of these so-called gullible young men to make it happen. But more than that, he wanted someone who had the brains to match his brawn.

Grebski knew right where to find them. A whole boatload of them, in fact.

* * *

CHAPTER 15

Tico's Place (formerly Hanratty's Irish Bar),
Jefferson-on-the-Lake/Aug. 30, 2:57 p.m.

"**They** told me you spend more time in this bar than you do in your office."

Haftmann was grateful he'd seen her framed in the rectangle of light before she entered his office. Being surprised in his bolt hole by the Grebski twins seemed to be a pastime. Fortunately, too, he hadn't imbibed as much as with the brother; something told him he'd need to be sharper with the feminine half of the duet.

"That 'they' you speak of, Ms. Boatwright, is it Hemingway's indeterminate, they're-gonna-get-you 'they' or did you have a specific 'they' in mind?"

"Heming—who? I didn't understand a goddamn word of what you said."

Haftmann felt her warmth despite the chilled air. The woman was a desert mirage, unbelievable yet compelling.

Bloody Mary," she said to Tico, appearing out of the darkened end of the bar. Haftmann discovered his new bartender had an uncanny ability to appear and disappear with the simple wiggle of the least digit of an upraised hand. That universal signal for a refresher that every bartender in the world hated. Raise it: *voilà*, one's glass was magically refilled without tedious conversation about weather, tourists, the heat, and so forth.

"I was wondering who," he said, feeling more confident, "whom you had been enquiring of my presence—or absence in the office, in this case." He also realized he'd been kidding himself about his relative sobriety; he was drunk, loquaciously drunk.

"That old guy who pushes the Kandy Kones cart up and down the Strip. He said you were here," she replied. "You must get shit-faced a lot, I reckon."

Piling on her Appalachian dialect for him. *Was she flirting with me now? A spitting cobra one day . . . a femme fatale the next,* Haftmann wondered. He scrunched up his face trying to recall the old gentleman's name, gave up, and said, "Kind of the old codger to keep business coming my way."

"I'm not your business, man," she said. "That's what I told you last time."

"Indeed you did," Haftmann said. "In and around the 'motherfucker,' 'cocksucker,'—and 'mind your own business, asshole.' I do well remember."

She made a noise that might have been a laugh. Even in the dim light of the bar, it was evident what a lovely profile she had. The teeth might be a little too prominent, however, and it suggested the *vagina dentata* image of a mythology class back in college.

"I came here to apologize. I was rude to you." She flashed that gorgeous smile again, and phony as it was, it flattered his ego because it meant he was worthy of being impressed.

"By the way," Libby added, before taking a big swallow of her drink, "don't blame my brother for the potty mouth. I ran with a wild crowd back in our high school days. Mitch and me, we were left to raise ourselves."

"I seem to remember." *Careful here, careful*—the little voice in his head whispered. *You saw how feral she can be and you do not want that lunk of a brother sidling next to you again.*

"Those were good days," Libby said. "Mostly. I felt free. I haven't felt that way in a long time. How about you, Mister Private Eye?"

"Not so free, I'm afraid," he replied. "I'm currently languishing in indentured servitude to my uncle. I can empathize with one part of your biography, however. I was raised by my grandmother, a very Germanic grandmother, in fact."

"What was that like?"

"She was crazier than a two-headed dog in a meat market. Always fussing about religion and the state of my soul."

"You seem to have turned out all right."

"No thanks to her." He smiled and raised his shot glass.

Christ, I'm flirting with her now. Haftmann mentally revised her power to enchant from heat mirage of an asphalt highway to a *fata morgana*, a whole city looming in the horizon.

"We're all Polacks on my father's side," Libby said. "Maybe Czech. I don't know for sure. What is that word when you look up ancestors?"

"Genealogy."

"Yep, that one. My mother's family is a mystery to us, Mitch and me. I don't give a darn, though."

From 'jizz-gargling son of a whore' to 'gee' 'darn' and 'gosh.'—

"Your brother—" Haftmann began, knowing he had to bring it up because she was right there waiting for it, after all. "He dropped by last week for a little chat."

"My brother's insane," Libby said. "I don't know if you could tell that."

Haftmann sipped his drink, not sure where the next *non sequitur* was going. He knew the few patrons in the place were looking their way, had been ever since she strolled in and sat down. Haftmann could have been invisible for all their stares said.

"I came here to warn you. He's dangerous. You can't believe anything he says. He's all mixed up in his head. Too many punches and blows to the head from football and our old man, whatever. He don't see things right. He twists everything around. It always comes out wrong."

Careful, careful . . . "He didn't seem . . . paranoid when we spoke."

"I didn't say 'paranoid.' I said he's dangerous."

"He seemed pretty concerned about your welfare and your husband's behavior."

"See? That's what I mean! He tried to ruin my marriage. Then he got involved with Marissa and me."

"The other day you made it sound as if Marissa was stalking you."

"Marissa was no virgin, man. You check out her little BDSM gig?"

"I'm afraid the police don't like it when civilians interfere in their investigations."

"Shit," Libby said. "I told her we couldn't see each other if she was going to keep doing that shit. Hell, it was no big deal, if you ask me. She has—had this one customer she makes put the tip of his dick through his wedding ring. Charges him a hundred bucks every time. Fuckin' crazy shit like that. Makes men stick pins in their balls and take selfies. I just couldn't have that shit around my kid, you know?"

Haftmann thought her smile was the most brilliant and deadly thing about her. He thought of Mitch's Black Widow description. Maybe the praying mantis was a better one; he unconsciously leaned away from before she opened those lips wider and clamped down on his head.

"What did you say?" Libby asked. "I didn't hear you. You mumbled something."

"Nothing. Poets in the past used to say about their women had 'bee-stung lips.' I was just thinking of that."

"What is this? So am I your true love now? Well, I did what I came to do." She finished her drink and set the glass down. The redness was fainter but visible like a tinted outline of a continent on a map. "I've got errands to run."

She spun around to slip off her stool, and it was all Haftmann could do not to crane his neck to watch her backside. She reached out and gave Haftmann's hand a squeeze. It didn't surprise him how strong her grip was, only the fact she didn't move a muscle in her body while doing it.

She seemed to catch his expression and said, "I had to work on that. A lot of guys used to think I was showing off. I don't know my own strength. Maybe I should have gone in for sports like Mitch. Too late now." She gave her belly a pat as if she were out of shape—or else fishing for a compliment.

"Remember what I said my brother." She headed for the door.

Haftmann deliberately did not watch her exit. Not a good-looking woman on earth who doesn't know she's being watched. No sooner had the door closed than the decibel level of conversation in the bar elevated a notch in pockets around the room as men here and there expressed appreciation.

Tico sidled over, a gnome in the dark with a huge smile on his face.

"On the house," he said and shoved the beer over to Haftmann. "You bring her in any time, *amigo*, and you drink for free."

Wonderful, Haftmann thought. *Now I'm a Judas goat for barflies.*

* * *

CHAPTER 16
Greyhound Bus Station,
Riverton, OH/ Aug. 31, 11:05 a.m.

"**Quit** sulking," Libby said. "I told you why I couldn't let you use his truck this time."

"I thought they were keeping your jailbird in for another week," Grebski said.

"His lawyer said he could bond out today. I told you that. His hearing's next week," she said. "Stop mumbling. You're freaking me out. If you have something to say, say it."

Grebski said, "All right. I'm breaking my back on that fucking ore boat night and day and all I do is provide money for you to give to lawyers or pay a bail bondsman for that shitbag husband of yours. What the fuck, Lib."

"It doesn't all go for that."

"Enough does, damn it," he said. "I'm tired of it, Libby. I've had it. I've had it with everything. I'm through fighting it. All this shit. My shitty life."

She reached over to caress his neck and back with one hand. "Hey, hey. Stop talking that shit. You know I couldn't do it without you. You know where I'd be without the money you give me. Probably on my knees giving blowjobs to bike trash out back of Annie's."

He put his hand over her mouth. "Don't say that, Lib. I mean it."

"You didn't always used to say that," she said. She let one of her hands fall into his lap. "You remember those times?"

Grebski's cock lifted at the proximity of her touch; it was horrible and it was wonderful. Grebski knew he was helpless. He knew he could never break free of her. *Not ever, not in this life.*

Libby brushed her knuckles over his crotch and laughed while he squirmed away from her.

"Jesus Christ, Lib. There are fuckin' people standing out here—"

"Yeah," she said. "I see them. A bunch of broke-ass derelicts going nowhere. Fuck them. Why the fuck are you going to Dearborn, Michigan for, anyway?"

"Arabs," he said and slammed the car door. "That's where they have Arabs."

Stupid, he thought. *She's too ignorant to guess but why do it?* Grebski cursed himself but at the same time he was exhilarated. He had a purpose in life, finally, after sports.

Grebski had hit pay dirt two days ago and after hours of combing through Islamic chat room full of *Inshallah's* and *Allahu Akhbar's* and garbled English about the Great Struggle and the Great Satan.

Then he found him—or maybe it was the other way around. The man was so easy to talk to and didn't judge him. In fact, he understood his rage. This Rafiq guy emailed him back right away.

After weeks and hundreds of attempts to engage one of these fire-breathers, these America-hating Arabs, he hit paydirt. Many were posers: like the African Americans who adopted the Muslim name in prison. He guessed they liked yapping to one another, but as soon as he asked for a meeting, they blew him off. Many called him an FBI informer. He wasn't into bullshit discussions with losers. The funny thing was, many of his initial contacts accused him of being an FBI plant, which was what he suspected they were.

When Rafiq contacted him, Mitch Grebski was just about at the end of his tether, mentally exhausted, ready to give up on his time-wasting, useless attempt to connect with a serious terrorist. Someone like him, somebody who didn't need to talk, talk, talk. Somebody who could bottle his rage and count to ten slowly the way he had done for years. On the verge of shutting Libby's laptop down and calling it a night around three in the morning in her upstairs room beside the nosepicker's, he felt a nibble. Tired of being ridiculed for his bad spelling and ignorance of this political crisis or that *mullah*'s name— tired of gibberish about the Great Satan. He wanted action.

"Everything is 'great' with these people," he mumbled to himself and shifted his position to remove the crick developing in his neck. Grebski was barely computer literate but he knew he was out of his depth in polemic. He was baffled by the AOL chat rooms spreading like toadstools after a summer rain. Libby grudgingly showed him how to join discussion boards on different topics. When he became adept enough to do it on his own, he made sure she was out of the room and told her to butt out of his business.

"I thought you picked up your women in bars."

"This isn't about dating women, Libby. Fuck off."

That was when Rafiq and he met. A less vocal debaters, he called himself "Scimitar." He seemed too moderate to Grebski at first because Scimitar rebuked those who condemning Arab Americans for failing to follow *shahid* or join any movements overseas since America's invasion of Iraq last March. "We each can serve in our own ways," Scimitar suggested.

* * *

Scimitar was careful with the man Grebski. He found it incredible he didn't use a handle but his real name. He rejected every request for an online chat except Grebski's. Scimitar could have engaged almost anyone in several languages. He was fluent in French and English besides his native Lebanese Arabic. He also possessed a smattering of Kurdish, Greek, and Syriac growing up in Beirut. He was a cultured man, not a dilettante.

Scimitar's letter from his cousin Habib sailing on the Great Lakes had wormed its way into his mind and given him a dream that he could not easily interpret. Somehow this boorish American, fumbling around chat rooms with his blunt queries intrigued him. When Grebski revealed enough biographical information to reveal himself as a sailor on the Great Lakes, Rafiq threw out some hooks, nurturing him with compliments while exploring his ham-handed grievances against the world, little by little grooming him for potential use. One dog feeling out another in his own comfortable language.

He had done the same with others who passed into his purview, but always they were found wanting in something necessary, and that something was easily defined: rage. He wanted to see it there, hovering like a scent above or below the words spewed forth that implicate the writer's hatred, that kernel of unmitigated hatred that could be channeled for use.

When he was convinced that Grebski had the right material and could be useful to bring his holy mission to fruition, he told him that they would be through some steps with careful explanations every step of the way. Grebski was angry at first. He didn't like taking orders, even those couched in compliments. It was like being a child led past dangerous creatures down a narrow path and he wasn't afraid to take on any foe at any time, he told Scimitar. He didn't comprehend Scimitar's lessons in an era before real-time texting and encrypted conversations out of reach of the FBI's cyber intelligence monitoring software. He gave Grebski an address in Dearborn where he could send a letter. He told the relative at the address a letter from Ohio would be coming from him soon.

As soon as Grebski began to explain in his crude language in a phone call to Rafiq what he intended to do with a lakeboat loaded with explosives, Scimitar shut him down with a curt command to be silent and told him where to meet him. He ended all contact on the web and closed down his accounts immediately. He told his friends without any of the Arabic lushness he preferred to use with him that he "had business that would take him out of town for a while."

Grebski didn't know if he himself had been baited for a trap. He knew he couldn't turn back whether Scimitar was real or an FBI plant. He had not completely convinced him he was serious about Grebski's project, always thinly veiled in their communications in the first chat-room talks, but Grebski wanted to believe it. Tell a Norwegian rat with a dropped pizza slice to let it go and get back in the sewer. He knew the man at the other end was probing, testing, finding out whether he was authentic, so he played the same game with him and answered every question as honestly as he could. The idea of destruction had bitten too deep by then. If the human limbic brain was all about reproducing and surviving, Grebski had shut his down. He wanted nothing more than the exhilaration of a final act that would cancel out all the swamp muck that stuck to his boots since he left high school. He had a time clock in his head that was set to go off. He told scimitar "no more delays or I go alone."

Shit or get off the pot, motherfucker.

He knew Detroit. The *Gött* used to tie up for winter layup there along with the *Roger Blough* and the *American Spirit*. He didn't like the city. Too many dope fiends, gangbangers, and homeless derelicts addicted to heroin and meth. People huddled near fifty-five-gallon drums burning wood salvaged from empty houses on streetcorners, sipping cheap wine or forties in paper bags, and smoking cigarettes or shooting up in broad daylight on Woodward Avenue. The whole inner city was one abandoned neighborhood after another, squatters fleeing from empty houses to score like cockroaches scattering when the lights came on. People wandered around the blighted, vacant lots like extras in a zombie film.

He found a room in a downtown hotel for $45 a night that lacked all the amenities except some off-white towels and a ragged cotton coverlet on the bed. Tomorrow he would take a taxi to Dearborn, the self-proclaimed Arab capital of the American Midwest.

Henry Ford must be shitting himself in his grave, he thought.

He thought of Libby's hand that morning at the bus station. He freed himself and within seconds shot a spurt of jissom across the cheap bed.

* * *

CHAPTER 17
Haftmann Investigative Services,
Jefferson-on-the-Lake, OH/ Sep. 1, 8:30 a.m.

He was doing penance. He was in early, sober as a judge, and going through his uncle's pending cases in a belated attempt "to organize and prioritize," as he muttered to himself. His uncle was a people person, not a bookkeeping person, as Haftmann considered himself. He looked in dismay at the file of bills paid and outstanding. His uncle was practically working for free in some cases, and the nephew suspected these were favors for a lifetime of friendships on the Strip and elsewhere. He tracked down a few payments his uncle routinely made to persons in Connecticut and North Dakota.

It turned out these were men he had served with and he was helping them out with medical bills. One client was a Nam veteran with PTSD, who had suicidal tendencies. His uncle had left a letter from the man's wife in the file, and it was heart-wrenching to hear her speak of her suffering and the gratitude she felt toward his uncle for the help he had given all these years until the past month when her husband had finally done what he had threatened so often. She found him hanging by a belt in their closet. Haftmann wondered at the resolve of a man who was so determined to die that he kept his knees from touching the floor so that he wouldn't merely pass out but die of strangulation. Even in his blackest despair from drink, Haftmann never felt the urge to end it.

On this day, he was feeling good about life, himself, and even the future—a post-private eye career, that is, when the phone rang and the reporter from the local paper who had blown him off a week ago was calling to see what he knew of the murder.

"You're asking me?"

"Hey, don't bite my ear off," the reporter said. "I thought maybe you had some contacts you could give me. Somebody your uncle's tight with—to get a head start on. There's all kinds of action around here, see. Panel trucks with Cleveland news logos. Somebody at this end got the word out to the big guys first, so I—"

"What the fuck are talking about? Marissa Toensing's death didn't even make the back pages of the *Plain Dealer*."

Even if the nurse-*domme* angle had been known, Haftmann guessed, which seemed unlikely given the indifferent reporting on her death, it was unlikely to garner much more ink.

"I see you're out of the loop," the reporter said.

Haftmann could hear the disappointment in his voice. "There's a dead body, a woman in her twenties, hog-tied to a pole out in the scrub where you—according to a little birdie I know—found Dean Boatwright's little dogfighting operation."

Haftmann felt ice in his belly. "I didn't know anything about it."

"Obviously."

Haftmann jumped into the pause before he could be cut off. "What girl?"

"The cops are saying a runaway but they don't know."

Haftmann racked his brains for the guy's name and thought it might be *Earl*. "Look, Earl, I might have something for you."

"It's Roy. I think if you really had something I'd have had something too, but I haven't got time to wet nurse you, Junior G-Man, so *adiós*—"

"Hang on, hang on," Haftmann pleaded. "I'm not just saying this, and I don't have proof of anything. Give me this much. How did she die? How was she found? You said she was tied to a pole."

"Not quite," Roy said. "The pole was inserted through her rectum and penetrated all the way through her body's internal organs until it came out through her mouth."

"*Je-sus Kee-rist Al-mighty*," Haftmann said, enunciating the syllables.

"*Nooo*, I'd say more like his opposite number," Roy said and broke the connection.

* * *

CHAPTER 18
Awad's وداس كوفي Coffee House,
Dearborn, MI/ Sep. 2, 1:31 p.m.

Grebski was on his fourth or fifth demitasse by now and running out of patience with these chickenshit assholes. *Fuck's sake, they were just punks, college kids. What a fool he was to think he could put this together with a bunch of children . . .*

Grebski heard Arabs greeting Arabs with the same sounding words and he asked Rafiq what it meant. Rafiq repeated it for him: *"As-salamu alaykum wa rahmatullahi wa barakaatuhu wa maghfiratuhu.*

It's our way of greeting and saying farewell," he said.

Even worse, the little bit of English conversation he was permitted to engage in was more an interrogation. He was peppered with questions from all four of these baby jihadists, these wannabee terrorists. Yet not one word of his plan had been solicited for discussion—at least not in English. He and Rafiq had conversed in private, adjourning to an outside table with a candy-striped umbrella.

Rafiq had then introduced him to the others as they showed up: three males. The female was the last to arrive. She was apparently the girlfriend of Rafiq if he could judge from the looks exchanged between the two.

Each one pointed at his chest as the names were announced by Rafiq except for the girl who stared at him as though he were a zoo animal. Grebski had his own system for memorizing their names. Samir Hamoud was "Moustache" for the thin strip of dark fuzz above his upper lip. Tariq Bazzi was "Spectacles" with his U Michigan ball cap worn backwards. The girl Ginnah was "Black Eyes." All had brown eyes but hers were so deep as to appear black. Grebski visited a whorehouse in Duluth where Mexican and Filipina girls worked. He wondered if Arab girls were as thick-bushed downstairs. Libby's dark bush was shaved into a Mohawk or trimmed it into a wedge with Playboy bunny ears.

He knew they were discussing him at times because they raised their voices a notch and cast hard looks his way. His size was intimidating. He could have bench-pressed them at one time. "Raff" quieted them down whenever they became too loud or aggressive, the alpha male of this crew of baby terrorists.

Grebski understood they were college students at Ann Arbor and lived in the international dorm. The one called Selim glared at Raff for saying that. The smallest one, Tariq, looked frightened or brave by turns, depending on how Rafiq talked to him. The fact they didn't reciprocate with false names convinced Grebski that he was one step closer.

They took courses over the summer instead of going home to Beirut, Abu Dhabi or Hubba Bubba or wherever camel jockeys came from. Grebski didn't care and didn't react even when they raised their voices or gestured at him.

The only thing that mattered was whether these clowns, however American they looked or acted, had the goods. Could they get him what they needed? Did they have a contact—a real guy back there among the sand dunes and the spiders—who could supply what Grebski told Raffi they needed for the job? Somebody important.

He would let them gabble in Arabic a little bit longer. Then he would tell Rafiq and his friends to fuck off. He would go back to his shitty hotel in Detroit and resume the search for the Big Terrorist. After a while, the discussion among them becalmed itself. Rafiq resumed a politer, more conversational tone. Grebski waited. He addressed him in his formal English:

"We want you to come back to the dorm with us, Mister Jones. We have some more questions for you."

"No more questions," Grebski said. "I'm done. I'm leaving now."

The impulsive one, Samir, stood up to confront him. Grebski was close enough to chest bump him over the table but refrained himself.

Rafiq grabbed Grebski's forearm. Grebski looked down at Rafiq's hand as if it were a tarantula. He quickly withdrew it.

"I'm sorry, Mister Jones," Rafiq said, using the name he had introduced Grebski to the others with. "Let us all be civil, please. We have only a few questions and then we can—outline the proposal you have brought us. We can discuss it more freely out of the public eye, agreed?"

"I'm tired of talking and I'm really fucking tired of listening to you four talking in A-rab like I'm a chair in the corner. I haven't heard a single word yet that convinces me you can do what I'm asking."

"Mister Jones, what you are asking is that we surrender our lives into your hands. Surely we can work out some details together that will satisfy all of us before we make a commitment to your most interesting proposal."

Grebski rode up front with Rafiq in a new Honda Civic. Ginnah sat in the back with her hands folded over the purse in her lap but her dark eyes were focused on the rearview for any look from Rafiq. Grebski felt the hairs on the nape of his neck standing up. It dawned on him she wasn't window dressing and that she might have a gun in the purse. When he glanced at Rafiq, the look he gave him confirmed it. Would she have pulled out the gun and shot him in the back of the head if they thought he was an FBI informant? Grebski didn't know the answer to that.

Coming into Ann Arbor on East Madison, Rafiq pulled into the parking lot next to Samir's Focus. Grebski understood that Samir was the most volatile of the four, and if he had to guess from the tone and the gestures that indicated himself, he probably despised Americans more than the others.

Up in Rafiq's dorm, Grebski talked of his special project to Rafiq, who asked frequent questions. Rafiq then translated a word or a phrase for the others. It seemed to Grebski he went into far more explanation than Grebski had provided.

"If you have a contact back there . . . back home," Grebski said, "somebody big who can arrange for a speedboat and weapons, I can force the wheelsman and the mate to slow the boat as we leave Duluth. You and the others board near the forward end. I'll have a Jacob's ladder over the side. From there, we take both ends of the boat. Everybody but the chief engineer goes into a paint locker in the stern. I'll take the deckhands, mates, and anybody else not on watch below to the dunnage room. We lock them in."

"I know," Rafiq said, still smiling. "You have told me this plan many times by now."

Grebski ignored him. "If we can concentrate enough explosives—"

"Mister Jones," Rafiq interrupted, "the deck plates of a lakeboat are a foot thick at the bottom of the hull, solid steel. How do you propose we pack enough explosive down there to do that?"

"I don't know," Grebski said; "you're the fucking engineers. You figure it out. When the *Gött's* heavy with taconite, it'll go straight to the bottom of the locks like a dart and drown everybody below the Plimsoll line. That's all I care about. But I want the people in the grandstands. I want to see heads and arms flying off in every direction, understand?"

"Oh, I do," Rafiq answered and smiled at Grebski.

He imagined the scores of cameras filming from the grandstands all the action from every direction. It would make the six o'clock news for weeks.

"The lockers, as you say, might not empty in time. That is, we need to be at ground level for the maximum impact to the grandstands. Wouldn't it depend on the timing of the locks and the vessel's draft when the . . . action commences?"

Always with the fancy words, Grebski thought, yet he had a tight lid on his emotions unlike the others and that was encouraging. "The rest is gravy as far as I'm concerned," Grebski replied. "You can spray them with lead inside those paint lockers once we reach Sturgeon Bay."

"Mister Jones, ignoring the fact that the bullet trajectory of the ricochet effect inside a closed steel container might be dangerous for the shooter, we haven't even discussed an exit strategy yet," Rafiq noted.

"I'm not interested in an exit plan," Grebski said. "You work that out with your team. I'm staying aboard for the whole ride. Just leave me one weapon and extra clips. What you and your gang do afterward is up to you."

His expression never changed. He turned to the others and babbled in Arabic for a long time. Several times, Grebski heard the words *shahid* and saw them turn their heads to look at him, this time with a new respect. Even Samir smiled as he raised a glass of mint tea to salute him.

Fuck you and all of you, Grebski thought, although he managed a grimace of smile back, thinking: *I don't give a fuck about you, your idiot cause, or anything else. Just help me make this happen...*

As the meeting concluded, Grebski watched them embrace and go through an elaborate farewell that sounded like the same words of their greeting at the coffee shop. But this time there was a solemn undertone that even a tin eared Grebski could hear. Something had happened to transform these baby-faced college kids into—something different—into four terrorists with a spine for what was coming up in a just a week's time.

He heard a chorus of *Aleikhum A-salaam* as they left Rafiq's dorm.

"Peace be upon you, brother," Samir said to him as he and Tariq left together.

Christ, Grebski thought with something like bittersweet amusement, *I really am one of them.*

* * *

CHAPTER 19
Port of Duluth/Superior, MN/ Sep. 5, 12:16 p.m.

Grebski was to meet his boat at the Port of Duluth/Superior, the western end of the shipping hub that connects the lakes to the St. Lawrence Seaway. It was where the *Gött* was loading gravel bound for Northtown Harbor.

With forty-nine miles of waterfront, it took him some time to find the dock boss who knew when his boat was due in and which dock he was loading. He had an awkward meeting with the first mate on the Texas deck instead of in the mate's quarters, as if Grebski were infectious in some primeval way. He gave Grebski papers to sign. Grebski used the portside winch to scratch out his signatures. The mate took the papers and paused; he made no sign that Grebski was welcome back. It didn't matter in the least to Grebski whether he was welcome or not because this vessel was about to be manned by dead men who had a reprieve of one week to live—providing the *Gött* stayed on schedule. They'd offload the gravel in Northtown and head back uplakes through the Soo for the next run. All that he had learned at home from a few calls made to his union rep and someone describing herself as the company ombudsman, whatever the fuck that was.

The last run of the J. Beaufort Göttlieb, Grebski thought, smiling.

His watch wouldn't start for another three hours and forty minutes, so he headed down the length of the boat for the afterend ladder. He had time to put away a few beers and contact Rafiq for a progress report. If half of what Rafiq told him was factual, things were moving fast. The urgency in Rafiq's voice told him everything was on schedule despite a few hitches. The weapons, AR-15s Army surplus, were already secured. Rafiq had wanted Uzis "for the easier recoil and dependability," but his contact couldn't arrange delivery as fast. Now there would need to be time for one trip to the woods outside Ann Arbor for some practice shooting.

At first, Grebski tried to talk Rafiq out of it, arguing that four Arab dudes with submachine guns would draw attention even in gun-happy Michigan woods. In the end, he caved and begged Rafiq to make sure his charges didn't shoot their feet off or do anything that would jeopardize the mission. "Mission" was Rafiq's word, but Grebski didn't care what they called it if they showed up in a fast boat outside Duluth Harbor armed with compact submachine guns and carrying the buckets of explosive material for detonation. When Grebski enquired about the kind of explosives, Rafiq turned evasive in his responses.

"Trust me, Mister Jones," he said. "With four graduate engineering students on that vessel, we'll make a big explosion for you."

Grebski's idea of a big explosion wasn't a few five-gallon buckets of ammonium nitrate laced with diesel fuel, however. He told Rafiq that the port of Sandusky was known as the major coal storage deposit on the Great Lakes but it also held a warehouse full of fifty-five-gallon drums of ammonium nitrate for the state's soybean farmers. The rich soil of western Ohio was made for growing soybeans as generations of German-descended farmer shad discovered and China was a major purchaser of those beans. Farmers needed the ammonium nitrate for their fields and so Sandusky accommodated the spurt with a warehouse full of fifty-gallon drums of the stuff. Rafiq agreed that it was "tempting," but Grebski's timeline was prohibitive. A whole other plan would be needed for liberating vast quantities of it and getting it on to the boat. "Too many risks," Rafiq told him and dismissed any further discussion.

Grebski and Rafiq met by a prearranged code at the Seven Sons Bar with a deck overlooking the harbor and the marina. Rafiq seemed calm, whereas Grebski was ever conscious of a tightening in his chest.

"I do think of the devastation just one barrel of the nitrate compound and one barrel of diesel fuel to enhance the impact could create, Mister Jones," Rafiq told him, "but the logistics are too difficult at this late date."

It was ironic, Rafiq said to the others later, that after Nine Eleven, the nuclear power plants in Perry and Oak Harbor had been fortified against attacks from the air or the sea, but this unguarded warehouse sat there wide open with nothing but an old security guard and a barbed-wire fence around it. He imagined a few of those vacationers at Cedar Point next door would be interested to know that each one of them could be catapulted into the next county by the explosive power in that single building.

Grebski came to realize that Rafiq wasn't just a leader who talked. He did his homework. He let "Mister Jones" remain in charge of the plan, but the improvising and small touches were all his, and in the end, Grebski knew that Rafiq was right about everything he proposed.

Grebski was blinded by the goal, the obliteration in the grandstands and the pain tossed out randomly by the flying shrapnel. Details were never his strong suit. The coaches always told him what to do and he did it without fail. They took the credit for his victories on the gridiron and track fields and he was left with blinding headaches and a brain that jammed when anything more complex than tying off a bowline was involved. Raff never answered Grebski's questions directly. Grebski figured that each member of Rafiq's team was engaged in a crucial task, but it would not be revealed to Grebski until the last moment, if at all. He tolerated the James Bond need-to-know bullshit because he couldn't take over an ore boat with a crew of thirty-seven alone, even with the bloody engine of his heart's madness driving him relentlessly forward.

They drank in silence for a while. Grebski looked at the vodka tonic Rafiq had ordered.

"I thought you A-rabs didn't drink booze."

Rafiq smiled. It would not be an easy thing to explain a *takfiri* terrorist to a man like Grebski, so he said, while watching a two-masted sloop, a Bermudan, tack into the wind a hundred yards offshore in the harbor. They sat on a park bench while dogwalkers passed by.

"All is permitted to kill the infidel, brother."

"*Inshallah*," Grebski said, and saluted him, finally getting into the swing of it.

* * *

CHAPTER 20
Haftmann Investigative Services,
Jefferson-on-the-Lake, OH/ Sep. 6, 2:54 p.m.

She wore a pair of Levi shorts that were faded and ripped exposing tawny thigh flesh.

Haftmann hoped she wouldn't cross her legs. Too late. She swung one long muscular leg over the other and then did something he's never seen a woman her size do: she tucked the ankle of her crossed leg under her bottom. It stretched the fabric across her crotch and showed the outline of her labia. Haftmann realized he'd been played like a schoolboy and raised his eyes to meet hers boring straight into him. What was communicate there went straight to the neocortex and it was untranslatable into polite words.

Now he was sweating under his armpits and hoped it didn't show. He was shish kebab and she was turning the fork this way and that for her own amusement.

"What—what can I do for you, Ms. Boatwright?"

"Libby, please. I thought we were on a first-name basis after our date in"—she craned her neck past him to read the new neon sign that had replaced Hanratty's—"Tico's Place."

"That was a date?"

"Sort of," Libby said. She gave Haftmann another hi-beam smile that showed more teeth.

"Is there something I can do for you, Libby?"

"Maybe we can help each other."

"How would we go about doing that exactly?"

"I can tell you used to be a lawyer. You ask a lot of questions, don't you?"

"To answer yours, yes, I do. It comes with this job too."

He stared into her smile and realized what a prissy answer that was. If she was flirting, he was responding, and it embarrassed him like being dragged backwards to middle school.

She took a few sheets of paper out of her purse and handed it to him.

"My brother wrote this before he went back to the boats."

Haftmann looked them over. Big block letters, a childish hand with misspellings. "I don't quite see what this is, Libby."

"Mitch is gonna do something. He uses my laptop and phone. He never showed any interest before and couldn't even open my flip phone, not that reception down there's worth a shit anyway. He's always been Mister Antisocial. Don't talk to nobody he don't have to. I had to explain what a *facebook* page was. He thought it was a paperback. Now he's all into chat groups, goes to Detroit—"

"Detroit?"

"Dearborn."

"Interesting."

"You trace calls, right? Check out who these numbers belong to?"

"I must ask you why you want me to. That might be a better place to start."

"OK, I'll make it official, like. I want to hire you to check these names and numbers."

She began rooting in her purse for a retainer.

Haftmann felt a rush of adrenalin to his stomach. She was unemployed and her husband was cooling his heels in the county jail. He was also under suspicion for the gruesome murder of a runaway found near his dogfighting ring. If what she was proposing meant she intended to pay him in cash or sex, which is what he had picked up in bar scuttlebutt about how Libby Boatwright managed things financially while her husband did time, he didn't know whether he had the strength to refuse. The specter of his uncle leaning over his shoulder wasn't enough to banish the lust-crazed gnome sitting on his shoulder gaping at the cleavage she displayed.

"I have money to pay," she said, reading his mind. She came up with a fitful of bills. "I know what people say about me."

With that, Haftmann's miserable celibacy seemed engraved in stone. He was partially relieved. The woman might be guilty of murdering her lover. Haftmann banished the term *red-handed* as soon as Libby caught him staring at her hand instead of her breasts.

"It's almost healed."

"That's good. You can get a serious infection from a burn. Sepsis, I think."

"I said I'm fine."

"We can work out the pay schedule later, Libby. Right now, I need you to tell me what you think these papers mean and, again—sorry, if I'm being blunt here—why you want me to investigate your brother."

"I've got Child Services on my ass again," she said. "If I find something out—I mean, if you do—and it means lives are saved or something, I can use that to help my case, right? It could help Dean's case, too, when he comes up for his hearing."

"I'm not sure it works that way," Haftmann said. "The law would expect you to be forthcoming about any knowledge you might have that would involve imminent danger to persons or property." Haftmann suspected she wasn't up on Good Samaritan laws, of which Ohio had either few or none, depending on the jurisdiction you were in.

She bit her lower lip, thinking, affecting a pouty look that Marilyn Monroe must have patented in 1955.

"I still want to hire you to look into it."

Haftmann drew a standard contract out of the desk drawer and handed it to her. You can take it home to read it over if you like. I just need your signature at the bottom of the second page.

"I'll sign and date it right now." She set the paper on the edge of his desk and wrote her signature in big loopy letters. "There."

Without another word, she stood up and pulled her shorts down where they bunched, outlining her pubis. "Shall I call you tomorrow— is that too soon?"

Haftmann suspected sarcasm. No client had walked in that door since Marissa Toensing, and as though reading his mind, he thought of petite Marissa writhing in bed with that blonde Valkyrie. Guilt washed over him. He thought of demure Marissa, secret dome in black Lycra, sitting in the same chair as Libby Boatwright.

He'd made only one follow-up call to his uncle's contact in the police department and was told the autopsy report had come in yesterday from Cuyahoga County where indeterminate or suspicious deaths were posted. Her death was ruled suicide and no further investigation was warranted. Her remains were cremated and she was put in a vault at the Angels of God Cemetery in the next county. She was already forgotten, replaced at the hospital, and nothing was going to change that.

Except that burn mark on Libby's hadn't altogether cleared up, and try as he could, Libby standing at a stove was not an easy image to conjure. The cop might have been in a good mood because he didn't blow off Haftmann's questions about the "hog-tied girl," as she came to be known in the media.

"Any suspects?" Haftmann asked him.

"Sure. Every deadass, lowlife biker coming through here in summer. That's about forty-, fifty thousand give or take a few hundred."

"What's the time of death?"

"Pathology report from Cleveland can't be precise. You know Elizabeth Bhargava, the Cuyahoga M.E.? She's had hands in more guts than Attila the Hun. It's close to the time you were starring in *Custer's Last Stand* out there in the brush. Your uncle know what an idiot you are, by the way?"

Haftmann coughed. *He'll know soon enough. Uncle Sam's coming home in a week . . .*

That put Boatwright right back under the klieg lights as prime suspect. The paper said the "investigation was ongoing"; in other words, the local cops were stumped and BCI was taking over the investigation. So far a Missing Persons canvass of every police department in the Midwest had turned up zilch. The trouble, Haftmann and everyone else knew, was that places like JOTL were a magnet for runaways, dopers, and lost kids. They passed through in summer in the tens of thousands, hung out in bars, scored dope, exchanged sex or money for it near "Little Minnesota," the area known for blonde hookers at an intersection on the Strip. A few were known to shack up or else squat in one of the many abandoned houses ringing the resort town. Most left, a few got tired of their road adventures and went home to Mommy and Daddy. Some disappeared forever. Rape and assault statistics weren't suppressed but the chamber of commerce did everything in its persuasive power to make sure that publicity was kept to a minimum, which usually meant a back-page paragraph in the local rag and Northtown's *Herald-Tribune*. Most crime stats wound up buried in some state-produced government report. That was one reason his uncle had set up shop in a one-horse town like Jefferson-on-the-Lake. Runaways provided a steady source of income from concerned parents.

He worked on Libby's notes and was able to decipher most of the names and numbers. By midafternoon, saturated with coffee and feeling a nervous headache coming on—another disturbing sign of the steady boozer—Haftmann learned that Grebski had had called his union hall in Cleveland twice, an Inland Steel company representative in Indiana Harbor, Illinois and ordered a large pepperoni pizza on Wednesday. Haftmann assumed the figure next to the phone number—9,0 indicated a big withdrawal. Not even buying rounds at Tico's Place could he go through that much money in a season, so he figured Grebski was gathering money. But for what purpose? Too much for a man simply rejoining his boat.

Haftmann called the Army Navy store in Northtown and with a little subterfuge about "his cousin telling him about the fantastic gear he'd just bought there," he described Grebski and learned from the chatty clerk "his cousin" had made about "several hundred dollars" in purchases, including work boots, heavy socks, and several pairs of work gloves. Haftmann thought it strange he didn't buy thermal underclothing or heavy outdoor gear for winter. Labor Day ended summer for the recreational sailors, but sailors on the lakes knew this was the time to have your heavy clothing stowed for the coming cold weather. It might be a sunny fall morning on the Strip, but it could be below freezing at the Soo before sunrise.

On a hunch that Libby Boatwright wasn't a top-notch housekeeper, he called her.

"Ms. Boat—I mean, Libby. This is Tom Haftmann. Do you have the notepad your brother wrote on by any chance?"

"It's still on the nightstand. Why?"

"I'd like to get it if that's all right with you?"

"No problem. You finding out what all them numbers and names mean?"

"Uh, still working on it," Haftmann said. "I've got some things to do up here, but I'll drop by around four. Is that OK?" He'd miss Happy Hour—

"Are you always this polite when you're sober? That'll work. See you then."

It sounded like a date. Haftmann controlled his "celibacy gnome" this time. The blood, instead of surging south, went north to his brain where he figured he needed it more. Libby Boatwright was far more interesting than he had credited her for being.

He had a few items left on the notes she'd given him to check: her brother had written down some names but used code names. *Black Eyes? Moustache?* Grebski scratched them out with heavy pencil lines. Haftmann tried a dozen combinations of the letters that he was able to make out but went oh-for-thirty on the attempts.

He felt guilty doing it, but he drove home at 3:30 to shower and shave before heading for Libby Boatwright's house in Riverton off Route 11 south.

Libby met him at the door. She had changed from her shorts to a summer dress that was clingy to her curves. Her sandals looked to be made of sisal. Her hair was combed out and Haftmann suspected the perfume she wore wafted straight to his nose from her cleavage.

She told him where her brother's room was. He thanked her and told her he'd find it "just fine" without her bothering herself.

"It's no bother."

She preceded him up the stairs. At the top landing, Haftmann realized he wasn't breathing. The house was dingy, a cluttered mess everywhere he looked, once he was freed of the spell of her swiveling hips. Cleaned up, a makeover on the right way to dress and apply make-up, hair done in a way to accent her face instead of the buttery mess on top of her head, she was a trophy wife without a rich mate. How that white-trash loser Boatwright managed to beat out the competition for her from scores of better men was a mystery that, like so many others, Haftmann guessed he'd never live long enough to find out.

With Libby standing in the doorway watching, one hip cocked, Haftmann picked up the notepad and used a pencil to trace the furrows and channels. Grebski did everything one way, like a bull, straight ahead, no finesse. Haftmann recognized the names and numbers. He tore off the two top pieces of paper and put them in his shirt pocket.

"Libby, did you or your brother dump the wastebasket since he was here?"

"Nope, not likely. He don't like me coming in his room. You know, surprising him if he was in here jerking off or something."

The smutty reference about her brother made Haftmann blanch. He asked her if he could have the contents.

"Knock yourself out. It's right next to the bed."

Haftmann leaned over the bed to fetch it while he felt Libby's eyes boring into his back. *What is it about this damned woman*, he wondered, *that unnerves me?* Libby was more than the flesh and blood that nature had generously distributed to make her what she was. She had ignored him in high school. Most girls did. Never looked at him once when she passed by in the hallway, although he must have had eyes bugging out of his head like the rest of the boys.

He had an uneasy moment at the doorway when he wasn't sure she was going to move aside to let him pass. He covered his confusion by thanking her excessively and babbling something about "hoping to have some results for you very soon."

Back outside in the heat and surrounded by the lush smell of summer fading into another perfect dusk, the forsythia and lilac bushes gently stirring in a light breeze, Haftmann realized he was sweating profusely. All he could think of was Libby's knowing, bright smile in the doorway and the decomposing body of a young girl in the weeds just a hundred yards from where he was, not to mention the phantom of Marissa Toensing looking down at him from an upstairs window and shaking her head as if to say, "You're no match for her."

Haftmann shivered in the car once the air-conditioning kicked in. He sped off from Libby's driveway with too heavy a foot on the gas from the rooster tail of pea stones clattering against the side of her house.

Back in high school again. Will I ever grow up?

* * *

CHAPTER 21
Awad's وداس كوفي Coffee House,
Dearborn, MI/ Sep. 7, 8:34 a.m.

"**Are** you sure he's all right back on the boat?" Ginnah asked.

Ginnah was speaking of Grebski's mental state, not his health.

Rafiq looked at his Garmin watch as if he had Grebski on the GPS locator. "I'm sure. Right now, I suspect," he added, "he's probably still cursing me for all the people he saw in the stands on Labor Day when his boat docked at the Soo."

"Tariq thinks he's a fool. 'A foul-mouthed, rutting goat,' he calls him. Samir says your Mister Jones knows nothing of politics, but it would have made sense to go when he wanted."

Rafiq didn't like to explain, and he didn't like to be contradicted. He thought that Ginnah's independent spirit, her courage and conviction to his cause were admirable traits. But he also thought she could use some proper humility for her male partner. He blamed her wealthy family in the Emirates for spoiling her when she was young.

"You're right, *habibti*, of course," he said. "The casualties would have been at their maximum. Our American fool is not a complete fool. It was difficult to get his mind off Labor Day as the target day. But even a dozen more or fewer casualties will not have nearly as much impact on the American public as striking on Nine Eleven. They have grown to fear that day."

Already the news media and Homeland Security were hyping their usual theme of "vigilance." Rafiq loved their slogan: "If you see something, say something." He planned on giving them something to say very soon.

"He doesn't yet know, does he, we're not bringing a bomb with us?"

"No, he doesn't," Rafiq answered her patiently. "Mister Jones still thinks we're going to blow a hole in the bottom of the ship and sink his boat. Mind you, I do like the idea of hampering their cargo shipping lanes for a while, but that isn't the point."

"What do you think he'll do when he discovers you—we—lied to him?"

"He'll be upset. It won't matter much at that point. I expect he'll be busy as will we all. When I first met him, it took me hours to dissuade him from using his boat as a battering ram to knock down a bridge. Then he insisted we use the *Göttlieb* like a big missile and crash it into another freighter on Lake Superior. He thinks like an American football player, doesn't he? Smash into things, make your point that way."

"I doubt he could drive a boat that size going eleven knots into another lakeboat at a distance," she said.

"You'd be right. I tried to teach him the Pythagorean Theorem. For a sailor, he doesn't even seem to comprehend that distances over water are deceptive. It would take skill to do that, and I seriously doubt we could threaten any wheelsman sufficiently long enough to stand there and steer the boat into another freighter. He speaks of a 'grand suicide.' He must have read it in a book."

"He doesn't strike me as a reader of anything but American comic books and pornography. I don't like how he undresses me with his eyes every time we meet."

Rafiq called her *ya rouhi*, the love of his soul, and squeezed her two hands in his. "Allah bless your patience for that. I'd like to slice his neck open when I see him do that."

"He's very big and he looks strong—" Ginnah began, her voice subdued, anxious. The strain was telling on them all. She saw the signs of anxiety even in Rafiq's face. She knew he didn't like being provoked. "What I mean is, what if he decides to . . . do something when he finds out we're not following his plan?"

"*Azizity*," Rafiq said, finding the right tone of condescension and patience for his charming woman. "Grebski will have no weapon in his hands. If he asks for one, I'm giving him the Glock with the bent firing pin. He's too unpredictable. Did you see how he looked at Samir when he asked him if he understood the concept of entropy? But when he hears those grenades he has carried aboard with the weapons broken down and tied in bubble wrap in his duffel bag—*Inshallah*—he'll understand that all his crew except for the two we require in the pilot house and the one in the engine room are blown to pieces in their metal cages, he'll be more—how shall I say?—amenable to commands."

"You still intend to kill him?"

"Of course. Our American comrade-in-arms must not survive. No one must know he had anything to do with helping us. I've given my cousin Ammar money to go back to Lebanon for a while. The FBI will be interviewing very Arab American in Dearborn including my mother's relatives. It can only help our cause."

"I fear Tariq lacks courage and will not see this through, Ginnah said. "I have kept an eye on him as you suggested."

Rafiq said, "Do you know the surah that goes, 'Allah does not charge a soul except with that within its capacity'? He will do fine, you'll see, *ana bahibik.*" He kissed her hand.

"*Ana bahibak, habibi,*" she said to him. *I love you very much.*

Rafiq personally did not mind that Grebski wanted to die. *Shahid* was for true believers, martyrs for Allah and the Prophet, not for infidels. Rafiq's plan was designed for his and their survival. In the chaos of the attack, after their grenades were tossed into the stands and then they came out from behind the hatch covers and blazed away at the people cowering or, most likely, running for safety, they had to escape in the confusion. Tariq, the least courageous of their cell, was chosen to cut through the cyclone fence with the bolt cutters. Ginnah had arranged for their motel rooms in Sault Ste. Marie at a Days Inn on the St. Mary's River. Rental cars under assumed names and paid for with MasterCard numbers stolen by a skimmer at a gas station on the Ohio Turnpike last week completed her tasks. She and the others were passing themselves off as Ontario University students, entomology majors, studying the migrating habits of the Monarch butterfly.

Rafiq would have been happy with any reasonable body count. It was less about the amount of blood spilled that it was about establishing his reputation among the warriors of the Middle East and Africa—al-Qaeda, ISIS, the Taliban, Boko Haram, or the next splinter group to emerge as champions of Islam. This would put him into the forefront of the war against the infidels. Rafiq knew how to keep secrets. Not even Ginnah had any idea of his true ambitions. He had only indulged himself once, a modest bit of harmless bragging, when he told Grebski that replacing one holiday with an anniversary every American schoolchild knew would add luster to the deed.

Rafiq did not hate Americans like Samir. He thought they were a fun-loving, arrogant, but stupid people. Their time was up. Chinese was rising. He liked what American culture offered and he reveled in their freedom to do and say things that would get a limb amputated in his part of the world. But they were basically sheep grazing under the eye of the butcher and their time was at hand, even though they continued blithely along in their mindless pursuits of pleasure.

Rafiq knew he was born for greatness, not merely privilege. He spent his spare time studying the schematics of nuclear power plants obtained online before the government put an end to that kind of access in the aftermath of Nine Eleven. Rafiq knew what a well-placed bomb could do in a feedwater system. By sending contaminated water back into the loop, he could cause a moon-sized crater to be blown into any power plant in the world. His long-range goal was to find a pipefitter with Grebski's psychological profile, one he could manipulate and train as easily. The attack at the Soo locks would surely bring him to the attention of other leaders, even he whose name was spoken throughout the Muslim world with reverence, whose whereabouts were unknown by all but his inner circle since fleeing the hideout in the Tora Bora caves. His source at *Al-Jazeera* told Rafiq that bin Laden would release a lengthy video later that fall. Perhaps his own *nom de guerre* might be mentioned by the great man.

He also had no doubt that Grebski, his own ugly American, would go along with the program once he realized there was no other way. As he had told Ginnah earlier, it did not matter one way or the other. Grebski was going to die on the boat as soon as he had served his purpose.

They call them Judas goats no matter what part of the world you come from.

* * *

CHAPTER 22

Haftmann Investigative Services,
Jefferson-on-the-Lake, OH/ Sep. 10, 1:53 p.m.

Rafiq Djibouti. Who in hell was he? More importantly, why would Grebski discard the paper he'd written that name on, not just pencil it out? His surname was one of those tiny, patched-in countries along the Horn of Africa that no one ever heard about unless some virulent disease originated from there.

Haftmann called the FBI Field Office in Youngstown rather than Cleveland, which would have been the logical choice. However, his uncle had often spoken of the former SAC down there in Mahoning County as one of the bravest law enforcement officers he'd ever known. He'd survived an assassination attempt in his own kitchen one night. He'd cleaned up mobster Lenny Strollo's gang back when Youngstown was the Murder Capital of the United States and "a Youngstown tune-up" had nothing to do with servicing your car.

He was put through to the SAC, an agent named Fielding who took down Haftmann's information, spoke quietly, and asked a few pointed questions about Haftmann's background.

"Look, I have no back story for you, Agent Fielding," Haftmann said. "It's just that some things have been happening up here including a recent murder and a suicide, and I wanted to err on the side of caution."

When he hung up, Haftmann felt like a royal fool. He'd just wasted a federal officer's time on a hunch—no, more likely the agent would see it as a cop groupie trying to make himself sound important. *If that agent checks me out*, Haftmann realized, *he'll come to the conclusion that call I made was something borne out of hurt pride.* Cops distrusted FBI agents as grandstanders who took all the glory; cops, on the other hand, considered private eyes nothing but motel window peepers and little better than mall security guards. Still, Haftmann had an itch in his belly recalling the conversation with Grebski in the bar a few weeks ago. That brief flash of smile like a statue cracking open before returning to stone. He didn't believe Libby wanted her brother in a jam because she was so concerned about her husband. About her kid, Haftmann just didn't know enough, but nothing in Libby spoke to the maternal instinct of womanhood.

He looked through the rain-spotted plate glass window of his uncle's office for the thousandth time in a week. His gaze wandered from the few passersby, now well thinned out after Labor Day, and finally focused on the orange and green neon sign of Tico's Place. The rain was falling from the gray sky. He could swear he could hear the hiss and sizzle of the fat raindrops hitting the sign all the way from here.

"It's just the booze calling to me," he said to his empty office.

Haftmann got up, stretched, and put on his windbreaker. The offshore breeze brought a tang of Lake Erie and dead shad with it. This was the time of the annual die-off when they piled ashore by the hundreds of thousands. Even the gulls grew weary of their rotting little silver bodies.

"I'm coming, I'm coming," Haftmann said as he locked his office door and headed across the slick, greasy street in what was now a wind-driven, sideways rain.

* * *

CHAPTER 23
Port of Duluth/Superior, MN/ Sep. 10, 2:09 p.m.

Grebski was on deck washing off the loose taconite pellets spilled from the three-ton booms that dropped from their silos as the deckhands shifted the cables up and down the dock to maintain proper ballast. Like thousands of little gray marbles that could get under your feet and send you flying to the metal deck and leave you with a broken back or a cracked head. In the early days of unloading ore boats in bad weather, a slippery dockside sent many dockworkers into the drink to drown, electrocutions resulted from working high above on Hewlett, and many limbs and bodies were crushed, a commonplace occurrence all along the ports surrounding the Great Lakes basin.

The boom was finishing up the last of their cargo into the three forward holds.

Grebski tried to control his temper and his thoughts; neither was behaving well on this, his penultimate day of life on the planet. The more work he did, he figured, the sooner the boat would batten hatches and exit the harbor into a fierce headwind and rolling waves that would shave off a couple knots of speed overnight.

If they arrived too early in the morning or too late in the evening, the result was the same: nobody in the stands to be killed in the explosion. Grebski wanted to grab each crewman returning to the vessel from shore, one by one, most with a good buzz on from binge drinking on their limited time off the boat. He liked the fact that they would be too fuzzy headed in their bunks to know what was happening when *it happened*. Even the ones showing up on deck for their shifts might not be drawing many sober breaths, which was also good. "Channel fever," sailors called it. Too much time on the water without a chance to get ashore, get drunk, get a woman made the men touchy and mean.

Grebski's seniority among the forward crew ensured he'd always have dog watch, which most of the men didn't prefer anyway. There was nothing he could do about the pace of things at this point, and he was already working ten minutes past his first shift. Rafiq's advice to the others was to trust to the will of Allah, but Grebski would have spat in God's face if he thought He was going to interfere with the project. He'd found his Arab terrorist, by God. The trouble lately was that Raff acted as though *he* did all the finding and the planning.

* * *

CHAPTER 24

Haftmann Investigative Services,
Jefferson-on-the-Lake, OH/ Sep. 10, 7:02 p.m.

"**Mister** Haftmann," the voice on his recorder said, "This is Special Agent John Larrimore of the Youngstown Field Office. I'm on my way up Route Eleven right now. Where are you?"

Jesus, I knew I shouldn't have answered my phone. He was halfway to saying, "I'm sitting in a bar—"*where I've been for the last five hours getting shit-faced.* Something in the agent's tone made him bite off the second half of his response.

"What—what can I do for you, Agent Larrimore?"

"Let's talk in person. Give me the name of the bar so I can get directions from my Garmin."

Haftmann told him but could not altogether keep the slur out of his speech.

"OK," Larrimore said, "I should be there in . . . thirty-five minutes," he said. "I'm just leaving Trumbull County . . . coming up on a sign now. It says Kinsman five miles, Orwell eighteen, so I should be there in under thirty minutes."

Haftmann did the finger trick with his pinkie and a new drink appeared brought like the others from the owner lurking in the shadows.

"You're like a trap-door spider," Haftmann said to his disappearing back.

Kinsman. That rang a bell. Clarence Darrow was born there in 1857. Scraped the cow dung off his boots and headed for Chicago and glory.

Just like me, Haftmann mused. *Except for the glory part.*

Haftmann pushed the drink away and signaled the bartender again. "Can you make me coffee—strong, black?"

He didn't know what was arriving with that agent from Youngstown, but it already smelled like trouble.

* * *

CHAPTER 25

Tico's Place on the Strip, JOTL, OH/ Sep. 10, 7:38 p.m.

"We did some checking," Larrimore said. "We take any call about Nine-Eleven plots seriously. This Rafiq Djibouti comes from a wealthy family in Beirut. His real name is Kaddoura. The Arab linguist at headquarters says it's a common Lebanese surname. It means "seller of vegetables.""

"He must have wanted something more swashbuckling for his internet handle."

"Like most of the egoists and terrorists, yes. He's attending the University of Michigan, although he's in his late twenties, older than his peers. He's charismatic. He switched from political science to engineering like the rest of his group. He's bright. Mensa bright. He and one of his math professors co-authored a paper last year. My source told me he can be as adroit in conversation about Khalil Gibran at an academic soiree or discussing wave propagation theory or the culinary arts."

"So he's on the Watch List?"

"No, nothing has come up to put him on it. He has a small circle of friends in Ann Arbor, mostly academics and students. He has his own apartment. His closest contact is a female with a Lebanese connection to a family named Simon. She's lived in the U.A.E. most of her life. But so far, her boyfriend has never walked into a Home Depot and bought parts for a bomb."

"You guys can get all this from somebody's electronic footprints?"

"We have our ways. Haftmann, we already have the technology to take a photo of every letter mailed in the U.S. Soon we'll have server farms big enough to collect every email sent or received by an American citizen."

"Big Brother, huh?"

"You bet. Big Brother with a big swinging dick."

"I suspect you wouldn't be up here talking to me if you hadn't found something interesting."

Larrimore chewed on that for a bit. Haftmann was a civilian, after all, and wasn't entitled to know anything even if he did initiate the visit. "Let's say we have other databases we check. Let's also say he knows some interesting people back home."

"And those people, I take it, are on the Watch List," Haftmann said.

Larrimore paused again. Haftmann squirmed on the stool impatiently. "Let's say some of them most definitely are."

"Let's say you tell me exactly why you dropped by our fair little town, Agent Larrimore. I assume it's not for the soda water Tico or his wife Marta down there is serving this evening."

"OK, let's talk as we drive. I want to visit this sister of Mitchell Grebski first. The report of his fight he got into has me worried."

Worried about what, Special Agent Larrimore?" Haftmann was pleased he said it without slurring.

"Ever heard of something called 'lone wolf operations'?"

* * *

CHAPTER 26
Four nautical miles out of Duluth Harbor/ Sep. 10, 8:07 p.m.

Clusterfuck.

That's what Grebski mumbled to himself watching from the starboard winch. The wind was whipping taconite dust into tiny swirls, baby dust devils skipping across the big steel hatch covers and disappearing into the cobalt blue skyline of the descending nightfall. Venus' Belt was a bold crimson band just above the horizon and the sky above was streaked with a reddish gold from the last dying rays of the sun now below the horizon.

"Fucking Arabs," he said to himself, much louder, and with pure disgust.

Duluth was a spackled canvass of pinprick lights on the hillside above the harbor. The headlamps from cars below the streetlamps and building signs were no longer visible. Taking a boat out in this chop against this wind was risky even for experienced sailors.

"So glad to have you back aboard, Grab-ass," said the third mate as he bumped past Grebski at the railing on his way back from the galley. Grebski didn't say anything. He glanced at the Ace bandaging of the mate's hand. Even if he had to go alone, the mate was going to die screaming in his own blood.

He gave the mate a big smile. "Glad to see you're feeling better than the last time we had a chat belowdecks."

"Cocksucker."

Grebski had told Rafiq several times how to approach the big vessel in his speedboat so as not to have his own boat sucked under the wash from the rolling waves. "You've heard of keel-hauling sailors back in the old days, right?" Grebski asked him.

"I understand, Mister Jones," Rafiq replied, peeved at his condescension. "I told you I'm an experienced sailor. I understand that too much of a bump alongside a boat that size and we would get rolled under the bottom of the *Gött*."

"You'll come out in the stern wash behind those big propeller blades, a gooey chum even the fish won't want, if you come out at all," Grebski said for effect.

Rafiq didn't let Grebski's frayed nerves affect his own his temper. "I understand perfectly, Mister Jones. I shall be cautious, I assure you. We have too much at stake." Rafiq hoped this was his last conversations ashore with the unpleasant oaf.

He didn't bother explaining to Grebski he drove a fifty-foot Marauder in cigarette-boat competition and owned the latest in design, an AMG Vision Gran Turismo, built on the supercar concept. "'Do not be a bragging boaster,' Qur'an, thirty-one, eighteen," Rafiq thought to himself.

It wasn't the danger of boarding that concerned him; rather, that prospect electrified him. Lake Superior's waters are so cold no one survives long in the water. "I'd rather die in the depths of the lake than be rescued on deck and die gasping like a fish from the shock," he told Ginnah. Ever since the first meeting at Awad's Coffee House in Dearborn, he, Tariq, Samir, and Ginnah had all practiced rope climbing drills in the woods behind an abandoned farmhouse until they had knots of muscle in their forearms. One had to trust to Allah for the rest, he knew.

He didn't want to call attention to himself. It was enough to get tongues wagging just being alone out here on deck in the chill wind but binoculars aimed at the shore would have been too much. Rafiq gave him a new camera phone and told him to snap the three men who would be taken captive.

Rafiq quizzed everyone endlessly in his cell on the men aboard the boat and their positions. Grebski memorized everyone's position but told Rafiq it wasn't possible to be exact with more than two-thirds of the crew.

"I know math, Mister Jones," Rafiq replied confidently. "I trust probabilities and statistics more than human behavior."

Grebski bristled. He knew he had been demoted from team leader in the eyes of the others. Samir, Tariq, and Ginnah no longer listened to anything he had to say unless Rafiq affirmed it. They would handle everyone in the stern. Grebski had given them a couple names to be careful of and he told Rafiq in their final meeting where each man was likely to be as well as the chief engineer. It would do no good to move the levers of the chadburn in the pilot house if no one responded in kind down in the engine room.

* * *

Grebski on shift. The sky is black. He watched, straining his eyes against the horizon for a single dot moving. *There it was!* His heart hammered with excitement.It seemed to be moving, growing larger as he stared. After a minute, he saw the creamy bow wave of what was no speedboat but an inflatable rubber dinghy moving fast over the black water.

That fucking Rafiq lied to me . . .

Grebski gripped the steel wire of the railing and nearly tore it loose. He had to get below and get the Jacob's ladder he had stowed in the dunnage with the duffel bags of weapons and grenades he had re-assembled in secret obscured behind dangling coils of tow rope draped over a pipe that ran the length of the room.

Grebski flew from his post as soon as he could make out the four black-masked, bobbing heads of the dinghy's crew riding the big waves.

I'll settle with you, Rafiq, when this is over—

Grebski flew down the first set of metal stairs to the sleeping quarters of the forward crew saw no one about, the card table with decks of cards on top. Agile as a big cat, he let his momentum swing him down the second set of stairs to the paint lockers and dunnage rooms.

He found everything undisturbed as he had left it, scooped everything up in his big arms and took the steps two at a time back up to the fo'c'stle.

He heard men talking behind him in the deckwatch quarters, but it sounded like ordinary conversation. No one would have challenged him regardless, even if he'd had to brush past them to the stairs. Again, this time with his breath coming in a timed rhythm to his accelerating heart and his churning legs, he went up these stairs two at a time despite the burning in his thighs.

The light was falling even faster now, and he saw the dinghy make a sharp intersecting turn to run parallel to the *Gött's* starboard side. Someone would have to be leaning out the window of the pilot house and even then, the dinghy was lost in the size of the mounting waves and the incipient darkness. All sound was smothered at the source in the wind.

Grebski threw the ladder over the side and tied it off at the deck winch. Its clanging against the side of the boat was barely audible even to him leaning over the rail as Rafiq leaned the boat into the metal wall of the *Gött's* side.

Grebski admired the seamanship of Rafiq deft maneuvering at the helm, a foot at a time, timing the waves just so, easing it beside the flopping ladder.

First up the ladder was Samir. Grebski handed him the duffel bag and he ducked behind the first hatch cover to extract the weapon and remove the grenades. Tariq had to be encouraged, however, and Grebski leaned half his body over the side to shout to him. Tariq's eyes were the only thing visible behind his mask and they were looking up at Grebski wide open in fear. He had separated from the boat, and he seemed frozen at the bottom of the ladder. The waves were smashing against his boots and banging him against the side of the boat. His knuckles were white from his rigid grip.

Grebski hollered *Climb! Climb! Climb!* at him and held out a hand for him to grasp even though Tariq was too far away to clutch it. He didn't dare to take his eyes off Tariq, whose glasses behind the eyeholes shimmered in the light.

Rafiq and Ginnah were fixated with Tariq's slow progress despite their own danger in the bucking craft. One big wave would knock him loose at any second, Grebski thought, and then, as if Tariq had been injected with a spike of adrenalin, he began to climb, slowly but steadily, making progress by inches. When he was just beyond Grebski's outstretched hand, Tariq looked up and Grebski saw he had the last three rungs to go with what had to be the last of his puny strength. As soon as he was within reach, Grebski reached down and gripped his black jumpsuit at the shoulder and he began to pull him upwards by sheer physical strength with no help from the flailing limbs of Tariq. With all the strength of one arm, Grebski heaved him over the railing onto the deck where he lay gasping and crying in Arabic.

Grebski kicked him in the ribs and rolled him over to Samir. Grebski tossed a duffel bag at him that hit Tariq in the chest, but Samir immediately went to work removing the AR-15 and the grenades.

When Grebski, panting now from the exertion, staggered back to the rail, he saw Ginnah climbing steadily upwards, masked like the others. Her long, chestnut hair tied off at the nape of her neck. Grebski drew her up and over; she was light as bamboo but just as strong. She hit the deck and went down on one knee. Looking side to side as if she were about to sprint down the deck. She grabbed the third duffel bag, which held just the two remaining ARs, and handed Grebski the Glock, which he shoved into his pants.

Grebski just got back to the rail in time to see Rafiq speed up the dinghy and then in a move so reckless it reminded Grebski of a graceful move by a confident athlete, something he hadn't seen since his football playing days, he was impressed for the first time by the leader of his student terrorists.

Rafiq took the dinghy over the crest of a huge wave; then he tied off the outboard motor handle at an angle that would ensure it would collide with the *Gött* when the next big wave hit. He pulled out a serrated combat knife from his right boot, leaned over the side of the dinghy and thrust the blade into the fabric below the waterline. He straightened up, balanced himself, took two high, fast steps over the dinghy and leaped toward the Jacob's ladder. He was in midair when he caught it about waist high and began climbing, pulling himself with one arm and then the other in a perfectly timed climb with just his upper-body strength.

The boat slammed into the side of the boat just under his legs, went vertical from the first wave catching it under and standing it straight up in the air and overturned. It was gone in two seconds, caught in the swells against the side of the boat, and carried down the length of the boat to disappear forever in the blackness.

Rafiq was barely breathing hard when Grebski hauled him up by the fabric of his jumpsuit. All he said behind the mask in his perfect English was a single sentence: "Time to go to work, brother."

Ginnah tossed him his weapon and they split into their two teams and without another word were gone.

Grebski and Rafiq went straight to the Texas deck and knocked on the first mate's door. His quarters were next to the captain's and almost as large. He came to the door in his underpants and a tee shirt.

"We need you in the pilot house," Grebski said as soon as the door had opened wide enough to allow him to insert a foot if need be. The mate, a forty-five-year-old with a pocked face, looked at Grebski and then at the smaller masked figure next to him. Grebski kicked him in the stomach and he went flying backwards in a heap knocking over a table with charts on it.

"Remember, don't kill him yet," Rafiq said.

Before he could get off the floor, Rafiq set the barrel of his weapon on the bridge of the mate's nose. "Don't make a sound and you will live through this," he told the man.

Grebski pulled the man by the arm out of sight of the doorway and thrust him into the utility bathroom which was nothing more than a toilet and shower. He tied him at the hands and feet with the nylon cuffs from the duffel bag.

"Lie there quietly, don't move and we'll be right back for you," Rafiq said. "If I find you've moved so much as an inch, I'll put a bullet in your head."

Grebski hoped the mate would say something. The man merely craned his head to see what was coming next. Grebski barely move toward him, but it was enough to alert Rafiq to throw his arm across Grebski's chest and prevent whatever mayhem he had intended.

"Not now, brother. Think of the mission. Time for that later."

They moved to the second mate's cabin. Grebski had to pound on his door to wake him, but when he saw Grebski, he seemed to instinctively understand he was in danger. He made a move to slam the metal door shut. Grebski was too big for him and much too fast. He threw the smaller man off the door as if he were swatting a fly. Before the mate could recover to say something, Grebski stepped right up to him and threw a punch to his face that snapped his head back and dropped him to the floor.

"I never liked you either," Grebski said and kicked him hard in the temple.

Rafiq, standing behind him, didn't say a word.

"I don't think we'll need to tie him up," Grebski said looking down at the man on the floor.

"The plan, brother. We stick to the plan."

He tossed a pair of nylon cuffs to Grebski who handled the unconscious man like a rag doll.

They crossed through the windlass room where the chain anchors were secured by a massive winch. The smell of the open lake mixed with diesel fuel was strong. Grebski banged on the watchman quarters where two men were housed for their twelve-hour shifts. This was one of the men to be wary of, Grebski had told Rafiq and the others at one of their final meetings.

Rafiq stood off to the side to get a clear shot in case something happened.

He opened the door. He had been drinking heavily in port and was unsteady on his feet. Even before Grebski got a word out of his mouth, the stench of alcohol was rife in the room along with a sour body odor smell.

Grebski said, "They need you in the pilot house."

"What the fuck're you talking about, Grebski?"

His eyes were trying to focus on the short man in black beside the surly deckhand.

"Who the fuck is—"

Grebski hit him with the Glock's butt in the forehead. Instead of going down, he took a small step backwards and shook his head, whimpering, a bull in the kill chute stunned by the bolt gun but a long way from dead. Grebski drew his weapon back for another swing when the bullet from Rafiq's barrel jerked and spat out a single shot that went through the wheelsman's right eye. He sat down as if he were a child ordered by a parent. His head lolled once and then he died in that position with a geyser of blood pouring down his face and over his chest.

"What the fuck," Grebski said and whirled on Rafiq, who seemed unaware he was now casually levelling the barrel at Grebski.

"Never mind," Rafiq said. "He would have given us trouble eventually."

Grebski pushed the wheelsman backwards to the floor and picked up his left foot to drag him over to the bunk. A blood smear was evident even in the darkened room.

"Now the difficult part," Rafiq said.

He meant the two deckwatches, the two crewman who handles the power boom and belt of the self-unloader, and the other two deckhands in opposite quarters below.

They approached the deckwatch quarters first. The steel doors to both quarters were usually kept open when the weather was good. The two men were sitting on the edges of their bunks when Grebski stood in the doorway.

"Hey, Grebski, what's up man?"

Grebski stepped aside so that they could see the black-clad man with the machine gun cradled in his arms.

"We're taking over the boat," Grebski said.

"What the fuck are you talking about and who is that?"

"He's someone who will kill you if you don't get off that fucking bunk right now and stand up with your hands behind you," Grebski said. He pulled out the Glock and aimed it at the deckwatch's head.

Both deckwatches were cuffed and told to sit on the lower bunk side by side.

"We'll be right over there," Grebski said, pointing at the other quarters. "If you move, you'll die."

Rafiq lingered behind to make the impression stick while Grebski walked over to the last of the men they needed to secure before the pilot house occupants.

When the deckhands were brought out cuffed, Rafiq motioned for the two deckwatches to join them at the poker table. He held the AR out and assumed a firing position for effect. The men talked, all of them incredulous. Curses were hurled at Grebski and names were called in the fashion of men who are brave in numbers. Rafiq said nothing but kept the barrel of the machine gun at the ready. His calm and silence told them more than threatening words would have.

In a few minutes, Grebski was marching the two mates downstairs to the dunnage room. The second mate was being supported by the first on one side and Grebski on the other. In his free hand he held the Glock aloft. The side of the mate's head was swollen and he was glassy-eyed. His mouth was bloody from the streams of blood that had poured from his nostrils. His nose was broken and canted at an angle from the rest of his face.

"You're going into the locker down below," Grebski said. "You won't be there long. We have some demands to make of the company. You'll be set free when we get what we're asking for."

The men looked at one another as if they expected something more sensible coming from their captors than the hijacking of an ore boat at the locks. Their question was the same: *Where would you take it?*

The clothed men were frisked for phones, knives. Grebski walked down the stairs backwards with his Glock pointed at the front man while Rafiq brought up the rear.

Once the men were walked into the paint locker, Grebski handed the last man, one of the two watchmen, a soft-spoken man Pierce, a battery-operated lantern for light. It was all part of the ruse to make the men think they were getting out of this. He looped a chain through the door handle and secured it to an eye bolt with a padlock from the same duffel bag. They could barely hear the curses and yells coming from the room.

Rafiq used his walkie-talkie to call Ginnah. He spoke a few words in Arabic, looked at Grebski and gave him the thumb's-up sign. It amused him to think that this dumb American had no idea it was an offensive gesture in the Middle East.

"Check," he said to Grebski. "Ginnah and the others have them secured in the stewards' quarters."

"They're supposed to put them in the supply locker in the stern, God damn it!"

"Easy, my brother. This will work just as well. They are locked in and that's what matters, no?"

"Where's the Chief?" Grebski asked.

"Ginnah says he is cooperating. Now let us proceed to the pilot house. Your friend, the third mate, and the captain await us," Rafiq said.

Grebski turned without a word and headed up the stairs to the pilot house. Rafiq trailed behind.

Grebski could swear he heard humming behind the mask . . .

* * *

CHAPTER 27

Residence of the Boatwrights,
Riverton, OH/ Sep. 10, 9:38 p.m.

"**She** seems to like you," Agent Larrimore said as they walked down the front porch steps.

"Shut up, Agent Larrimore," Haftmann said. "That woman, I don't know. Something's wrong here."

"You mean a woman like her living in a place like that?"

"That's not what I mean," Haftmann said. "She knows more than she's saying, don't you think?"

"You mean she's smarter than she looks?"

"If her brains matched her body, she'd be teaching quantum mechanics at Cambridge. I meant that her brother borrows her car for these mysterious trips to Dearborn, Michigan. Yet she somehow knows how many miles are put on the odometer. She's holding out," Haftmann said.

A gas bubble in his stomach caused Haftmann to burp. The alcohol still cavorting in his system made him woozy in the damp night air.

"I'm calling the Coast Guard in Cleveland," Larrimore said. "They can contact Grebski's boat when it docks. Have him questioned, do a search of his quarters."

Larrimore made several calls to the Cleveland Coast Guard on the way back to Jefferson-on-the-Lake. Haftmann volunteered to drive so he could use his phone undistracted, but the agent told him that writing a report on the passenger who managed to get an OVI while driving a government vehicle signed out to him wasn't *on his agenda that evening, thank you.* The Coast Guard called Larrimore just as Haftmann was fashioning a rejoinder to that insult, which forced him to swallow it.

Why argue the truth? Haftmann told himself. *The dog returneth . . .*

Larrimore asked Cleveland to call him at his number as soon as they knew something. This much was known already, he told Haftmann: Grebski was reinstalled aboard the *Gött* as a deckhand and the boat was currently loaded with taconite, whatever that is, en route to Sault Sainte Marie, the locks there, and then it's heading downlakes for its next port-of-call, Northtown.

"Look, I've got to make a courtesy call to the Cleveland field office when we get back. Shall I drop you at the bar where I picked you up?"

"Sounds like a plan," Haftmann said.

"Everybody should have one."

Haftmann was back on his bar stool in Tico's Place but that something he felt back at Libby Boatwright's shabby home was still nagging at him.

He got off the stool and walked outside into the nearly deserted street. A donut shop and a sidewalk pizza parlor seemed to be the only business still open besides the bars.

"Libby, it's Tom Haftmann."

"What do you want now? You were just here with what's-his-name."

"Yes, I know. I have one or two more questions to ask."

"Fuck, man, it's late. I'm tired."

"OK, really quick," Haftmann said. "Did you find Marissa Toensing's suicide note?"

A long pause—*she's thinking of how to answer this one*, Haftmann knew.

"No."

"Did Marissa have any life insurance?"

"Hey, fuck you," Libby said and ended the connection.

"I just got my answer," Haftmann said to a dead phone receiver.

He called Agent Larrimore—Haftmann silently thanking his uncle for that bit of good advice: "Always, always get a phone number for everybody you deal with in a case, no exceptions, laddie"—and waited without breathing for him to pick up.

"Special Agent Larrimore."

"Look, we have to get over to the county jail tonight—*Right now!*"

"Haftmann? What, are you drunk? Do you know what time it is?"

Haftmann had to think hard. He knew he had one chance to press this agent's button: "Yes, I do. It's almost the anniversary of Nine Eleven." He kept the panic out of his voice.

"I'll be right there," Larrimore said.

Damn, he didn't even ask where I was. Another sure sign of a drunk.

* * *

CHAPTER 28
Sheriff's Office,
Jefferson, OH/ Sep. 10, 9:56 p.m.

Boatwright wasn't happy about being disturbed this time of night. He was "going out on a chain" tomorrow with some other prisoners, in his case to his hearing for parole violation and Libby had promised to meet him before he boarded the transfer bus.

"Mister Boatwright," Larrimore began, "we have to ask you some questions. It's vital that you answer truthfully. It's a matter of national security."

"Ask your questions," Boatwright said. "I might not answer them without a lawyer. I'm just saying that up front."

"Sir, if you fail to assist this investigation, charges will be brought and they will be far more serious than a parole violation," Larrimore said.

"What the fuck is he doin' here?"

"Mister Haftmann here is a special investigator assisting my investigation," Larrimore said and acknowledged Haftmann with a curt nod of his head.

Haftmann kept his face still, but it was obvious Boatwright was thinking he should have placed his shot with more accuracy that night. Haftmann decided not to reveal how he and Boatwright were acquainted. Judging from the look he got after Boatwright's response to his presence, he was sure he was going to get an earful from Special Agent Larrimore for withholding that tidbit of information.

After badging half the officers and the watch commander on the late shift and using his best command voice, Larrimore was able to drag Haftmann along without interference. "Just keep your mouth shut. I'll do the talking," Larrimore said.

"What's this about?" Boatwright asked them.

Larrimore had been briefed by Haftmann's theory en route but he had not had time to formulate a good strategy for confronting Boatwright. Haftmann could see he was going to wing it and hope for the best.

Larrimore put both hands palm down on the stainless-steel table in the interrogation room, and said, "Look, we need your help. I'm not asking you to implicate yourself in any way. But what I'm asking you, if you help us, can do some good for you too. First, did Marissa Toensing name your wife Elizabeth—Libby—as beneficiary of her life insurance?"

"Yes."

"How much was—"

"Libby said it was a quarter-of-million," Boatwright said.

Haftmann was as surprised as Larrimore at the rapid response from the husband, but he showed no emotion.

"Does Libby's brother have insurance on his life?"

"Yeah, I know that for a fact. Libby told me he gets it through his union. It's another hundred thousand, I think. Maybe more. I don't know. Libby told me one time." He yawned.

"Do you know . . . if she is the beneficiary of both policies?"

"I think so. Why? What's this about?"

"Libby won't collect on either policy," Larrimore said, "if the ruling is suicide. You—she knows that, right?"

Haftmann remembered the burn mark on Libby's hand.

"I don't know jack about that." Despite the shackles on his wrists and legs, he twisted uncomfortably in the metal chair.

"If the ruling on Marissa's suicide is changed from 'indeterminate' to 'homicide,' she'll get all the money."

"So what . . . does that mean?"

"I think your wife Libby is setting you up for a murder indictment on Marissa Toensing. I think she's hoping to collect on that money and she may also be involved in something that is about to happen with her brother, and that is the only reason why we're here," Larrimore said quietly.

Boatwright hung his head until his forehead touched the metal table. Haftmann held his breath watching him. Boatwright began making soft gurgling sounds and Larrimore reached across to pat his shoulder.

"She killed our baby," Boatwright said and began sobbing. "She killed our baby girl. That's how we got to the house and I got the new pickup. Just to shut me up."

"What—what are you talking about, Mister Boatwright?"

"Libby told me she accidentally rolled over on the baby. She said she fell asleep while she was breastfeeding her. The baby suffocated. It was an accident . . . she said."

The last sentence was said with such bitterness that Haftmann knew he must have been simmering with suspicion for a long time.

"You—Libby had taken out life insurance on your child?"

"Yesss," Boatwright said, bitterly, the sibilants lingering like hissing snakes in the cramped space. "That bitch ain't got a soul, man."

"How do you know it wasn't an accident, Mister Boatwright?" Larrimore asked.

"Because she got a check for fifty-thousand dollars about four weeks after . . . after the funeral. Libby, she looked so heartbroken . . . the evil bitch has got everybody fooled."

Boatwright raised his cuffed hands in some kind of dark emotional pain wracking his body.

Jesus, Haftmann thought, *she's a match for her brother . . .*

"Tell us about your brother-in-law," Larrimore said. "What is he planning to do tomorrow? You know, it's the anniversary of Nine Eleven?"

"No, no, I didn't and I don't give a fuck, neither. I got my own shit to worry about. I can't be worried about sand niggers too."

"The brother . . ." Larrimore encouraged without betraying the impatience he must have been feeling then.

"Mitch. I always thought he and Libby were—you know, like, way too close. Way too close for brother and sister. It used to freak me out when I saw him in the house. Libby always had this look on her face, like when she's pulling something over on me or someone."

"You think they were . . . intimate?"

"That's a pretty way to put it, now ain't it?" Boatwright almost spat on the table.

"Tell us what he's planning to do?"

"All I know is Libby said he was up to something . . . something 'real big,' she said. She can't keep her mouth shut when she's in a bragging mood. You know they's twins, right? She could practically finish his sentences for him before he got through speaking. Used to creep me out, man."

"What is he planning to do tomorrow, Boatwright? We have to know right now if we're going to do anything to stop it."

"Libby and me, we got into an argument before . . . he, your guy there, come running out of the bush shouting 'Po-lice!' at me. It was about how many miles her brother had put on my fuckin' truck. I might have been drinking that night, but I never hit Libby. Fuck, I made that mistake one time. She's as strong as her goddamn brother. The whole fuckin' town thinks I beat her but—"

"Boatwright, we have to know what Mitchell Grebski is doing right now."

Boatwright gazed into Larrimore's face and then he shifted his gaze to Haftmann.

"I think he's planning to kill a bunch of people on that boat of his."

It's much worse than that, Boatwright, Haftmann was thinking, as Larrimore's face lost a shade of color right in front of him. *He's got a bona fide terrorist with him.*

* * *

CHAPTER 29

"**You're** fucking crazy, Grebski," the third mate said for the twentieth time holding himself back from pacing in the tiny confines of the now crowded pilot house of the *J. Beaufort Göttlieb*.

Grebski didn't react. Some of Rafiq's cool was rubbing off on him. This was better: *drag out the revenge, let the shitbag wonder what was coming. And oh boy, is it coming for you, bucko.*

The captain and the wheelsman were silent. Whenever a radio communication had to be made, Rafiq positioned himself right behind the captain and tickled his neck with the barrel of his weapon. "I understand the language of the sea, Captain. Don't say anything that will make this gun go off and punch the back of your brain into a stew because I *will* shoot you."

Grebski felt at peace for the first time in a very long time, longer than he could remember. He had not had one of those blinding headaches in days and his mental confusion and episodes or irritation were lessened by the events of the last few days.

Rafiq called Ginnah in the engine room and spoke in Arabic.

"Why don't you just speak English to her," Grebski said to him. "What's the point now?"

"I merely told her we were at the first checkpoint coming to the Soo locks," Rafiq said.

What he had said to her was to tell Tariq and Samir to ready the grenades forward and aft. As soon as the captain communicated to the tugboat bringing them into the lock channel, each was to toss in a grenade, slam the door, open it for another grenade toss. Three grenades apiece in each locker. That should make for quite a spectacle when the doors were opened again. "They'll be identifying femurs for weeks," Tariq joked to Samir out of Grebski's hearing.

Samir was all for doing it as soon as the men were herded into the lockers, but Rafiq told him they had to wait. "Grebski is too unpredictable. I don't know how he will react when he hears the grenades go off and knows I lied to him. One of us must stay in the pilot house with the captain and the wheelsman. We can't both be off the boat. It's far too risky. We need him to walk the cable right to the grandstand. After that, he's expendable."

Tariq was to go astern and keep watch. One tug was all that was necessary given the *Gött's* powerful bow thrusters once they cleared the harbor breakwall and the piers were in sight. Grebski was forward deckhand. The mate would swing him and Samir over the side in the bosun chair with Rafiq holding the gun on the mate. Grebski would take the forward cable and walk along the cement pier until it came time to through the cable over the bollard. Samir was to imitate Grebski's walk and actions, dressed like a sailor in the dungarees and heavy flannel shirt. Walking along the stern wearing a yellow hard hat and life jacket vest, he'd look like any deckhand or dock worker. The third mate would have to operate the after-winch as well, and if he failed to hustle down the deck after swinging the men over the side, the AR-15 pressed into his ribs should speed him up.

Rafiq had given in to Grebski on this and it worried him. He knew Grebski wanted to give this man special attention, and that was fine when the time came, but of the three mates aboard, this one was the only one who had the size and temperament to mount a revolt. He intended to back up Tariq while the mate operated the steam winch for the afterend cable.

It was the only part of the plan, Rafiq believed, which put them all at risk once the men were contained. Americans loved to think of themselves as more heroic than anyone else. The schoolboy nonsense of their films, he supposed. The mate also was an ex-Marine and might have that *Semper fi* motto locked in his mind. Rafiq would put a bullet in him and kill Grebski right after if he had to.

They were way too close now for failure. *Alhamdulillah.*

* * *

CHAPTER 30
Residence of Dean and Libby Boatwright,
Riverton, OH/ Sep. 11, 12:02

Haftmann stood just behind Agent Larrimore on Libby's porch and spoke through the screen door.

"I've called the Coast Guard and the entire Sault Sainte Marie area will be on lockdown in just a few minutes. If there's anything you want to tell us about your brother, now is the time. It could help save some lives."

"Go fuck yourself," she said through the screen. Even in the shadowy mesh of the screen, Haftmann saw the brilliant flash of her perfect teeth.

Larrimore turned to go. But Haftmann wasn't through with her.

"You held Marissa down. You poured the lye down her throat and some of it splashed onto your hand. Even as strong as you are, she fought you."

"Get off my porch, fucker."

"You know those hesitation marks people see on suicide's wrists when they aren't quite sure yet, before they make the deep cuts down the veins?" Haftmann asked her. "Those splash marks on her face will help convict you someday."

"How many times do I have to tell you to get the fuck off my porch?"

"You wrote those names and numbers down, not your brother," Haftmann said. "You forgot about the insurance company number I traced on the paper behind it. I don't know how you got your brother to tell you, but you did."

"Wouldn't you just like to know?" She flashed that smile once more and the screen door slammed in his face.

"C'mon, Haftmann, let's go," Agent Larrimore said and pulled him by the elbow.

"Nothing I said to her is evidence," Haftmann said to him. "She's going to get away with it no matter what's happening up there with her brother. Just like she killed her baby and got away with it."

"The pathologist will keep Toensing's death 'indeterminate,'" Larrimore said. "She won't get any insurance payout."

"I don't know about that," Haftmann told him. "I've never seen anything as deadly as that woman that wasn't confined in a steel cage or a concave-shaped building."

"We probably saved Boatwright's life anyhow," Larrimore said. "Where he was going, there are a lot of bad guys who'll kill you for an extra sandwich in the chow line."

Haftmann remembered Libby's father was tied in with the Aryan Brotherhood. He wondered if she had strings to pull to see to it that Boatwright never came out of the joint. His uncle told him the Brand had a special trick of getting their enforcers assigned to the cells of the men they intended to deal out punishment or kill. Boatwright found garroted in his bunk wouldn't disturb his own peace of mind much, Haftmann realized. He remembered those grisly dogfights.

"You're right about that, Agent Larrimore," Haftmann said. "She's a chip off the old block."

But it was the absent brother up north that preoccupied both their thoughts on the ride back to town.

* * *

137

CHAPTER 31

The Soo Locks, Sault Ste. Marie, MI/ Sep. 11, 2:05 p.m.

Grebski held his binoculars on the stands. They were still too far away to see much.

He hoped there would be hundreds of them—mothers, fathers, grandparents. College-aged youth who were on the threshold of their best years just as he had been before his were blasted away from him in the loss of mental faculties. It brought home the horror of his future: the worsening mental confusion that made him sometimes forget how to tie a simple half-hitch knot when collecting the deck ropes. Most of all, his increased memory loss, the impaired judgment, impulse-control problems, sudden bursts of aggression for no reason, long bouts of depression where he swam alone in a cesspool of darkness and filth, and, eventually, the worst thing—progressive dementia, a pants-shitting husk relegated to a nursing home. Today, finally, it would all be over. Rafiq promised they would have the bomb waiting at the Soo. He could set the timer himself, Raff promised.

The forward tug was churning up a nice bow wake, all ninety tons of thrust power strained through the thick towrope hauling the massive boat overshadowing it below.

Grebski stood on the number-one hatch cover wearing his vest and hard hat waiting to be swung over the side. Samir, looking nervous and small beside him, seemed lost inside his red-and-black plaid jacket that was too big for his small frame.

The third mate stood glowering at him from the winch. Whenever he took his eyes off Rafiq, he'd look over the side to see the narrowing distance between the *Gött* and the dock wall. Rafiq hoped that the pride surging up through his belly was not offensive to Allah. He could not help but be proud of what he had accomplished so far—especially with his erratic American.

He used the walkie-talkie to have Samir go down to the engine room where Ginnah was faithfully keeping the chief engineer at his post. Only when he had to urinate was she allowed off duty so that Tariq or Samir could replace her in a situation too indelicate for a good Muslim woman. He was fed by her hand, however, while he was cuffed to a rail. He was nothing more than a big donkey with a single task to go round and round the millstone. Ginnah told him she could handle things down there if he needed to be killed. He had no doubts she would strap on a bomb vest, like the Black Widow *Shahidka* martyrs, as the Western press called those brave women of the Russian schoolhouse bombing in Chechnya. But Rafiq was not the marrying kind like his idol Carlos the Jackal. She did not adapt well to American ways and that, Rafiq lamented, was her single flaw.

Time. Time for the bosun chair. There wasn't more than a few feet between the dock and the *Gött*'s side. Samir worked the ropes to the boom that would swing Grebski and Tariq over the side and lower them to the docks.

Rafiq held his breath while he watched Samir plant his feet. Grebski was twice the weight of Samir so he needed to use every ounce of strength to get Grebski free of gravity and moving in the small plank of a chair.

Slowly, Grebski moved to clear the railing with his boots extended. At that point he was about twenty-five feet above the ground as Samir began heaving at the other rope to lower him. Too fast and he would fall to the cement pier and perhaps be injured. That would jeopardize everything. Samir's forearms were strained from the effort as Grebski dropped a couple feet at a time in jerks. From his bouncing chair Grebski shot Rafiq a look that said, *Fix this.*

Rafiq, without a word, slipped the AR over his shoulder in its sling and jumped onto the hatch cover where Samir was struggling to hold Grebski in place. Just in time, he reached the rope and set himself. Grebski took one drop and then stopped dead in mid-air as Rafiq lent his strength to the effort. Between them, they managed to lower

Grebski to the pier but his descent was still too fast for him to get his legs under him in time and he wound up sitting in the chair on the pier.

Grebski sprang to his feet and headed toward the winch where the cable was hanging like a large steel tongue waiting for the mate to throw the lever. Everyone on the deck heard him say "fuckhead"; fortunately, they were too far from the crowds of people already enjoying the view, milling about on the grass near picnic tables, or ascending the grandstands for the best views of the boats raised and lowered for their ongoing journeys across these inland seas.

Rafiq stood on the starboard spar deck and spoke rapidly into his walkie-talkie in plain sight of all. It would look perfectly normal on a thousand-footer where this was the normal means of communicating with the crew along the vast expanse of steel boat where different duties were ongoing all day on the water or in port. Inside he was tense despite the outward calm.

He closed his eyes for a moment and envisioned where everyone was at that precise moment—Ginnah with the engineer belowdecks, Samir back in the pilot house with the captain and wheelsman, both cuffed, by the time the boat came to a full stop in the assigned lock. He always found time to rehearse what he would do in the sequence of things in case of contingencies. It was why he was the leader of the group. Ever since Grebski had showed up in a discussion board with his infantile notions blurting out hints of a violent "project," Rafiq assessed the situation and understood that destiny had just taken him by the hand. In just minutes, he knew, things were going to be happening very, very fast . . .

Two helicopters appeared out of the blue sky, coming from the town of St. Mary's. One was a medical helicopter that hovered over the grassy area behind the grandstands. The other, a larger one with Coast Guard markings, separated and swung over the stern of the *Gött*. Rafiq took his eyes off the smaller helicopter to watch it circle the smokestack.

Something wrong—

* * *

CHAPTER 32
Soo Locks, Sault Ste. Marie, MI/ Sep. 11, 3:48 p.m.

The Navy SEAL Team repelled from both sides of the Coast Guard helicopter in pairs, one after the other landing on the boat deck of the ship's stern and splitting into two three-man teams to descend the steps on both sides. The portside team headed for the galley and crew's quarters.

Ignoring the booby-trapped grenade rigged to the door handle, they went down the catwalk to the engine room. Team leaders made sure each man was familiar with the ship's schematics faxed from corporate headquarters moments before boarding the helo. It was easy to get confused in the claustrophobic crisscrossing pipes in an engine room regardless of the tropical heat, the hiss of steam and clanking of metal. All the six-foot brass pistons of the *Gött* were stilled in the locks so the noise level was much abated from a moving boat.

This was a six-man team assembled within an hour of Special Agent Larrimore's last call to the Cleveland Coast Guard alerting them to a possible terrorist situation at Sault Ste. Marie. He also notified his field office SAC, who then notified the FBI's HST team in DC. The call to his office was protocol and mainly of the cover-your-ass sort when competing bureaucracies are at risk of clashing over jurisdictional rights and deciding who had strategic command in emergencies.

But once Homeland Security was notified, it was a done deal and the call to the Michigan Air National Guard base in Lansing, where a staging operation could be set up, was made within minutes. These SEALs were one-third of Team 10, stationed near Virginia Beach, and already available with their gear because of training exercises in a joint exercise with Canadian commandos. The plan was to drop them by Coast Guard helicopter about a hundred yards from where the *Gött* would be settling into the assigned berth at the Soo.

The rest was not in any agency's playbook, never considered a contingency for an American vessel in a home port or in an international commercial enterprise like the Soo locks. History had something to say about failing to mind the lessons of the past.

* * *

CHAPTER 33

The Soo Locks, Sault Ste. Marie, MI/ Sep. 11, 4:02 p.m.

Grebski's hands were sweating in his gloves. He could see where the last three mooring posts painted a bright hunter's orange were lined up down the end of the dock. As soon as he dropped the cable loop around the bollard post, he was heading back aboard by way of the Jacob's ladder Rafiq would toss over the side in the same place he had helped hoist them aboard last night. Let the rubberneckers in the grandstands watch him climb and wonder. They wouldn't be wondering for long. Rafiq assured him several times already that his "contact" would be there. "He is high up in his organization," Rafiq had told him. He is eager to see this happen. We will all be famous."

Grebski had known something of fame in his young life as an outstanding athlete with a promising future at a Big Ten school. *You can have it*, Grebski thought. *I just want to kill as many as I can.*

Grebski heard the whirling blades of the chopper at the same time everyone else did. People in the stands pointed at the chopper as it hovered over the boat amidships. He watched the men in combat camos repel from both sides of the chopper—three on each side. In no time, they would be on the deck. Grebski looked up to see if Rafiq were aware of what was happening. He saw no face leaning over the side. Hundreds of tons of water were being siphoned from the lock compartment per second to lower the boat and it made hearing difficult. He shouted "Rafiq! Rafiq!" but no response came back to him.

Grebski turned one way and then the other. Tariq was too far away at the stern to hear or see anything except the helicopter and his view of the men descending might have been obscured.

No! No! No! Grebski screamed internally. *They won't take this from me. Not now.*

Just as he was turning away, he heard the sputter of a machine gun and saw the barrel extending over the stern winch. He saw Tariq fall backward to the pier with his arms and legs flopping. The cable swung harmlessly into the boat's side without a sound. No one in the stands could see the shooting from where they were.

Grebski pulled out his Glock and held it up at the third mate's face. He pulled the trigger but nothing happened. The gun was jammed. The startled, terrified mate stepped backward out of sight. Grebski stood there, helpless son the dock, not knowing what to do or where to go next. No sounds came from overhead. He dropped the gun and ran toward the cyclone fence separating him from the grandstands. His only thought was surviving so that he could kill whoever had betrayed him.

He flung himself at the fence and climbed it to the top; his hands gripped the top strand of barbed wire, which cut into the palms of his hands. Oblivious to the pain, Grebski swung his body over the wire and landed feet first on the other side. People were looking at him and pointing. But the action on the boat's deck was more compelling—and then the gunshots erupted in a steady staccato of bullets being fired.

Screams, yelling, panic—chaos.

Had Grebski stopped his mad run through the fleeing crowds, he would have seen something close to what he had hoped for. Except that the killing was being done by the SEALs and the bullets were finding their targets. Ginnah had put her weapon to the chief engineer's head as soon as the SEAL came crouching toward her along the overhead gangway, weapon raised, and bellowed at her to drop her weapon. She screamed back that the engineer was her hostage when a round took the back of her head off. She never saw the second SEAL.

Samir was shot through the pilot house glass when a SEAL made a distracting noise at the entrance door. He fell face down without making a sound or firing a shot despite his finger being on the trigger. The SEAL had put the burst exactly where it needed to go to shut down Samir's motor reflexes.

Rafiq knew death was coming for him once he spotted the ropes emerge from the sides of the chopper. He would die *shahid*—a small balm to his sorrow at this failure. He wasted a fraction of a moment thinking the captain must have made a surreptitious call or said something in code despite Samir's vigilance. He did not know that the captain was just then lying on the deck of the pilot house gasping for breath. The stress of the terror had given him a major heart attack. An emergency quadruple bypass at the hospital in St. Mary's would save his life but his career on the Great Lakes was over.

Rafiq figured the engineer and Ginnah were both dead at this point and that the American commandos had secured the stern saved the men in the steward's cabin. It was a vain hope that Ginnah might have been able to detonate a grenade before she was killed. He, however, would not die without shedding infidel blood. The men in the dunnage room—deckhands, two-man shuttle-boom crew, two deckwatches and the two mates—would count for something when his name was mentioned.

Allahu Akbar . . .

* * *

CHAPTER 34

Haftmann Investigative Services,
Jefferson-on-the-Lake, OH/ Sep. 13, 9:00 a.m.

His uncle said, "One case, eh? That's all right, Thomas. This is the slow season, after all."

Haftmann almost snorted at that but covered it with a cough.

Haftmann was sober and made every effort to look it. He had kept his uncle in the dark about everything pertaining to Libby Boatwright's case except the fact she hired him to look up some names and numbers "for a family matter." Haftmann liked and trusted his uncle, but he didn't know exactly where he and the law—or some ethical compass most private eyes subscribed to—had gone erratically off the beaten path. *Better to let sleeping dogs lie*, he told himself, an adage he preferred to the one that usually came to his mind with his hangover that had to do with dogs and regurgitation.

The fact that he wasn't even mentioned in the papers was a huge relief.

"Sorry, Uncle, I didn't hear you?"

"I asked if she paid yet," his uncle repeated.

"No, actually, I'm delivering the report today."

"You feeling OK, Tom?"

"Never better, Uncle, why?"

"You look a little . . . pale is all."

Boozer's pallor. One drunk recognizing another the way motorcycle riders give each other a wave in passing.

It didn't help he dreaded the thought of seeing Libby Boatwright again. He thought of mailing the report and washing his hands of her forever, but that would have aroused even more suspicion in his uncle.

You always gave an oral report with the bill—no exceptions. Haftmann smiled to himself: he liked the idea of formulating rules like that. Maybe one day he'd have his own little portfolio of rules to live by, an existentialist handbook of sorts.

"You off already? I thought we'd have coffee and chat a little about things. I'd like to have a talk with you about what I learned out there in Arizona. Mostly about myself."

"Sure, Uncle. I'd like nothing better but, damn it, I promised this woman I'd have the report ready for her this morning, so—"

"I understand," his uncle said. "We'll talk later."

I'm sure we will, Haftmann thought, as he rose from the chair, to leave. His uncle looked happily ensconced in his big desk chair once again.

Out in the bright sun of a beautiful fall morning in Northern Ohio, he started to feel good despite the tiny tremors in his hands and twitching nerves. Fifty-two hours and counting without a drink—wasn't that how the real alcoholics did it? *But I am one*, Haftmann reminded himself.

Before he'd picked up his uncle at Cleveland-Hopkins, he'd pried what new information he could out of Agent Larrimore, but he could tell from the FBI man's tone, he was coming to the end of their partnership, if it ever had been one. Haftmann was relieved he was kept out of Larrimore's filed report, the FD-302, and was named only in the FD-209 as a confidential informer. That suited him fine.

His thoughts segued to Libby Boatwright. It struck him as unbelievable that a woman who had collected $50,000 insurance money on the dead infant she "accidentally rolled on in her sleep" had her name as beneficiary on four other policies: her husband's, her brother's, Marissa Toensing's—and, scariest of all, her young son. Larrimore told him that the head claims adjustor at the insurance company where Marissa's policy had been taken out assured him that their lawyers "would fight her claim tooth and nail if she even dreamed of filing it." Boatwright's lawyer was in the process of getting his client's name removed from her policy on him, and the brother was still officially a missing person implicated in the "Dearborn Plot," as the media were calling it, still clamoring authorities for more information. Every news channel and paper in the country wanted more details.

Statements from the surviving crewmen were still being assessed by the FBI and Homeland Security, but it was apparent to all he was more than a willing dupe of the four plotters from Michigan. Libby's name had appeared in a *Plain Dealer* article ascribing "suicidal tendencies" and "anger management issues" to her brother. She added that he was "easily influenced by the wrong people."

Haftmann thought the psychobabble TV lingo was a nice touch. A firestorm of protest over the issuing student visas to international students, especially from those regions engulfed in the political fury of the relentless tensions in the Middle East. The ripples were widening out and innocent people were likely to be hurt in violence inspired by what she said.

Larrimore's theory was that Grebski was freezing and starving to death in the woods surrounding St. Mary's. "Right now, he's being eaten alive by deer flies and mosquitoes. He'll come stumbling out of the forest up there any minute now."

Haftmann knew from news reports that the blood left on the razor wire was from Grebski's leap to safety after the debacle of the plot. He remembered Grebski's sly smile on the bar seat next to his and the rapid, graceful exit. Had he been on the boat, Haftmann wondered, would he have let those SEALs riddle him with bullets? Larrimore told him the Glock he had was useless and theorized the plotters meant to kill him. "He was seconds away from getting a bullet in the head like that wheelsman. This way, it'll take a decade longer when we do get him. His next berth will be in Lucasville on deathrow. He's got the steel ride with a needle coming."

The "hog-tied girl" had been finally identified through facial reconstruction. She was a twenty-five-year-old, part-time bartender at biker bars on the Lake the year before. Fired as an LPN for stealing patients' drugs at her nursing home, she had four kids by three men, all being raised by the woman's mother because of her worsening meth addiction. A crowdfunding benefit effort was set up online to help the family. No one could remember where she had been or who had seen her last when she disappeared. It wasn't unusual, according to the dead woman's mother, for Susie Stockton to go missing for weeks at a time. Police were asking anyone with information to come forward . . .

Thinking about that dead, lost woman and her abandoned kids made Haftmann realize something: he wanted to know. He wanted to know what happened to every murdered, lost, missing runaway. How could anyone live their lives in peace while all this mayhem was going on.

It dawned on him, too, that he liked being part of an investigation into mysteries. He knew that police academies were having a hard time finding recruits. *Well, if the law is a wash, maybe I can be a cop*, he thought. A brief sidebar article in the *PD* noted that the next class for the academy in Columbus was still taking applications. Cops were in short supply Haftmann did the math: his birthday made him eligible by three weeks. Fate, serendipity, luck—something was pushing him toward a career change. Why not? He couldn't share his uncle's office. That was strictly a one-man outfit.

He was feeling good about this decision and decided he'd talk to his uncle about it; after all, he'd been a cop himself long ago before he decided to hang out the private-eye shingle.

"It's in the blood," Haftmann told himself as he pulled into the driveway behind her car for what he hoped would be the last time he'd clap eyes on Libby Boatwright. She was that witch in a tragedy he read as an undergraduate.

He knocked on the screen door with his much-abbreviated report and waited.

He saw the husband's pickup truck sticking out of the garage. He thought of tucking the report under the doorknob—to hell with the oral report—but the slightest pressure of his hand on the door swung it open.

He stepped inside and looked about for a clean place to set it, but the entire kitchen was a mess and the table was cluttered with dirty dishes. He saw grease congealed to a gray color on some pans on the stove. Beauty and orderliness obviously didn't go together in Libby's genetic make-up. He moved some dishes aside to clear a space and set the file folder down.

149

The scrape of a chair from an upstairs room made him jump; he almost bolted out the door. This was trespassing and Libby might come bolting down the back stairs with a gun in her hand. He quietly walked out the door and was down the steps when he heard it: a child's cry.

Fuck, shit, piss. Decision time: he turned around and went back inside.

He took the steps two at a time while his heart began pounding in his chest; he started to get the tunnel vision of an adrenalin jolt.

No sounds . . . he approached one bedroom and peeked inside. An unmade bed, glam rock posters on the wall.

He heard another sound but unlike the child's cry. More like a gurgling noise.

He headed down to the last room at the end of the hallway stepping around discarded clothing, toys, video game cartridges and an Xbox console. Smells mixed in the stale air. Libby's stale perfume with another, stronger—a goatish smell wafting from it.

Libby was on the bed, Grebski was nude, filthy, crisscrossed in healing cuts, straddled her, choking her neck with his big hands. Her body shook on the bed. Haftmann's neocortex took in the knotted muscles of his arms, the spittle drooling from his mouth, his body crisscrossed with fresh cuts and bruises. A thin, keening sound from the corner alerted him to the boy standing there watching the horror.

Haftmann flung himself at Grebski. The impact was like running into a granite boulder. Grebski seemed unaware he had been attacked. His face was mottled; his eyes were the craziest thing Haftmann had ever seen in a human face. Haftmann threw an arm lock around Grebski's neck and tried pulling him backwards. That managed to free his grip from Libby's throat, but that was all it did. Grebski was too solid and Haftmann knew he had seconds to do something. Even twenty, thirty pounds lighter and malnourished from his days on the run, Grebski was still too strong for him.

Grebski barely moved his torso. He snapped an elbow into Haftmann's jaw that sent him flying into the wall where he sat stunned. Grebski lifted himself off Libby and it was one of those curious reflexes of a mind in distress that made Haftmann realized he had been killing her while he was trying to rape her. Haftmann noticed the muscular thighs of Grebski coming toward him and wondered why he couldn't get off the floor. The kick to his right eyebrow from Grebski's heel, a blur he just managed to see but not escape, made the skin puff up instantly like a car fender buckled in a collision.

Haftmann didn't remember the next few moments because his brain was sending signals in all directions to his limbs. His limbic brain was screaming for him to do something but his coordination was still in flux. Another kick to his chest made the air escape from his lungs in an audible sound. Haftmann's brain was still demanding some action from him when Grebski's fist caught him squarely on the bridge of his nose. This time he didn't hear the sound because his brain was abandoning the citadel too fast like a scorched dog fleeing a house fire when there's nobody left to save. Haftmann thought he could hear the Doppler effect of the little boy in the corner whose screams seemed to drop an octave down the scale as his consciousness completely abandoned him.

When he came to, his one eye enabled him to make out Libby's prone body on the bed; her breasts were no longer bouncing. They were flattened out on her chest as if she had decided to take a nap in the nude. Haftmann tried to move his head but it wouldn't swivel on his neck the way it was supposed to. The boy was no longer standing in his corner. Haftmann's tongue told him his teeth were cracked; his lips were swollen, bloody. He had no idea what his nose looked like or even where it was. He doubted it was still in the center of his face. He passed out from the exertion of thinking about locating it with a fingertip.

He came to again. It was a nerve-searing, painful thing to do, he realized, like being born into world created by Hieronymus Bosch. The pain rocked him in waves. But he had no more terror. Something named Death was coming for him, and he was trying to recall who Death was when the thought arrived like a student late for class: Grebski.

Grebski is my death—

"You're awake now, stay awake," Grebski demanded and slapped his face. "Look at me."

Haftmann tried to look at Grebski's face staring into his own.

"Am I—sitting down?"

He had to cough it out.

"What did you say?"

". . . *sitting down* . . . ?"

"Do you want me to pick you up?"

Without waiting for Haftmann to attempt to reply, he hoisted him up by the chest and walked him over to the bed where Libby lay still sound asleep.

Grebski shoved her legs aside and threw Haftmann against the bed railings at the bottom.

"Hold on to that if you feel like fainting."

Haftmann spat some blood out of his mouth. "OK, I'm good . . . you . . . motherfucker."

"Not you're not good," Grebski said. He held him upright against the railings.

"I've had concussions," he said. "You think you're OK but you're not."

Haftmann tried to say, "fuck you," but it came out like a baby gurgle, full of fricatives and bloody spit because of his missing teeth. Pain wrapped him in its embrace like an electrified boa constrictor.

"What color . . . are . . . your eyes?" Haftmann asked Grebski.

"Be quiet. You don't know what you're saying. I've been saying things like that to people for years."

He's talking, Haftmann thought somewhere in his back brain, hiding from the pain, *so maybe he won't kill me—*

". . . k-killed her?"

Grebski turned to stare at Libby's corpse on the bed. Her tongue stuck out between her lips as if she were mocking him, having the last word.

"It looks like it from here," Grebski said without emotion.

". . . boy?"

"In the kitchen pantry. I told him to stay there and be quiet. You can take him away from here."

". . . let . . . me . . . live?"

Grebski's mood plummeted. He was a man holding an anvil stepping through a trap door. For years he wanted to kill the world. Now he was sparing a single man. Neither made sense. Nothing made sense.

Haftmann's brain was coming back like chips in a kaleidoscope tube. Grebski's calm was eerie, terrifying. Haftmann knew he was living on a bubble of the man's mood swings.

". . . say so . . . " he blubbered, the words slippery as eels.

"Bet you want to know?" Grebski on haunches, staring into Haftmann's pulped face.

"Y-yes . . . no . . . don't . . . care—"

Grebski grinned. He grinned, showed teeth. Haftmann couldn't see him clearly through the waves of pain. The man shape-shifted, half-wolf, half-human.

Then Grebski loomed above him, a gun in his fist. A wobbly cannon. Haftmann closed his eyes, waited for the bullet to obliterate his pain, remove him from the cosmos, this bizarre world he'd stumbled into on a summer day.

"There is no fucking why."

The old Grebski back in charge—angry, deranged, the personification of mayhem. When Haftmann opened his eyes, he knew the barrel would be pointing at him.

"Libby," Grebski said. He shot himself in the temple.

* * *

CHAPTER 35
Riverton General Hospital,
Riverton, OH/ Sep. 15, 4:04 p.m.

Haftmann had been removed from ICU and brought down to his room. They wouldn't let him see himself in a mirror because his head had swollen to the size of a beach ball from edema; they call it third-spacing in medical lingo, but it was result of three separate surgeries, the last one for facial reconstruction.

Haftmann's uncle sat in the bright green Naugahyde vinyl chair and looked at his nephew in bed. When he saw his eyes open or as far as Haftmann could open them, he cleared his throat.

"How are you doing?"

Haftmann tried to focus on his uncle, but he seemed to be shimmering like an angel. Then his face dissolved into another person's, like Libby's. She was dead—or was she? He couldn't remember. His brain was too fuzzy. She was that witch in a play he read as an undergraduate. His uncle's words brought him back.

"People always say dumb things like that, don't they?"

Haftmann sent a message to his mouth to reply, say something to prove he wasn't a vegetable, but no words came out.

"Hey, Tom, don't try to talk. Just listen. I'm so sorry I got there too late."

Haftmann tried to speak again but it was all mush.

"The boy? Is that what you said? Look, he's OK. He's in Child Protective Services, all right? He's better off there than . . . Look, you did a good thing. Who knows? Maybe Grebski would have taken the kid with him, killed them all. He was a rabid dog."

Haftmann lay there in silence, taking in his uncle's words like the steady drip-drip-drip of the morphine bag. But he didn't think so. He had a hunch that a DNA test would reveal something no one suspected yet: the kid might be Grebski's, a child of incest. Another reason that made him expendable. Deep down, he suspected Grebski himself thought so, and maybe that was the only reason the boy was left alive. Libby wouldn't risk her brother's wrath until she knew she was safe from him.

"Tommy, they won't let me stay long. You need to rest and get your strength back. I heard from an Agent Larrimore in Youngstown. He told me what you did while I was gone. I want you to know I'm proud of you. One more thing Larrimore told me. There was a decomposed body found in town while I was away—some woman. They found her DNA in Libby's house. The cops don't know if the husband's guilty or he abetted his crazy wife—"

"Sis-ter," Haftmann croaked.

"That's what Agent Larrimore thinks."

"Look, I've got to go. I'm getting black looks from your nurse in the doorway here. I just want you to know there's a place for you in my office. Someday I want it to be yours."

Haftmann watched his uncle leave. He thought: *There goes a good man.*

Haftmann closed his eyes; he was cocooned in pain. It seemed that was the way of the world now. All this suffering, for what? He thought of Grebski's last words about resolving mysteries: *There is no fucking why.*

All the same, he thought, *we can try to get a few answers before the light fades.*

His head merged with the pillow's fabric and he felt himself falling into a swirling black vortex that was not like sleep but more like death. Before the light faded, he knew he'd be back for more and so he took that small comfort with him into the black waves closing over his head.

* * *

Haftmann's convalescence lasted through the autumn of that year. He stayed sober. His uncle died in the spring. As his uncle's heir, he inherited the office in Jefferson-on-the-Lake. Haftmann gave away the furniture and applied for an opening in the next police officer training class at the academy in Columbus. Two months over the age limit, he was at first denied. Unknown to Haftmann, Agent Larrimore wrote a letter that resulted in the denial being rescinded.

EPILOGUE

Reuters –May 2003. *Journalists petitioning release of an FBI report on last summer's attempted terrorist act aboard a Great Lakes freighter in Sault Ste. Marie, Michigan were denied access to the report. Despite the Freedom of Information Act filed, the director of the U.S. government's Information Security Oversight Office stated the report will remain "undisclosed and undisseminated" in the FBI's vault for "the indefinite future." FBI Director Brian Sechrist affirmed the decision by stating it contained "sensitive information" that might assist future terrorists on Coast Guard preparedness and security operations along the Great Lakes.*

The End

In Football-Crazy East Brangton
by Robb White

My father used to say Ohio was the biggest nothing state in the union. I should have listened to him and gone sailing on the ore boats when I was eighteen—maybe got off in Duluth and stayed for good among those happy Minnesotans. But he also used to say he could make a better world than this in six days. Maybe he was right about that, too. I was reading the front page of the *Plain Dealer* when I got the call from the parents of a girl who was kidnapped across the Ohio River in West Virginia by some high-school boys who dragged her from party to party, stopping now and then to rape her in the back of a car. The rapists, they said, were football players from East Brangton High School, a football powerhouse in the state. The town was stonewalling the investigation by clamming up or going public to line up behind the accused footballers.

I was slugging down my third cup of morning coffee when the parents of the girl called. It was a sign. The stars were lining up and a booming voice from the clouds was ordering me to take the case. Instead, I told the parents I was sorry for their pain but that I could do nothing. This was a police matter. I guessed the FBI would be called in soon if they weren't there already.

"*Matter*? You're sorry about this 'matter'!"

The father's voice boomed at me. When we used to use wires to send sound waves, it had a different effect, less anguished, softer, as though the something in the ether sapped its energy. Bu technology isn't my strong suit. Before those idiotic words *I know how you must feel* got past my tonsils, I said, "I'm truly sorry for your suffering, sir, but this kind of investigation exceeds my purview by a long mile."

Purview—now, why did I have to trot that word out? I sensed his disgust at my insincerity. The girl's mother took over from there.

"The police aren't doing anything, Mister Haftmann. No one's cooperating. Those boys—"

The father must have grabbed the phone then. "Everybody knows who did this to Shawna, but nobody will help us, God damn it!"

I heard her say *Frank, Frank* and then she came back on the line. "What's wrong with people—what kind of people are they that would do this to my little girl and not say a word?"

She got it out before a sob choked her off; then I heard the father's growl in the background followed by soothing noises. I guessed she was trying to calm him down.

My guts twisted. All the religions in the world haven't been able to answer that mother's question, and I had stopped wondering about human beings and their motives after my first tour on the Cleveland police force after my abortive, short-lived law career. That's for the real lawyers to fret over in criminal trials. I was a glorified street sweeper then, and I'm less than that now. I almost quit being a cop when I found myself spending half my days sitting on my ass on a bench outside one courtroom or another in the Justice Hall, even if the overtime doubled my salary. When I made the grade of detective in homicide, I thought I was finally going to be doing something useful. It took me another year at crime scenes to show me how blind I was to that delusion, too. You hear people say a lot about bringing justice to families on TV and "closure." There's no closure, there's no justice. That's why I'm an existentialist. But that's my non-paying calling. I still have to work to eat.

I said I'd take the case. Every instinct I had as a private investigator and ex-cop said this was stupid. Just how stupid I was going to find out. But two hours later, I packed up my gear and headed south down to the Ohio River.

Over the years I've driven through East Brangton a few times on my way down or back from a case. Once upon a time it might have been a nice place to live and raise your kids, but today it's just another rustbelt city with a rundown main street, shuttered store windows, and a bunch of clapped-out houses that could use a new paint job. You see skinny meth heads on the corner and raggedy-looking kids with tattoos and Kool-Aid-colored hair cadging quarters from cars on the interstate exits near the river. The steel and glassware factories have all gone to China. The cement and furniture factory took about ten years longer to pack up, but they headed south to Mexico after NAFTA and, cruel irony, when the doors in Ciudad Juàrez closed because of cheaper labor overseas, they headed for China too.

America, baby. Free enterprise. Capitalism. Get used to it, the politicians said. They turned us into a barren landscape of closed-down factories, shuttered houses, and junkies reeling from Oxycontin to the latest drug craze—fentanyl and the zombie drug, xylazine.

So it wasn't my big heart that sent me down here to see what I could do for this family. It was the fact that my cases are dwindling down to subsistence level, especially in the off season of my resort town on Lake Erie where I work. My bank account shrinks in proportion to the leaves turning fall colors.

I met the husband and wife at my motel off the freeway. A big row of clouds with gray bellies and white tops had followed me into the Ohio Valley and now their bottom edges twisted in the October winds like dirty rags. It was their sixteen-year-old girl I really needed to talk to, but they decided to leave her in the car until they had talked things over with me first. I understood and clucked in sympathy. My face wasn't much to look at, thanks to my first big case when my uncle still held the reins of the business. Making a sympathetic noise was the best I could do.

I already had the outline of events from the Cleveland paper's investigative reporter: no names were publicized because these were juveniles, and it was early in the investigation. Two of the varsity starters, both sophomores, were already under sealed indictment— but an open secret in this town. "Jimmy Radcliffe and Wayne Steeson," said the mother. "Those bastards got Shawna from her girlfriend's house and took her to this party."

"Was this here or in West Virginia?"

"Here," said the father, "in your state." He said it as though I held some of the blame for what had happened.

I've gone through this routine many times with grieving parents. One parent interrupts the other or tries to finish the other's sentences—usually the man, but not always. Real sorrow takes away words; it doesn't lend you eloquence, so I tend to listen harder to the quieter of the two. I made the right listening noises, all the while scribbling in my notebook even though I had a tape recorder going in my pocket; this was all for show. People need to get it out of their system first. Later, I'd interview them and get the answers to the list of questions I had composed on the drive down Route 11, which is one lonely ride across barren farmland with corn fields blighted from the summer drought and where you feel there's nothing between you and Canada but a barbed-wire fence and an occasional wild dog to look at.

There would be things the girl would not want to say in front of them. I've had experience with runaways. As I escorted them from my room into the early afternoon sunlight, the mother's occasional hiccups of grief echoed across the parking lot. Traffic made a Doppler-like sound whizzing by on the interstate. He had signed the contract I brought. He wasn't interested in the details. His eyes were red-rimmed and his voice was tight with suppressed rage. I wondered if he was going to be trouble for me down the road.

About hallway to their vehicle, I watched a slender girl exit the back seat of her parents' car. She shielded her eyes from the morning glare, Injun-style, before noticing me. She approached slowly, taking small steps, her head slightly bent showing the zigzag of part in the center. I'd asked the parents to give me an hour with her. Out of the corner of my good eye, the father scowled driving past. The last thing he said was for me to be "careful" about how I asked my questions. I didn't want the girl thinking about them sitting out there while we spoke inside.

As she got within handshake distance, I completed it by habit: one-oh-five, brown and brown. Shawna wore the skinny jeans the kids all wear nowadays, and her tennis shoes were pink with the Nike swoosh. She wore a WVU Hilltoppers midnight-blue and gold sweatshirt that looked too large for her until I realized, with a slight shock, despite her slender physique, she had womanly breasts that stretched the fabric of her sweatshirt out. My ex-wife used to dress down for her court appearances and always made a point of buying blazers two sizes too large to disguise her cup size. "Male jurors staring at my boobs aren't listening to what I'm saying," she often reminded me.

"Hello, Shawna," I said, "I'm Tom Haftmann. Come inside, please."

She had a small hand, the bones like a bird's beneath the skin, and her palm was clammy. The bed was undisturbed and my change of clothes was tucked out of sight under it. I offered her a bottled water, but she declined in a small voice.

"Shawna, I'm working for you and your parents now. I want you to relax and know that everything you tell me is said in complete confidence and will not be revealed unless I have your permission."

She nodded, her ponytail bouncing on her neck.

"Tell me what happened that night from the time you left your house. I know you've told this story to the police and the district attorney already, but it's important you tell me everything. If I have questions, I'll stop you. You must not hold anything back, do you understand me?"

She nodded her head a couple times. "Okay," she said in that same small voice barely above a whisper. She sat demurely on the edge of the seat near the door. I sat on the carpet and crossed my legs and laced my fingers together. With vulnerable children and nervous animals, you try to make yourself smaller.

She began with the details of leaving her house to go to her girlfriend's. They had arranged to meet that afternoon during last period study hall.

"Why were you going to meet her?"

"Her parents were out of town," she said. "We were going to have the house to ourselves."

"Were you planning to have friends over?"

"No—no, nothing like that," Shawna said in her whisper. "Just hang out and stuff, y'know."

"I see. Go on."

They were watching a reality show about spoiled California trophy wives when a friend from school called. "Some kids from school were going over Randy Dumont's house and so me and her thought we'd stop by, check it out, you know?"

"Uh-huh, go on," I said.

"Like, there was no party goin' on or nothing like that," she said, "but when we got there, some kids were smoking weed and these two guys from Ohio were there, friends of Randy's."

"That would be Jimmy Radcliffe and Wayne Steeson."

"Yeah," she whispered and lowered her head.

"Shawna, I need to know how you left the party with Jimmy and Wayne."

She shook her head back and forth a couple times wincing at the memory. "I—I can't remember."

"Try. Tell me how you left Christine's house. Did you say anything to her? Did she see you leave with them?"

"I don't know—I don't know!"

"What do you remember?"

"I remember coming to in the back of a car. I remember somebody being on top of me. I remember the car moving and I remember how—how he kept shoving . . . his—"

"He was having sex with you. Was this Jimmy or Wayne?"

"I don't know! I can't remember!" She collapsed into sobbing, covering her face with her hands.

Frigadoon. Fuck a duck. My bedside manner needed a refresher course. That was it for the remainder of the hour. She couldn't remember. I planned to see the emergency room nurse later to find out what drug they had spiked her drink with and its effects.

Shawna's memory wouldn't matter legally. These boys had put everything on the internet. The ten-minute video of Shawna being hoisted out of a house and carted off by ankles and wrists that night was taken down by *YouTube* and classed as evidence. They also took photos of her nude body with their cell phones and passed them around. There were dozens of these cyber bystanders who witnessed the crime; some videoed her, others tweeted. Wayne and Jimmy were toting her all over East Brangton like a prize deer they'd bagged.

When they dropped her off at her girlfriend's back in West Virginia, the deed was finished off with a final act of urinating on her unconscious body. Every avenue of social networking via *Facebook*, blogging, tweeting, re-tweeting, and online posting the highschoolers frequented was filled with vile, obscene references in the days afterward. Wayne Steeson's teammate, not one of the participants, sent him an encouraging message after the police came to school that Monday to arrest him and Jimmy: "We got your back, bro. Some girls deserve to be pissed on."

The big joke at school that week was to download Nirvana's "Rape Me" for their earbuds or ringtones. All of this, text and video, was being subpoenaed as evidence by the DA's office. Every cell phone ping was going to leave a lovely trail right back to these boneheads like breadcrumbs in Hansel and Gretel's fairy tale.

On the other hand, the town's lone juvenile crimes cop was getting zilch. Nobody was talking—at least, not to him, a short-timer with a month left to pension, although the whole town was busy phoning and texting among themselves. By the end of that week, everybody knew and nobody was talking. The code of silence was in full effect and any would-be snitchers knew to beware.

On my way to the hospital, I drove past the school. It was lunchtime and I was hoping to catch Coach Niesbaum in his office. A revered figure in town, the Cleveland paper had quoted him briefly as "treating each of his players like his own son." According to the article, he knew nothing about what happened that night and didn't seem to know much about social networking as a concept, much less how it was practiced by his entire football squad, not to mention the rest of the world.

I parked in the stadium lot, a ten-thousand-seat affair that would rival a Division II college's shrine to its athletic prowess. A silhouette of a blue-caped rider on horseback with rapier point extended above the horse's head occupied the center of the massive scoreboard.

Two students, a boyfriend and girlfriend, were coming my way. I'm an addicted reader of everything, especially TV chyrons and people's tee shirts. The boy's said: *I Do Whatever the Hell I Want*. Hers said: *Who's Taylor Swift Anyway? Ew.* They directed me to Coach

Niesbaum's office at the end of a long corridor past the gym. I passed a glassed-walled room where some older males with buffed physiques were slinging iron and grunting in cadence. They all wore the same cutoff tee-shirt with the Blue Raider logo on the chest.

I knocked and stuck my head inside the door. Coach Olsen was reading a newspaper dwarfed by two wall-sized white boards filled with X's and O's in red and black marker colors. As soon as I identified myself, he threw the paper across the room in disgust. Before I could identify myself properly, his hand reached for the phone. Temper tantrums like that mean nothing to a cop, but a private eye is no better than Joe Schmoe. I don't know what it is about a high-school coach that causes a red mist to drop over my eyes. They are easy to dislike as a species. The coaches in my high school didn't have the combined brain power of three guinea pigs. I left him there scowling, his hand gripping the receiver like a baton he'd rather use on my head. No point in making local law enforcement aware of me before I had a chance to get the lay of the land.

It would turn out to be a day of being rebuffed, ignored, and verbally abused. By the time I made it to my car, one whole side had been keyed. I saw a knot of boys watching me from the fence.

The desk sergeant who met me at the station told me in no uncertain terms I was "intruding" and wasn't welcome in his town. I insisted I was merely making a courtesy call at the station and nothing more—just letting the law know I was in their town and working a case. He said that "they knew how to solve their own crimes without my help" and the smart thing for me to do, he strongly suggested, would be to stay out of the way of law enforcement altogether.

"Go back home if you want work. Try Cleveland."

"Sergeant, but that girl's family isn't paying me sit in my motel room all day writing a redaction of the district attorney's charges."

"Write a—huh, what did you say?"

"Never mind, Officer. Thanks for your advice. Cleveland needs cops, by the way. I see your talents are wasted here."

He mumbled something unkind about private eyes behind my back—just a little tap on the fanny to help me on my way.

I wasn't going to wear my face out smiling in this town, and I also knew the clock was ticking down on me faster than I would have believed. By sundown, the gossips would get wind of my presence, so any hope I had of gleaning a few real nuggets of information from the rubbish would be lost once they closed ranks out of loyalty to the football team—or just plain old fear.

Cops know how to shut out an outsider like, say, some snoop from Internal Affairs. I know how it works. But this felt different. It was a smug little town on the ropes clinging to Friday night glory on a football field. The morning paper mentioned "the ongoing investigation into the alleged incident" but immediately piled up a litany of testimonials about their beloved team and sons from all and sundry. The few who dared to cross the line from sanctimonious rage or full-throated condemnation of "the lies and distortions" of this girl and her parents, who were "obviously out for money" did so in a tepid way by feigning a handwringing over youth and "modern times." The editorial, in fact, was a letter from Wayne Steeson's father. He said he would carry a placard proclaiming his son's innocence in front of the courthouse until his son was vindicated and released. There was a lot of mawkish drivel about "our noble sons" and "the virtues of team sports," but there was no denying his sincere outrage.

I needed to get inside this closed circle of parents and boosters of East Brangton H. S. somehow. Shawna's parents couldn't help me there.

I went back to the motel and ate a meal from the vending machine outside my room. A faded decal, GO BIG BLUE GO was slathered across the glass. I was hoping this place wasn't a sleazy party joint for trysting lovers and cheating husbands. I set my alarm for three in the morning. That was the time Shawna had been taken to the emergency room in her drugged state shortly after being dumped off in front of her house. No one had tried to clean her up, but she somehow managed to get off the ground, stagger into the house, and try to clean herself up. Her mother broke down and wept when she described to me shampooing her daughter's hair; it was matted with semen. I hoped I'd find the same E.R. staff on duty.

I took the bridge across the river. No one else was on the road. A few stars glittered between ragged patches of cloud. The water below looked black and oily from the bridge lights. Her name was Patricia Gleason and she seemed OK about talking to me "off the record." The FBI had already taken her information. I told her I'd wait for her break time downstairs in the lobby.

"Break time? Does this place look like a factory to you?" She said it with a smile. I had my first glimmer of hope in a long day of having a shutout pitched at me.

About forty minutes later, she found me alone in the lobby. Half the fluorescent lights were off unlike the emergency room area, which was lit up like luminol sprayed on a bloody crime scene. I was grateful for the dimmed lighting. My eyes are bad and tire easily. Even in the desolation of three in the morning, a cop knows an emergency room is no place for a quiet conversation. The business from the passing night was still in evidence: a black eye and split lip from some barroom brawl, a feverish child, and a dyspeptic baby being crooned to by a worried mother, and a whole clan rallying in support of some kin who needed to be sewed up or medicated into tranquility.

"Always this busy?" I asked.

She was about forty, attractive, short, and wore her hair in a bobbed cut that came to a pair of matching points below her ears. She bristled with energy, whereas I was feeling raw and itchy with too little sleep. "For the beginning of the week, I'd say typical enough," she said. Cops and emergency room nurses are natural allies, and I don't mean in the fight against the forces of darkness. They often find their way into bed; it's the aphrodisiac of violence and death.

I asked her about the girl's injuries that night and she gave me a precise, exactly worded list of bruises and contusions as if she had crammed for a quiz.

"Shawna Rae wasn't your first patient, I take it?"

"No, sir, I've done this a few times."

"What did they drug her with?"

She hesitated.

"Come on, Pat," I said. "This isn't my first rodeo either."

"Well, all right," she said. "It'll be public anyway. Toxicology's not official and I might have to testify to this, so don't quote me."

"OK, off the record, as you requested."

"It'll come back GHB, I'm thinking."

"You sure?"

She gave me an arch look—professional to dumbass rookie. "There's an odor on the breath," she said, "despite what those internet recipes all say. I've seen meth, crack, heroine, and oh-so-many cases of marijuana you can't believe. We have more than our fair share of Oxyheads over here, too."

"Did she say anything at the time you can tell me?"

"No, she was confused in speech. Lucid in short intervals but nothing out of the ordinary comes to mind."

The date-rape drug would explain Shawna's memory loss. "Wouldn't she have had a terrific headache coming out of it the next day?"

"Not necessarily," Pat said. "Depends on the dosage and whether they mixed it right."

"You say her breasts were mauled. Any bite marks?"

"No, just manual pressure," she said and wagged her fingers for effect. "Her vaginal area wasn't bruised. No bleeding or bruising. The inner labia weren't torn."

"Anal sodomy?"

"No, I don't think so—but . . ."

"But what?"

"She looked at me. Sometimes you can't always tell rape from consensual, especially if the body is totally relaxed as it would be in this case."

"Because of the drug, you mean?"

"Probably, yes." She said it in a musical way and hissed the s at the end, as if still deciding the question.

I was tempted to ask her out for a meal despite the wedding band. I said I was an existentialist, not a saint.

Back in my motel room, I tried to grab a couple hours of shuteye despite the mattress squeaks, headboard bangs, and moans of orgasming ecstasy coming through the walls of the next room. Like supermarket lines with some old geezer tying up the cashier, I do know how to pick them.

Day One: Haftmann zero, East Brangton one.

But not game over. I was hoping for day two to improve things in my favor. I had a ruse worked out to see one of the boys involved, Wayne Steeson, the team's linebacker and all-state honorable mention last year.

The boy's father was a local big shot contractor with city hall connections. I had picked up a little gossip in the diner across the street while nursing my fourth cup of joe and waiting to see if anyone coming or going looked promising. Some of these retired old farts turned out to be good sources occasionally. I look for the kind who have a sneer on their faces and wear their pants up to their nipples. That morning, I had zeroed in on a table of geezers talking about the death of Number Thirty-Two, the great Jimmy Brown, golf, how-hot-it-is-in-Florida, and the presidential debate. I was silently cursing my luck. One table over, a bunch of older men were having a conversation just out of earshot. Men gossip as much as women, and I knew there ought to be plenty of buzz about their beloved football team at every watering hole, McDonald's, and diner in East Brang, as the locals call it.

About ten, waterlogged from java, I headed across the street at a bar that had just opened. I'm not the boozehound I used to be, but every time a neon sign outside a tavern lights up for business it's winking at me like a summons to temple to a Buddhist monk—or, if my ex's point of view still mattered, to a hog when it hears the stick rattle inside the swill bucket. The irony, I suppose, is booze didn't kill my marriage; my wife opening her legs for a colleague did. They were working out of the prosecutor's office on a big bribery case. I was outside in the rain standing in the shrubs, holding a directional mic to the window glass listening to the seduction as I did to so many cheating spouses on the job. When I confronted her with the evidence, she laughed at me and called it ironic. If irony means what I think it does, it's still operating because after the collapse, she ran off with another colleague, only this time a woman.

I asked the barkeep where the nearest ATM was situated. He gave me more directions than you'd need to plan a Chinese wedding in the T'ang dynasty. I was pretending to understand when, out of the corner of my good eye, I saw him sitting on the farthest bar stool around the U-shaped curve. My radar pegged him as a problem drinker, although he didn't wear the badges of a serious alcoholic. For one thing, he was young, late twenties, early thirties, conservatively dressed, with skinny arms poking out of shirt sleeves, and sporting an unfashionable haircut. One glance told me he had what I needed: a mousy demeanor hunched over a glass of morning brew, his twitchy head bob when he picked up my scoping him, and a morose expression on his mug all said he was flying the loser flag. Somebody, you could say, who might have trouble getting past the velvet rope.

I cut the bartender's endless directions off and had him send down a whiskey with chaser. He nodded at me, uncertain, not unfriendly, but I knew I had my man.

He had a cautious look on his face when I took the stool next to him and extended my hand. I could see him thinking this might be some kind of gay pickup move. I ignored the wet noodle of Wade's handshake and rattled off one of my put-'em-at-ease spiels.

We did the small-talk routine for a while. I waited for an opening. He struck me as a shoe clerk without a shoe store. "At the moment, I'm between jobs," he said.

"It's tough," I agreed. I let it trail off, buying the lie. He was washing dishes on night shift at a Perkin's "to make ends meet in the meantime." He did his sleeping after noon.

"I understand," I said, and signaled for two more shots. "Your circadian rhythms need adjusting."

That remark elicited a droll "Whatever," and we drank in silence for a moment. He hadn't given me anything to broach the subject yet, but I knew him—rather, his kind: a man that my ex would describe as a loser, isolated, socially maladjusted, bitter. She called them "Alfreds" because of T.S. Eliot's J. Alfred Prufrock, who wanders around London in the poem, pissed off because he's sexually hung up and doesn't dare "disturb the universe" or some twaddle about despair and modern life that still appeals to our society of overwrought neurotics.

This Alfred was named Wade Buckney. He got up to leave—nappy time, I guessed—and I reached out to hold him back. I immediately relaxed my grip on his bicep when I realized how thin his arm was. My hand easily circumscribed it, and I could imagine the bone snapping like a toothpick with a little pressure. I laid my pitch on him, casually but fast, and hoped that the whiff of derring-do might lure him in. I snapped my business card on the top of the bar under the cone of light for him to read. I sensed he was half in the bag by then from the way his head swiveled on his neck trying to read it. I tucked the card away and told him not to reveal my identity to anyone in town, "or I could be in serious danger." He liked that. Then, like Satan whispering into some unsuspecting soul's ear, I told Wade what I wanted from him.

"You—you want me to help you investigate?"

Pathetic, I know, but you do what you must if you want results in this business. None of my pawns had ever been hurt helping me out. I like to think I brought a little spice into their dreary lives.

He bit, as I hoped he would. So I had myself a confidential informer, although my term to Wade was "silent partner." I added a hint that a generous "bonus" was due when "our case" was concluded. I avoid smirking every time I mention the bonus bit. On the rare occasions I get a wealthy client, these bastards always have their lawyers do a line-item analysis and more often than not, I wind up getting less than my fee, never mind the theoretical bonus.

Wade and I met that night during his half-hour break at Perkin's. I told him what I was driving and where I'd be parked to lace a little more conspiracy into our meeting. I didn't want people to see us together "for his safety," I had said that morning in the bar. His eyes bulged like a mackerel's and I knew I had gone too far with the gig at that point so I walked it back to a fear that he might be the subject of "malicious gossip." That worked better.

"Screw what these jerks think," he said and winked at me as he left the gin joint.

I was parked near a dumpster out back when I saw him come out. He lit up and I followed the cherry glow of his cigarette tip. A few feet from the passenger side of my car, he flicked the barely smoked cigarette into the weeds. *Good*, I thought, watching the bravado of his gesture, because I knew he'd been role-playing undercover cop day and dreaming of it in his sleep.

"Hey, Wade."

"Bro," he said. "What's up?"

I told him a little, leaving out most of what I did know, and spoon-fed him information anybody could have had from reading the Cleveland paper. I said the local paper had one short column on page four about the latest developments with the word *alleged* used five times. It devoted a half-page below the fold to fracking for shale oil in the south county.

He snorted. "That rag wouldn't get the story if Putin's boys parachuted over High Street at noon and took over the town."

"Wade, my razor-keen instincts tell me you're not too fond of your hometown."

"Ha, this cesspool? Let me give you the skinny on good old East Brang..."

I let him rant for five minutes. When he was primed, I directed him toward what I needed from a local source. Wade confirmed the obvious about the investigation being stonewalled. The sex crimes cop was not going to work the case right, and the rest knew which side their bread was buttered on. The criminal court judge who had the prelim hearing might recuse himself because of connections to the families, and according to Wade, the sheriff was in the bag to the county commissioners who also took their cues from East Brangton's power brokers, so there would likely be no multi-agency task force.

"A couple FBI guys had supper here last night," Wade said.

"Can you pick up anything from them?"

"Like, how? I'm in the back scraping shit off plates."

"I was thinking of a friendly waitress you might recruit on the sly to eavesdrop a little."

"Man, the chicks here are all stuck-up bitches."

It would figure, I thought. My loser sidekick had probably made moves on every eligible female and been given the smackdown.

"Listen, Wade," I said, "I've got to get inside the circle. This isn't about boys beaming dick pictures to their girlfriends from their cell phones. It's about kidnapping and raping a young girl. Tell me everything you know about these football players and their families."

"You'll never get anywhere that way, man. Don't you have, like, secret microphones and shit?"

"I do, Wade, but you can never replace human intelligence in the field. Now tell me what you know about these people, and I want to know everything. Where they buy their groceries and what churches they attend and whether they wipe their asses with their right hands or their left."

"OK, man, your call. Let's start with our backfield. QB's name is Timmy Harding. His dad runs a shop on River Street where they do laser cutting on milling machines with computers . . ."

I did my scribbling routine for effect, but my pocket recorder was catching it all. I hoped there'd be some nuggets among the gossip to sift for later, so I didn't ask questions. Twenty-five minutes into it, Wade checked his wristwatch. "Oh, shit, man, I've got to get back inside. That fat-assed prick night manager has it in for me."

"I'll see you tomorrow at MacTeague's," I said, meaning the bar where we first met. "Your money's no good."

I watched him get out. He did a right-look, left-look thing I assumed was part of an ace undercover agent's repertoire for spotting surveillance. I didn't feel much better, though. I didn't have a handle on anything yet, and I knew Shawna's family couldn't afford a long investigation.

The nightly news channel led off with the report that began with East Brangton's chief of police asking for cooperation. The newscaster mentioned that the Monroe County prosecutor was so far refusing to ask the Ohio attorney general for help. They replayed Coach Niesbaum's interview from the practice field where he professed to treat every player like his son. When the reporter asked why no other player besides "the two indicted" were suspended from this week's game against Cleveland's tough South High School, he trotted off. That was followed by an interview with the superintendent of schools, who bragged about East Brangton being "among the highest academic performing districts in the state." He said he would not provide students with information about dating violence or sexual assault unless it, meaning "the incident," interfered with students' education. Technology, he said, was "a gray area." The piece ended with a shot of the frumpy sex-crimes detective trudging up the courthouse steps with a thin manila file folder in his hands; he looked like my unmade bed.

I slept badly but at least the heavier sex was farther away. Even so, muffled, urgent whispers came through the walls and penetrated my dreams. I heard Micah begging or demanding me to do something, but I couldn't tell what it was she was asking me to do, and her frustration was all too evident in that familiar scowl across her eyebrow ridge. When I awoke at dawn, Tom Junior, my one-eyed southern head, was poking up from the sheets like a sub commander in his conning tower. Any sex, even masturbation, is ashes in the mouth, so I started my day a little edgy.

When I stepped out of my room to get my breakfast from the vending machine, I beheld a gorgeous fall day of red and yellow trees with leaves that glowed in the morning sunlight as if somebody had waxed them overnight. That mood didn't last long because, as I drove out of the lot to meet Wade at our place, I saw a dead raccoon in the middle of the road, his guts streamed behind him all the way to the curb. It was so fresh that the rancid smell of death hadn't polluted the air. Sometimes the olfactory memory of too much decomp from my cop days in Cleveland comes flooding back and I seem to smell it everywhere. It's strong enough to send me out of a diner from time to time with my cheeseburger left uneaten on my plate.

Wade was chipper when I greeted him, so I had to keep my flattening mood in check. He was already nursing a whiskey. I worried I might have made a mistake in choosing him.

"What's the plan?" he asked me as I ordered a club soda with a lemon twist.

"We're going to crack this case today," I said.

"Fuckin'-A, bro," Wade said and started to bring the shot to his mouth. I caught his wrist in mid-air and the drink splashed all over.

"Hey, what the fuck," he said patting his shirt front as if he were on fire.

"I said 'we' and I meant *we*, sober, are going to crack this motherfucking case," I said and gave him a cop stare I hadn't used in a while.

"Bro, I am in this house of war with you."

Oh fuck me.

While we drove, I told Wade what I had in mind. I had done some checking on my laptop after our conversation in the parking lot. One of the names he gave me turned out to be an IT expert, still living in East Brangton. The guy I normally use for technical gee-whiz stuff lives in Youngstown just fifty miles north. His name is Danny Gumataotao. He's a bronzed, wheat-haired Solomon Islander who's a genius with computers and who happens to be a little shady. I am as unable to negotiate in cyberspace as Danny is unable to avoid legal problems in the real world. Danny always needs money for lawyers when his computer scams backfire. Thus, our mutual kinship despite our mutual dislike. This time, however, Danny was not returning my calls at his residence. He tends to skip town whenever a cybercrimes cop comes sniffing around.

I had another lead I was going to seek out once Wade made the intro to his former classmate for me. I found the website for the Ohio Alliance to End Sexual Assault and sent an email from my motel asking the director to call me on my cell. She lived in Columbus, which meant I might need to drive up there. It was going to be a busy day. I knew Steeson's and Radcliffe's parents were daily visitors to their sons. I planned to confront them outside the jail during visiting hours. I was looking for a reaction, an angry one that one of these couples might blurt out—something for me to follow up. They would not be happy that, of all the boys who must have been involved that night, their sons were the only ones whose lives could possibly be destroyed. Dominoes won't fall unless you get that first piece to topple.

On the way to meet Wade's guy, I asked him what he knew about the woman who was the advocate in the Ohio Valley for sexual survivors.

"Don't know anything about her, man," he said. "Don't even know who she is."

"That's odd, Wade, because she graduated with you and the rest of your senior class ten years ago. I went to Riverton High myself."

"A shitty school, man. We beat their dicks into the dirt every year."

"I remember but let's focus on my question, shall we?"

I cut my eyes to my laptop on the floorboard next to his feet.

"No shit, Riverton? Were the girls as stuck up there?"

"Wade."

"OK, man. Chill. What's her name?"

"Angel Delrocco. She's a part-time advocate, works for a real estate firm in the Valley."

"I do remember her. She was in my sixth-period study hall. A real rugburner."

"A what?"

"A raging lez."

In case I was unfamiliar with that term as well, he clamped his hand over his mouth and wiggled his tongue between his fingers. It was not a pretty sight.

"Next road, man. Turn right," Wade said. "Bos Darc." He pronounced it like "Boston."

"I can get him on my cell."

"Let's surprise him."

"I get it. In case he's doing some illegal or pervy shit, we can make him do our bidding."

I let that one ride.

Wade's old classmate's house was a small Craftsman in brown with yellow trim. The lawn was neat, the flower bed trimmed, and bird bath out front were reassuring. We weren't going to find a doped-out meth cook at home.

Richard Detweiler turned out to be a good catch. He wasn't just a run-of-the-mill geek. He was a national social media and web analyst. Even better for me, he knew, or accurately suspected, that a lot of the players were not going to be indicted. Knowing that, he used his blog as a repository for some of the texting traffic that went on during and after the rape.

"Screen grabs," he said after I had introduced myself. I noted the sideways look he gave his old classmate. No bosom-buddy thing there.

As soon as I could do so without appearing presumptuous, I moved Wade to the background because I didn't want any high-school reunion chatter interfering with the mission. But I didn't have to entice Richard to help. He seemed relieved he wouldn't have to expose himself to the town "as a traitor." He showed me the tweets on his screen and the obscene comments he had collected. I watched the ten-minute video he had snatched before *YouTube* deleted it. I have images of it in my head I wished I didn't. She was hauled in and out of homes by the wrists and ankles and, once, dragged down a carpeted cellar steps to a rec room where teens were drinking and videoing their fun. Hoots of laughter and derisive comments about "the dead body" were easily picked up.

"These idiots really believe the delete button works," he said.

What was it Danny said to me all the time, *The geek shall inherit the earth* . . .? He had a sunroom in the back with a table converted to a cockpit of laptops, notebooks, cables, and various speakers, modems, and printers attached to three desk computers.

"I've got a robot doing a deep search on that one right now," he said pointing to the end computer. "Check this out."

He took me over to one of the screens and hit the keyboard with fluttering fingers. He scrolled through tweets, postings, and blogs. All the same in bad or telegraphic English and most of them laced with obscenities and crude references to "the dead body." One tweet, however, seemed to come from a highschooler with a conscience: "Who the fuck raised these people? You help someone you don't take advantage of them."

"This one," Richard said, "went to Steeson right after the cops arrested him and Jimmy."

I peeked over his shoulder. "Fuck 'em. I got your back bro. Someone took shit too far."

"Are all these from classmates?"

"No, not all," Detweiler said. "Some are from recent graduates. I grabbed one from a guy in a dorm at OSU. Also, I've got disks of The Ohio Valley Athletic Association sports-talk website I've been monitoring."

"Anything there interesting come up?"

"Nope. They're all playing dumb, you know, by being super-careful not to talk about it."

"Keep an ear out and an eye out for me," I said. "They'll have to start talking. Something will shake loose sooner or later."

"I wouldn't be too sure about that," Detweiler said at the door.

"Why not?"

"The governor gave his state-of-the-state address in the school gym last year. People here have connections."

I left him at the door, and while it might have been a trick of the light as walked into bright sunshine, I thought I saw him move his head left and right checking for nosy neighbors.

Not even halfway through the day and I was ahead on points. What was it Micah used to throw at me—something from a Greek tragedy? "Count no day good before it's done." I used to hate it when she was right.

Many of these supporters and friends of the accused raised a similar concern, although not for Shawna Rae's welfare. Inside city limits nearly every other telephone pole bore a GO BIG BLUE GO decal and tree limbs all over town were wrapped in blue bandannas. The flags above the stadium attested to three state championships. Wrote one: "We're not gonna let dumb shit like this spoil our chances for another state championship."

Richard put it all on disk for me. By the time I was ready to leave, Wade was nodding off on the sofa in the next room. Richard looked at me and rolled his eyes. "If you hadn't shown up at the door with him, I wouldn't have let him in," he said.

"Come on, Wade," I said and tugged his shoulder. "Let's get you home to beddy-bye."

"Huh-uh, OK. See ya, Richie."

From here on out, I didn't want my partner around. He'd be a boat anchor on anything that required finesse. I dropped him off at the corner of from his rental apartment, keeping up the notion that we had to be discreet. Our next rendezvous would be at the dumpster to compare notes. I told him to start people talking, eavesdrop as much as possible, but get me a lead to somebody no matter how insignificant he thought it might be. I know something about connections too.

Angel Delrocco was dressed in a blue blazer and a white pleated skirt. I remembered Wade's face-mashing description and realized how off it was. If she were gay, nothing in her looks or dress betrayed it, but in a small town like this, she'd know to keep herself professionally safe.

Her office was on a side street a couple blocks from the river. I could smell it as I exited my car. A mix of fish guts, smoke, and diesel. We met at her desk and, my luck still running, her two colleagues were out on "shows" at the moment so we had the place to ourselves. It was a miniature house—bigger than a child's tree fort but a house only by suggestion. She occupied the corner desk and I had to keep looking over my shoulder for fear of hitting it on the faux crossbeam.

"We don't spend much time here," she said watching me duck again. "It's just for paperwork."

She was heavily made up with a pert, pretty face that didn't need it. I guessed the make-up was part of the job description. Her legs were thick in the calves but her hands were small, very shapely. I've always noticed a woman's hands for some reason.

The a/c was blasting morgue-temperature air all around us, but she sniffed and wrinkled her face in disgust. "Some idiot dumped a fifty-gallon drum of liquid cyanide into the river a couple weeks ago because the city wouldn't pick up the barrel from his front yard."

"I read about it this morning," I said. "The paper said thirty thousand fish dead in a two-mile stretch."

"How can I help you, Mister Hoffmann?"

I told her why I was there and what she know about "the incident."

"Now you sound like a townie," she said. "You mean the rape of that West Virginia girl."

"Yes," I said.

"I've been getting a lot of flak and dirty looks from people around here," she said. "But I think we need to talk about it honestly. At the very least, we need to make young people aware of how things like this happen and how they can be stopped."

"You're right, Ms. Delrocco. Things like this happen everywhere in Ohio, not just here. And this isn't the first time I've seen people try to sweep dirt under a rug."

She told me her boss was stopping just short of asking her to drop the matter and "maintain professionalism until this thing passes over."

"But it's too important an opportunity to have a real conversation with the kids," she said.

Angel told me something else. Two years ago a rumor was floating around about the soccer team and a female sophomore at a party. The girl involved later dropped out of school and committed suicide.

"She got into the goth lifestyle and started doing Oxy and then meth," Angel said. "Then she started prostituting to pay for the drugs. She was a mess. Her parents kicked her out."

"I've seen that happen to a lot of runaways," I said. "But I've never seen so many young people involved in a major crime incriminate themselves all over the place. That's new."

"They feel they can get away with it now," she said. "They don't care. The parents aren't in charge anymore."

I asked her for some names of people who might want to help Shawna but might be afraid to speak out. "The whole town turns out for the Friday night football game," she said. She couldn't think of anyone offhand, but she took my card and said she'd call me at the motel if she had anything to give me.

It was a beautiful day and I was still riding a big lead going into the fifth. It was time to brace the parents. That would shake things up. One of Haftmann's Rules is that, when you've got no leads to follow or nowhere else to turn, find a stalking horse and watch.

And so I did. My luck continued gold: both sets were heading for the precinct door. I recognized the linebacker's father from the newscast, the father who was picketing the courthouse and claiming his boy was "a credit to the school and an A student." I did what birds do when they want to look bigger: they "bill" with their beaks stuck up higher than the bird they're trying to intimidate. I timed my approach, sucked in my gut, and invaded the space of the bigger of the two men just in front of the steps.

"I want to ask you some questions, sir," I said in a not-very-polite tone.

He stopped in mid-stride before we were nose-to-nose. "Are you a cop?"

"No."

"Are you a reporter?"

"No."

"Who are you?"

"I'm working this case as a private investigator for the family of the girl who was drugged, kidnapped, and raped by several members of the football team," I said.

He started to ball his fist, but his wife was there to clutch his arm before he could swing it. I was close enough to him to appreciate the close shave he had given himself. His face was mottled with color like bits of dark glass beneath the surface of his skin, ochre where the beard showed a blue-black haze.

"Get the fuck out of my way, you asshole—"

His wife pulled him away at the same time the other husband was moving toward me. The little bounce of his feet told me he was on the verge of combat too. I had to be quick. It's one thing to stir a simmering pot but another to wind up being boiled in it.

I tossed my card with the motel's number scrawled across it in front of them. "I'm staying there," I said. "I'd be interested to know if any of you folks would like to get justice for your sons or whether you're going to let the town make them the scapegoats for what half the team did, not to mention—"

"Get the fuck out of here, you!" screamed Steeson, Sr. This time it looked as if he were going to bowl his wife over to get to me. I sidestepped the approaching Radcliffe male and nearly tripped making a fast exit. At that point the glass doors of the precinct opened and I heard, "Hey, what's going on out here?"

Micah used to say I had a Messiah complex. I think it's just my existentialist self.

stretching his tiny, fragile wings inside me occasionally. "Do something," he seems to be saying to me.

I was pulling out of the station house parking lot when my cell went off. The director of the state chapter against sexual violence was returning my call. What I wanted from her, I said, was the right psychological approach to get at Shawna's memory of that night. I told her I was an ex-cop and out of my depth at this kind of interrogation. I know how to scream through the veins of my neck at lying suspects in a closed-off room or cajole some deadass into confessing by pretending to be his friend, but young rape victims require something I don't have in my nature and I needed to unlock Shawna's reluctance to speak to me.

She didn't have any "tricks," she said, but she said I was doing the right thing by not pressuring her. "Listen to her," she said. "Believe her! People should know to believe the survivor when she says she's been assaulted."

I told her about the offensive posts, and she said these needed to be removed from social media, especially in a small town where everybody knows everybody. She made some suggestions for my next interview with Shawna. I've driven hundreds of miles in cars with teen girls, runaways I was returning to their families, and I remember a lot of silence as the miles rolled by. It's like driving home with somebody who's just been told about a cancerous tumor. Words fail.

I went back to my motel and slept for a few hours. I had some more research to do and I needed to think through the next stage. I kept coming back to Shawna's memory loss. Something didn't sit right, but I couldn't fathom what the secret of unlocking her reservation might be, and I hoped the professional advice I heard was going to work.

I met Wade by our dumpster that night at break time. As soon as he got in the car, he told me he was in trouble with the manager and "on probation" for various infractions of work-related policies that had come to his attention.

"You're a dishwasher, Wade. How could you be violating company policies?"

"I know," he said. He looked worried. "This job is shit, man, but it's all I've got."

"Do you want to stop?"

"I think—I think maybe I should cool it for a while, ya know?"

"No problem, Wade. You've been a great help. I appreciate it," I said. I stuck three hundred dollars in folded fifties into his front shirt pocket.

As he got out of the car, he looked immensely relieved. "Thanks, man," he said leaning down to look at me. "I'll be in touch."

No, you won't, Wade, I thought as I watched him go back inside. No Bogart impressions this time with a cigarette flicked into the dark. The steel door closed on him and I had already dismissed him from my mind—even a little glad because I didn't like him but I didn't want him connected to me if things did start to get hairy. He might be the grand marshal in the losers' parade, but I felt responsible for him.

About eleven or so, when I stepped out to get some ice cubes from the machine, I felt, rather than heard, footsteps behind me. When I turned around, I was coldcocked by a fist wrapped in something and that fist must have been curled around something heavy like brass or steel. It clipped me on my jaw and sent me sideways like a dolphin breaching. Lucky for me, I landed on grass and missed pavement or hitting my head on anything as I went down.

I wasn't out for very long; in fact, I heard the car screeching out of the parking lot. I was dizzy and my jaw throbbed but I was not badly hurt. If anyone in the motel noticed the mugging, no one came outside to assist me. The night air was chilly and everything felt the same as before except that I was slightly concussed and very much aware that my good luck had abandoned me very abruptly in that place. I was even a little afraid. Violence always does that after the adrenalin jolt wears off. You feel a little less sure of the ground beneath your feet. My rule about stalking horses has some disadvantages if you're the horse instead of the observer so I keep in mind another rule I borrowed from Jack, my ex-partner. He had an old Marine Corps saying he used to bring up when we were working Cleveland's Eastside: "If you pull a tiger by the tail, you better have a plan for his teeth."

The ice that was supposed to go into my nightcap went into a t-shirt that I held under my jaw. The mirror proved no teeth were cracked despite the blood I kept spitting into the sink. I downed some Tylenol and put a chair against the door to wake me in case I had more company coming. I slept with the lights on.

In the morning my face hurt too much to shave and the note I found taped to my door was brief and to the point: GO HOME, it said, in big block letters. It was done with a blue Magic Marker.

I was thinking about coffee from somewhere other than the vending machine when the phone rang. A man's voice said, "You should get in your car and go home. This is none of your business." A few minutes later, another call was put through to my room, a different voice this time: "We clean up our own messes." I didn't recognize either of the speakers except that neither one was the linebacker's dad's voice.

I called Shawna's parents and gave them a summary of my work so far. I left out names and I didn't mention being suckerpunched, the note on my door, or the phone calls. Occupational hazards.

The father wasn't satisfied with my progress. I told him that kicking down doors happened in Hollywood movies, not in real life.

"Don't get lippy with me, Haftmann. I'm paying you, remember?"

I heard the wife's voice in the background repeat his name, but Frank wasn't through telling me how to do my job yet.

"So what's next in your so-called plan to bring these scumbags to justice?"

"Well," I said, "I thought I'd take in a football game."

"You're kidding me, right?"

"No, sir," I said. "That is the plan."

I should have been a little less sarcastic with him, but my jaw was killing me and I was still a bit woozy from the blow. The liquid filth that passed for coffee I used to down the pills was swirling in my stomach and adding to my bad mood. I was a little apprehensive about wade, too, and I was fighting an urge to call him in case I had put the spotlight on him. Warning him might send him deeper into an alcoholic abyss and I didn't want to be responsible for that or risking his job any more than it was. I had some things to do today besides changing motels, and I wanted to be ready for the Friday night football game. *The whole town turns out. . .* I could hear Angel's words; they sounded less sinister then.

I had stirred the pot; now it was time to see what floated to the top. I had xeroxed last year's East Brangton H. S. yearbook, and I was trying to fix some names and faces into my head before the game. The banalities and traditional clustering of photos around clubs, sports, programs, and highlights like homecoming or other such sentimental nonsense belied that other, darker side to student life in America: the boozing, doping, risky sex, bullying of the weak, hazing of unpopular students, contempt for learning and teachers, the cliques, and divisions of classes by status and money. All of that went on twenty-four, seven beneath the surface. I could not see behind the smiling faces of these young athletes the same boys who had taken advantage of a young girl as if she were some kind of barbarian war prize.

The aftereffects of the punch to the jaw were almost gone except for a slight puffiness under my jaw. I was amazed I hadn't been brutally kicked all over once I went down and given a serious, first-class beating. Maybe something had frightened my attackers off. Maybe those feckless gods who rule us, as my ex used to say, don't want to annihilate us too soon. She'd usually quote something afterward, like Shakespeare, about boys pulling wings off flies for sport. Being a recent convert to existentialism, I don't believe in the gods. We have all the trouble and demons we need right here. No need to go to Mount Olympus or heaven.

This Friday night was another specimen of beauty, and I almost pulled back my belief in nothing more than the high cold stars above us. All day long the maples and oaks of the Valley were emblazoned in gold and red, and the air had held that tang of smoke that makes nostalgia inevitable. The soft afternoon light shone through the leaves and the wind was just brisk enough to rattle them and make you feel that something surely wanted us to feel the beauty of nature besides its wrath of endless eating, sex, and death. I thought of the dead raccoon in the road, now a foul-smelling husk of desiccated fur lying near the sewer grate and remembered that winter would be coming to us all soon enough.

The mob of people heading to the entrance gates was a bright blue snake stretching from Riverview Drive near my new motel all the way to the stadium. Youth were everywhere I looked and it made me stand out despite my camouflage of blue jeans and blue windbreaker. Micah used to laugh at me for getting colors mixed up and I saw I had misjudged the shade of blue I wore. This blue wasn't as deep and reminded me of Lake Erie's waters before a summer storm. *Good enough to blend in*, I thought.

South is a mostly black school on Broadway southeast of the city. It's a poor area with its inner-city problems, mostly gangs, drugs, and dysfunctional families. The faces of their supporters driving to town stood out against the mostly Appalachian white faces. I saw a lot of mothers and fathers, aunts and uncles working their way toward the visitors' gate. It seemed that football offered a hiatus from life's bigger concerns and brought some respite to the struggles of daily life in Cleveland. Some of these kids would go on to college on scholarships just like their white counterparts down here. The energy in the air crackled. For a moment, I felt the tension easing out of my shoulders.

I followed a gaggle of girls who looked like freshmen or sophomores. They were doing the equivalent of cruising in cars, sauntering behind the stands, watching, and aping the older girls, hoping to be noticed but half-afraid they would be mocked for something in their speech or dress that wasn't quite right. Nothing as cruel or insecure as a pack of teenaged girls. Three girls peeled off from one group and headed for the refreshment stand. I followed a few feet behind, trying to overhear what they were saying. It was a lot of gossip about certain girls and several boys' names were mentioned.

As two of them got in line, the third drifted over to the side. I walked over to her and asked her if she knew Wayne's dad. I put a big smile on my face and said I was supposed to meet him here tonight. No, she didn't know Mr. Steeson, she said; her eyes boxed my face looking for some sign that might tell her who I was.

"It's a darn shame," I said, "about Wayne and Jimmy."

"Who are you?"

"I'm a cousin of Wayne's dad," I lied easily. I said I lived in Salem and was at the game to support my cousin "during the crisis." I put on a concerned face as I pretended to fumble around for the right word to describe "the incident." She didn't bite. I saw her cut her eyes to the line where her two friends were buying popcorn.

"Yeah, well, I have to go," she said.

I disappeared into the crowd before she could point me out to her friends as that old man who had just creeped her out with talk about Wayne and his dad.

I tried this little ruse on a dozen groups of high schoolers right up to halftime. I was careful to avoid anybody with a letter jacket or anybody who looked to be more than a couple years out of high school. I picked up nothing useful and I was pushing my luck. I saw several teens I had accosted in this way avoid me as the stream of people moved past me and more than once I got the fisheye from a teen. The Blue Raiders of East Brangton were crushing South, so the mood among the crowd was jubilant and that helped my little charade. But nobody wanted to talk about "it." And nobody blurted anything out. I was surprised that one girl, obviously not popular because of her weight and her thick glasses, expressed support for that "poor girl." Her companions, equally unattractive and overweight, ridiculed her immediately. "Charlene, why are you defending that white trash?" She blushed and immediately lapsed into silence while her two chums reviled the "ho" and "bitch across the river."

By the end of the third quarter, I was getting anxious. There were fewer people moseying around behind the stands and walking the track by then; everyone was settled into the game. The cops on patrol were starting to eye-track me along with some older men who fit my stereotype of boosters.

I checked my watch and decided I'd give it fifteen more minutes and then scoot. I was walking toward the nearest exit when I saw him, a teenaged boy, oddly alone, and clinging to the one-inch cable wire toward the end zone. At that moment, East Brangton was on their opponents' five-yard line threatening to score again and the roar of the crowd was accentuated by the drum corps beating time near the far sidelines.

As I approached him, I saw a pool of liquid vomit at his feet. He retched again as I came within a few feet of him. He was mumbling something that turned into a monotone of *O fuck O fuck OfuckOfuckfffuuuuck*, as another stream of projectile vomit arced over the wire.

He repeated his vomit-mantra but apparently he had emptied himself out.

"You need a hand, son?"

"F-Fuck off."

His jacket reeked of sour wine and marijuana.

"Let me help you," I said.

"Fuck off, faggot," he said. He tried to turn his head to look me over, but he was wobbling on his feet.

"You look like the Irishman holding on to a blade of grass to keep from falling off the earth," I said and smiled at him.

I held my palms up: see, no weapons, nothing but a Good Samaritan here. I was considering my play, thinking I had hit the motherload with this pup, because I knew I could wring every morsel of information he had before he knew what hit him. I just had to clear the environment of obstacles first. I was considering what to say when I caught movement out of the corner of my eye. A knot of men was moving slowly but definitely my way; they ranged from twenties through thirties to some gray-haired or gray-bearded types. These weren't your aging hippies with the gray ponytails and pot bellies. These looked like working-class men. The biggest was lurking behind the pack, and that's when I knew I was busted. He had fists the size of wrecking balls and he didn't want me spooked so he lingered behind. Maybe these were the men from my motel adventure the other night.

I didn't panic—but I almost bolted. I wasn't going to be jumped so publicly. I was betting on it. You don't have as many subconcussive events, as my medico likes to say, as I have had in my lifetime and not worry about the consequences in old age. Drooling from a corner of the rec room in an Alzheimer's clinic is not how I want to end my days.

The men stopped a few feet from me and casually formed a semicircle. The big man stepped out from the others and gave me a hard look. Without looking at the boy, he reached out and with one hand grabbed a bunch of shirt fabric near the boy's shoulder and whisked him out of sight the way you'd brush a fly off your dinner plate.

"Let's have a talk," he said to me.

"Sure," I said; "here's a good place."

The man next to him said, "No, asshole, the parking lot. It's a better place for a quiet conversation."

"So you can stomp the shit out of me? No, thanks," I said. I think they thought I was stupid enough to go with them.

One of the older, smaller men stepped in front of me. "You need to get back in your car and go home to your Cleveland niggers," he said.

"Now, Jess, that ain't very nice. Mister Huffman here is a guest in our town. We need to show him some East Brangton hospitality." This was from Wrecking Ball, said slowly and with a razor-slit of smile.

"I've seen your hospitality to strangers," I said. "I've felt it, too. Come to think of it, there's a mother and father of a sixteen-year-old girl across that river who know something about your hospitality when it comes to unconscious girls in your fair city."

The men looked to him for their cue. He didn't flinch except for a tightening around the eyes. He placed a finger the size of a small bratwurst on my chest for emphasis.

"Jess here is right. You should go back home. You should go tonight. We'll take care of our own mess."

You know that little voice in your head that pipes up and says to you, "Shut up right now"? Well, I was hearing it in stereo in both ears now. Too bad I don't know how to follow good advice. Their backs were turned when I said, louder than I intended, "What if it was your daughter?"

The big man whirled back and without much effort, he parted his companions on either side like a bowler handling the seven-ten split, mule ears, I think they call it. He got to me so fast that I didn't even react before I found him chin to chin with me—rather, his chin to my nose. I expected the knockout punch. I debated a swing to his midsection and ruled it out. The beating afterward would be terrific and I knew in my guts the cops would let it go on if they broke it up at all. I had a better chance fighting him in a closet. For a long, long moment nothing at all happened. Then he stepped backward, turned away—this time, more slowly, and looked back once before he and his happy little posse of like-minded citizens ambled up the track.

My knees were weak. Whether he was a team booster or not, he was definitely an ex-player and most likely a former tackle or middle linebacker. The spit was gone from my mouth, and I had to settle my breath down and get my pulse in order. Adrenalin works nicely when that old limbic brain fires up for the flight-or-fight syndrome, but you can't think clearly when it happens. I know that from years of cop work.

I walked, or maybe staggered, to my car and didn't leave the cover of streetlamps. I took off and headed back to my motel. I started to do a zigzag route back to pick up any tails when I realized that would be futile. If they had my name, botched or otherwise, they would know where I was staying and probably had my itinerary ever since I confronted Steeson and Radcliffe in front of the cop station. I wasn't sure I needed to do more than keep myself safe with a little extra surveillance when I was out and about. I knew it would come to this eventually. It's just the immediacy of violence that always takes you by surprise. It's never the same twice.

But the gloves were off and I'd need to be careful with everyone I met from now on. I thought again of calling Wade and giving him a head's-up, but I didn't know how to frame it without panicking him. *The less of me, the better for him*, I thought.

I drove across the river to West Virginia and found a new place to stay. Next door was a Denny's. I ordered a pot of black coffee, chugged it with some aspirin for a fast-blooming headache, and called Richard Detweiler.

He answered on the eighth ring.

"You're not at the game," I said when he picked up.

"Who is this? Mister Haftmann, is that you?"

"In the flesh. Calling you from wild and wonderful West Virginia."

"I've got something you need to see," he said. "I'll be gone all day tomorrow so we can set a time for Sunday if you like."

"I'm coming now," I said. "Put the porch light on for me."

"I've been sifting through postings ever since you left," he said when he admitted me into his back room. He had the fidgety look Danny gets when his computers have made his day. "Look at this." It was a collection of tweets, blogs, and online postings in text-English. I skimmed through them.

"What am I missing, Richard?"

"It's like a code," he said.

"You mean computer code?" I asked.

"No, nothing that sophisticated," he said. "They're using some terms in odd patterns. Even with all this mangled English, it didn't make sense to use certain words over and over."

I looked again but it all sounded like teen gibberish: young girls getting into hysterics with exclamation points over "this awesome pair of sweatpants at Dillards!!!" I've never figured out why anybody feels compelled to blurt to the world what kind of day they're having on their social platforms. I misjudged karaoke, too, so don't go by what I think.

"Look," he said, "it works like this—or I'm offering a theory that it might work this way."

"Go ahead," I said. "You couldn't surprise me now."

"OK, well, the word *window* means 'girl' or 'a specific girl' or somehow correlates to a girl. 'Ride' seems to refer to some kind of initiation, I think. I'm not sure. Going for a 'time out' has several meanings, but it sounds to me like an acknowledgment of the—of this 'initiation,' or whatever it is—that it's been successful. Here's another thing. You've got football players—not normally known for math skills anyway, right? Well, they're talking about grades in 'algebra,' 'linear calculus,' and 'geometry' as if they're happy with these courses, but nobody ever mentions a theorem or an equation."

"Why would they bother using any code or any indirection when these knuckleheads blurt out every nasty thought in their tiny little minds?" I recalled some of those vile descriptions and obscenities from his previous gleanings.

"I know," he acknowledged with a head shake. "It doesn't make sense. They didn't hesitate to incriminate themselves before, during, and after the rape of that girl."

"Unless they were afraid some adult or parent might confiscate a cell phone or accidentally come across it, whatever they're really talking about," I suggested. That theory was weak as rooster soup, too.

I thanked him and left. I was irked I'd gotten my hopes up. Day Four: Haftmann 1, East Brangton 3. I was losing the series.

The idea that what happened to Shawna might have involved a sexual initiation occurred to me, but there was too much else that implied she was a victim of opportunity. Wrong place, wrong time, as the old saying goes. I needed to find out a little more about Christine, the girlfriend, but her home phone wasn't picking up messages and nobody answered my calls. I had asked Shawna's parents to contact them for me, but no luck yet.

When I got back to my motel room, something clicked—Angel's rumor about the soccer team and a sophomore. I called her number at work and left a message on her machine. Before I was about to drop into that black whirlpool of sleep, my cell phone buzzed from the dresser.

"Mister Haftmann, were you asleep?"

I love that question. "Why, no, and thanks for calling me back so soon. I didn't expect to hear from you until tomorrow."

"I have call forwarding from my office phone. The job, you know. What is it you need?"

I gave her a rough outline of Richard's theory and asked her what she remembered about the girl's suicide.

"It started, I think, from the basketball team. The rumor was they would pressure a girl at school to sext nude photos to one of the team members. If she refused, they'd ruin her reputation."

"Are you telling me that a girl would do this—send a nude photo of herself—out of fear of hearing herself gossiped about? I've heard of peer pressure but that's too much."

"That's what my source said. She was a senior herself at that time."

"Was she one of the girls?"

"No, she's gay. She would have told them to go fuck themselves, excuse my French."

The sexting led to demands for sex, then to parties, where the entire team would expect to have sex with the girl. Sometimes one girl who was victimized would be coerced into acting as a friend to another girl to lead her to the team for sex.

I've been out of high school too long, I realized. Talking in line, chewing gum, missing homework deadlines—those used to be the crimes in high school. Now it's pregnancy, school shootings, suicide on *YouTube*, boob-shaking competitions on *Tik Tok*, drugs, bomb threats—

"It's all different now," I said. "It goes deeper than a football team."

She agreed. "The whole cultural mentality is different. It's an age of helicopter parents, latchkey kids, and single moms. The kids are raising themselves and the parents aren't in charge anymore."

"You said that before."

"Doesn't make it less true," she countered.

"Have you heard whether these boys go recruiting in West Virginia?"

I was thinking of Jimmy Radcliffe's postings before the rape. He was bragging about "dogging out an '89 Camaro IRoc Z over in West Virginia."

The trouble with that is you'd have to drive south all the way to Highway 50 between Clarksburg and Parkersburg to find a stretch of flat road. They didn't call it the "Mountain State" for nothing.

Radcliffe's post used the word *window*, but he was talking about the view from the Camaro's window, not a 'girl,' as Detweiler believed. The math thing bugged me, too. On Jimmy's *facebook* page, Richard showed me an exchange between him and somebody named Doug going back and forth about "geometry" and "algebra." You took those courses in certain years, I remembered. Math wasn't my strong suit either but geometry was in sophomore year, algebra in junior, and calc in senior year.

I had an hour to kill before my meeting with Shawna in her house. The father was giving me fits because he wouldn't agree to a private discussion between just Shawna and me. I finally got him to agree to staying in the next room. "But the door stays open, Haftmann." Her parents were worried about PTSD and were smothering her with attention. She'd been checked for STDs and her gynecologist did not think she was pregnant.

I checked the yearbook and found the girl from the game last night, the one who expressed sympathy for Shawna before her companions put the kibosh on it. Her name was Janna Mulqueen, and her house wasn't that far away. I wasted a little time on wrong turns but got there with a half-hour to spare before my meeting with Shawna. *Worth a chance*, I thought.

No one picked up after several attempts to get them on the phone, but I could see a Hyundai in the driveway.

What the hey. I got out of my car and crossed the street and walked up the sidewalk splitting a postage stamp of lawn. The place was shabby but nothing unusual about it in this working-class residential neighborhood. It seemed to be holding its own despite a few houses here and there having given up the struggle and gone to seed.

The girl herself opened the door.

"I'm not allowed to talk to you," she said before I could open my mouth.

"You know who I am?"

"You're a cop."

"A private investigator, Janna. There's a girl across that river I'm going to see this morning. She's badly traumatized and I'm just trying to help her and family. I know you're made of better stuff than your friends from last night."

"I don't know anything," she said, but her homely face twisted in pain; the struggle was evident.

"Janna! Janna! Get back in here right now!"

The basso-profundo voice of her father, no doubt.

"Sir, would you come out here and talk to me for a minute?"

"Get out of here or I'm calling the cops!"

Janna gave me an anguished look and slowly closed the door in my face.

My batting average was zilch-point-shit so far. I was wandering around town like an idiot looking for the lost head of John the Baptist. I was tired of getting nowhere. I needed a walk-off home run.

I met Frank and his wife at the door. Their faces told me all I needed to know about the heavy atmosphere in that house of late. I was sorry for Shawna's sake. These people were in another state, they were isolated from the gossip, but they might as well have been camping out in the middle of the high-school stadium. East Brangton was like hell. It was everywhere in that house and I could smell its stink in my nostrils.

Shawna stood in the doorway to her room, half-leaning against it, looking at me. Her hair was parted in the same zigzag way and she wore a faded, terrycloth bathrobe pilled from wear.

"Shawna, I told you to get dressed an hour ago," her mother said, apologizing. "I'm sorry, Mister Haftmann. We can't seem to get organized this morning."

"That's all right. You should see my place."

Shawna led me into her bedroom, and as soon as I entered the room, I shut the door behind us. Let Frank open it if he dared. He'd only add to the brooding distrust I felt. Shawna's pale eyes were highlighted by the dark semicircles beneath them. I threw away my bag of tricks for this interrogation. Nothing was going to work in this place and I knew it. Another K for the opposing pitcher, chalk up another victory for the blue-caped rider back in Ohio.

When I looked at her, Shawna made the unconscious gesture of clutching the robe tighter against the bulge of her chest. I smiled at her, not knowing how to begin. Then I saw it. On the shelf. A Brutus Buckeye stuffed doll. It was the Ohio State University mascot. Something clicked. I couldn't say what.

I went into my spiel, used my softest manner, but produced nothing. It was the same thing as before: "I don't know" and "I can't remember." After twenty minutes of the gentlest interrogation I've ever conducted, she was writhing in anxiety and flustered. She had raised her voice several times at my questions and I knew she was on the verge of tears. I couldn't stop myself. I was jabbing my thumb into an open wound and I knew it, yet I was forcing myself to intimidate this little girl.

"Shawna, I need to know why you were at Christine's house that night," I said for the third time.

"I told you! I told you! Stop asking me that!"

She was agitated and rocked back in her chair, the distress so overwhelming her that she accidentally opened her legs and displayed her sex. Shawna ceased squirming and looked at me. A look of cold contempt crossed her face. She closed her legs and arranged the hem of her robe over her knees.

"Is everything all right in there?"

No, Frank, God damn it. Nothing's all right in here.

I made small talk with the parents afterward. I told them what I had left to do and said I'd call them at the same time tonight to report on what I had learned.

"You're getting nowhere, aren't you? This is all a waste of my money," Frank said to me at the door out of his wife's hearing. For once, he wasn't glowering or sneering at me. His face was drawn and pinched. I had a prevision of how old he'd look in twenty years.

"It might be," I said. "I'd like to give it another day or two. If I don't get some hard evidence by then—well, I think we should call it off and let the police handle it."

I saw his face change color. "Those East Brangton cops—"

"I meant the state police," I said. "I'll contact BCI myself. I've spoken with the *Plain Dealer* reporter who did the original story. He's very interested in a follow-up. We can get them to put the spotlight on that town and that high school. I'll go to the governor if I have to."

"One more day," Frank said. We didn't shake hands.

You try not to get used to losing. But sometimes the forces of darkness are pitching a shutout and there's nothing you can do with a chin-high fastball but get out of the way.

Still, that Buckeye doll on her shelf bothered me as I headed to my car.

I was having a couple cheeseburgers in the same diner where I had hoped to recruit an informer that first day. By now, everyone knew who I was. Imagine a rabbit surrounded by wolverines and you'll get the picture. I ate fast, left a generous tip, and stopped at the door. When I turned around, there were twenty pairs of eyes boring into mine.

I was reaching for the key when some motor in my head started first. Geometry could mean a sophomore girl. That doll—

I called Richard.

"One of those websites—I don't know the name of it—had a thing pop up in the corner."

"A logo bug," Richard said. "It's like the Nike symbol, a corporate logo."

"Bring it up," I said. "I'm on my way over."

I'm sure I was followed by a beat-up Ford 150, but I blew through two red lights and left it behind.

Richard met me at the door. "Wow," he said, "That didn't take you long. I've got it. It's a teen sex website, crude, but the Buckeye logo is in the lower left corner. I ran down the IP address and the real address. It's out of Columbus."

The next three hours were dismal. Don't get me wrong. I'm not a prude but watching two hours of amateur, herky-jerky camera action featuring teenagers rutting in the woods isn't my thing.

"Whoa, right there," I said. "Freeze that."

"What is it?"

"Look."

The kid doing the filming with his cell phone panned the overlook where the cars were parked. I caught a flash of Ohio license plate as he came behind it. Then I saw it: McKinley Stadium, the blue-caped rider on the scoreboard barely discernible, but the stadium, the high school, the town—it was all there. It was shot from a high hill in a small clearing, a lovers' lane created out of a switchback on some hillside, but it had to be in West Virginia. The stadium was a bright bowl of white lights below amid a nexus of streets bordered by parallel rows of sodium arc lights casting an orange glow. I recognized Main Street and River Streets easily.

"It's local."

Another hour of viewing erect males in coitus all shot from the beltline, no faces, pants around knees, humping girls from behind against cars—and then my stomach lurched. After one gangbang, I saw the top of several football mascot dolls in the backseat. Brutus Buckeye, his familiar toothless Halloween smile gaped from a stupid ovoid face. I had seen it a hundred times over the years watching Buckeye football on Saturday. His red and gray striped shirt with his name etched in white across the chest wasn't visible but there was no doubt. Geometry meant sophomore girl. Algebra meant a junior . . .

"This is really piss-poor-quality porn," Richard said.

"I know, Richard."

You hope things won't go a certain way and that's a sure sign they will. I try not to let superstition corrupt my existentialism, but sometimes I think my ex was right. The gods do like to play with us, like pulling wings off flies.

I didn't recognize the wanton boys but I guessed Jimmy Radcliffe and Wayne Steeson would know the girls well enough. I saw her just as I was about to tell Richard I had seen enough, and I had. Enough to last a lifetime.

Shawna wasn't camera-shy. She was filmed front and back, literally. In a sequence that lasted for almost an hour, she was nude and backed out of the passenger side window. The entire lower half of her body was extended out the window so that the male could easily penetrate her.

Two other males in the vicinity were maintaining erections awaiting their turn at her. The facial shots showed the same zigzag part in her hair and her expression as she accommodated the thrusting from behind. She made low noises in her throat unlike the theatrical moans of a porn actress. She crossed one arm under her breasts to prevent their swaying motion. Her face held the same earnest expression—not joy, not pleasure—but something else. She furrowed her brow once and I recognized the look she had given me when her robe parted and she knew I was looking. I was no different from these boys, the look said. The part I couldn't read then was still a mystery but part of it had to do with power and sex, the joy of getting away with something, tasting the forbidden fruit, if you want to throw a religious gloss over it.

When all the males had climaxed on her face, she situated herself in the car and smiled for the camera dabbing with a Kleenexes at the ejaculate that dripped down between her large breasts to her tawny pubic thatch. The last thing was to blow a kiss and look away as the boy filming walked over to the other car. I saw the logo bug pop up once more and then a fade into black.

"When was this filmed?"

"No way to tell," Richard said. "It's her, isn't it?"

"I want to thank you for all your help," I said. I reached into my wallet and peeled off some bills. "Buy a new—whatchamacallit, router on me."

I threw up at the curb, ashamed of my weakness. How many sex websites were there? Dozens? Hundreds? It seemed half the world was filming the other half having sex. Richard told me that *YouTube* uploaded three hours of video every single minute of the day.

I drove straight to Christine's house. Her parents were both working. She knew me at once and let me in. I showed her a disk and said I had everything they did on that hilltop on it. I told her if it came out in court there was no way those boys would see another minute of jail time.

"Level with me, Christine."

She did. She introduced Shawna to Jimmy and Wayne. It started in her senior year, last year, with a group of kids from their high school. They were having sex anyway, so this was no big deal, the filming of it. At first, they exchanged videos of one another, always careful not to show faces, but after a while, one guy suggested they film themselves and send it off to a guy he knew across the river, a former football player on a scholarship to OSU. Pretty soon it was a contest among them to see who could make the most outrageous video. Having sex while on hands and knees inside the vehicle was her idea, but Shawna went for it when she showed her the video.

"Are you going to go to the police?"

"I'm working for the family," I said. "I'm not an officer of the court, so I don't have to turn anything over to the defense." Besides, the disk was empty; it was just a prop.

"What's going to happen?"

"That's a question you should have asked yourself a long time ago," I said and left the house.

It was a short drive back to Shawna's house, but it seemed like a hundred miles. I could see how the scene would play out as if I were going to film it. Hysteria from the mother, chest-beating wrath from Frank. They'd both collapse on the floor, blaming me.

Or maybe not. Maybe they'd be stunned to silence. But it was time for a lawyer to take over now. I couldn't advise them. I was astounded these teenagers kept silent, knowing this record of wild fornication existed in cyberspace for anyone to see it and grab it. They knew so much more than any adult in the school or anybody I had seen interviewed. "The kids are in charge," Angel had said to me.

I figured on getting stiffed on my bill, but that didn't bother me then. It was the squirmy distress in my belly, a feeling I was in another dimension, an upside-down world, and I didn't have my bearings for it.

The long drive north back home to Jefferson-on-the-Lake gave me time to think things over. Part of me was glad I wasn't a father raising a daughter in these perilous times; part of me wanted that no matter what and wished that Micah and I had worked things out.

All things considered, I didn't lose the game. Nobody won. Haftmann's Rule for existentialists: *You didn't ask to be here, so don't whine about it. Do something.*

It was going to be another lovely fall day.

* * *

The End

Crème de la Merde
By Robb White

The beautiful people, I really hate them. Miami's South Beach, its snobbery, glam and glitz—all of it makes me sick. I'd never set foot on this expensive pile of sand if the job didn't take me here occasionally. If I had my way, I'd bulldoze the whole city straight into the Everglades, art deco buildings included. I'd rip down every Givenchy and Gucci logo on every boutique window. As for the hoochie-coochie girls, the trophy wives, the blue-haired widows, and the millionaires with their old/new money, I'd give them all thirty-six hours to get out of town or face deportation to Barrow, Alaska. I'd burn everything except the mansions, the yachts, the Lamborghinis, and Porsches. I'd let the residents of Little Havana and Liberty City loot everything and whatever's left can be won in a big lottery. Ticket money would go to build retirement houses for aging greyhounds from Hialeah.

I track runaways. I'm a private eye from Northern Ohio where a lot of the flabby, melanoma-prone snowbirds live. I despise them, too, for what it's worth. But here I am, once again, in the land of sunshine and clubbing 'til dawn.

The girl I came down here to find and bring back to her parents died in a motel room far from the beach. She was malnourished, scabby, and riddled with STDs. I was twenty-four hours and some odd minutes too late. Miami-Dade PD was obliging enough to let me see the autopsy report. A promising life, albeit in boring Ohio, was what she left behind to follow a hustler named Max to the sunshine state. She was seventeen when he seduced her. His age, according to the parents who hired me, was somewhere between twenty-five and thirty.

When she wouldn't drop him, they threatened to bring statutory rape charges, which of course resulted in their flight. It's not a new story even with the sad ending for Kara Levesque.

Her family is distantly related to René Levesque, the French-Canadian minister who founded the Parti Québécois. I don't read much besides political memoirs and biographies, which hobby might seem strange for my profession. (I'll dignify what I do for a living with that word instead of "job," which is all it is to me nowadays.) It was René Lévésque who said: "There is a time when quiet courage and audacity become for a people at the key moments of its existence the only form of adequate caution. If it does not then accept the calculated risk of the great steps, it can miss its career forever, exactly like the man who is afraid of life."

That might seem like a roundabout beginning to what I am going to tell you, but it's important to what happened. You see, I was enjoying a cold draft beer out of the suffocating humidity in a dark neighborhood tavern close by *Calle Ocho* where no one from the trendy SoBe crowd would even dream of entering; it was a place where you are more likely to hear Frankie Yankovic's "Roll Out the Barrel" than that thumping, autotracked rave music in the clubs. I suppose I was close to crying in my beer over the fact I had just missed another one. I mean saving a lost girl who needed saving; it wasn't the money, either. I've failed before. I'm not an egomaniac. I'm a realist (but a closet existentialist as well). The number of runaways I do find and cajole or forcibly bring back is less than a third of the total. Kara wasn't the first one I've found dead in a sleazy motel room with the walls spattered with dried, cast-off blood from the needles. I've found them dead in otherwise perfect health and dead with dirty needles sticking out of their unwashed arms. The smell in that room, however, was so foul that a rookie cop upchucked his breakfast outside in the bushes. I told myself that, even if I had found Kara in the nick of time, rather than staring up at the ceiling from a lousy mattress with eyes glazed like a dead bird's, soiled from her own bowel movement, would she have gone with me no matter what persuasion I tried to use on her?

Because hers was an unattended death, the lead detective told me the body would be kept in the cooler downtown until the final ruling. They wanted to talk some more to the boyfriend Max, who occupied the room with her but whose condition was much less dire when cops kicked in the door. Their money for the drugs most likely wasn't earned working at a fast-food franchise or panhandling in the street. Cops were curious how these two homeless drifters could afford a two-hundred-dollar-a-day habit between them. Kara's family had money, but they cut her off after her promise to come home with the money wired through Western Union had also gone for dope.

I asked Raymond Navarro, who got the call-out, if there was any suspicion of homicide in the death.

He shook his head. "Not likely. You saw the room after it was partially cleaned up and I'm surprised you didn't heave your cookies. Both of those birds were one hot shot away from death long before we got to her."

I showed him her high-school graduation photo.

He whistled. "Pretty girl. Not so much in the after photos they shot of her in the room and downtown on the meat slab."

I asked about Max Marovitz.

"Who?"

"The boyfriend," I said.

"His real name is Max Aaron Cole. He uses a half-dozen aliases. Got a sealed juvie jacket and did a two-year bid in a real prison before he lit out for the greener pastures of your state."

"What was that for—the conviction?"

"Conned some widow with Alzheimer's out of twenty-four thousand," Navarro said. "His lawyer tried to get him county because of no priors and a non-violent felony charge, but the judge wasn't buying it. Then the lawyer thought he could get the judge to recuse himself because his own mother died of dementia. Cole wound up doing his time in Starke, that's Raiford, where the bad boys go."

"Sounds like a charmer."

"Lucky for us Cole likes tattoos. You can't drop those so fast when you change your name," the cop said.

"Any chance I can have one or two personal effects to bring back to her parents?"

"You told me you used to be a cop up there," Navarro said. "You should know better than to ask."

I did but I had to try. Somehow it makes the grieving hurt less for the parents.

While I was nursed my beer, I plotted my next course. I didn't want her parents to pay for my time down here anymore than necessary, but if they were to enquire about this Max Cole's whereabouts, what could I tell them? They already knew he wasn't good enough for their daughter. Telling them he preyed on old ladies as well as young girls—how could that help? I was playing devil's advocate with myself and figured, at the very least, they'd want the satisfaction of knowing he was possibly going to face charges greater than drug possession especially if he had any responsibility for Kara's overdose. One or two days at most should do it, I told myself.

I took Raymond Navarro's card and asked him to call me as soon as he had any word of the pending charges against Cole.

I returned to my motel and stripped down to my shorts and put the a/c on high. I had a six-pack for company and that's about all I remember until Navarro's call around five in the evening woke me out of a fuggy, sweat-soaked nightmare.

"The D.A. won't indict on the drug charges," Navarro said.

"You told me that room had about fifty used needles in it and bindles of heroin everywhere there was a flat surface."

"All true, my friend, but it turns out the manager of the motel got in there after the paramedics left. The cops couldn't stand the smell. He messed around in there. Cop who answered the dead body found call says the guy was probably in there to steal drugs or money."

"What did Cole say?"

"Cole told his lawyer the guy was messing around in there. Anyway, the D.A. doesn't want to waste time on a felony possession his lawyer intends to fight so they pled it down to a chickenshit misdemeanor charge and the lawyer's taking it."

"No shit? He doesn't even have to bond out. Where is he now?"

"He's being cut loose now. A little paperwork I can delay for about fifteen minutes if you want to tail him but that is it, brother."

"I'll take it," I said.

I thanked him and got going fast, barely dressed, still groggy in the merciless heat of a Florida late afternoon and sped over to the precinct three blocks away. Navarro told me where the prisoner discharge exits were, so I should blend in there. I couldn't find any shade so I had to park curbside and watch for him.

News people in a van showed up and presented credentials at the gatehouse. Minutes later, a cruiser pulled into the area where the cameras could shoot the latest perp walk for the six o'clock Miami news channels.

Max Cole didn't know me from Adam much less have any idea I was working for the parents. It would be an easy tail if I didn't pass out in this blinding heat. Only the tourists got tanned down here. You stayed out of this brutal heat if you were a native.

There he was. I hated him the moment I had laid eyes on his photo the Levesques had given me along with those of their daughter to take down here. The bastard was handsome—Brad-Pitt-twenty-years-ago handsome. Long surfer-boy locks, a gold loop earring that caught a glint of sunlight as he stood in the street looking this way and that, blinking like an owl after a day inside a cube where all the lighting was fluorescent. He had a dark shirt, blue or black worn loose over a white tee and several layers of chain hanging from his neck. Navarro didn't have to use the ruse of paperwork to hold him for me. The guy would take that much time adorning himself in gold.

I had envisioned a junkie pallor and a scrawny body type, not this *GQ* cover model with a trendy three-day beard. His clothes were stylish, casual, and fit him better than anything I had ever hung on my own body even when I wasn't a middle-aged, out-of-shape ex-cop fighting and losing the flab wars. I wanted to call Navarro and ask him what gives—how does a guy practically OD on heroin and maintain a physique like that? If he had lost weight through a long drug binge, his male model leanness would be replaced by a gym rat's bulked-up size.

One answer made sense: he held back and let Kara sink deeper into her addiction's increasing demands for a high. That wasn't murder but it was cold enough to be murder's little brother. I had no proof of anything just then.

An orange Dodge Challenger pulled up to the curb in front of him and Max got in. They sped off and I followed. We were traveling away from my area of shabby gentility toward something much better. Bigger houses, more palmettos in the yard, and landscaping that must have cost the owners a bundle. The chamber of commerce welcoming sign we'd just passed nailed it in any event: Coconut Grove.

Max and his driver turned left into a Marriott parking lot. I followed, not too close, but I had to get the room number.

Max's friend parked and they got out. The friend was black-haired and wore a similar amount of gold chain around his own neck where a blue glyph in Chinese characters started under his ear. His shirt was black and the gold cufflinks were quarter-sized. He draped a white sport coat over his arm and the two headed for the lobby.

I had to double my speed if I meant to catch them at the elevator. My timing, for once, was perfect. The elevator had a couple young women waiting to go up and a guy my age and wearing my face was invisible among them. I slid around them as they took a few moments to eyeball one another and exchange greetings. From my corner I thumbed the button to the top floor and waited to see what numbers the males pressed. They spoke a language that was almost unintelligible to me, but I inferred some club names or restaurants were involved in the short conversation. The girls mentioned a place and the two males mentioned a different place; then they got down to talking about times and it occurred to me I was witnessing a mating ritual.

The girls got off on four, which left me exposed to the view of the two men but it was a risk I had already taken. I kept my back to them as much as possible and hoped they'd resume their conversation, as men tend to do, when the females they've been flirting with are out of earshot. Not a word between these two. That, for some reason, made me feel a chill despite the sweat trickling down my back from the exertion of my brief dash to the lobby.

They exited the elevator on seven. I waited for the doors to close before I hit the Open button. I stayed there and listened for the sound of talking or the sound of a door shutting. I heard nothing, thanks to the plush carpeting. I stepped out and tried to look like the lost tourist I intended to play if confronted by staff. The corridor turned right about forty yards ahead so I had to bolt for it if I wanted to catch up. The carpeting buffered my footsteps. At the corner, I dropped to my knee, pretending to tie my shoe. I risked a fast look down the L-shaped corridor and heard a door shutting about fifteen yards off. I headed straight for it and put my ear next to the door. I just managed to catch a man's voice speaking in normal tones, although I couldn't hear the words themselves. That had to be it.

I headed back down to the elevator, pressed the button, and waited. When it arrived, no one was inside, so I had it to myself all the way down to the lobby. Some couples were entering just as I headed for the revolving glass exit doors. For all intents and purposes, I was the Invisible Man. I felt a little pride in being totally ignored by the few people around.

The tools I carry in the trunk of my car would get me arrested if I were a civilian but being a private investigator, I figured, I stood a chance of having a chinwag with any cop who might brace me over the possession of burglar tools.

I returned to my car, which was parked a couple rows over from the Challenger. I had beef jerky and soda water in a bag behind me. Surveillance food. I dug in. It was a joyless meal but I was happy—that is, until I thought of Kara's photo in her ballerina tutu. Her strong, muscled body, so graceful in the pose she struck, and her eyes held the smile her face couldn't show made me think of her juxtaposed to the autopsy photos in Navarro's file. Shit," I said aloud, for no reason. Then I remembered something: dancers in the ballet world say, "Merde" to one another before going onstage, their equivalent to "break-a-leg." Ten years ago I'd picked up a biography of Maria Tallchief at Barnes and Noble. The jacket cover said she was America's first major prima ballerina and a Native American. I flicked through it before putting it back on the shelf. But that expression was all I recalled from the book.

I was relieving my bladder for the third time into one of the plastic jugs I'd had the foresight to get as soon as the rental car contract was signed near the airport. An old cop's experience there. Around ten-thirty, the two came out of the Marriott's doors and headed in a different direction for the spot where the Challenger had been parked.

I fired up my Honda Civic and drove parallel to their direction. Neither seemed in any kind of a hurry. From what I could tell, we were going clubbing tonight. Since no bouncer has ever let me past the velvet rope of even a modest night club, I had no delusions I was going in with them, wherever that was. It looked like more surveillance ahead.

The driver of the Challenger looked out the window in my direction as they passed in a black Jaguar F-Type Spyder convertible, taking me by surprise. My little Honda, so good at blending into traffic, was not so good at keeping up with a supercharged V-8 that could probably top out at 180 miles per hour. I hoped the two up ahead of me were not inclined toward some macho display of testosterone and would cruise at speeds where they could check out the women. I watched with some anxiety as the Dixie Highway/95 Interstate junction sign appeared ahead, but they kept going and turned onto West 40th Street.

They made a sudden, sharp right onto the Tamiami Trail highway and roared off straight toward Biscayne Bay and the bright lights of downtown Miami. Fortunately, heavy traffic slowed them down enough so that their bursts of acceleration came to nothing. I imagined Max in the driver's seat showing off for his buddy, talking and laughing about his good luck at walking out of jail and thin king of the night's adventures ahead, whereas there was a dead girl stiffening on a sliding steel board in the Miami-Dade morgue he had some moral responsibility for putting there. But, as the saying goes, if you don't feel a responsibility, you don't have one.

My guess about the clubbing was right. We hit three different clubs that night and I watched from my car while my beard grew a little more each time, but nothing happened. I listened to the music booming through the mammoth speakers as the door opened each time to admit new people. The women were gorgeous and they came in pairs and groups. Sometimes they exited from a silver Rolls or a cobalt-blue Porsche with the men they came with, but they were very much the beautiful people everyone else in America admired and wished to trade places with, especially the naïve and the gullible who think this life is free and doesn't ever have a price tag that has to be paid sooner or later.

By the time Max and his pal left Mojito Joe's at four in the morning on Collins Avenue, they were both loud and a little tipsy—or else Max's friend was. Max seemed to hold his liquor better or else he had a higher tolerance for mojitos. The two women with them looked to be in their early twenties. Both wore summery dresses with a lot of thigh and cleavage on display. Both were very drunk and practically staggered alongside the males. I wondered how they were going to pack all that flesh into a two-seater without an excess of arms and legs sticking out to draw the attention of the cops. But somehow they managed it. The Jag roared to life in a burst of speed that left me in the dust without much chance to follow. I watched their lights shrink and disappear in the almost empty pre-dawn streets. I drove back to my motel, took a fast, hot shower, and collapsed into bed.

Decision time again. I could catch up on my sleep in a real, if lumpy, bed—or I could do something that would help a father and mother understand what had happened to their beautiful little girl. I toweled off, looked in the mirror to see if there was someone left I could still recognize. I went out to the parking lot and grabbed the bag of tools from the trunk. I threw it into an attaché case and set it in the passenger side well.

The Marriott's lobby was brightly lit but no one was about. I saw no clerk behind the main counter and figured he or she was cooping in the back somewhere. *Sleep on, kiddo,* I said to myself and took the elevator to the seventh floor.

My fingers aren't what they used to be but why should that surprise me, I thought; nothing else was—reflexes, muscle tone, faith in myself, belief in a world of decency and kindness. All gone over the years . . .

The master card key I had with me would not open the door, not to save my life. I couldn't stand outside the door of Max's room jiggling it into slot much longer. We were some minutes away from dawn when the non-partyers of the world wake up to go to their jobs, but I was riding a thin wave of luck here. Max and his amigo could come back at any time for all I knew. I hoped they were rutting at some distant place with those two girls.

Click, finally: red light to green and I was behind the door in a heartbeat. I stood with my back against the door, not sure if I was even breathing. I let my eyes adjust and I listened for any sound. Just because those two had left didn't mean no one was left behind. Track lighting illuminated the kitchen but there was nothing to see except a bottle of Johnny Walker on the countertop. Max's friend had expensive tastes.

My attaché case held some other tools that might be useful but right now it was just a prop to be set down. Worst case, I'd say I had mistakenly entered the wrong apartment and see how that went down with a surprised occupant. I took a walk down the dark hallway, my hand brushing the walls lightly for balance. A rectangle of light under the door of one room made me hold my breath again. Probably a bedroom light left on.

I approached the door and pushed it gently. I could make out an unmade bed and some rumpled sheets near the bottom of the bedstead. Then, the slightest stirring of movement. As my eyes adjusted, I knew what it was: a foot—a small, human being's foot sticking out from under the bed covers. My heart hammered so loudly in my ears at that point that I was terrified the person in the bed could hear it.

Turning around as slowly as I could, I had that déjà vu sensation of being in one of those dreams where you're stuck in quicksand and you can't escape fast enough.

Then I heard it—an unmistakable sound: a whimper. Not someone in a dream but someone who was crying out softly in pain.

Going back to the room, I took a deep breath and walked through that door with an icy fear in the pit of my stomach. If this were a mistake and there was someone with a weapon pointing at me, I don't know what I would have done but begging not to be killed was at the top of the list.

There was no weapon. Just a woman, nude, gagged and bound to the bed.

Rushing over to her, I removed the sodden gag she'd managed to work loose enough to make the sound. Her eyes bore into mine while I loosened the knots. My peripheral vision took in the disposable syringes on the nightstand opposite the bed.

When I had her freed, I lifted her to an upright position and looked around for something she could cover her chest with. It didn't seem to matter to her because her head lolled on her neck like one of those bobble dolls. I crouched down to see if she could focus on my face. Her eyes were dark from the lack of light in the room and from whatever she had been given. The iris had almost disappeared into the pupil.

"Who are you? Who are you?"

That got me nowhere, although she seemed to want to look at me for some explanation. I helped her to a sitting position and kept one hand on her back so she wouldn't collapse backward.

"H-help . . . stand," she whispered.

That I understood. I lifted her to her feet, putting her hands on my shoulders for balance and asked her if she could stand up by herself.

Her head nodded once, then twice. She seemed to be struggling to come back from whatever dope abyss she had been wallowing in for who knows how long. No doubt, they'd shot her up thinking she'd stay out until they returned but they underestimated her will to survive this ordeal.

"Clothes?" I pantomimed dressing.

She made another of those bobble-doll gestures with her head. Then, slowly, as if it hurt to lift her arm, she pointed at the closet door. I was afraid to let her go completely, so I walked her over with me like two kids in a picnic sack race. I opened the doors and hit a closet switch. Rows of pressed slacks, suit coats, shoe racks of men's shoes of all kinds and all one size. The smell of cologne wafted out. I rooted around looking for anything to give her and then saw a bundle tossed in the corner. I fetched it out to look at it. From the feel of the fabric alone, I knew it had to be her things. I disentangled a bra, panties, and dress and set them next to her on the bed. She craned her head like a robin eyeing a worm to look at the pile of her clothes but made no move to dress herself.

If it sounds like an erotic idea you'd like to try sometime, let me disabuse you of the notion. It took forever to get her things on her. It was like trying to hold water in place. Everything kept sliding over the wrong limbs and it seemed to take hours to get her clothed. She tried to help but it was hopeless. I was just grateful she remained conscious. When she was dressed except for her shoes, she let me hoist her to a standing position and then, hip to hip, I walked her to the front of the apartment. I reached down to grab my case and almost lost her right there.

We made it out and the door clicked shut behind us. The walk to the elevator was as long as the Mogadishu Mile—or felt like it to me. I propped her into a corner of the elevator and we rode it down alone—almost. It stopped on the second floor and a woman, very professional-looking in a navy-blue blazer and bone-white blouse got on. She looked us over and sniffed in disgust. I didn't even have to make an excuse.

Getting her to the car was easier because the salt tang of ocean air seemed to snap her out of some of that drug-induced lethargy.

Strapping her into the passenger seat, I drove off. Me with a smiley face.

From the very second that I walked back into that room, I knew what I was going to do. Don't ask me how it came to me like that. I've never had a thought or a plan like that in my life. I don't know if you can suppress rage just so long before your heart turns black. All I had to do was pick up the phone, dial nine-one-one or just drop Detective Navarro's name and wait for the cavalry to arrive. I'd even get the satisfaction of seeing Max and his scumbag friend cuffed and taken downtown to the precinct for their own perp walk. *Finito*. Job done. I could go back to Ohio and report to Kara's parents that, indeed, justice will be done for their dead daughter.

Bullshit. I had a better plan.

I took her to the emergency room of Mercy Hospital on South Miami, the only hospital I knew I could find from there. I'd once brought a beautiful girl named Raina there and I was thinking of her as we drove. One of the few good endings I can claim to be responsible for. I told the nurse at the registration desk I had found her wandering in the street. Before she could ask me another question, I was out the door and running to my Honda.

The next part of my plan was already in motion. It was as if I had been given an injection of adrenalin. I wasn't tired or sleepy or hungry anymore. Something had wormed itself into my brain and I was going to feed it until my plan was executed. I saw sheet lightning in the massive cumulus clouds rolling in from the Atlantic. It was another sign that things were lining up for me—rather for my plan. Why is it, I have often wondered, when you go to do a good deed, everything combines to put obstacles in your path? But plan an evil deed and it's as if nature itself goes out of its way to assist you. I remember a grumpy old nun from my grade school years; she had a face like an apple doll with two red spots in the center of her cheeks. She hated us kids and we hated her right back. After one class where disruptions came from all corners of the room, she smacked her fist on the glass top of her desk and shattered it. She lifted a bloody hand to show us what demons we all were. Then she said something I've never forgotten: "The greatest trick the devil ever pulled was to convince us he doesn't exist." She never gave Baudelaire credit for that quote, but it didn't matter to me then because it seared itself into my brain letter by letter where it's been ever since.

* * *

Want to slow somebody down in a fast car? Take a good-sized Idaho potato, peel it, cut it in half. Now jam it up the muffler as far as you can get it to go. Once the smoke starts to pour out of the tailpipe, you'll know that vehicle isn't going too far. A Jag sports car requires four potatoes but the effect will be the same.

Max's pal was blowing a plume of blue smoke I could see from fifty yards behind, which is where I was trying to keep him in sight. He'd made it to the Julia Tuttle Causeway heading for Miami Beach when the car trouble started. He swung the Spyder over to the shoulder. Cars blew past at eighty; no one stops here and no one intends to who doesn't have car trouble. People have cell phones, however, so I had to be quick.

I pulled onto the shoulder right behind him.

"Hey, can I help?" That's me, the Good Samaritan.

He eyed me and decided I was a harmless tourist. I was even wearing a shirt with parrots on it.

"Naw, I'm good," he said. "I'll call a tow. Fuckin' car's worth a hundred grand and it craps out on me."

I suppose I should have pitied him. Instead, I hunkered down by the exhaust pipes and said, "Hey, friend, here's your problem. Look."

He squatted right next to me so close his cologne stung my eyes and peered into the pipes at the lumpy black mass in one. Then the other. I stood up to make room for him.

"What the fu—"

He never finished his curse because I took him across the back of the head with my stainless-steel baton. He rocked on his heels for a long second and then pitched forward with his forehead touching the license plate.

Remember what I said about the forces of darkness abetting evil? I used one knee to keep him balanced like that until a break in the traffic allowed me to lug him under the arms to my trunk. It was a dead lift to get enough of his mass over the lip of the trunk to enable me to shove the rest inside and slam the lid. All in all, it took fewer than twenty seconds. It took me five full minutes gasping for air and sweating profusely in the driver's seat before I could control my muscles to haul ass out of there.

I told you I've been to Florida before. I know places where people go who don't like to be found and places no tourist brochure will list.

After I put nylon cuffs on his ankles and wrists, I drove Max's friend to one of those places. There's a fisherman's bar not more than half a mile from where I took him down by the docks. The water's filthy down here. Oil slick collects around the pilings and sewage, dead things in the water, bleached of all color, white as a fish's belly. Plastic water bottles bob in the water. I suspect someday they'll make it all the way to the South Pacific Garbage Patch.

There's a row of abandoned and desiccated cabins rotting under the Miami sun down here. The fading graffiti on the walls inside is the usual mindless swill of young minds disturbed by a violent pop culture.

I popped the trunk and looked at Max's friend. He seemed to recognize me. The size of his eyeballs suggested it anyway. I threw a hasty gag around his mouth although there was no one to hear him, but I couldn't take the chance on a squatter lurking somewhere in the tall scrub hearing. I told him I'd help him get out of the trunk, that I just wanted to talk to him, ask a few questions and then I'd let him go. If he complied, he'd be OK, not counting what must be a mild concussion banging away in his head. I showed him the baton flexed to its full length. I said if he tried anything stupid, I would hit him again. His eyes pleaded for mercy.

Keeping the baton held high above him, I slit his ankle ties with my knife and helped him out and kept a firm grip on his triceps. I led him toward the closest cabin, which still had a roof but the door was long gone.

I pushed him inside and told him to sit on his ankles.

I ripped the gag from his mouth.

"Listen to me, man, I don't know who the fuck you are or what you want but—"

My baton caught him on the side of the jaw and left a crimson welt about seven inches long.

When he snapped to again, refocused his eyes on me, he didn't whimper or plead or curse—none of those things they do on TV. That told me, along with the iron in his upper arms, he was tough and able to take care of himself.

"I talked to Janessa Søndergaard," I said. "I know what you and Max planned to do to her."

That was a lie. When I called the hospital enquiring of her, fobbing myself off as a relative, I was told to hold the line, which told me the cops wanted to speak to me. I clicked off. I made a couple discreet enquiries about her later and got her name but that was it. She was gone like smoke and there was nothing I could do about finding her without disrupting the plan.

"W-who?"

"Don't play dumb, moron, or you'll get the baton again. How many girls do you keep drugged on ice in motels?"

"That was Max's idea, man! He said we could put her on the street. Make money off her. Max, like, does this whenever he's gotta get the monkey off his back."

"You need the money that bad, do you?"

"N-no, man. I make good money! I'm a booking agent for some of the biggest DJs in the country. Listen, man. I'll give you ten thousand to cut me loose right now! No cops, no nothing."

"Keep your money. Tell me one thing and I'll let you go."

"Anything, man! Anything! Just name it!"

"I can't do the potato trick twice, so how do I get Max to come to me? Somewhere he won't be suspicious of. Think about it for a couple seconds and don't talk."

I smacked the meat end of the baton against the table—*Crack! Crack! Crack!*—to help keep his mind focused.

"You meet him in Dewey's Bar in West Miami," he said. "He makes his drug connect there."

I heard no deception in his voice. I heard the voice of someone selling out his crimey.

"OK, Dewey's Bar, West Miami. What day and time?"

"Thursday or Friday, around three. He buys from the bartender on duty then, a guy named Jimmy."

"What does Jimmy deal?"

"Everything, man. You fuckin' name it, he sells it."

"Last question," I said. "What's your name?"

"My name's Derek. Derek Parr."

That relaxed him. You wouldn't ask a man his name if you intended to harm him, right?

"Now, man. Let me go. I did what you said. I won't call no cops either, man. We're square."

"Derek, I lied."

* * *

Derek never mentioned Dewey's was a bar for rough gay trade. I didn't panic. I saw a few middle-aged types in there. Some were dressed as if they'd just left their high rises after sealing a good deal for themselves or their companies. I overheard a conversation at the bar that suggested the two guys talking were forex traders discussing how the US dollar was holding up against the deutschmark in an arbitrage. Shop talk in your average leather bar.

Max came in wearing expensive shades on his handsome face. He looked around, greeted a few people, and headed for the bar where Jimmy was on duty, having just replaced a girl with pink hair.

Jimmy put one hand over Max's and slid his drink toward him at the same time. It was a slick move and I had seen him do that to other customers at least five times before Max walked into the place. Max took a big sip of his mixed drink and walked over to a small crowd of men at the end of the bar. I got up and left.

I went to my Civic and waited. It wouldn't take all night unlike the time Max and his chum went clubbing. Alcohol takes time. GHB, the date rape drug, works a lot faster.

A half hour later, I saw Max stagger out of the bar. He went around to the back where the cars were parked in a lot surrounded by a cyclone fence. I watched him clutch the links of the chain fence and double over. A spume of yellow vomit ejected from his mouth. He stood up and wiped his mouth. I watched him head to his car—the orange Challenger.

He drove out of the lot and zigzagged between lanes going east on Highway 41. He made it past the Orange Bowl Stadium before he had to pull over.

I pulled up behind him and walked very casually over to the driver's side window. I rapped on the glass. His head jerked up; he had a wild look in his eyes.

"Hey, man," I said. "I saw you weaving back there. Are you OK? Is there anything I can do?"

Mister Good Samaritan at work again.

"Fuck off, shithead," he said. "Mind your own fucking business."

He was slurring his words badly. Jimmy the bartender charged me five hundred to drop the right amount into his favorite drink, a sloe gin fizz, a ladies' drink that, I imagined, he'd used in his predatory nights looking for women to seduce or turn out like Janessa Rose Søndergaard. Part of me was glad she'd booked because it forced my hand in the direction I was already going.

"In a few minutes," I said, "you're going to pass out, Max. Is there anything you'd like me to tell Kara's parents in Ohio?"

"F-f-fuh—fuck . . . you, ash—asshole. F-fuuuck them too—"

I had the baton at the ready, cupped in the palm of my hand with the shaft tight against my forearm. But I didn't need it. I watched his lights go out.

Decision time: Civic or Challenger?

I left my Honda parked against the curb and opened the Challenger's door. Max's head lolled toward me but I shoved him back against the seat and then climbed in. I pushed his heavy body over to the passenger side and tried to get him down out of sight, but I couldn't manage with the strength of one arm. I took off even burning a little rubber.

I made a few wrong turns until I got to familiar territory. Max never made any sounds or movements except for the *shushing* intake of breath now and then like the sound of a broken pipe.

The Challenger followed the dirt track much better than my sorry little Honda so I pulled right up to the desolate cabin where I'd brought his partner in crime.

Taking my time lugging him out and getting him arranged inside, I had my tools already stored inside the place.

I'd resupplied my kit of surveillance food but with the difference I had brought along a Styrofoam container packed with dry ice and stocked with bottled water and cans of soda pop for the sugar high I might need. GBH sometimes lasted a full day and more if the drugged person couldn't shake off the effects of memory loss and nausea. Max was a big boy, well-muscled, so I hoped for sooner rather than later.

Waiting is part of the job. Patience, discipline. Once upon a time I believed in those traits for good ends.

He came to eighteen hours, thirty-four minutes, and sixteen seconds later. I timed him for no other reason than having something to do during the interim of watching the sky change colors while a canopy of stars replaced our daylight sun with its optimism with their own kind of cold, indifferent beauty.

The sunrise that day was gorgeous: big streaks of crimson and golden light washing over the harbor. The stench of diesel fuel was taken down a notch by a gentle sea breeze. It was a day you could feel good to be alive. Max stirred, began to shake off the effects. Lots of old timers in nursing homes and hospitals die at dawn because the body's circadian rhythm can't put up the fight even one more day. Her slender dancer's body had taken a lot of drugs to bring down to the level where she finally died. A slow death interrupted by mad blitzes of highs that passed and left her craving the drugs that were killing her. It took a cold heart to watch that suffering, yet Max had done that.

Gurgling sounds, then a coughing noise like a generator that won't catch. He opened his eyes, bucked in his ropes, and then started to gag. I rolled him over to prevent him from choking to death on his own vomit.

"Recognize me, Max?"

"N-no . . . yes," he finally said.

"Take your time, old son," I said. "I want you to recover your strength a little."

I helped him drink some water, although much of it was slopped down his chest. He looked at me with gratitude. I lay his head back and told him to rest some more.

Moving one of the chairs over to a window, I could watch the daylight grow until the pale lemony light turned into another beautiful fucking day in paradise.

An hour passed. I turned to look at Max still in the prone position I had placed him.

"Are we all set?" I then proceeded to the next phase of my plan.

* * *

You never get used to it despite the number of times you bring news like that to parents always hopeful of a good outcome. I said the usual things to Mister and Mrs. Levesque, told them I would have more information from my contact in Florida in a week or so. I asked them to be patient. I left them in the doorway holding each other and sobbing.

Detective Navarro came through for me. He sent me copies of what I had asked him for. I would redact some of it, change some cold clinical words here and there—try to soften the blow as best I could about their daughter's last days and the cause of her death.

At the bottom of the packet Navarro included something I didn't ask him for. It was a back-page item from the *Miami Herald*. I am including it here. Navarro is a cop's cop. He doesn't like people playing dirty games in his backyard. Those were his exact words to me in our phone conversation when I asked him to send me what he could for the parents' sake. I was lucky there, too. Navarro has two young girls.

Courage and audacity, René Levesque once said about the need to act. Those words mean something to individuals as well as nations. I don't want to be a man afraid of life.

BODIES FOUND BURNED IN CABIN

Miami Fire Rescue crews responded to a burning cabin on the waterfront opposite 400 S. Biscayne Blvd Thursday night. Crews found two bodies inside the abandoned cabin, neither yet identified. Cause of death is unknown as the bodies were charred beyond recognition. Arson investigator Jody Lewis said an accelerant had been used to obliterate facial features and fingerprints of the victims. Both are believed to be males between the ages of 18 and 34. Miami-Dade police are asking anyone with information to call their anonymous tip line number: 305-TIPP.

Someone named J. T. Nunez signed the piece with a *Miami Herald* email address and a phone number to call.

The End

Fight Your Way Out of This One
By Robb White

Sean Roby reminded me of a weasel. One of those South American weasels that like to jump on the back of a parrot and ride it as it flies through the jungle. It's like those cat videos people love on *YouTube* except that the weasel isn't joyriding; he's waiting for the exhausted bird to drop to the floor so he can rip into it.

Sean was a former client of mine. I'd handled a few unpleasant tasks for him in the past and he'd quibble about the bill every time. He'd go through each item in front of me while I waited for the astonished look to subside and then patiently explain why I had inserted such-and-such in the final tally. I don't recall any bill over two hundred dollars for any of the jobs he hired me for, but his fretting every nickel and dime made it seem that I had just penned the most unjust bill since the Removal Act of 1830 that kicked Native Americans off their land. Sean could give seminars in goosing billable hours. Roby, by the way, was a lawyer if I haven't made that clear. He was in fact the town's leading defense attorney and the go-to guy if you were caught with a meth lab in your garage. As a trial lawyer, he was masterful—a preening banty rooster with a bad dye job in a courtroom.

But Sean had his own legal problems, too. Most recently, he was caught mixing funds with an estate he was probating and the state's ethics board summoned him for a hearing in Columbus.

I bumped into him at Tico's Place the evening he returned. You'd think it was Caesar returning to Rome after the Gallic Wars. He told everyone in the place how he handled himself against those "chumps"; Sean called them white-shoe lawyers who'd never been in a courtroom fight in their entire careers. "You have to have big balls like mine to

223

win in that arena and I know how to win," he bragged. He also knew how to womanize and he wasn't very discreet about it. Of course, our resort town is small and gets a lot smaller when the summer tourists go away. More than one of my jobs as a private investigator involved smoothing over messy domestic situations because of his sleazy adulterous liaisons.

When he showed up in my tiny office on the Strip one hot morning in early August, I wondered which unhappy husband had to be appeased. Secretly, I was hoping it would involve some out-of-state travel because I was going through one of those slumps where nothing much interested me, and I have often found a temporary cure for depression in driving for long stretches on the open highway with no real destination in mind. After Micah left me, I drove all the way to Maine and back with an occasional stop for a piss and a bottled water.

"Christ, Haftmann," he said, before the door had shut behind him; "crack open your checkbook and get a new air-conditioner in here."

"Hello, Sean," I said. "Trouble at the Motel Six?"

"Ha, ha, I'm about to roll on the floor laughing."

"I don't recommend it," I said and pointed at the aged carpet that came with the office when I set up in the private-eye business more than ten years ago. "It's the maid's day off."

"I can see. Maid's decade off you mean."

He paused to collect himself, as it was his habit to do that even when he was tossing them back in bars late at night. I could see him preparing to fix the jury with one of those patented looks in behalf of his long-suffering client.

"I've got a small job for you, Tom. It's not much of a thing so don't go crazy with your line items the way you usually do . . ."

That was how it started. How it ended still has me bolting upright in bed on sleepless nights.

Roby had a promising "business opportunity in Cleveland," he said. The offer had come from a "source" high up "in certain prominent government circles," but the chance to get in on it was going to expire by the end of the month.

"I've got to decide fast if I want in," Roby told me.

"Who's your source—or is it partner?" I asked.

"Somebody who prefers to remain anonymous. My silent partner," Roby said. "But I'll be handling the day-to-day activities and making all the decisions."

"What's the investment?" I asked. "Something that's going to expire by the end of this month sounds more like baked goods than venture capital."

"Haftmann, don't worry about it," he said. "It's over your head."

Since most things nowadays seemed to be out of my depth, I shrugged. "Better not be illegal, Roby," I said.

He looked offended—if a lawyer can look offended.

"Don't worry about it. Just get me the information I'm asking for and your job is done."

Cleveland's fifty miles west of us on Interstate 90. I had spent most of my career as a homicide cop there. But that was a long time ago. Not the travel I had in mind but it would have to do. Roby stopped by that afternoon and dropped off his list. He watched me look it over.

It was just a computer printout of all the major downtown hotels.

"What's this?" I asked.

"I want you to get me a list of all the guests who've booked those hotels for the last two weeks of this month. I don't care how you get it but I need it by next Thursday, latest. You're on the clock for this one, Thomas. Work fast. I don't care how you get it but get me all the names."

"I'll need some up-front money," I said.

"What for?"

"I'll need the money," I said, "because hotel staff will need to be pieced off. I'll have to find the right contact at each place. Or do you think I can just go up to the manager and say, 'I want a list of all the Presidential candidates, their staffers, the delegates, every big shot Republican in town, and every lobbyist trailing them like hounds, if you please and right now because my client Mister Roby is in a hurry.'"

"How—how did you know?"

"I was born, Sean. I just wasn't born yesterday."

Even the dumbest crackhead, stoner, and biker-gang trash in our tiny resort town knew that Cleveland was the site of the Republican National Convention during the last week of August.

"Look," I said. "I don't need to know why you want the names. I'll get you the names and what you do with them is your business."

I sometimes must appease my clients with a little Pontius Pilate routine like that. But if I had known what Sean and his silent partner intended, I would have gone whole hog on the Pontius Pilate routine and washed my hands of the sordid mess he was bringing me.

But that's hindsight and right then, all I knew for sure was that my money was tight, the clients few, and my to-do list was reduced to deferring the bigger bills flooding in through my mail slot and waiting for Tico's bar to open. My instincts at the moment were telling me that, behind Sean's outwardly calm demeanor, was a man about to take the biggest leap of his life while clutching me by the pant leg.

I've bribed hotel staff before. Busboys are my preferred choice but they wouldn't help with a guest list—especially if some of those guests were household names and came connected to the most powerful families in the country. I had some sense of the urgency of Sean's need when he ceased bickering over the goodwill cash I had asked for. That was just a knee-jerk reaction. He wrote me a check for five hundred, scratched it out, and rewrote one for seven hundred on the spot.

"The bank charges you seventy-five cents for a voided check nowadays," I said, just to lighten the mood.

"Don't worry about it. I'll take it off your bill," he said.

I admit I was curious. On the ride to Cleveland that evening, I tossed around in my mind what the purpose of such a list could mean. Because my mind tends toward the nefarious in life and in people, I assumed Roby had some Ponzi scheme, some big deal he wanted to get backing for and these were the kind of people who could make things happen as well as write big checks. I didn't give much thought to it after that. I had to worry about time and the means of obtaining a list of names for the hotels. Roby also suggested a bonus if I could get him some of the biggest names staying at luxury hotels.

When I suggested he find a hacker to get into the hotels' databases, he dismissed it with a wave of his hand. "Hackers are blackmailers without balls. You I can trust."

I'd had a job like this before. It involved discovering some celebrities and their prescription medicines. One pharmacy tech, well bribed, at a local drug store, gave me everything I asked her for and she did it all through her workstation computer.

Before I left JOTL, our acronym for Jefferson-on-the-Lake, I called a *Plain Dealer* reporter I kept as my own personal stringer. He was an unpaid intern, just like all the ones before him, and I asked him to keep his ear out for any names who might be staying in town. The top journalists would get assigned to handle the party nominee and track his whereabouts and movements between the conference center and the hotel at all times; that was public knowledge.

This job was going to involve some shoe leather and some drinking in the hotel bars and local taverns. Bartenders, bar flies, disgruntled staff, and cops are people I know well. I'd scout the right places and see what scuttlebutt I could pick up and then I'd zero in on the people with access to this kind of info. Every hotel would prep its staff about which delegates were coming and who among them had to be given special attention. People talk. It's what we do.

By Wednesday of my deadline, I had a lengthy list of names of delegates staying in Cleveland's hotels. There were some who booked the cheaper franchise hotels along Interstate 27, a good twenty minutes from downtown. I'd made a few calls to some of the chains and the smaller places to see if I could get a nibble. I passed myself off as a reporter. At small cost, I located a couple dozen names that way of people in town for the convention who seemed to want to stay out of the limelight or who had failed to reserve at the pricier hotels in time.

I was feeling good about the names accumulating on my list. Only a couple names meant anything to me because they were big media people from New York's major networks. All the CNN staff were staying in one place, but for the most part, one delegate's name was no different from another's. Roby wanted the big people, I knew, the insiders close to the power brokers in the party, so I kept at it through one more night of drinking at bars where people hang out after work and kept my ears open. I bought rounds of Mojito's for groups of professional men and women, the advance teams for the news outlets and the politicians, mixing at the trendy bars in the Flats and the Warehouse District. Blitzed and barely able to see well enough to write down what I overheard, I managed to fatten my list with some names of real big shots heading to Cleveland in the next few days. Two of the women I met were part of an advance team for a candidate who had missed the brass ring but whose name was rumored to be Vice President material.

When Sean came to see me at four o'clock in the afternoon the next day as promised, I was still hung over.

"You look like shit, Haftmann. I hope you did more in Cleveland than drink yourself blind on my money."

I handed him the names I'd printed out for him.

"The disk, too," Roby said. "That was part of the deal, remember?"

"What if I made a back-up?"

"You watch too many crime shows, flatfoot," he quipped. He used the corner of my desk to write out a check for my services.

He stopped just before adding his signature and picked up the bill again to scrutinize it for padding.

"Roby, damn it, my head is pounding like a bongo. Just give me the damn check and get out. I need to sleep."

"Hair of the dog, Tommy," he said. He handed me the check—without the promised bonus.

I knew some of those names had tripped a response, but he kept his reaction cool.

I looked out my picture window at the neon sign of Tico's Place blinking its orange and green message to my neocortex.

Why not? Roby's check was big if not generous and I could pay some bills. I deserved a treat, I told myself.

The treat turned into an all-nighter; the all-nighter turned into a two-day bender. The little progress I had made in the last couple of months as a controlled alcoholic, which is what I call myself, crumbled around my ankles like a child's finger-drip sandcastle.

I remember watching the convention on various television sets in various bars on the Strip, although I do not follow politics. I remember a few bar stool conversations with other patrons about what it would mean but overall, I didn't care. Those names on the list I had given Sean Roby a couple weeks back were lost in the booze fog. I couldn't name ten to save my life.

The detectives who came into my office on Friday in early September weren't young; in fact, I was surprised to see Pete Moisio at all. He was a lieutenant and he ran a good team of men and women out of the sheriff's department in Jefferson City. If he was lead detective, it had to be important.

He handed me a file folder containing some eight-by-tens of a body that was burned beyond recognition. The corpse was in the familiar fighter's pose of muscles contracted under enormous heat. The body could have been a man's or a woman's. It was inside the trunk of a car.

"Charcoal in the lungs," Pete said. "They cooked him alive."

"Nasty," I said. "Who is—was he?"

"You know him," the younger detective said, Pete had introduced him to me but I didn't recall his name. I'd closed a different bar last night after Marta—she's Tico's wife—kicked me out. That corpse's brain was fried instantly in its skull like a chunk of stew meat in a boiling ragout. My own brain was getting the crock pot treatment— a little cooking over a longer time.

"Sean Roby," Pete said.

"You did some work for him in Cleveland a couple weeks back," the young cop said.

"That's right," I said.

Client confidentiality disappears when the client is found dead. Besides, cops don't like us gumshoes, and in a small town like this, I can't afford to alienate them. I felt bad that my first thoughts weren't for poor Sean's ugly demise but my own paltry livelihood.

"These all your notes?" Pete asked when I showed him my file folder.

"It wasn't much of a job, Pete," I said. "Go to Cleveland, find out where the delegates were staying, come back by Thursday and give Roby the list of names and hotels."

"Any idea what he planned to do with the names?"

"None whatsoever?"

"You didn't even ask him?" The younger cop regarded me as if I had just magically transformed into a balloon-blowing goat.

"No," I said. "I generally don't pry into my clients' personal affairs."

"What do you think he wanted them for?"

"No idea. Some business deal Sean and this silent partner I mentioned had in mind."

"Tom, that doesn't make sense. These names could have been grabbed off the internet in a hundred ways."

"I know," I said. "Roby said he was under some pressure to get the names before the convention. Maybe whatever he had in mind had to happen before everyone flew the coop."

"What's the partner's name?" The young detective asked me. He had his pen and notebook out.

"No idea," I replied. "Sean didn't say—or wouldn't—who the person was."

"OK, then give me a copy of the disk with names," the cop said.

"I gave Sean the only disk," I said.

"For a private eye, you're not very good, are you?"

"Why don't you take a flying fuck at the moon," I replied but without any heat. Sean knew me.

"Easy, easy," Moisio interjected. "Let's behave like adults."

The lieutenant asked me a few more questions and that was it. He told me Sean's body was being flown home for burial. Roby had an ex-wife in town still named executor and she had agreed to take charge.

Moisio described the crime scene as an isolated dirt road in the heart of Wine Country going up a hill next to a vineyard in Napa Valley. The car was a late model Mercedes Benz. Sean had rented a Shelby Mustang the day before in Napa that was later found in a chop shop in Mendocino.

"Funny," I said. "I never took Sean as a wine drinker."

"He travel to California much that you knew?"

"No, actually, I didn't think he traveled at all. He seemed stuck in this place." I almost said *like me*.

"You think of anything about this mystery man Roby was involved with, give me a call," Pete said. He handed me his card. I smiled. I was thinking of the hundreds of cards I had handed out over the course of my career in homicide with the same words and the same meager expectation of results.

"What's so fuckin' funny?" This was from the younger cop.

"Piss off, Junior," I said.

Moisio just shook his head in dismay at my losing my cool so easily and led his younger partner out of my office.

I felt bad I didn't feel worse about Sean Roby's awful death. I felt bad I had lost my cool with that cop. I felt bad that I needed a drink to stop feeling bad.

About a week after that, I started getting hang-up calls late at night after I'd left the office. I set my phone recorder to ten rings to keep the telemarketers and bill collectors at bay; they'll quit at six or seven. But this was odd because the caller would hang up after my recorded message began.

Then one night I was staying late—I had just finished doing the bill for my last client—but I was delaying my urge to cross the street to Tico's owing to some vague feeling tickling the hairs on my neck. For days, I was moping along the strip, hitting different bars along the Strip, walking around like a cartoon character in a comic strip with a black cloud over his head. Roby's death made a big splash in the local papers but since then, nothing, no follow up. I called Pete several times but Roby's death wasn't his problem and he had not talked to a detective out there in weeks. He had nothing new to tell me. I called Roby's ex and she was even less cooperative. Their divorce was less than amicable, and I knew Sean had come out the winner in the settlement because he'd crowed many times over drinks about "skinning" her lawyer.

The Republican convention over, Cleveland was still basking in its success as host city. Millions of dollars from the convention had poured into the city's coffers and the mayor could finally relax knowing that his trigger-happy police force hadn't tripped off another street protest by emptying their guns into some fleeing crackhead's windshield.

This time the caller left a brief message. It was a woman's voice and she sounded drunk or high. There's a nasal twang that some women get when they've exceeded their limit. Hanging around bars will fine-tune your ear for things like that.

I called the number she left and asked if I could help her.

"You work for Sean Roby," she said.

"Not exactly," I replied. "I worked a few cases for him a few times. What is it you wish to talk about?"

"My name's Cecelia Bowers. I go by Ce-Ce. Sean ever tell you about me?'

The nasally twang was gone but it was replaced by a shrillness she was holding back.

"No, Sean never mentioned a Ce-Ce or a Cecelia to me."

"You sure?"

"Yes. Now what can I do for you, Ms. Bowers?"

"He never talked about—about our Cleveland job?"

"What? No, what Cleveland job are you referring to?"

Remember those cheap cardboard games where you jiggle tiny metal balls so that they fall into slots? The balls were dropping into the slots in my brain, and I was sure I was talking to Sean Roby's silent partner and the Cleveland job she was referring to was the reason Sean had left this earth so abruptly in his burning metal coffin out in California.

"Maybe you should come into my office where we can talk about this," I said.

"No—no—no! Absolutely not. You don't understand. They're watching me. They're following me. I can't leave this place."

Made-to-order TV crime show dialogue, I thought, but her fear sounded genuine.

"Then I'll come to you," I said.

"No—no. This was a mistake—I shouldn't have called."

"Wait! Don't hang up. Tell me where we can meet. Pick a place, somewhere safe. Out in the public."

She gave me the name of a bar in the Flats and a time. I knew the place, had even done surveillance there a couple times when I was Cleveland PD. It was not my kind of bar—a trendy, college-grad, electronic-dance place with crisscrossing laser lights and expensive mixed drinks with obscene names.

I told her I'd be at the bar right at that time.

"How will I know you?"

"My clothes will give me away and I'll be at least twenty-five years older than everyone else around me," I said.

Cecelia Bowers approached me with a drink in her hand and a nervous smile. She was a pretty, brown-eyed twenty-five-year-old with a nervous smile. She wore skinny jeans and black sandals. Her sheer top had dangling stings that tied around the biceps. Lots of other women there wore the same kind of see-through blouse without the blocking white undergarment and showed far more cleavage. It was a typical Cleveland watering hole for young professionals. It was noisy for a mid-week evening, but as I said, it wasn't my kind of bar.

She led me to a small booth against a wall but there was nowhere to escape the thudding voiceless song coming through the speakers. Every so often the synthesized sounds would change and go off in a new direction. It was the musical equivalent of hysteria.

"I was the one who approached Sean," she said. "He worked a case for me two years ago when I came to that resort. I got drunk with some friends. I had a one-nighter but the guy didn't want to believe it was just that. I called a law office here but they suggested I call a lawyer there because the guy was local and so I got Sean's number. He handled it and the guy stopped harassing me."

I was surprised Roby would waste time on something like that. It was something he'd normally dump off on a guy like me. I had a feeling it was Ms. Bowers' personal attractiveness that made the difference.

"We—I had this idea from a friend of mine who had a gay friend visiting her. We all went out for drinks. He was a staffer for a Congressman who liked to swing with married couples. That night he got wasted and told us all about his Congressman's adventures and how he was such a hypocrite. You know, spouting family values and all that."

"I understand. What was your idea?"

"Sean, well—Sean seemed like the right kind of guy to talk to about something like this. You see, we were just dating for a while, and I got to know him a little bit. I hadn't heard from him in a while when he called me out of the blue one night. I guess it was around the time of his divorce, maybe six months ago, and we started talking, you know. Just exploring ideas, ways to make some money. Not being all that serious."

You have to let them get to it in this business. I continued to smile and sip my lousy, watered-down, very expensive drink and smile gently at her. She'd say it sooner or later and after about three more drinks, I had it. Maybe not all of it but the essence of the scheme she and Sean had cooked up one night out of happy bar talk.

The Congressman's staffer had proof of his boss' infidelity because he's made a copy of a printout the Congressman kept in a safe in his office. It was an online profile in which the Congressman had advertised himself as "attached male seeking couples." It turned out that an anonymous hacker had threatened some very prominent people with disclosure of their illicit sexual activities on this cheaters' website if they didn't pressure the parent company into abandoning its "full delete" fee for cleaning out the user's profile—including sexual preferences. The fee was a whopping twenty dollars, but apparently, this geek was so teed off by it that he threatened to expose the site's entire database for the world to see. All thirty-seven million names, their real names, and identities. Exposed as cheaters, to their wives or husbands, colleagues, to the public. It would be an endless tabloid nightmare for some and create some overtime work for the comedy writers of late-night TV. Careers would be trashed in an instant. It was dynamite in the form of blackmail. To say that there had to be, statistically speaking, some very well-known names involved in that number was an understatement of the decade.

Now factor in Cleveland, the Republican Party Convention and for one week in one city packed in a few blocks you had—statistics again here—the very likely possibility that some of those website cheaters were in town and they would not want their masks as the respectable, God-fearing elite of society to be exposed as adulterers, cheaters, and sexual perverts. Try looking a voter in the eye after you've been pegged as a BDSM *domme* or bondage freak.

"How did Sean hack the website? He's a lawyer."

"He didn't. The fact that it was hacked and all over the news was all we needed. Everybody was talking about it. I was going to make contacts with as many of the convention-goers as we could manage in a week. Sean was going to make the pitch we had that person's sexual information and we would delete it for a 'small fee.'"

I said: "I assume more than the full-delete fee the website was asking for?"

"A lot more," she responded. Her brown eyes turned watery with more than drink: the memory of what a colossal, dangerous mistake she and Sean Roby had made, the fear that her life was turned upside-down, and the bitter knowledge it would never be possible for her to live the same way.

"How did you expect people to believe you?"

"Remember the staffer I told you about? He got so drunk he forgot where he put that copy of the Congressman's printout. My friend had it and she gave it to me."

"Where is she? Did she know what you and Sean were going to do with it?"

"Sean said we should give her a 'finder's fee' for it. Just enough money to implicate her so she couldn't claim to be innocent of it."

"How did that work out?"

"They found Beth dead in a swimming pool in Camina del Mar two weeks ago. She drowned. She had enough heroin in her to kill three people."

"I'm sorry," I said.

"Beth wasn't a user. Hell, I never saw her drink more than three wine coolers at a time," Cecelia said.

I knew Sean was a salesman; his whole life in a courtroom was selling juries on the stories he wanted them to believe. Sean, like most good trial lawyers, didn't give a tinker's damn about the truth. Courtrooms are about lawyers, not truth, and Sean always thought he could talk the birds out of the trees.

"How much did you get?"

She stared at me.

"Look," I said, "give me a dollar. That means you're retaining me. That makes you my client and that means you have complete confidentiality. I can never betray you."

"Betray," she said. She almost whispered the word as if it were a foreign term with exotic connotations. She dug into her purse and came out with a five. "I don't have any ones," she said.

"That's fine," I said. "I'll write you a receipt when I get back to me office and establish you as my client."

She gave me the rest of the story despite my repeated requests for her to clarify something or repeat something she had said. The music was making it hard to hear, but I didn't want to relocate; you change venue, you can change mood, and she was already talking in a monotone despite the high-energy, frenetic techno beat.

By the end of the week they had made over a hundred thousand dollars from at least a dozen people, not all men. Sean had set up a shell company and the checks they wrote on the spot in their hotel rooms or downstairs in a swanky bar with mood lighting. They used aliases and slight make-up to disguise their looks. Cecelia had urged Sean to wear a hat to hide the hideous orange hair he favored. She'd be waiting in a car in the parking lot in case he had to bolt, which happened a couple of times, she said. One dignified-looking bald man in a dark suit, a TV pundit who had directed a major presidential campaign told Roby to go "eff himself" and went looking for hotel security. I was really pissed at Sean because we had several good prospects at that hotel but we couldn't risk going back.

They were going for volume over "quality," Sean told her, but she wanted one more score—a big one. Here, she paused and looked at me as if I were her confessor.

"Who was it?" I asked. "Who did you two decide to tag for the grand finale?" I was trying to keep her mood from sinking but it came out mockery.

She told me.

"Holy Je-sus Christ," I said. "You're shitting me."

"No, I'm not shitting you," she said. "I accidentally encountered him in a hallway at the hotel. I was just leaving. I had a check in my purse for ten thousand and I guess I was feeling too confident. He didn't have any bodyguards with him. He said he was looking for an ice machine. I could tell he'd already had a few by then. You could have lit his breath on fire."

I was still astounded and barely taking in her words. You get jaundiced as a cop. That goes without saying. You see the worst in people. My second career was hardly better. People either wanted me to take something away from somebody or help them keep somebody from taking something from them. Dante and the Seven Deadly Sins all the time.

"I let him think our meeting was no accident. I showed him the Congressman's printout. That was something Sean said we should do every time to establish trust. We could never pass ourselves off as computer experts. By then, I had the spiel down pat. I was ticked at Sean for hogging all the glory. I was just his secretary, according to him, and he always let me know he was the one doing the heavy lifting and taking the big chances."

"How did he react—your, your mark?" I couldn't even bring myself to say the name aloud.

"He rocked back on his heels a bit. He couldn't believe that it was all coming undone. He was having the greatest political week of his entire life and here I was with a pin in my hand about to burst his balloon."

"I have to ask. Did he pay you and Sean?"

"We were asking three hundred thousand. He said he'd pay. I wouldn't go back into his room, though, not with his entourage and bodyguards in there. I said to call me the next day and we'd meet for the delivery."

"I couldn't believe how lucky I was," she said.

I could see in her eyes she was drunk. That sober-drunk when the knowledge you're carrying won't permit the alcohol to do its work.

"When I got back to our motel to meet Sean, I told him. I'll never forget the look on his face."

"You mean because you'd pulled in the big fish?"

"No, no," she said and shook her head from one side to the other. "No, not envy. Not the look I expected. He was terrified. His face went blank and he said nothing for the longest time. Then he walked away from me and looked out the window."

Sean Roby speechless was hard to imagine. "What did he say, finally?"

She looked at me and her eyes no longer glittered like a drunkard's eyes. "He said, 'You've just killed us.'"

I drove back to her place with her. She claimed her condo was broken into, things slightly misplaced. She was sure her phone was tapped. I waited for her to gather a few things and I drove her to a motel twenty miles from my office. I'd used the place before and trusted the managers, a husband and wife from Madras.

I called her at eight the next morning and said I'd pick her up in an hour.

When I pulled up to the motel, Garjan and his wife Aadita met me in the lobby and handed me a note from Cecelia. It said she had "a change of heart" and was leaving town. It was signed Ce-Ce Bowers and had a five-dollar bill paper-clipped to it.

When I asked Garjan a few questions to verify the authenticity of her note, his answers were vague. The look on his wife's face, however, spoke volumes: she was terrified.

I left them and returned to my office. I had a feeling that things were spinning out of control and the condition of my office confirmed it. The room wasn't tossed; it was ransacked and everything in it was strewn around the floor. My olive-green file cabinet—a heavy steel bastard—was busted up and all the files were tossed around the floor. They'd even found my brand-new directional mic still in its package and smashed it. My big picture window with Thomas Haftmann, Private Investigations in Baskerville Old Face was crisscrossed with x's and o's in Day-Glo orange.

I called Moisio and told him everything and Cecelia Bowers and Roby's blackmail scheme. I told him I found my office vandalized.

"You think it's kids?"

"No, do you?"

"There've been some break-ins along the Strip lately. One of our CIs said some meth heads staying at the cabins on Erieview are responsible. It could be them."

"C'mon, Pete."

A coincidence stinks like a Chinese egg in a cop's nostrils. I didn't know what to think. Somebody knew how to act fast to put me in check like this. I spent hours cleaning up my office and walked across the street for a liquid supper. Cecelia was using a burner phone when we met and her cell phone number was no longer in service. I left Tico's with an hour of drinking time still on the clock, but I wanted to wake up sober and use a contact in the US Attorney's Office for the Northern District of Ohio. That was the plan anyhow.

I had my hand on the door when the first punch hooked into my liver. I remember dropping to my knees to the gravel and feeling as if a whole toilet tank of nausea had been dumped into my bloodstream. There were more punches and kicks from two men after that but when your conscious brain is trying to escape the body's punishment, it makes the counting difficult.

What mattered was the message and the message was clear: *leave it alone.*

The painkillers handled the worst of it, but I couldn't go out in public with my face looking like a slit-faced bat. I stayed home on my couch and brooded. Would they kill me next time? I suppose that was the biggest, most unanswerable question I posed to my ugly face in the mirror. Gradually the eggplant bruising subsided. I hesitated about making the call. Had they gone that high up to quash three murders? The only reason I wasn't a fourth was that two dead men from the same small town might have sparked some interest in one of the big papers.

I admit I'm not a man of much courage. I became paranoid and started to see strangers lurking in shadows everywhere I went. I haven't rubbed shoulders with the rich in my life, but I know how they work: they'll get three or four people above you and you'll never know what hit you when it all comes crashing down around your ears. In case I was slow on the uptake, I found myself in front of an ethics board about a year after Sean's body was discovered in its burned-out Benz.

The complaint was a phony. A guy had hired me to follow his wife and she claimed sexual harassment. The husband turned out to be a fake and the woman was induced to report me. My license was suspended for six months in Ohio. It wasn't revoked by a single vote, and after the hearing that one vote in my favor told me "I had a friend who was looking out for me."

Another not-so-oblique message to keep my nose clean. If this were a movie, I'd say, "To hell with my license" and go get the bad guys and the film would end with me, battered, and bruised but triumphant, just before the credits rolled and the final jaunty track of the musical score began. However, this was my life, my only means of support, and I had nowhere else to go. It's a bitter drink going down your gullet that reminds you that you traded all your heroic dreams for security.

I see him on TV all the time. The gods do like their little jokes. He's always smiling and waving to the crowds of his adoring public. I must have been really drunk that one night when he came on the news because I swear he was winking right through the camera lens to me on my bar stool.

Somebody mailed an anonymous letter to me about three weeks after that. Not a letter. Just an envelope. Inside it was just a newspaper clipping. It said hikers had found plastic garbage bags in the Mojave Desert. The bags contained bones of woman's skeleton. Forensics put the woman's age at between 20 and 30. The teeth were missing from the skull. The police were searching through all missing person reports. Many women that age disappear in California every year, the reporter wrote. The police spokesperson concluded the piece by saying she was not "hopeful" the crime would be solved unless new leads came.

The sender underscored the last sentence of the article in red.

The End

Tom Breneman's Restaurant Is No More
By Robb White

Fifteen years a cop, five as murder police, had shown me every variation on human wickedness short of some Aztec torture trick or cooking someone alive in the brazen bull of ancient Greece.

I gave all that up when a bullet put me on disabled duty behind a desk. I bounced around a bit after that—a couple years in Youngstown as a private eye before transferring my act to this tiny resort town in Northern Ohio at a place called Jefferson-on-the-Lake. I liked cop work, got promoted fast to detective sergeant, not because I was that good, but because my fellow officers would have trouble finding a solar eclipse if they were standing in the path of totality. Lucky for me, my homicide pension carried me through the dry periods. My practice in JOTL, in the shorthand of locals, often ran short of paying clients. But one thing held firm throughout my address changes: I never left human vice very far behind.

I don't have many gee-whiz electronic devices and spy stuff. Besides a directional mic that I never figured out how to use and left in the closet, I keep few photos in my office. For one thing, it's small and I'm not given to sentimentality, not in my business, which leads all other jobs except my detective career by a long shot when it comes to human depravity.

After my wife divorced me and left town with another lawyer she prosecuted cases with, I had even fewer photos around. But one I do keep one and I'll keep it around to remind me of how things are not what they seem. It's a photo of Tom Breneman's famous Los Angeles restaurant where hoods like Mickey Cohen and his gun thug, handsome Johnny Stompanato, used to hang out. On Sundays, there was a radio program broadcast from there. In the photo, there are hundreds of people, the men in suits and ties, their women in dresses and jewelry—all dressed to the nines, as they used to say in those days. The restaurant's long gone, but the building still exists. The Doors played there in the seventies. The most infamous racketeer of his day, the Mickey Cohen is in there, but I have three candidates for the Mickster's pet thug, Johnny Stomp, because he had the dark good looks of a Hollywood cinema star that men cultivated at that time. There they are: the hoods and flunkeys, politicians, and crooked cops, ordinary, squarejohn citizens rubbing shoulders with famous actors and rich degenerates. People on the edge or looking for an edge. A snapshot of their time and ours, too. The fancy duds and smiles don't fool me.

The photo was a gift for services rendered from a man on death row who was convicted of killing eight prostitutes and dumping their bodies in ravines and lakes. I had to cross all the way from one end of Ohio to the other, down near the Ohio River where the Lucasville pen houses Ohio's most dangerous mend.

I believe if I had asked him about the murders, he'd have told me every detail. I didn't ask. He had the photo taped to his bunk. I asked about it once. He told me his old man gave it to him from a trip out West. He pointed to a man in a black-and-white checkered suit and said that was his old man. To me, the guy looked like Bugsy Siegel but I said nothing.

He wanted to hire me to work a case for him. I carried his letter in my jacket pocket; he wrote in a childish block letter style with a lot of misspellings in it. I've had letters from convicts before. Half the losers in lockup think they can work on your sympathy to do some investigative work on their cases, and over the years, I've had some doozies penned by every kind of criminal from axe murderers through check kiters to little lost girls who said they saw my photo in the papers and I knew at once that I had "a kind face" and would I please take their case so on. The fact is I have the face I deserve and you wouldn't know me on the street. I never write these hustlers back—until John David Poluga wrote to say he wanted me to investigate the disappearance of his brother and an office worker he was presumed (according to the facts of the police investigation) to be having an affair with.

Poluga's brother, for what it's worth, was a professional accountant with an MBA and a six-figure salary. I know. Go figure. I've seen it happen before in families. But Poluga had two things that convinced me: the first was money. He was able to pay. Cons are allowed to keep only so much money in their commissary accounts, but it was through his missing brother's probated estate that he could afford to hire me. Poluga gave me the name of his lawyer in Youngstown and told me he had given instructions to the probate lawyer to draw money in the amount of five thousand dollars. He promised me a bonus if I discovered what happened to his brother when he disappeared seven years earlier. Poluga was unable to touch the money until the court ruled his brother deceased.

"Now," he said to me in the standard lime-green conference room, "if I wasn't in here, they'd have declared him dead four years ago and the trail wouldn't be so cold."

I didn't say it but, four years or seven years, this case wasn't cold; it was in the deep freeze locker where it would most likely remain forever.

I had to ask him although it was nothing to the case: "Why me?"

He looked me in the eye, and I suspected he was cooking up some convict story, but he seemed to decide against it. He was a bull of a man, about 280 pounds. He had small hands. He told me to feel his side where he had a mesh net grafted into his skin after a cancer operation. He was taking all kinds of medication and a doctor had to come in once a month to lance his knees for the swelling. He was strangely calm about all of it, his health problems, and the fact the Grim Reaper was keeping watch from the other side of his tiny cell.

"Article in the paper said you found that runaway, the girl from Youngstown. You took a bullet in the head for your trouble but you got her back, it said."

That second thing I mentioned that drew me to his case was the fact that the girl who disappeared with him was from a loving, middle-class family. I had the case file from my detective pal at the precinct,

Lt. Pete Moisio, who also showed me the clippings from the Youngstown *Vindicator* before it went belly up. The family—sisters, brother both parents—were devastated and their lives went downhill from the day she never returned with her lover from their weekend tryst. The sisters' divorces followed the accidental death, due to intoxication in the brother's case with his motorcycle, and the mother died of cervical cancer within two years. The father wound up losing his job and drowning himself in a bottle and when that wasn't enough to dull the pain, he shut himself up in his garage and duct-taped a tube to the muffler and sucked gas. A whole family wiped out because of a mystery.

By all accounts, the convict's brother was a model citizen. "He was trying to make up for his scumbag brother," Pete told me when he handed me the girl's photo. It was taken somewhere on a beach the year before. You can't call a young woman "pretty" nowadays without all the political correctness harpies coming out of the woodwork to attack you as a sexist pig. I'll risk it by saying she was attractive, not stunningly pretty in a typical way, but striking in her asymmetrical features. A nose too sharp for one thing. High cheekbones, maybe Slavic, but I found it hard to look away from those blue eyes that smiled back at the camera and yet were calmly assessing at the same time. My wife was dark-haired and I always measured other women's beauty against hers. The photo was a head shot only, no body evident, but she was brushing away a lock of her hair while sitting on a granite slab of a breakwall in the bright light of a summer day. I saw white blurry flecks in the background and assumed these were gulls in the distance. Her ash blonde hair was tied back in a ponytail.

I don't know why it struck a chord in me. It was just a photo of an average-pretty girl in a ponytail. I wanted to do one more big case besides the usual skip-trace jobs, the endless telephoning and emailing, the bail jumpers, and all those unhappy husbands and wives who wanted me to peep behind windows at their cheating spouses in sleazy motels.

"Look, Poluga," I told him, "I'm a private eye, not a magician. That's God you're thinking of. I'll do what I can but I make no promises I'll find out what happened to your brother. If I think I'm just milking you like a cash cow, I'll stop and give you my final report."

"Just so you know," he said. "My last appeal was rejected six months ago. It's one more pass at the governor and then I get a date for the needle."

On my way to the parking lot, I said what I was thinking inside: "No great loss to society, Mister Poluga, when you do get the needle." Poluga's brother's girl could just as easily have been one of the photos in the file that had put Poluga on death row. One thing you need to know about us private investigators is that we don't have to like our clients to do our jobs.

Seven years. Seven years for everything to fade or disappear—the memories and the records alike. If you think your life is unforgettable, stick your finger in a bucket of water and pull it out. When those tiny ripples subside in a few seconds, that's your impact on the world.

I called Poluga's probate lawyer and asked if I could meet him in his office tomorrow. He gave me a brief slot in the middle of the afternoon for my interview. I had to start somewhere.

He had the creepiest comb over hair I'd seen on a man in years. It was flattened and slicked over his bald spot like sticky cotton-candy and dyed a Day-Glo orange. But he was a pleasant guy, for a lawyer, and gave me what information about Poluga's brother he had. He confirmed what John David had already told me, but with cons, you can never be sure what their end game is. For all I knew, this was a snipe hunt that served Poluga's whims and nothing more. The lawyer knew nothing about Chloë Randall, the girlfriend, that wasn't noted in the police murder book in Youngstown. As far as I could tell from my conversation, Poluga considered her collateral damage; it was his brother he wanted found. I knew deep in my guts that, after this much time, where the one was, the other would be too.

It was just after high season in the Outer Banks but still mid-August and very hot and humid. My rental SUV blasted chilled air in my face all the way across the state. It was time to get acclimated, so I shut the a/c down and opened the windows. My first real lungful of North Carolina had a tang of mud river, diesel, and gardenia, an unpleasant mix. I stayed a long week here with my ex three years ago and the stink of gardenia was constantly in my nostrils on the drive down and back. I can barely recall the ocean's salt-scent thanks to this olfactory memory.

I decided not to cross to the Outer Banks until morning. There's about 120 miles of roadway from the Northern Beaches to Ocracoke Island. Then it's ferry hopping to the southern end, down to the Cape Lookout Lighthouse. I had a dozen photos Chloë's family provided me, but this was unhelpful as it had been to the police. People still used those cheap throwaway wedding cameras in those days before selfie sticks and iPhone videos. The cops found these on the dresser of their motel before they disappeared leaving all the contents of their luggage behind. Except for the famous Cape Hatteras and Bodie Island Lighthouses, the latter a black-and-white swizzle-stick, and a couple snaps outside restaurants where the names were visible, like Tides and Full Moon Café near Manteo, they could have been tourist shots taken on any beach on the Atlantic Coast. I was grateful to the family and tried not to let them get their hopes up, but these were not going to be much help to me so many years and hundreds of thousands of tourists later.

I was tempted to burn Poluga's money on the per diem, but I resisted. A client on death row is still a client. I found a Motel 6 but the Marriott was tempting. He said nothing when I mentioned expenses, which is unusual in my experiences. The wealthier people are, the more they scrutinize the line items of the bill I give them.

Since the cops had their motel in Nag's Head, I was going to concentrate on thirty miles of area from that motel. I tied a string to a pencil and made a circle that covered Roanoke Island, north to Kill Devil Hills, and south to the village of Frisco near the end of Hatteras Island.

I dreaded flashing the photos of the two smiling lovers at every beachfront restaurant and souvenir shop. The report Pete secured from his Youngstown PD colleagues said they did canvassing, but I know how cops handle that chore because I did it enough myself. After a half-hour of hearing yourself say the same thing and getting the same head shakes, you go on automatic pilot and then you miss things. I'd save that task for later.

First, there was a retired cop I wanted to see. He was lead investigator at the North Carolina end, and if anyone had a memory of anything about these two, he'd be the one.

Det. Sgt. Bobby Thorpe retired two years earlier and was cordial at the door of his double-wide in Creswell on Route 64, one of the two main arteries to The Outer Banks.

We drank a beer and sat in what he called his Florida Room, but it was a patio deck he'd built from a kit. The awning, he told me with a wink, was a separate purchase.

"I saw it advertised on the Home Shopping Network," he said with a smile, and I bit. An impulse purchase, you might say."

I slugged down the beer and was grateful for it. The day was blistering hot and the traffic was bogged down by the tourists leaving the islands to get the kiddies back to school. Thorpe told me the "low season," in the spring is the best time to visit. "The food," he said, "is even better and it's damn good all season long as far as that goes."

We talked restaurants and seafood dishes for a while. I mentioned some places from my visit years back and he approved of some, gave that wave of the hand for a so-so impression I thought only us Yankees did.

"The girl—hell, she was gorgeous, and people remembered her. Not so much the guy, her boyfriend. He was older, a bit standoffish from what I picked up. She had a smile, though, that people remembered." That was saying something. Living in a resort town myself, though nothing like these regulars with their snobby OBX license plates, I know that one Ma-and-Pa tourist family with their brood of squalling brats or teenagers with ear buds plugged in their heads texting their BFFs back home looks just like the next batch rolling past on the boardwalk.

"What's the brother's angle—that psycho you-all workin' for?"

"I didn't ask," I said.

That made Thorpe laugh. It goes against a cop's grain *not* to ask. But I trained myself to not ask. It isn't any of my business, for one thing. Thorpe wrinkled his brow, so I gave him what I thought might be a plausible answer.

"I think he's looking for forgiveness. I think he wants to make amends for being such a vile piece of work and causing his brother so much shame."

Thorpe nodded but didn't say anything, but it sounded lame even to me.

"Here's what I'd do, Mister Private Eye," he said and leaned toward me, his beer bottle held by the fingertips between his knees.

"We had shit and we knew it. No lead rang the cherries, nobody knew anything after they checked in. But something happened to those two, and I had a case the night after we got the call about the missing couple. A break-in at a sports shop. A guy in his twenties, ex-jarhead who got a dishonorable from Parris Island, and his girl. That chick, man, she was a piece of work, let me tell you. The little bitch was class valedictorian, Mom and Dad from Beaufort, country-club types, lots of money."

"What was it about her?"

"Besides the fact she didn't belong with that tattooed stud, nothing," Thorpe said. His face wrinkled at the memory. I knew the expression: cops call it different things in different places. We used *JDLR* in Cleveland back then: Just Doesn't Look Right.

"Anything connect to the couple?" I asked.

"No," Thorpe said, "not a goddamned thing. The stud had a big ole Nazi swastika on his chest and a buck knife in his boot. They had their van half-loaded with Nikes and jerseys and shit. He pretty much took the fall, said his girl was a lookout he "threatened" into the caper."

"What happened?"

"He got three, did every day of it, I heard. Got himself chalked up for various infractions and mainly fighting. Daddy brought in some big gun lawyer types from Raleigh and the girl got five years' probation, not a day in jail besides what she served."

"That it?"

"Yeah," he said slowly. "I liked him for it—I mean, for *something*. He was an asshole but there was something mean about him, you know? Crazy mean."

"His alibi pan out?"

"Oh yeah, the girl, she confirmed everything and everything I and the guy from Robbery-Homicide on it could check, did check."

"Any recent word on Nazi boy?"

"My info's dated," Thorpe said, "but he got cracked for armed robbery down in Mobile after he got out—maybe a month—and he's still doing time. Got a Buck Rogers sentence this time. Somebody shot a teller."

"What about her?"

"No idea. After Mommy and Daddy cleaned up after her, she disappeared. At least, she never turned up in our databases again."

"Got an address for her?"

Thorpe gave me that cop smile when one cop asks another for a favor. "You try the phonebook?"

"No," I said, "but I was thinking her parole officer would have a recent address."

I was hoping he still had the bug and wanted to see where this would go.

"Call me tomorrow, same time. Another beer?"

"No, thanks. I hear you Southern cops are ferocious on drunk drivers."

"Ferocious drinkers," he repeated. "We don't like to share the highway with other drunks."

I thanked him and left.

I ate at a Denny's near my motel and drank too much coffee. I had to have a plan for what I'd do after my talk with Ms. Saffron Priscilla Fordyce; you can't be poor and have a name like that. First, I'd have to see if she'd talk to me at all.

That night I found it hard to sleep. So close to the ocean yet so far from the soothing waves rolling up on the beaches that all I recalled were the sirens of cop cruisers and ambulances wailing in hi-lo tandem throughout the long night. When I stayed on the shore with my ex, I remembered her telling me the entire Outer Banks are strung along a single highway called the Virginias Dare Trail. I asked who she was and Micah—after informing me of my ignorance of our nation's earliest history—told me she was the first baby born on American soil in the Roanoke Colony.

"Is that why the highway is named for her?"

"No, dummy," my sarcastic legal-eagle wife replied. "She disappeared along with the entire colony. No one knows what happened to any of them. It's a mystery."

I was thinking of that little baby girl, born in a rough land, when I finally fell into a deep black hole around dawn. By midmorning, I was shaved and ready to get to work for my client. A mockingbird was trilling a combination of notes as I locked my motel room. He steals the songs of other birds and takes them for his own. John David Poluga back in his cell was like that: he enticed each call girl, escort, or prostitute to his motel room with a different story, sometimes a hard-luck tale but often a grand lie about traveling incognito because of his wealth and his greedy relatives. Each girl believed him despite her street smarts or knowledge about men. We know this because Girl Number Nine survived; she had to write everything out in her testimony in court because her larynx was badly fractured by Poluga's small but powerful hands around her throat. The paper reported Poluga dozed off during her testimony—he'd had a big lunch, according to his defense attorney—and when he fell to the floor, he took down both of his attorneys with his big body.

Priscilla Fordyce was married to a general contractor and lived in a nice house in Elizabeth City about twenty-five miles from Thorpe's trailer in Creswell, which is on the other side of the Abermarle Sound.

I did a little homework on her: married, three kids, husband high-school educated and three years younger, house bought on a foreclosure from the bank; it displayed double rows of ginger lilies on both sides of the driveway. She was a teacher's aide, going to the local community college (nursing program). Three vehicles sat in the driveway, an SUV, and a Prius, along with his work pickup, a shiny new black 4 x 4. An older gentleman in the town's only diner knew him because Johnnie Ray had done contracting for the remodeling of his kitchen and kept his workers on time and under budget without a hitch. "A good boy," the old gent concluded with fork upraised like a conductor's baton before he dived back into pecan pie.

I couldn't get much word on her. She didn't have friends or club acquaintances, and the local library ladies had no gossip to dish up for me. I used my charm on one plump staffer and learned she had a library card in the name of Pris Fordyce and used it for self-help books and nursing DVDs.

When I had my questions rehearsed, I waited for her husband to leave for work in the morning. Luck was with me: school had just started and all her kids were leaving the house in the morning, packed into hubby's truck, but teacher's aides weren't assigned until the second or third week of school. She was home alone.

I've used various ruses over the phone and in person to elicit information in my day, but my instincts told me to hit her directly and hit her hard.

I pulled into her driveway as soon as the husband pulled away from the first intersection. I'd seen the long gun in the rack behind his cab.

I went to the walk-up deck on the side of the house. The glass doors were opened and a light breeze blew the sheers away from the screen.

I knocked on the aluminum door.

"Priscilla Fordyce," I said when I noticed her approaching.

It's hard for me to look small and unthreatening, so I gave her what passes for my friendly smile and dropped the name of her former parole officer to relax her, make her think this was official business.

"What do you want?"

She had a cell phone in her hand. She could hit nine-one-one with a couple twitches of her thumb if this didn't work, so I gave it my all-in-one shot. "It's about Billy deWitt, Ms. Fordyce."

"What—I haven't had any contact with Billy, with him, in seven years," she said. "Who are you?"

I badged her with my private eye's license the same way I used to do on the street with my detective shield. If she knew how easy it was to get one of these things, she'd have slammed the door in my face.

"We're looking into a possible crime Mister deWitt might have committed just prior to the time—before you and he were associated—in that other thing," I said. "You know, the Outer Banks thing."

She was hard to read. Dressed casually, her red-blonde hair tied off in a bun just to get it off her face, a petite woman with an oval face and very intense ice-blue eyes. I could see them through the screen boring into me.

"I told you I haven't seen him since his trial. Leave! You had no business coming to this door instead of the front door."

"I'm sorry about that, Ms. Fordyce. You didn't hear my knock at the front door just now, and I wanted to save you the trouble—"

"What trouble?"

"Billy's talking. He's implicated you in the double homicide of Leonard Steven Poluga and Chloë Alice Randall on August twenty-two, two thousand eight."

She stood rock-still. Her eyes flashed, looked down briefly and then back to my face.

"I don't know what you're talking about. I served my sentence."

"Ms. Fordyce," I said, pausing to adjust my tone. I pawed a flapping sheer out of my face. "I'm not down here all the way from the Ohio Bureau of Criminal Investigation because of some stolen sneakers. I'm talking lethal injection and you're on the line for it.

"Wait a damned minute now—"

"Billy gave us every detail including where you two dumped the bodies, so cut the shit, and start talking to me. If he signs that plea deal the Alabama attorney general is considering approving by this afternoon, your insides are going to burn like fire once that needle pushes in the first drug. It's called pancuronium bromide and it'll paralyze your muscles but your mind is totally aware of everything. Then the potassium chloride goes in and, baby doll, when that hits you, you're in major trouble. It's like drowning. Half the time the damned drugs don't work and—"

I was winging it, not to mention impersonating an officer of the law, which is jail time. But sometimes you risk gambler's ruin, as they say, and go for it.

"I have . . . some money," she said in a shaky, little-girl voice.

"It's a crime to bribe or threaten a licensed investigator," I said calmly and hoped she didn't read "gumshoe" into that.

252

I took a step toward her, one of those Mother-May-I kiddie steps to see if she'd panic.

"Look, Priscilla, it's Billy we're after, not you. Just tell me what happened to those two people who disappeared from their motel the night before you and DeWitt were helping yourselves in your little midnight requisition at the sporting goods store on Delphine."

"I—I paid for that."

"Billy deWitt, think. Did he show any violence during the time you and he were together?"

Her eyes told me. Bingo. Pay dirt. She almost stepped backward from an invisible slap. You don't react like that unless you have something to hide. Something big.

I went for broke. Worst case, I'd be out of this state before she could summon the authorities to have me jugged.

I made a show of checking my watch. "That Alabama AG isn't going to wait all day for your decision, Ms. Fordyce. Shit or get off the pot. Billy's a singing canary and you're the name of the tune."

The lies were tumbling out of me like clowns out of a Volkswagen but I kept my voice and my breathing steady.

"When I leave here, Priscilla, your last hope is gone and your three kids will be state-raised when your husband decides to divorce you.

My next lie was going to be a whopper, however, and I said it fast and evenly so that I could watch her reaction in the smallest detail.

"DeWitt said that you and he robbed the couple in their motel room for money and things got out of hand. He said you and he then ... did something, something bad to the couple."

I watched this married soccer mom, this nurse-in-training blanch. A redhead is pale in the first place but the blood drained from her face so fast I thought she might faint right there in her kitchen. One hand reached out to clutch my arm. I noticed a blue tattoo on the inside of her wrist—a scorpion. That wobble brought her oval, fox face close to mine. I saw freckles spattered across the bridge of her nose, the pale blue eyes moisten. Take away the crow's-feet, and she was a teenager all over again.

"Billy said *that*? He said that I—that I *helped* him k-kill those people?"

I nodded.

Then it was like the heavens split open for me and I saw the hand of God.

"Billy did it," she said in that tiny voice. "He killed them both. He said he'd kill me if I didn't help him."

"May I show you a photo?" I was all feathery touch and politeness now.

She nodded. I reached inside my jacket pocket and came out with the top photo of the couple smiling in front of a restaurant that showed hand-drawn smiling crabs in white bibs with knives and forks in their claws eager to dig into a meal. The crabs were oblivious to the fact that they were the meal and their own plates were empty. Poluga's brother wore a smile, one hand up to steady a straw beach hat in the breeze; she had her hip touching his leg and a bigger, sincere smile spread across her face. Her high cheek bones and even white teeth were prominent. She wore shades, however, and I silently cursed myself for not choosing one where both were clear face shots.

"Yeah," she said it like a gum-chewing teenager. "That's them."

I was almost gagging on my own spit. It *never* goes like this.

"How did Billy—?" I left it unfinished.

"Billy shot the guy in the back when he was running to the bathroom. He shot the girl right after him. She was, like, hunched over in the shower. Begging for her life. Billy stood over her and put the gun right to her forehead. I was screaming, I was so scared."

I felt as if somebody had shot ten-penny nails through my shoes. I couldn't move.

Sitting on her sofa, holding her tiny hand in mine, she told me how it all started. It was a game she and Billy played, one Billy made up— for fun, he said. Billy called it the Purse Game. They were lovers, she said, and Billy convinced her to run away from her parents' home. They drifted from one resort to another, partying, occasionally swapping with a friendly couple, having drinks, and flirting with each other's partner; then they'd go to one or the other couple's hotel room for more drinks after the clubs closed. Billy would give her the signal and she'd exclaim that her purse was missing. Just after Billy made eye contact, she'd stuff her purse into the sofa cushions or kick it under a chair while no one was looking. Then Billy would accuse one or the other of stealing his girl's purse. Billy would rant and rave, act like a madman. The couple meanwhile would be protesting their innocence. But Billy refused to believe them. That's when the gun would come out—a big silver-and-black Taurus with a bobbed hammer. She said that way it wouldn't stick in Billy's clothes when he drew it out.

"Why did Billy want to play the Purse Game?"

"Billy loved to see the fear in their eyes," she said. He loved it when they begged for their lives. Sometimes he'd demand a blowjob from the girl, you know. That way they'd be reluctant to go to the cops after."

"I see. Go on." ... *with your sordid tale of this lowlife, worthless fucko.*

"If he didn't like the guy, he'd beat him up—you know, pistol whip him. Beat his face to a bloody pulp. Billy liked to humiliate people. He used to hit me, too."

"What happened to the bodies?"

Make or break time.

"He wrapped them in this old canvas sail we found in a dumpster. He got boat anchors from the marina. He drove them to a swamp," she said. "He made me go with him. He said he'd kill me if I ever mentioned a word of this to anyone. I've been holding it inside like a bomb for seven long years."

She broke down and sobbed for a long time. I let my hand rest on the nape of her neck for comfort.

I called the police from her house. I mentioned Thorpe. Inside, my guts were churning. I staggered off her deck and had to use the rail to steady myself.

The next five or six hours were a blur: city cops, sheriff's investigators, an FBI agent, and whoever else wanted a go at me and the story I had to tell.

They didn't arrest her at that time but she was told to bring her lawyer and her husband with her to the precinct.

I didn't dare to look back. She must have been watching me all the way to the driveway.

Once inside the car, I started to shiver uncontrollably. The sweat popped out on my forehead, but I was chilled to the bone by the story she told and the way she told me.

I called Thorpe as soon as I was back in my motel.

"You believe her?"

"I believe her."

"Man, if her lawyers are good, and if she's from money, you know they will be, you could be in some deep shit yourself, partner. You ever hear of fruit-of-the-poison tree back in Ohio?"

"Now you sound like my ex-wife, a trial lawyer."

"You think she'll remember where they dumped them?" Thorpe asked me. "You said she told you they stopped just before the Intracoastal."

"I think she'll remember," I said but it was mostly a hope. "I'll see you get the credit for this," I added, hoping to assuage some of the guilt I had for using his name in my own little sadistic game of coercion.

He laughed. "I'm ex-officio now."

"Now you really sound like my ex-wife."

"Hold up a sec," Thorpe said.

"What is it?"

"You didn't—look, I got to ask. You didn't do anything to her besides the bullshit, right? You didn't do anything to really fuck this up for the prosecution? I've seen good lawyers go after a loose thread like a junkyard dog. They'll shred you on the stand. You better be ready in case you so much as whispered something nasty in her shell-like ear."

"I understand. I'll be ready," I said. I wanted to say: *I wouldn't have touched her with a ten-foot barge pole.* I thought of that tiny blue scorpion on her wrist.

I spent four days down there going over the same things with Thorpe's people and never once got to see the ocean or hear the waves. I had detectives, investigators from the DA's office, state cops, FBI agents, and a dozen other people taking my statement until I could have recited it backwards and forwards like one of those long epic poems they used to recite from memory. I begged the county cops to let me ride with her when they took her to find the dump site.

It took three trips in a sheriff's cruiser to find their remains but they did find them. It was a lonely place filled with the reek of muck and wild swamp flowers and the sounds of insects whirring in the brush. I was bitten on every inch of exposed skin by mosquitoes so aggressive that they tried to fly up my nose. The deer flies bit even harder and at night, in my inexpensive motel, I discovered my ankles were bitten up by chiggers. I grew sick of eating crab cakes but I'd lost my appetite anyway.

On my final day in North Carolina, I read in the paper that Billy deWitt was going to be charged with double homicide. There was a mug shot. Not the youthful one from his sports store heist but a recent prison mug shot. He'd aged badly; his eyes were lost in folds of fat and his head was shaved in that high-and-tight Marine Corps cut. A long white scar snaked across his neck from an old prison tussle. Not a word about Priscilla née Fordyce. Her parents' money was already at work for their little lost princess.

I drove back to Ohio the next day and fell asleep in my own bed. I made it to my office sober from a good night's rest. I spent an hour itemizing my bill and stapling receipts to it. I put the whole thing in a manila file folder and prepared to mail it to Poluga's lawyer in Youngstown. I'd already called him and given him a verbal report to pass on to his client. I said my full written report would accompany my bill. Poluga's lawyer called me back three days later to express his thanks "for the good thorough work," and added, "He wants to see you in person."

My debt to my client was over, I reasoned, and the bill was paid in full. I had the check as I spoke on the phone, and it was a burning a hole in my wallet. My stomach was getting back to normal and a well-deserved drunk at Tico's Place was on the agenda.

"I don't want to see him." I put too much heat into it.

"I understand, believe me, but he's very insistent. Do you know he's got his date set? The governor won't consider a stay."

"Poluga was expecting it. He didn't get there singing off key in the choir."

But in the end, I caved. Tico's would have to wait. I had a five-hour drive down to Lucasville in the morning.

It took an hour from the time I arrived to the time they led John David into the same tiny conference room. My shirt was stuck to my back. The sounds and smells of a prison are the most dismal in the world.

"You did it," he said.

I nodded, waiting.

His braying laughter boomed out of his massive chest in waves.

I admit I was astonished. I had watched them hoist his brother's skeletal remains out of that swamp muck along with the disgusting corpse of that once-lovely, sweet girl. I watched her decomposed foot in its shoe fall off. I recall a vile stench so pungent it took three hours of hot showering to cleanse it from my pores. Every article of clothing I wore that day went into the dumpster out back.

"What's so funny, Poluga?"

"You."

That provoked another round of harsh laughter.

"What are you talking about?"

"My brother. Shit, I hated him. I paid Billy to kill him. I told him to do it slow, use his knife, and not rush it. Saffie called me right after from the motel while Billy was cleaning up the mess. She said Billy shot him in the back. That pissed me off," he said.

Saffie. Saffron Priscilla.

"You—you knew? You knew all this time?"

I couldn't get my mind around it.

"I'd been planning to kill that fuck of a brother of mine since I was a kid. Hadn't been for that whore who tripped me up—"

"Why?"

"Don't you listen, idiot? I hated him. Besides, he wasn't married— yet. I knew he didn't have a will because I broke into his office and looked for it in his private papers. But I knew he planned to make one right after his marriage, so I thought—why not? Do him, get the money, but that fuckup Billy deWitt. He had to go dump them where the bodies couldn't be found. I had to wait all this time to file a claim."

"So I was just—?"

"You were my tool, my little monkey," Poluga said and gave me a big smile. One hand reached between his legs to grab his genitals in case I didn't get the point.

"It was a million-to-one I'd find the girl. You could have ratted him out at any time."

"Convicts rat on each other all the time. Nobody cares. Besides, I didn't want a snitch jacket."

I didn't believe him. Somebody would have started to investigate Billy deWitt and his girl.

Poluga read my mind. "Hey, I was going to let you fumble-fuck around down there. My lawyer would get a message to you. I'd drop the cop's name, and if that didn't work, I'd 'remember' a girl my brother mentioned in his last phone call to me just before he went missing. Some girl—"

"—some girl," I finished for him, "who happened to be dating a psychopath with a big Nazi tattoo on his chest."

"Saffie's one tough little bitch, man," Poluga reminisced. "She did double with me and Billy after we all got high on meth. I should have taken her away from him. Billy was too soft for her."

"You couldn't predict she'd blurt out all that shit. Seven years. She changed, Poluga."

"You stupid fuck," Poluga growled—and I could see the rage inside the killer those dead girls had all seen before he choked their lives out—"if I had to keep dropping big fat clues in front of your stupid face until you made the connection, I would have done it and you'd never know I was playing you."

"Do me a last favor?"

"Sure," Poluga said, "you did me a solid in getting that shitbird deWitt slammed with two murder indictments. Man, he ain't ever gonna leave his cell now and nobody can say it was me."

"Let me come to your execution."

Poluga gave me another belly laugh. "Sure, why not?"

I went. I'm not ashamed of it. But I'm not going to describe a man's final terrible moments on earth here—even a shit-sucking, evil bastard like Poluga. Let's just say it was the last piece of business between me and my former client and let it go at that.

It turned out there was still one more piece of business. A month after Poluga was interred, I had a call from his lawyer—his criminal lawyer, not the probate one. He said John David left me "a gift." He was putting it in the mail that afternoon. Before I could tell him I didn't want it, he clicked me off.

It arrived a few days later. It was marked *Fragile*, and I knew right away what it was from the shape of it. I'd seen it often enough in his cell: that long, old-fashioned rectangular framed photo of Tom Breneman's restaurant with its palm-tree wall murals and a rotunda ceiling. Breneman himself, in a natty tweed sport coat with a boutonniére in his lapel, smiles with his open, round face, looking benignly in two cameos in each bottom corner of the photo. There's his faint but elegant ego-trip of a signature, too, and above—immortalized forever like flies in amber are the hundreds of smiling, happy guests dining in his restaurant. The only words are *Hollywood, California 1948.*

I keep track of Priscilla Fordyce. She turned state's evidence against her former lover. Her team of lawyers defended her as an abused woman and she was given a year of house arrest and five more years of probation. Her husband did divorce her but she kept custody of the kids. She's living with them in California now. Her parents send her money every month. She owns a flower shop in Encino.

The End

A Planet for Barnard's Star
By Robb White

The spider in the corner of my ceiling seemed confused by the crown molding and kept bumping into it and backing up. I'd kept half an eye on him all afternoon. The other half of my attention was directed outside my plate glass window where the rain came down in sheets. If this were summer, not chilly late autumn, the weather woman on Channel 8 would have called it a gully washer. But it was November, and the rain was sleety ice, clumps of dirty slush built up in the streets and ran overflowing into the sewers. The empty street outside wasn't exactly a ditch, but that's how I sometimes thought of the Strip in Jefferson-on-the-Lake, a place where the human flotsam and jetsam flowed into a common gutter.

I was a little depressed. Business was slow even for this dark season, and I hadn't had a client walk into my office in ten days. The messages on my answering machine were all from telemarketers in the technology end of private investigation shilling the latest gadgetry in the technology or offering more deep-dive options in databases I couldn't afford and would never use. I still have a partially assembled directional mic in my closet with instructions in three languages more complicated than a recipe for catfish Couvillion in Tagalog.

Tico's nephew Alarico opened the door and stomped in, spraying droplets in all directions, cursing the wet weather. I wasn't happy to see him. He was under the impression he was training to be a private investigator under me. I didn't give him that impression. One fat droplet arced high enough to land on my computer screen. It followed the same law of gravity pulling everything toward the center of the earth. I had a fleeting hope the annoyance he brought with him would offset the monotony of spider-watching. He brought news from the sheriff's department where he still had a toehold despite his habit of running afoul of his boss. Rico's career was sliding downward like that fat drop of rain because he'd gambled in a power struggle some years back and came out on the losing side. Sheriff Johnson had a long memory. The trouble is, every time Deputy Cardona got into a scrap on the job and wound up patrolling the county's back roads, he would show up in my office campaigning for a partnership. I couldn't afford me, much less him.

"He show up yet?"

Rico never read an epic, not even a graphic novel version of one, but he starts every conversation *in medias res*. I wiped away the rain drop with my fingertip.

"He *who*?"

"The guy, you know, the guy."

Communicating with Alarico Cardona, which I've been doing since I met his uncle in the bar across the street, required the sixth sense of identical twins. Thunder rolled in sonic booms from nearby Lake Erie and the rain intensified. My plate glass shivered with the thunderclaps, not a good sign.

"No, I don't know which guy you mean, Rico."

"Jesus, Tom, you can't miss him. He looks like the Scarlet Pimpernel."

"Your Aunt Marta heard you calling me 'Tom,' she'll crack you across the mouth."

"She's old school, all right."

They say the kids from Generation Z are a bunch of self-centered, lazy, disrespectful fuckups. Alarico's not lazy.

In fact, he impressed me that he knew the Scarlet Pimpernel at all. Normally you could put the totality of Rico's knowledge of history and literature inside the circumference of a shot glass with a fat crayon.

Before I had time to ask the obvious, the door swung open behind Rico. A man taller than Rico but not as broad slipped inside and stood there looking at us beneath the brim of a velour fedora with a sodden feather. Rico wasn't far off in his description. Water sluiced forward, spattering his belted camel overcoat that looked expensive when he nodded at Rico first, then me.

His name was Roald Colen-Briscoe. In his late fifties or sixties, he wore his hair in a long, gray-blond ponytail. He bore no real resemblance to the dashing aristocratic figure on horseback Rico had indicated and which I'd filed away in a dim memory long ago in boyhood in front of the television. When he opened his coat and flapped the ends to shake off more rain in my tiny foyer, I rescinded my dismissal of Rico's allusion to Sir Percy: a black satin ruffle shirt tucked into black leather pants which folded into a pair of calf-length black boots. An outfit you'd ignore on Melrose Avenue but this is a Midwestern resort town, not even Cleveland. I pegged him as an unreconstructed hippie, but I couldn't recall seeing a hippie under seventy in years. Even that impression was belied by a ruddy complexion in a lived-in face, big hands, the confident manner, and smile of someone used to creating a scene and not being shy about it.

Introductions made, he said his hyphenated surname was an homage to his mother, a fan of Roald Dahl, whose books she read him as a toddler. That garnered no reaction from Rico, who could imitate a cigar-store Indian as well as any cop when confronted by the bizarre. The name aside, it didn't explain the sartorial splendor in our little town, a working-class resort with no pretensions. Thunder boomed all around with an occasional lightning flash to add to the surreal effect. I knew Rico well enough by now to know he was amused by Mr. Roald Briscoe. I glanced at Rico, my "fisheye," he called it whenever I wanted to usher him toward the door. Instead, he took up a position beside my desk, pulling one of my plastic chairs to him to settle in for the show. His way of claiming a finder's fee. Grudgingly, I felt compelled to refer to the deputy as a "part-time associate," dreading the benchmark I'd just set for the next conversation with him on the topic of his joining "the firm."

Briscoe impressed at once as an intelligent man. He didn't waste time on small talk, picked his words carefully, as if he were choosing from an outsized mental rolodex, and he didn't seem inclined to do what all my clients did by embellishing facts. Neither did I detect any virtue signaling in what he asked me to do for him, "if I wanted the case," and took full responsibility for what he called "a regrettable failure to act." Best of all, he didn't presume up front what the parameters of the investigation had to be, as if to do my job for me, or as was true more often from my clients, to curtail future expenses.

It sounded simple. Most complicated things do in the beginning. He wanted me to find a missing man, a friend of his "with whom" he was riding across the country on Harleys. Ron said he was a department chair at a small college in Kentucky. Jesse Moorehead, his colleague and friend, was from Sandusky, sixty miles west of Cleveland on Lake Erie. He said they planned to meet up in Northtown. Ron detoured to visit relatives in East Brangton on the Ohio River about fifty miles south of Youngstown. He expected to meet his friend at the bar up the street from my office.

"I never heard of this place," he told me. "But Jesse rode through here on his way to the Finger Lakes once."

But his friend never showed. Briscoe waited, made what he called "a two-day, utterly futile attempt" to find him or get some word from his family in Sandusky. The locals, he implied, were "unhelpful."

"I don't want to sound liked the chamber of commerce, Mister Briscoe," I replied. "But a million people a year pass through here."

JOTL-ites, as the year-round locals refer to themselves, number in the low hundreds.

Time was critical to the trip, he said, because both were on contract for the fall semester. He finished the cross-country trek alone.

"What day did you arrive, Mister Briscoe?"

"The day after I called Jesse from Youngstown. August sixteenth. I told him I wanted to stay overnight. I had a colleague at YSU and I said I'd head up to your town in the morning. Besides, I'd been drinking and it was late at night."

"What time did you arrive at Mickey Finn's?"

Mickey's has the name but the bar next to it, Annie's, has the real reputation. It's an outlaw biker bar. I've been in there dozens of times tracking leads on missing persons but always walking on eggshells, especially in high summer.

"Morning," he replied. "I recall a paper sign on the door stating the bar wasn't opening until ten o'clock, so I hung out around here on the Strip, I think you call it. When the bar opened, I spoke to a bartender. He didn't remember Jesse being in the place."

"Did you try later?"

"I spent a couple days, drank at the bar, came back at different times, asked again, went right up to closing time. Nobody saw him or remembered him."

"Did you speak to Ida?"

"Who?"

"Ida Zweiger runs Mickey's."

Ida manages the place but her husband Oliver owns it. He bought it five years ago from a Vietnam vet named Perkins. Customers say Ida lives in the bar, does all the hiring and firing. Oliver is in the county nursing home; he has severe dementia. I've never been in Mickey's that I haven't seen Ida's scowl behind the counter, usually close to the till. It struck me as strange that he never saw her.

"How did Jesse sound over the phone?"

"Stressed," Roald said. "But he didn't say why. He said he was getting out and he'd call me right after. He never did."

"Do you know why he sounded 'stressed'?"

"No, but I heard voices in the background—some shouting. Angry voices as though a fight was about to break out."

That wouldn't raise an eyebrow in Annie's. In Mickey Finn's it was extraordinary. The two bars were polar opposites. Annie's was rowdy. Lots of police calls, fights, drunk and disorderly arrests in the early morning hours, especially weekends. If a tourist in Mickey's cracked a cuticle picking up a fork, it was noteworthy.

"You're sure the voices you heard were angry voices, not people having a good time?"

"I heard male and female voices, but I couldn't tell the ages. I couldn't hear distinct words," he said. "I do remember hearing a woman in the background several times. It sounded like a banshee wail."

"What kind of whale?"

"Never mind, Rico," I said, wincing at his intrusion.

"Do you remember what Jesse said just before he ended the call?"

Briscoe followed my glance to Rico's bland expression, made whatever calculation he did about our "partnership" and resumed speaking to me.

"No. It was a short conversation. Definitely a woman's high-pitched voice in the background. Like Sumi Jo with a sore throat."

I can be disciplined when I have to be. I didn't swivel my head toward Rico.

"Nothing more than 'I've got to go, I'll call you later tonight.'"

"And you can't recall hearing any specific words spoken?"

"No. He didn't sound unduly concerned. Just that he had to go and he'd call me that night."

"This was ... three months ago?"

Cops fret if a person goes missing for more than forty-eight hours.

A much longer pause. The wind blew a styrofoam cup past my window. Rico shuffled his feet. Then Roald Briscoe broke the silence: "It was just before the pandemic closed everything down."

"You're shitting me," Rico blurted.

I clenched my jaw, avoided twisting around to glare at him. Instead, I kept my pen busy on the notebook page, but after hearing what I just heard, it was scribbled gibberish to offset the awkwardness.

Briscoe didn't respond to Rico's outburst. He looked steadily at me as if a four-year discrepancy were a minor detail.

"You do find people, right?"

"I try to."

When I asked Briscoe why he allowed "that much time" to pass before enquiring about his friend, he said he and Moorehead were in different departments. They'd only gotten to know each other during the end of spring semester. The idea of a drive to the East Coast before the start of school after Labor Day was a sudden, mutual decision made "during a lull in some dull, obligatory meeting."

"Did the college make an effort to locate him when he didn't turn up for classes?"

"That's why I didn't think anything of it," he said, casting a look at Rico. "The school replaced him with another non-tenure-track hire. Jesse said he never told his department chair he was interviewing in

Massachusetts for a tenure-track position at Tufts. He told me he'd had one phone interview, and said his chances were good. I didn't think anything of it. He wanted out, his chair was a dotard, his colleagues timeservers. I could respect that."

After several questions from me on the particulars of the day before and after the disappearance, our talk devolved into the pragmatic concerns of hiring—costs *per diem*, providing him with progress reports, and all the hum-drum activity that reduces life's dramas to balance sheets. Mercifully, Rico remained silent throughout this part of the conversation.

Our business concluded with a retainer check he placed on my desk, he left in the middle of another thunderclap while wind-blown sheets of cold rain splashed against the glass.

I looked at the date on my screen.

"Three years, four months and some change."

"You're shitting me," Rico repeated.

"I heard you the first time."

* * *

I barely heard Rico mention he was leaving for his afternoon shift. I had little to go on because my concentration was on the screen as my fingers tapped away at the keyboard. After an hour, my databases yielded nothing except confirmation of the facts Briscoe had already informed me of regarding his friend's past life, although I had refined "friend" to mean "acquaintance." Every license I tracked of the ones digitized from that era told me the same thing: someone living a normal life disappeared from that life as if he'd stepped off the Earth in mid-August of that year. I was willing to believe that sub-atomic particles could wander into other dimensions but not human beings.

Like Briscoe, Jesse Alan Morehead was a newly hired assistant professor from Indiana State University, whereas Briscoe's degree was from Princeton. An economics professor and an English professor whose paths rarely crossed until that one faculty meeting that brought out a love of Harleys. I looked at the photo I'd printed from a grainy faculty yearbook. Moorehead smiled at the lens through a wispy beard.

His features were asymmetrical, the smile genuine if crooked, and his eyes gave no hint of the wry intelligence Roald had mentioned Jesse possessed. Roald wrote some data on the back for me: Jesse's height and weight, and the make and model of his motorcycle, a rebuilt Harley 1986 FXRS with 100,000 miles on the clock.

Briscoe couldn't tell me why his friend sounded "stressed out," but indicated Jesse needed to make the call brief, which was neither abnormal nor illustrative of anything as the two had held only one prior conversation on the day before they left for the trip. I'd learned from one of Jesse's relatives in Terre Haute Jesse had given $500 of his traveling money to a cousin as a wedding gift. Jesse had given the money "right there, on the spot," according to the relative, now a man in his late fifties.

Was that typical? I asked Briscoe. "Jesse told me he was poor as shithouse mouse," he said. "The college paid non-tenured teaching staff slave wages. Every cent went into his bike."

* * *

Mickey Finn's used to be a grand old Victorian house unlike its poor cousin Annie's, a cinder-block rectangle that resembled a bunker to watch nuclear explosions from.

Mickey's is familiar to me for other reasons. Rico and I meet there whenever he doesn't want the boss to know he's slipping me information. Though the local population was few, small-town tongues wag, and he doesn't like to be seen going into my office. I remembered Ollie Zweiger behind the bar with Ida when I first arrived in Jefferson-on-the-Lake from Cleveland homicide, my little dream of finishing up as a private eye. I figured tracking runaway college kids would see me through until retirement. He was just beginning to show signs of memory loss and confusion, little outbursts of anger at vendors. Then Ida shuffled him off to the nursing home three years ago, claiming early onset dementia. Local scuttlebutt said something else.

Ida Zweiger's been running the place ever since along with her on-and-off boyfriends. Still a handsome woman despite the frizzy dye job, she's a fixture on the Lake. Some say that she carries clout in local politics. That I never understood, knowing her character as I do. She disliked me for reasons I've also never understood, not that I give off warm, fuzzy vibes everywhere I go.

The music in the place always reflected the tastes of the current boyfriend. The last time I met Rico here, steel guitar poured from the speakers. When I walked in that evening, skipping around the puddles like a goat, I didn't recognize the music.

"Hey, handsome," she said as soon as I took a seat. "Long time, no see."

"Handsome" was no compliment. I didn't need a mirror for that. She's used me as the butt of her humor whenever she has a crowd to perform for. Lucky for me, I suppose, only a few customers occupied stools, some hard-core drinkers, a few there to escape the dreariness of a gray sky and relentless rain.

She sidled over, leaning across the bar to stare but mainly to expose the generous cleavage as a taunt.

"I saw this ad on TV, Haftmann."

Even in Annie's, I get called "Tom."

"No kidding? An honest-to-God TV commercial?"

"Yeah," she drawled. "Some cosmetic surgery outfit in Cleveland. You should call 'em, see can they take some of those wrinkles out of your face. I wrote down the number in case you came by."

A big man with heavy shoulders and a blue neck tattoo a few stools down muttered, "A face transplant, you mean, Ida."

I didn't know him.

"What's up, lover boy?"

"Lover boy," another familiar jibe from Ida's bag of cheap wit.

My wife left me—for another woman. Small towns, small circles, as they say. More like poisonous Venn diagrams.

"Ida, was it true the staff on who handled prison mail used to cut the cards to see who got to open your letters?"

Rico has a contact at the Sheriff's who had a brother who worked as a guard at the state pen in Youngstown, a maximum-security joint. He told me Ida used to write to random inmates as a pen-pal until the administration blocked her because her letters and photos were pornography. They reserved a special "Ida's Board" for her censored mailings.

"Too bad you can't write your ex-wife," she simpered.

She made an obscene gesture with her tongue and her two fingers.

"Tom Collins," I said. "Unless you're too busy sharing gossip about my life with your beefcake down there."

"What'd he fuckin' say, Ida?"

"Nothing, hon," she replied, never even turning her head, or raising her voice. "Fix me a JB and a draft."

I looked at Ida. "Can't he make a Tom Collins?"

Not many bars know how today. That's one reason why I keep ordering them. He seemed to be flexing just sliding off his stool. Bunched around the bulk of his deltoids, his neck seemed abnormally small. After tossing a black look in my direction, he headed for the racks of bottles behind the bar.

"Hey, I'll swap gossip with you anytime, old man."

"No, but thanks for the offer. What's that noise coming through the speakers?"

The music was making my chest bone thump.

"Not your taste, huh? Denny's into indie music. That's Modest Mouse. The Kills are playing here next weekend."

"Whatever are they thinking at Severance Hall? I'll bet Khatia Buniatişvili is shitting herself in fear."

"Who?"

"Ida, before the health department—excuse me, before the pandemic shut you down, around the time Oliver bought Mickey's—"

"*We* bought Mickey's, jerkoff."

"Sorry, when you and your husband bought this place, did you work behind the bar with Ollie?"

"Hell, no. Ollie didn't want me near all them horny tourists. We got us a better clientele now."

Prescient Ollie, I thought, but there was no hesitation in her answer. I looked at her boyfriend behind the bar staring at the rows of liquor bottles like an ape staring at fire.

Her gimlet stare and bosom were Ida's most notorious features. She made a gesture that Rico called "squaring up the boobs." Scooching backward and stretching, Ida hunched over the bar top, leaning her elbows, and staring at me. With her plucked eyebrows and mascara she evinced a tacky harshness, but the lift doubled the cleavage as if an invisible pump had pneumatically inflated them. Ida knew men talked about her.

"Why you asking me that, Half-Man?"

"No reason," I said. "Curious."

"Bullshit."

"How's Oliver doing, by the way?"

"Like you care," she said. She hunched her shoulders dimpling the tops of her breasts. "He has good days and bad days."

"You mind if I pay him a visit?"

"Be my guest," she replied. "Just turn the lights down before you walk into the room. He wakes up and sees you, it might scare the shit out of him."

She said it loud enough to draw appreciative chuckles from Beefcake. Her muscle-headed boyfriend loomed into view beside us. He pushed a tumbler of whiskey and a glass of draft in my direction. He seemed more menacing when he wrapped an arm around Ida, a hand loosely cupping the bottom of her breast.

"Here's your Tom Collins. This ain't a fag bar. Drink up and fuck off," he said.

"Now, babe," she said, squirming into his hand like a puppy. "He's a nice man—ain't you?"

"Sure am," I agreed and toasted him.

The elaborate neck tattoo began with a fancy *D* in Italic script under an unshaven jaw and curled around. The rest of it slanted around to hide behind the rest of his thick neck but it was readable.

I finished the booze. Not a Tom Collins. Not even JB. Four Roses, the one she served late at night to the men too drunk to know the difference. I put a ten on the bar, looked at him, and got up to go.

271

"So long, creepo," Ida's new man said. He left her to greet some customers entering.

What was it, I wondered, *that drew some women to violent men?* Not *Denny* but *Demon* was inked on his neck. I'd asked myself a thousand times since my wife left me what solace or pleasure or happiness had she seen in a woman that I had failed to provide her.

* * *

The rain slowed from a deluge to a steady drizzle, like an ice-cold shower from a nozzle. By the time I crossed the facility's parking lot, I half-expected to see fat flakes tumbling from iron-gray sky. Winter leaves Northern Ohio with the same reluctance a squatter leaves an abandoned house he likes. Lake-effect weather in winter can turn on a dime. You might find yourself in a whiteout a mile from home and completely blinded by the fury of a squall. On the way over, running parallel to the lakeshore behind the treeline, I glimpsed ranks of whitecaps dotting choppy pewter water smashing into the breakwall farther down. Colossal shafts of crepuscular light, the size of Parthenon columns, created a *trompe l'oeil* effect of light and shadow. It looked like a giant disco light penetrating the bellies of cumulonimbus clouds blanketing Lake Erie as far as Canada beyond the horizon.

Oliver Zeiger's room was on the second floor at the end of the hallway. Gray flocked wallpaper and blue-gray carpeting with golden fleurs-de-lis created a lulling effect on the mind. Every other unit of the overhead fluorescent lighting was switched on which added to the somnambulistic effect on my nerves. That drink had made me dull-witted. I felt stupid enough for thinking a man with dementia was going to aid my investigation into a four-year-old case. I'd spoken to the supervising nurse from the parking lot on my cell phone. I wanted to be prepared for his condition before I saw him.

Ida promoted the idea her husband suffered from Alzheimer's when it was rumored to be syphilis in the tertiary and final stage of the disease. Oliver Zweiger rarely experienced lucid intervals now, according to the supervisor, who believed I was working for the family's trust-fund lawyer.

The only other bars near Annie's and Mickey Finn's operating from those days was the Step Down, a biker's bar where fights were common and sleek black choppers were lined up out front until the early hours of the morning. The darkest bar where drug deals were a common sight was the Windlass, now a vapes store. A sports bar opened and closed within a month, now an empty lot. A three-story apartment complex occupied land where the only other bar had existed from those days.

Like most bars and restaurants before the pandemic wiped out businesses like a giant scythe descending from the skies, it struggled against the forces of competition for a time before withering away. One other burned down, two more relocated. Back then, the Strip was not as family friendly as it claimed in advertisements. Since the pandemic ended, a new grill bar opened, also a restaurant which featured *pommes frites* rather than "french fries," and a microbrewery recently opened across from Freddie's Grill. A drunk could get hurt wandering into the wrong bar in those days. It didn't surprise me that Jesse Moorehead had chosen the safer-looking Mickey's for a rendezvous with his pal Briscoe.

"Ollie, can you hear me?" I leaned over the bed. His lips moved to my voice. Flakes of dried spittle caked the corners of his mouth. His lids were at half-mast, fluttered twice, seeing but unseeing.

His hair was a tangle of ringlets; purple bags like half-moons hung under his eyes. His tongue poked briefly from his mouth and withdrew, an albino eel popping out of a cave. Once a good-looking man, he was ravaged from within by microbes eating his brain. *Ollie, Ollie in free*, I thought, remembering the old childhood game of hide-and-seek.

"He wakes up now and then," said a voice behind me.

I straightened up. It was the LPN on duty. Her name tag said "Clarissa."

273

"Is he able to talk?"

"Mostly he just rambles nonsense and makes squeaking noises."

"What are these?" I asked, pointing to the drawings on the walls.

"He drew them when he was still mobile," she said. "Same thing all the time."

I looked closer. "My God, they're rats."

"Nothing but rats," she laughed. "Big rats. He liked it when we taped them to the walls."

A weird child's art gallery of crayon rodents. Sometimes a single rat, sometimes in pairs. Brown or gray ones at the head of a seething pack. The smaller they were, the more they resembled a scribbled swirl of loops, a vortex of rat frenzy. Some had ruby-red eyes, others revealed bloody jaws and razor teeth.

I pointed at a drawing. "What are these biting? It looks like—"

"People," she said. "Arms, legs, faces. We take them down when the state inspector visits," she said. "The wife insists we keep them up for him, though. I don't know why. She doesn't come very often nowadays."

That didn't surprise me, not with Beefcake around to tend the home fires. It didn't sound like a rebuke. Nursing home staff get accustomed to families abandoning their loved ones after a while. It might not be odd that Ida wanted the drawings to remain up. She wasn't squeamish. She had no qualms about picking up boyfriends on a whim and didn't care who knew it. But to insist on it to please Ollie despite the staff's disapproval didn't seem right, either.

"Nurse, did Mister Zweiger's wife ask you to leave the drawings up?"

"Clarissa," she said. "I'm not an RN. I've been here ten years."

I stepped over to the farthest drawing and worked my way from one wall to the next. In many of them, the rats fought each other or dined on jagged portions of human anatomy. Some were downright grisly as the feasting became voracious. The last two featured swirling gray masses of rats tearing up or dragging off loops of intestines and genitalia. I noted the squabbling among the rats over viscera, rarely acting in unison, as if they'd decided there wasn't enough to go around.

I turned smiling to the aide. "There's a certain *je ne se quois* sensibility at play here."

"Sorry?"

"Nothing," I said. "I was trying to be funny."

"Uh-huh."

She was young. The darker corners of the human psyche were still too new to her. She wore a yellow wool sweater draped over her shoulders and buttoned at the top. She suddenly clutched her elbows together in a nonsexual way, the opposite of Ida back in the bar. "Somebody just walked across my grave," she said.

"My old grandmother used to say that."

"Really?"

Her tennis shoes made no sound on the floor as she turned to go. I was left behind with Ollie Zweiger and his rats. He never spoke a word although several times I saw his jaw working. My little joke with Clarissa had boomeranged yet brought back another French term my ex used to use: *frisson*. That little thrill of skin-tingling called paresthesia. I contemplated this morbid gallery of rats rampant for a long time before I felt the need to go home.

* * *

Our spring was false. The skies unleashed snow churned up by the warmer waters of the lake coming up against the chilled winds from Canada. Tons of swirling flakes, every design different. It was staggering to think about like the varieties of shapes in the human face with eyes, nose, and lips being apportioned equally to every human face. I made it back to my rental house before the first snowplows took over the roads. I turned up the thermostat, fixed a drink and settled down on the couch. The nap on the arms is so worn it feels like caressing skinned animal hide.

After the second Tom Collins, I *knew* what it was. The rats had so dominated my attention that I missed it. They all occupied the same environment, a neglected ruin. A crumbling, soot-blackened brickwork, more a façade than an actual building. On one, Oliver drew the year: 1901 in black crayon. Fronds of wild sumac grew against the sides of an abandoned building where the rats cavorted below. Broken windows, a fire escape in another. Tunnels of foul, grainy dirt where the rats scurried back and forth from burrows.

How had I not seen it right away?

I drove past it every time I went to the county courthouse on Lake Road. Long abandoned to taggers and teenagers, the city of Jefferson fought with the JOTL township officials over whose responsibility it was to tear it down. Rico's uncle told me it was a textile factory back in the 1920's. Driving past, I never considered it much besides an eyesore. At the peak was a capstone in different shades of brick with the numerals 1901 cut into the center.

Tossing my glass's dregs into the kitchen sink, I deemed myself sober enough for the short drive back to the Strip. Mickey Finn's was barely a couple hundred yards from the factory.

I parked in front. The No-Trespassing sign was a suggestion. It hadn't escaped tagging, either. Entering by the ground floor was difficult because of the thickets of pricker bushes cluttered the entrance where metal doors canted to one side. The second level looked feasible with a fire escape leading to it. I decided to risk it.

The structure swayed under my weight but held. Standing on the small platform of metal strips, I looked through the broken windows at the giant bobbin machines that still stood in an array as they once had when the factory spun tons of fiber and wool into yarn for clothing merchants. I tried to imagine what those twelve-hour shifts were like for the children and the girls in those long dresses that could easily have been snarled in those spinning machines under deafening and very dangerous conditions. s

I crawled through and landed on tongue-and-groove boarding. Every window on this floor was missing or broken. Stones lay all about, hurled from generations of vandals. Taggers had scrawled their boats and paid tributes to this girl or that's sexual prowess and genitalia or to some enemy male's failures in those arenas. At the end of the vast room, I spotted a door that I hoped led downstairs.

Lucky for me, it did. The reek of stale urine and rotting vegetation fought with a dozen other pungent smells. On the first level, little machinery or furniture was left intact or undamaged. A few tables and chairs no one wanted to steal. Big gaping holes in the floorboards.

Mickey Finn's previous owner before the Zweigers talked to customers about the Vietnam War. He mentioned tunnel rats one time when I was in there looking for a bar before I made Tico's Place my preferred watering hole—those small, courageous men who climbed down into the Viet Cong tunnels on search-and-destroy missions. The teens who smoked their dope or spray-painted the building were oblivious to the hordes of rats they shared the space with—not your pet white lab rat, either, but cat-sized, vicious Norwegian rats that gnawed through steel fencing.

Something else tickled my memory like rat whiskers brushing my face. Something bad had happened in my resort town around the same time Roald Briscoe's friend disappeared after showing up in Jefferson-on-the-Lake to wait for his friend. It was a sordid tale of child molestation involving a little girl.

Ida Zweiger's stepdaughter . . .

* * *

The *North Coast Tribune*'s archives at the public library in Northtown hadn't been digitized. Microfiche provided the missing information. Dated August 16, 2020, in a single paragraph in a column below the fold of an issue with the headlines proclaiming a ground-breaking ceremony for the new animal shelter. Of the four county commissioners holding shiny spades and smiling at the camera, two names were familiar political figures in politics.

But there it was: a man was wanted for questioning in the case of a sexual assault on a child reported by none other than Ida (née Holland) Zweiger. Gossip said she was from one of the more prolific breeding clans in Northtown, one of the toughest, too. My ex-wife, a courthouse lawyer, told me Ida's "marriage" to Oliver Zweiger was a fiction; she was his common-law wife. Oliver's daughter by a first marriage was never connected to Mickey Finn's as far as I knew, and no one I knew ever mentioned her except for this one incident. She had been the sexually abused girl of rumor.

But abused by whom? The paper didn't say. I went forward eighteen months hoping to find a follow-up story.

I went back to my databases and found the daughter now living in a suburb of Cleveland with Oliver's first wife, the girl's mother. I used my access to BMV records to get her current address and phone number.

I called and reached the woman who took her second husband's name. I asked Louise Gambrell if we could meet to discuss a matter affecting her former husband.

"What's that crazy bitch done now?"

There wasn't much doubt about whom she meant.

"I'd rather discuss it with you in person."

"Who did you say you are?"

A child cried in the background. A man's voice ordered the child to "shut up."

"I work for a law firm in Jefferson," I lied. "My questions have to do with the estate of Mister Oliver Zweiger."

"When . . . when did he die?"

"Mister Zweiger remains incapacitated. The issue and my concern has strictly to do with the power of attorney. Your daughter is technically his only child and legitimate heir. She might have legal recourse to the estate in the event of her father's passing."

I'd listened to enough lawyers in my time. I hoped that sounded right.

"The bitch said she cut her out of the will," Louise said.

The heat in her voice convinced me I'd chosen the right ruse to worm my way in. Ida left a scorched-earth policy behind even with her husband's flesh and blood. It worked to my advantage because she reluctantly gave me a time the following day. I gave her the name of a restaurant in the Warehouse District where, I said, all chummy now, the sea scallops were the size of crab apples. I proposed to my ex there. She declined, however, pleading a doctor's appointment and errands to run.

"Sounds as if you're busy."

"Tell me about it."

"Mrs. Gambrell, I'm sure we can work the transaction out very easily to Jasmine's benefit."

I liked the word *transaction*; it carried as many meanings as it disguised. But I didn't like invoking the little girl's name. That made me an abuser, too.

* * *

I stepped inside the modest Craftsman. Jasmine answered the door and showed me in. Zweiger was a big man, a bully in his prime, and a bad drunk, but he had very pale blue eyes like sea ice that women found attractive. They tamped down or hid some of the brutishness lurking behind them. Jasmine had the same eyes.

The heavy tread of footsteps coming downstairs was followed by the mother's appearance. She looked nothing like Ida. They say men go after the same type when they divorce. Louise Gambrell had nothing of Ida's crass sensuality. Smaller, thinner, she had deep lines around her eyes that, I suspected, came from worry rather than laughter. The tunic blouse she wore seemed to swallow her up. She carried the haggard look of wives and mothers with too much responsibility and too little money.

The male's voice I'd heard in the background on the phone yesterday was the same one I heard coming from a room near the back of the house. I'd already discovered from my databases the house was in a rough neighborhood on the east side of Cleveland that used to be ethnic Polish but was now African American, Puerto Rican, and poor white. We called the Caucasians unable to make the white flight to the suburbs "city goats" when I served on the force. I inferred from a brief, gruff conversation after she introduced me that he didn't suspect I was there about Oliver's will. *Fine by me*, I thought. An old detective's rule: divide and conquer.

"Louise," I began, "I saw your former husband last night and I believe he's—"

"—dying, I hope. The rotten bastard. Satan has a special pitchfork ready for him."

"—very ill," I finished, determined to be unfazed by her wrath like a good lawyer. "He might not be . . . with us much longer. Can you tell me anything in his past that might be causing him mental distress at this moment?"

"You mean besides my slut of a replacement?"

"Yes."

"How about murder, him and a bunch of other drunken assholes chased a man out of a bar and clubbed him to death. Will that do?"

My knees almost buckled. Time stopped because I heard the beating of my heart. It synced up with the ticking of an ormolu clock on the fireplace mantle before I could find the words I needed. I dropped the subterfuge of a mealy-mouthed lawyer and put on my detective hat again.

* * *

It was a sordid tale. She'd had years to think it over, and a well of misery at being shoved aside for a younger, sexier model. Nothing stews like wrath. It was a tattered cloth of bits and pieces and part comprised of what she'd been told by Jasmine herself, learned from others in the bar that night after she went home to fix supper, and Oliver's own confession after the guilt became too much for him. In other words, their lies. What she thought she knew at the time, however, wasn't the truth of what happened to Jesse Moorehead—an acknowledgment she herself made, which made me trust her version completely.

In essence, this: Jasmine was used to wandering around the bar on her own while both her parents kept busy working the bar in those tumultuous years when Mickey Finn's was close to financial collapse. Ida had no sooner been hired by her husband as a barmaid than she had seduced him. They both worked twelve to sixteen hours a day, and every dime they had went into the place. Meeting the monthly note was a struggle and there was nothing extra to pay for a full-time babysitter for Jasmine.

The girl wasn't "neglected," Louise insisted, because she and Oliver tracked her movements even during the busiest times when the bar was lined with every variety of drinker—college kids, tourists, recreational boaters, JOTL businessmen, the resort town's big shots slumming—even some "bad-assed types" assuming Mickey's was another version of Annie's.

"There were a couple terrible fistfights out back," she said. "Guys beaten to a bloody pulp. For a while, Oliver and I were afraid Mickey's was going to be declared a nuisance and shut down."

Jasmine wasn't allowed outside, but she could play in the back rooms if she didn't mess with the beer or liquor cases.

One evening busier than normal, Louise recalled, a younger man, a stranger to Mickey's went out of his way to speak to Jasmine. Lou-Lou (as Oliver called her back then) kept a sharp eye on any man who approached Jasmine: "The world is full of sickos and pervs."

Jasmine was bored and tired by seven o'clock. She wanted to go home, like always, but she knew it would be hours before her mother would find a free moment to hustle her off to home and bed.

"Her teachers were always pissed at me," she said, "because Jasmine was exhausted from being kept up late. She sometimes fell asleep during lessons."

When I asked Louise what the stranger's name was, she said she didn't know. "He must have been young, in his twenties, but I don't remember much. He was someone I never saw before," she replied, "and I knew he'd come on a motorcycle because he wore leather like a biker."

"You mean like the bikers across the street at the Step Down?" I asked her.

"No, not like those guys. They were hardcore, mean-looking, with beards and greasy clothes. Some of them smelled. Sometimes they'd come in by mistake. Jas knew they were dangerous and never to talk to them. Oliver was on me all the time about that."

"This stranger," I pressed her. "How else was he different from them?"

The guilt of her daughter's lonely childhood in a bar full of noisy drunks and loud music came through in the pitch and tone of her voice.

"I still have the words of Frank Sinatra songs running through my head from those days. Some drunks played Frankie Yankovic's 'Beer Barrel Polka' every time they got shit-faced."

"What do you remember about that night?"

"It's confusing," she said, "because of what happened afterward— all the running around, people going nuts. Oliver threatened to beat me black and blue when he came home because I didn't take Jas with me when I left the bar . . ."

"Is this the stranger?" I placed Jesse's photo on the coffee table in front of us.

"Yes, maybe. Jasmine only described him a couple times to me. I wouldn't let Oliver interrogate her."

"You said 'confusing,' Louise. What did you mean by that?"

"There was . . . another man," she said. "He came in right after him. He wasn't a biker."

"Try to remember."

"He, the other man. He kept slipping away to the back room to see her. He brought her an orange pop and a bag of potato chips. Oliver found the bag and the empty bottle later."

"It wasn't the first man, you're sure?"

"Yes, she remembered that man's smile. They were the same age except he, the second one, had street clothes, not biker's."

I waited.

"He touched her—the second man. I don't remember what led up to it. She never said. All I remember is the pain Jasmine said she felt when he put his finger inside her vagina. She said the man's face 'twisted up.'"

"Twisted up?"

"That's what she said. Like he was crazy."

"What happened then?"

"Jasmine ran and hid in a hiding place, she called it. She made a fort out of cardboard boxes in back. She'd play with her dolls there. She waited until the 'scary man' went away. Then she went into the bar, crying, and told everyone. Oliver went crazy."

"Did you see him—this second man. Was he ever at the bar when you were there?"

"I wasn't there, God damn it! I told you!"

I meant, later. Did Jasmine ever recognize the man again? Did anyone know him?"

She had a faraway look in her eyes. "It was too late. All hell broke loose."

I had an idea what occurred after Jasmine went into the bar to tell her father, but I needed her to tell me.

"What happened?"

"You must know or you wouldn't be here, right? A bunch of those drunks, all respectable citizens. They formed a posse on the spot and they went after the stranger. Not the pervert. The kind man, the one who spoke nicely to Jasmine. She was too emotional at the time to know what was going on."

I had to wait while Louise sobbed out her guilt.

"Jasmine told me she remembered shouting . . ."

Years passed. Jasmine's memory wrote the narrative the only way it could to deflect more pain from overwhelming her young mind.

"So they—the men in the bar. They picked out a stranger, the nice man, the one who first smiled at Jasmine, the biker wearing black leather."

"Not just men," Louise said in a voice still strangled with grief. "Women, too. It was like watching a dog pack hunt down a wounded animal."

"They told her later, my little girl, as though she were part of that mob . . . he got what he deserved . . ."

"They killed an innocent man."

I could picture it: the frenzied, lynch mob atmosphere, outraged villagers grabbing their pitchforks and heading for the monster, a man who had defiled a child and who might have remained coolly sitting at the bar while a little girl informed on him. Someone confused the two men. Who would point a finger at an innocent traveler passing through? Only one man came to mind. Add the sultry Ida to that friction between parents over that awful evening. Neither wanted to confront responsibility for what had happened.

"You're no lawyer!" she suddenly screamed at me. "Get the fuck out of my house!"

Louise's sobbing began, which began as a low moaning, climbed the scale. When the husband came storming out of the bedroom, I apologized and headed for the door.

That's me, Tom Haftmann, spreader of cheer and happiness all around.

* * *

On the drive home, I had much to ponder as far as my next move. Ida was too volatile to confront in the bar with my information. Oliver was for all intents and purposes a rat-sketching vegetable. Louise had come right up to the edge of what she could clearly recall and be certain of. Others in addition to her own fragile memory had painted in the rest.

The paper mentioned a man "questioned" but not named the day after Jesse Moorehead disappeared. Louise had said Jasmine remembered "the nice stranger" making a phone call from the pay phone in the anteroom because her father dragged her out there by the hand and pointed at him, screaming: "Is it him, Jasmine?"

I could imagine the bloodless expression on Jesse Moorhead's face as he understood what the outraged father was accusing him of. He must have dropped the receiver and bolted for the door. Roald remembered the abruptly terminated conversation, a woman screaming, shouts in the background, all before the call ended.

But not a woman's screaming. An outraged father about to exact revenge for his daughter's violation.

The puzzle had a few more pieces. By the time I pulled into the lot behind my building, I had a way to get them from the only person who could provide them.

* * *

I spent hours scouring databases, put in long hours and neglected calls from three potentially paying clients. I did a deep financial dive on Ida Zweiger. I called in a favor from an IT expert who paid me to follow his cheating wife to her rendezvous motels. He was good. He said he couldn't cross the "air gap," whatever that meant, but he knew how to tickle information from computers as well as any FBI's expert. I risked losing my license if what I discovered became public. I was already past the point of no return when I showed her the documents revealing how much she had cheated the I.R.S. In return for my silence, she agreed to come clean.

"All I want to know is how he died."

She didn't bother asking who was meant.

She grabbed me by the arm and led me into the dimly lit storage area. I panicked for a moment, thinking Muscle Boy was in there waiting with a baseball bat. Jasmine played with dolls back there. "The stacked cases of beer were mountains," her mother told me.

"I wasn't there," she began.

"Bullshit."

The silhouette of her glowering boyfriend appeared at the end of the bar. "Any problems back there?"

"Go back to the bar, hon. If I need you, I'll call you."

"Your pet gorilla, will he keep out of this?"

"He'll do what I tell him just like Ollie does—did. Now as for you, fucker, I swear I'll take you down with me if this goes public."

"Agreed."

She breathed deeply, cut her eyes to me, a cocky woman who thought herself smarter than everybody, especially men who couldn't stop staring at her boobs. Brando's line to Maria Schneider in *Last Tango in Paris*, that she'd be playing "socko with those tits" when she grew old.

"Ollie went ape-shit," she began. "Running up and down the bar screaming he was going to strangle the son of a bitch with his bare hands."

I held up the photo of Jesse at her.

"Get that away from me!" she barked.

I put it away.

"Look, people started gathering around the guy out in the foyer. He's looking around at everyone like a deer in the headlights. He had no idea what was happening. Jas was sobbing her heart out."

"Why would he run?"

"Are you stupid, Haftmann? They wanted to beat him to death right in the bar. Some guys had broken bottles in their fists. He tried explaining, talking—but it only made it worse."

"You told a reporter from the *Trib* the next day," I replied. "You said, 'a strange man, no one knew him or saw him leave.'"

"Cops went after the bike trash next door, hassled the shit out of them. The owner still won't speak to me."

"So who stopped the investigation after Jesse was—dealt with?"

"Forget it, gumshoe. You go near him, you're toast."

She made me pry it out of her. Or as much as she was willing to spill. When Jesse felt those eyes boring into him, he knew he had to get out of there or he'd be surrounded by crazed drunks spoiling for a fight. He ran. He shouldn't have. The cowboy hero in a movie wouldn't, but Jesse must have thought he could outrun a bunch of boozed-up males. He almost made it. He'd gotten his bike started when Zweiger hit him like a linebacker and knocked him into the street. Jesse abandoned his bike and ran across the street down that road where the old textile factory was with a pack on his heels.

Some former track star from Sts. Stephen and Basil tackled him just opposite the factory, according to Ida, who saw it all. He fought off the miler but the others caught up, and then it wasn't a fair fight. Surrounded, he was beaten and stomped in the deserted street. Ollie, however, wasn't satisfied. While the men stood over Jesse's unconscious body, Zweiger went off into the weeds and came back with a piece of rebar. Before anyone could say anything, he brought it down on Jesse's head.

"Cracked him on the temple," Ida told me. "It sounded like a pistol shot."

I suspected she was right there getting her licks in.

"Was he dead then?"

"I don't know."

"What do you mean, you 'don't know'?"

"Ollie and them guys, they hauled him off into the weeds. Ollie told me that night he came back later and shoved the body into a big hole. He said the rats would devour him."

"Jesus Christ."

I forced her to reveal who else was in the posse that night. Not surprisingly, some of JOTL's finest citizens, some of whom punched or kicked the fallen body when they could get a shot in. Zweiger hauled Jesse's bike away the next day.

I know several of those men. I've seen them around the Strip. Ida said many of them still come into the bar with their wives or girlfriends. One's a full-time drunk now. He used to work in a plastic plant off before the pandemic closed it down. He had nine kids. Another runs a used car dealership and paints signs. I've used the towing company owned by another one of those men myself.

He came into my office one day and wanted me to break into a rival's office. I sent him to a lawyer across the street. Another one wound up with an MBA from Baldwin Wallace in Cleveland and is currently an office administrator at the local community college. Except for Vinnie Stallamattio, the wino, there probably isn't anything more damning against them than a slew of traffic tickets. Pillars of the community. Stalwarts of public decorum. All with families, wives, and kids grown up. People who pay taxes and vote, civic-minded folk who serve on juries.

* * *

I try not to be superstitious. Sometimes I look for patterns where there aren't any. Explanations for why things are the way they are. Why the world is the way it is. Why people act like dogs meeting in the road. It's like looking at the space station on a dark night. It seems to zigzag but only seems to; the computers aboard keep it perfectly synchronized on its relentless GPS track without the slightest variation. But the human mind needs to see patterns, so we think it moves helter-skelter across the sky.

On that August 16, the day Jesse Moorehead was attacked by a posse and left to rot beneath decayed floorboards in an abandoned textile factory, thousands of "true believers" led by an expert in Mayan cosmology gathered in sacred sites around the world to ward off global disaster by holding hands, meditating, and humming in harmonic resonance. It was also another anniversary of Elvis' death from an overdose. Nothing to connect, you say.

The tiny spider broke my concentration. He was only a few feet from where I'd first spotted him on the ceiling the day the Scarlet Pimpernel showed up in my office. I start and end my day with a routine: I check the news in case there's a thermonuclear war declared, or a Himalayan-sized asteroid heading our way. Disaster gives me hope. That evening, it happened a radio astronomer from the massive telescope in Northern Chile's Atacama Desert was announcing a new super-Earth-sized planet had been discovered for Barnard's Star, six light years out, as if it were lurking just beyond the Oort Cloud.

"It's an extremely cold planet," the young scientist burbled to the interviewer.

"Not as cold as ours," I said back.

The exuberant TV whiz kid nattered on about space travel in the coming generation. "Luxury meals served," he boasted. Way too optimistic for me on this doomed planet.

I shut off the computer, flipped the switch, listened to the familiar sizzle as the lights flickered and went out. I felt nailed to the floor by the whole dull, nighttime routine waiting for me upstairs in my loft. It hit me between the eyes like a fist. I wanted to stay there in the dark, not moving, lurking in the soft dark like the black spider on my ceiling. It knows nothing of suffering or of its universal cause: attachment.

In the end, I went upstairs, made a Tom Collins, and sat in my scuffed-up chair listening to a Chopin étude and thinking about how I would inform a client with a literary name he'd been saddled with of the death of a friend or just an acquaintance he'd wondered about over the years.

The End

The Day the Rabbit Died
By Robb White

"Hey, Tommy, I hear that new guy in Northtown is hiring. Why don't you see if he'll let you make his coffee or something."

"Hilarious, Fritzie. I'm falling off my stool laughing."

Fritzie Galway's booming voice could be heard all over the bar and halfway down the Strip. A few grunts here and there around me, although the bar's never full this time of day, especially in the raggedy end of the summer season. Add in the Coronavirus and you have what looks like a dying bar in a dying resort town. I should know. I've been trying to leave this place for years.

This used to be Tico's Place; now it's called Penney's Lounge, although the only one I've ever seen in here is that big bruiser at the end of the bar who not only can't mix a Tom Collins but he told me straight-faced he never heard of it. Tico's long gone. He put a shotgun barrel in his mouth when the pain from his pancreatic cancer got to be too much. His wife Marta went back to Guatemala City—God knows why. Their boy used to help out around the bar and, for a time, was a promising welterweight down in Youngstown where Kelly "The Ghost" Pavlik used to train. I haven't seen him in years.

Everything's changed for the worse. The tattoo parlor across the street used to be my office.

"Haftmann, what's new?"

Everything but Fritzie, that is. Still the same.

"How come you got a German nickname when you're always bragging you're ninety percent Irish?"

"You think I can't be German like you, you Kraut? Joe, another beer for this bad-tempered fellow. I'll have my usual boilermaker, top shelf, if you please."

Fritzie's little joke with the new guy. His idea of "top shelf" is either Seagram's or Four Roses. The first time Joe did reach for the lone Johnny Walker Red, he nearly pulled back a bloody stump when Fritzie leaned over the bar to stop him.

"What's new, gumshoe?"

"You asked me that already."

"How's your boy Jason Lee these days? Still running things from his stepdaddy's mansion?"

"You should see him, Tom. If there's a Barack Obama lookalike contest, he'd take first prize. His bodyguard says he catches him practicing Obama speeches in front of a mirror."

Fritzie used a polite term for ex-con Joseph "Ray" Reynolds, Jason's personal factotum. I had other words for him: "drug dealer," "criminal," "sex trafficker," "thug," "bully,"—and my personal favorite: "murderer."

Fritzie mumbled something about the date and slapped his forehead, hamming it up for the other customers. I knew what was coming up.

"Of course, it's the anniversary. How'd I forget that?"

He was referring to the morning paper's front-page article on the five-year anniversary of the unsolved murder of a young wife at a cabin close to where we sat. It made state-wide news. I was hired by the husband when the police investigation stalled. It wasn't one of my shinier moments. Cops blamed me for interfering, and the husband blamed me for exposing his wife's infidelity and what the papers delicately referred to as her "com plex interrelationships" with others, both men and women.

"I still say the hubby did it," Fritzie said, taking a swallow of his drink and staring at his image in the mirror.

"You don't know shit about it."

"Still galls you, don't it?"

"Fritzie, talk about the next big biker rumble you've been predicting for the last ten years."

"It's gonna happen, Haftmann. The pot is boiling now."

Jefferson-on-the-Lake used to be a big biker scene for Mongols, Pagans, Hell's Angels, and half-a-dozen other clubs. Half the Strip burned down in rioting when the biker clubs had enough of the truce and went after one another. That was 1969 and made the Cleveland *Plain Dealer*. Nobody except a few old-timers even remembered it now. The tourists come back every year, and occasionally I pick up a little business when someone's daughter or son doesn't come home. I even found a missing dog once.

"Yeah, I saw Bobby and T.J. talking on the corner of Annie's Bar. They had to be planning mayhem."

Bobby del Rio is in his seventies and "Buck" Larrimore is close to eighty now.

"Mark my words, the Day of Reckoning is fast approaching."

Sometimes I think Fritzie genuinely believes the nonsense coming out of his mouth. He's not the craziest person I've bumped into around town.

Fritzie knocked back the rest of his drink and left, nodding to a couple acquaintances on his way out. Penney's hadn't changed the interior; it's still dark and there's no music, thank God. You can brood in silence if you want and few people will bother you. That's how a bar should be. Like a church without sermons or choir or anybody talking to you.

"One more for the road, Tico."

"Name's Joe."

"That's what I said."

"That's not what I heard."

"Any chance when this scintillating conversation ends I can get a beer?"

He took his time replacing his face mask and walked off in silence. I was tempted to call him "Penney," but my days of tangling assholes ended when I resigned from Cleveland homicide two decades earlier from a hip injury. I was chasing a drug dealer in East Cleveland through a dark, abandoned tenement and I went down a steep flight of stairs, ass-over-teakettle, as my sainted grandmother used to say.

I thought living off my pension and opening an office in a small resort town midway between Cleveland and Erie, PA would be a good way to ease into retirement. I was wrong. I've been wrong a lot.

Six more beers and four hours later, I staggered out of Penney's and crossed the street. If this were two months ago, I'd be playing Russian Roulette to cross this street with a load at dusk. By nine, traffic was bumper-to-bumper. But twilight brings out the shift from families and beachgoers parading up and down the Strip to cars packed with teens on cell phones and hyped on adolescent hormones, not to mention the availability of illicit drugs from garden-variety weed to high-octane sinsemilla through an assortment of dipping specialties like Buda, candy blunts, and Bazookas to the hard-core druggies' choice around here between meth or heroin. Our tiny population has been adjusted downward by three pedestrian deaths in the last two years at spots within a fifty-yard radius of where I had just staggered between a restored Shelby driven by a white-haired man in his late fifties and a Honda Civic coming the other way. One of the girls in back, a cute blonde with a sheepdog hairstyle, gave me the finger. I smiled back at her.

Beer takes the edge off but it takes a lot of beer. I try to hold off on the hard liquor until weekends. Tico used to call me a "controlled drunk." His wife was less given to nuance. Dark-eyed Marta regarded me as either "the *borracho* at the end of the bar—or in a voice a couple decibels higher than Fritzie's, "*Otra cerveza por el beodo.*"

I have a cabin at the end of Erie Shores Lane, which is another cute chamber of commerce misnomer when they platted the village. Lake Erie is across the street and well out of view from my gravel street, which twists around the gnarled, dusty maples lining it where the cheapest cabins for rent exist out here.

The first steps into my cabin make me think of that degenerate nobleman in a Dostoyevsky novel who described hell as being tied to a chair inside a filthy cottage with spiders in the corner. I hate thinking of it as the hill I'm going to die on but every day that passes makes me think so. Like those nightmares where you run into quicksand or find yourself in a slurry up to your thighs while whatever's chasing you closes in. But time and memory can't be escaped no matter how fast or slow you try to run.

I state the facts nightly to this empty, sour little room as I pace from tiny kitchenette back to the single main room, circling the rump-sprung La-Z-Boy in the center of the room. To wit, as my ex-lawyer wife would say, Bonnie Van Ekdal, 24, was slashed to death in a cottage on Erieview she and her husband Eddie rented five years to the day. Somewhere between four in the morning, when she returned from the several bars on the Strip, to her husband's discovery of her body in that blood-smeared cottage at 9:10 in the morning, she fought a terrible battle with her killer, running and stumbling from room to room, leaving blood everywhere from her wounds, until she collapsed and died in the bedroom in front of her one-year-old's baby crib. The photo of her bloody handprints on the top rail of the crib showed where she last stopped before dying, virtually exsanguinated. The reporter who wrote for the Northtown *Herald-Tribune* speculated that "with her dying breath, she attempted to shield her sleeping infant from her merciless attacker." We'll never know.

She was seven months pregnant. The infant was a boy buried with her, laid in her arms in a white christening gown to match the mother's long white velvet gown to hide the slashes in her flesh. Her neck was covered in a white ribbon for the same reason. The family made much of the baby's resemblance to the father. That didn't curtail all the rumormongering on social media about who the "true father" of the baby was, but it dampened some of the meanest comments. The detectives took their cue from the family as well because the follow-up articles never went beyond referring to Bonnie's "complex interrelationships," as the reporter delicately put it.

But you couldn't stop people from wondering about a young mother's character who would leave an infant alone in a rental cabin to go barhopping while seven months pregnant while her husband worked the night shift at a bottling company in Northtown before joining the family in the daytime. The cops cleared the husband early on; he clocked out at 6:33 that morning. He was seen throughout the night shift. The drive to JOTL, as the locals call this resort, would have taken 25 minutes one way.

The cops looked hard at the father-in-law, a mean drunk who pounded back a pint of Jim Beam daily. Their theory was that she came home in the early hours and he confronted her. He demanded sex, maybe as a bribe for his silence, and she refused. She resisted and the assault occurred over the next agonizing fifteen minutes as he pursued her and slashed her; her fingers on both hands were cut to the bone.

Cops couldn't break him, however. He even tried to "assist" the investigation—an old interrogator's trick—by stating how he could have gotten rid of the weapon. Van Ekdal said he'd wrap the bloody knife in a towel and toss it off the cliff into the lake. When cops pointed out that he'd have to pass by three cabins full of partying bikers and tourists to get there, he switched and said he'd drop it in the first sewer he passed. Every sewer on the Strip was opened and searched, nothing found other than the disgusting debris of a lakeside resort's detritus: vomit, used condoms, beer cups, and used needles.

No one heard anything. Shocking to the average reader, I suppose, but out here, on a weekend of revelry in summer, you could play Tchaikovsky's *1812 Overture* with the cannons booming, and the people on the Strip 100 feet away wouldn't hear it. Getting information from transients, cheating spouses, college kids, and an assortment of runaways from three states, drug addicts, pimps, dealers, and the kind of mobile human trash that moves like a sludge through this place every summer and you have your three mystic apes who see no evil, hear no evil, speak no evil. Especially the latter because bikers out here might be swarming the geriatric population, but they cast the same cold eye on snitches.

I took out my file on Bonnie's killer, set it on the La-Z-Boy and fixed myself a stiff Tom Collins. It's a ritual made necessary by my failure, especially when an afternoon's drinking did nothing to assuage the guilt.

The Day the Rabbit Died

First, the photos. Mine, every one of them taken on surveillance. The day I got into it with Mookie Brown at the Jefferson Courthouse over their refusal to go after the man covering for him was the day all cooperation with the Lake cops, the Sheriff's, and every cop between here and Columbus ended. The blue line is real, trust me.

He looks like half the males trawling the streets of the Strip: shaved head, goateed, ear studs, ripped Levi jeans, black tee with some nitwit slogan on it. Joey Reynolds is older, mid-thirties, has a vocabulary mixed with jailbird slang and MTV gangster rap lingo. Mentally, he couldn't fire up enough brain cells to light a 20-watt appliance bulb, but he has the ex-con's sewer-rat instincts. He's been trouble since he terrorized his neighborhood as a twelve-year-old; as a teen, he went to one of the toughest juvenile facilities in Cuyahoga County. That's where Cleveland gangs like the Heartless Felons send their youth to gladiator school for more intensive training in the art of mayhem.

He's also strong. Not quite a gym rat because he lacks discipline and his protector wraps him in enough cash to keep him content. But beneath the belly fat there's muscle. He slings drugs on the side, which he's been doing since he was a youth, although he's more selective in his clientele nowadays and prefers selling to the clubbing crowd at the Lake. He doesn't smoke crack like the fiend he used to be in his twenties, but he's known to sample his own wares with teenaged girls, especially vulnerable girls he can hook with candy-flipping LSD and Ecstasy or bumping up Ecstasy with powdered cocaine.

The rest of his aberrant personality is best left to the prison shrinks. He has no mercy and he has no guilt. Liberal sociologists get their panties in a twist over it, refuse to acknowledge it, but there are rabid dogs on two legs who need to be put down. Joey Reynolds is one of them. I know he sliced Bonnie Van Ekdal to ribbons in that cottage five years ago. I just can't prove it.

Most of the rest of my thick file on the murder is devoted to one other man. I culled the portions on Bonnie's personal history (the papers were right: she had other lovers, including one woman), the husband (I don't take cases from anybody implicated in a crime without doing a deep dive on that person first), newspaper clippings, field interviews (mine, not the cops'), miscellaneous material gathered over an intensive 3 weeks that involved 16-hour days more than a few times.

It all came down to one man in that cabin doing the killing and one man masterminding it—if you can call reproducing a slaughterhouse mastering anything.

Joey Reynolds works for Jason Lee Morson. He takes his cues and his cash from that man. He's loyal as a dog to the wealthiest scion, one of the "Four Families" who control 90% of the Lake's business, its bars and restaurants, the arcades, and concessions. Public records revealed, as of last year, Jason's family owned 35% of the real estate on the Strip, including shuttered buildings like the old Burly-Q near Freddie's Grill where Tempest Storm and Blaze Starr performed for the steel workers who brought their families on vacation to Lake Erie from the Mahoning Valley. Jason, who's half-black, was adopted by the Morsons. He has bigger ambitions. The BLM march down the Strip was his doing. Besides the Northtown preachers and civic leaders, he had a couple state legislators, three county commissioners, and the lieutenant governor marching along with the BLM backers chanting "No Justice, No Peace" and "Say Their Names" through megaphones to a sparse, midday crowd on the sidewalks. The news coverage was wall-to-wall with Cleveland and Youngstown news vans and their logos and aerial whips. More reporters than onlookers. Jason's not-too-subtle way of informing the power brokers in state politics he's ready to make his first foray into their midst. Scuttlebutt around the watering holes claimed Jason was being groomed by the Congressional Rep for his slot in the 14th District in two years when he announces his own bid for a Senate seat. According to Fritzie Galway, Jason was cultivating a "Barack Obama" look and practicing Obama speeches in front of the mirror.

Last summer, I picked up barroom gossip from a biker who rode with the Mongols. He'd had a few; he said a runaway was being held prisoner in one of the cottages on Sunset Drive off the Strip. He didn't say who was holding her, but when I mentioned Reynolds to him, he clammed up, sobered up, and abandoned his bar stool as if he found himself sitting on a hot plate.

I made the call to the precinct from the bar. I asked to speak to Det. Brown. I knew Mookie was catching calls that night because he's have been sitting at the back table with his buddies otherwise. I told Mookie not to hang up and to listen to me first.

"Haftmann, you're a glutton for punishment. You got some nerve calling me."

"I trust you."

"You just can't let it go, can you?"

"That's right. Me and the husband, we have a problem with somebody butchering his pregnant wife in front of their child."

"Yeah? I hear he's got no great love for you after you dug up all that sex-swinging dirt on his old lady."

It made the papers. I got careless with a reporter looking for inside information, and she betrayed me. The look on the husband's face when he stormed into my office and swatted me across the mouth with a rolled-up copy of the daily didn't hurt half as much as the expression on his face.

"Water under the bridge now, Mook," I said. "Are you going to send a cruiser or do I have to call somebody I know in Columbus?"

"Ha, BCI will tell you to go shit in your hat. Call a Lake cop. Say it's a noise violation."

"Not a bad idea. Those assholes are in a permanent state of D & D, playing shitkicker tunes all hours of the night. But I need somebody to go inside and look around."

"Look, we need a reason to poke around in the Lake's jurisdiction other than some guy gets hammered in a bar and pisses some gossip into another drunk's ear."

In the end, he made a call and a cruiser was sent. It was a long shot at best. The girl happened to be tweaking between shots, and she heard people talking in front of the cottage. Her scream gave the cop all he needed to make entrance. Joey Reynolds was brought to the station, lawyered up, and was bailed out the following morning.

The girl was from a decent family in Girard, PA, traveled to the Lake with friends, wound up getting high and stayed after her friends left from college in the fall. Joey Reynolds kept her supplied, used her for sex, and was about to dump her back onto the streets when that cruiser rolled up.

I was living in my car outside the police station waiting for her to come out. She didn't want to talk at first but I offered her money "for the trip back home." Mary LaRue was convinced Reynolds intended to kill her. "I wasn't his first," she told me later. "He said that whenever I begged for the dope. He made me do things . . ."

"You don't have to worry now, Mary," I told her. "You can put this animal away for twenty-five years."

She nodded, beaten down, humiliated, but a brave girl who had endured hellish treatment at his hands for almost two months of her captivity. He'd chained her to the wall and gave her a plastic milk jug every other day for relieving herself.

The cottages on Sunset were privately owned, some rented out, but all six on both ends of the cul-de-sac were owned by the Morson family. I finally had leverage after all these years.

Then Mary recanted, refused to testify. She left town. Her number at the family home was changed. I drove down to beg her to return but was told there'd be a sheriff's deputy waiting for me if I set foot on the property again.

The night following Jason's choreographed protest march, I was in a bar at the other end of the Strip watching a true-crime show about Oscar Pretorius, the "Bladerunner," who shot his girlfriend through a bathroom door because a burglar had broken in—he said. An obnoxious drunk on the next stool said, "The bitch deserved to get aired out on the toilet," and I said that was harsh. One thing led to another until he called me a "candy-assed liberal, like those protesters, BLM scum and their white girlfriends." Long and short, I told him I'd meet him out back "for a quiet conversation." I was sober, one beer under my belt by then.

Big surprise. No sooner had I stepped through the back door than he assumed a fighter's pose and looked as sober as a judge. I got one punch in before he banged me around the lot with fists and flying kicks I never saw coming. In minutes, knocked to the gravel, I was gripped in a hold that wrenched my shoulder so badly I still can't reach the gin bottle on top of the fridge. He skipped town right after, no doubt after collecting his fee. Joey made a point of catching me in Penney's the week after. He drank a beer in silence beside me at the bar. He demanded the remote from the bartender and pointed it at the TV. The guy who beat me black and blue was doing a promo for a cage match in Cleveland the following week as one of the cage fighters. Joey flicked off the TV and left the remote on the bar top. Message received: mess with the Morson family and bad things will happen worse than a professional trimming in a parking lot.

My neck hairs were the only thing working on my battered body—every one stood at attention. One card to play and not much time. The forces of darkness were one out away from pitching a shutout.

* * *

"Haftmann, you look pie-eyed drunk. Even for you, it's early. What's up?"

"'lo, Fritzie. Sh-*celebrating* my . . . good luck."

"Oh? What luck might that be?"

"I just got a big birthday present in the mail. Gonna go collect it tonight. Your buddy Jason's gonna pay up to get it from me."

"Stop blowing smoke up my ass, Haftmann."

"'s'true! I swear! The guy calls me, says he's had it. No justice, no peace and all that shit—"

"What guy? You're making as much sense as a rat copulating with a grapefruit. What guy?"

"Bonnie—Bonnie Van Ekdal's old man, her hubby. Says he's gonna off himself. Fuck this corrupt town. He told me where the package is in the cottage. Bonnie hid it there in the cottage, been there ever since."

"He killed himself? When that happen?"

"Mookie Brown called me from the cottage, got yellow tape all around it. Told me they found him hanging in that same cottage where Bonnie got sliced up. Been there all weekend swinging away from the rafters. Not a pleasant smell, Mook says. Cops left the back door open to air it out."

"What did he say was in this package?"

"A note from Jason wrapped in cellophane asking her to meet him that night, his DNA all over it. Copies of emails from him denying he fathered her child and insisting she abort it. A pregnancy stick. Positive. The gal was pregnant by him."

"Jesus, Mary, and Joseph."

"Oh yeah. Papers'll be all over it like flies on shit. Big time. Bye-bye, state legislature, so long Congress, see you, future President, and newest darling of the Hollywood elites.

"You tell anybody about this, you lush?"

"Not a soul, Fritzie, not a soul."

"Better not, if you like your oxygen straight instead of through a tube."

"Gonna go get my present. My golden parachute, Fritzie. Gonna ask Jason if he'd like to purchase it off me for a small fee."

"How small?"

Back to his old smiling self—that is, if a Komodo Dragon could smile without his forked tongue falling out.

"Ten thousand . . . a hundred thousand. First, gotta go get it soon's I fish—*finish* my drinkie poo here."

For all his bulk, Fritzie slid off his seat like an alligator slipping down a ravine into the water. Gone. At least he was smart enough not to make the call right in front of me at the bar. I gave it another thirty minutes, my heart thudding like a bongo, my drunk act for Fritzie had worked. My pores opened and I began sweating despite the chilled air in the bar. I wiped my face with the mask I bought on the Strip from some junkie desperate for cash. I never wore it.

I gave up prayer years and years ago. But I wanted to pray just then. The words just wouldn't come.

* * *

"Stupid, stupid son of a bitch," Reynolds said. "Tell us or you'll get more."

He slapped the retractable steel baton against his leg as if it were a riding whip.

"Where is it?"

That question from Jason. He didn't trust his own fixer not to try to blackmail him.

"Hid it. Never find it."

"Say again, you drunk. I can't hear you if you don't enunciate clearly."

Jason's practice in front of the mirror was paying off; every word was succinct and dropped like golden coins from his mouth. He had arrived in a hurry. His suitcoat and shoes looked expensive. He removed the ruby cufflinks and rolled up the sleeves of his bone-white shirt.

I wasn't slurring. I had blood in my mouth and some cracked teeth that made it hard to talk. One flap of duct tape had loosened around my right leg. Joey's tub of belly made it hard for him to bend over while securing me to the chair legs. I planned to get one kick into his nuts if possible. My arms and hands, though, were immobile with layers of tape.

"Hit him again," Jason said, bored. "Do some damage this time."

They weren't concerned about leaving marks. That worried me more than anything said so far. It meant I wasn't leaving the cottage alive. My phone call to Det. Brown woke him up, grumbling and angry when he realized it wasn't the station calling him out.

Timing is everything, someone rightly said. I hoped Brown didn't go back to sleep or I'd be taking the long dirt nap.

Time passed, how I don't remember now. I recall how I came swirling up from beneath a cloud of pain to realize that the interior of the cottage had suddenly bloomed in light—turquoise, then cherry, turquoise and back to cherry—a beautiful neon display that could only mean one thing: the cop believed me.

Jason and Reynolds stood rooted to the floor, neither moving beyond exchanging a glance.

Pounding, a demand to open that could only come from a big cop's larynx.

"What should I . . . ?"

Jason gestured him into silence with a flick of his wrist.

What little mental energy I had left focused on the sound a battering ram made when it splintered a door off its frame.

"Open it," Jason said calmly.

"I'm not taking the fall by myself, Jason," Reynolds hissed back.

"Relax. My lawyers will handle it."

"How . . . how you . . . handle that, Morson?"

I gestured with my chin to the upstairs loft railing where a pinhole camera was attached to a dowel. Three cameras covered the place from every angle, and a recording device played to a tape hidden outside the cabin in case they spotted the cameras.

When the door exploded with Reynolds' hand still on the knob, I laughed, although Mookie Brown, telling the story to anyone in Penney's who would listen, said I was sobbing like a baby.

Maybe I was.

* * *

They brought in a duo of interrogators from CBI to break down Joey Reynolds after five hours in the interview room—a cop euphemism I always liked. It's not like they bring you in their for a job.

Jason's lawyers were good. He pled to an aggravated menacing charge and got probation, which resulted in house arrest at his deluxe estate. But it put the kibosh on his political aspirations. He was radioactive after that.

Reynolds received a 20-year sentence. Not exactly justice.

I told Fritzie the county prosecutor was a chickenshit for not going after it. He reminded me too many years had passed, witnesses were gone or dead. She had no family left in Northtown.

"Her reputation alone would have sunk the case, Haftmann. You know that."

"Sounds like pot calling kettle black to me."

Reynolds' addiction to crack back then would have been another barrier to a first-degree murder conviction.

"How'd you know about her pregnancy?"

"I took a wild guess. Things added up. The cops should have put it together, not me."

"So there was nothing the husband left behind?"

I didn't answer. I thought of her 6-year-old being raised in another state. I'd been studying Bonnie's case like a monk working on the Book of Kells. I hadn't done anything else for so long that I didn't realize until Jason's arraignment that I had no life or any other purpose.

If I were a more moral person, I should have blackened Fritzie's eyes for him instead of letting him buy me a drink. He even clinked glasses with our boilermakers as if we'd been on an adventure together.

I'm healing up OK. I'll be walking around with missing teeth for a while yet. Haftmann the hillbilly, Galway called me when he saw me out and about afterward. I'd missed all the legal action in the courthouse, even though there wasn't much to see, but I did get to glimpse Jason doing the perp walk for the cameras on his way in and out of the courthouse.

People always say that when you manage to crawl out from under a heavy burden, you feel lighter as if that weight had suddenly been lifted from your shoulders. It'll come to me in time. Maybe it won't. It won't matter to anyone else one way or the other.

The End

Author's Afterword

In *The Dearborn Terrorist*, the John Donne sonnet Haftmann recalls in Chapter 5 is from *Holy Sonnets*: "Batter my heart, three-person'd God."

Haftmann's reading of Camus' "The Myth of Sisyphus" occurs in Chapter 9.

Portions of the dogfighting scene in Chapter 12 were adapted from "The Dog Returneth to His Vomit," published in *Thomas Haftmann, Private Eye* (Key West: New Pulp, 2017): 175-201.

Haftmann lying doped to the gills in his hospital bed in Chapter 35 is unable to recall Hecate, the witch from Greek mythology who appears in Shakespeare and brings about Macbeth's downfall.

Haftmann recalls his ex-wife quoting Sophocles and Shakespeare in "In Football-Crazy East Brangton": *Oedipus Rex* :"Count no man happy, until he dies, free of pain at last" (ll. 1678-84) and *King Lear*: "As flies to wanton boys, are we to the gods./They kill us for their sport" (4.1).

Finally, I'm grateful to Kerry and Chuck Carter, publishers of *Mystery Weekly Magazine*, one of the best print magazines in detective/mystery fiction, for publishing "Crème de la Merde" in *Mystery Weekly* in February of 2016.

—R.T.W.
Ashtabula, Ohio

tomhaftmann@hotmail.com

Thank you for reading.
Please review this book. Reviews
help others find Absolutely Amazing eBooks and
inspire us to keep providing these marvelous tales.
If you would like to be put on our email list
to receive updates on new releases,
contests, and promotions, please go to
AbsolutelyAmazingEbooks.com and sign up.

About the Author

Robb White lives in Northeastern Ohio. Many of his stories and novels feature private investigator Thomas Haftmann: *Haftmann's Rules* (2011), *Saraband for a Runaway* (2013), *Nocturne for Madness* (2015), and *Doggerel for Dead Whores* (New Pulp, 2019). *Thomas Haftmann, Private Eye* (2017) is a collection of 15 stories. In 2019, White was nominated for a Derringer. A crime novel, *The Russian Heist*, won *Thriller Magazine's* Best Novel of 2019 award, and a short story, "Inside Man," was selected for inclusion in *Best American Mystery Stories 2019*.

2nd Place Winner, Whodunit competition, for novella *Burning Girl*, 2020.

For sales, editorial information, subsidiary rights information
or a catalog, please write or phone or e-mail
New Pulp Press
Manhanset House
Shelter Island Hts., New York 11965-0342, US
Tel: 212-427-7139
www.NewPulpPress.com
bricktower@aol.com
www.IngramContent.com